HOME INVASION

A. AMERICAN

PRELUDE

FINALLY, IT LOOKED LIKE THINGS were ready to start calming down. To start the long walk back to a normal life. Or at least what we all took for normal in the Before. Not that that was the end goal. It was just unrealistic to think we could get back to the same point. But something closer to a normal, calm life was the goal.

With the victory over the DHS now complete, Morgan's greatest threat was vanquished. Or so he thought. The world he and his friends lived in was small in relative terms. For many in the new world, it consisted of wherever they could walk in a day. And for most, it was less than that. We were used to speedy transportation. To being able to hop in the car on a whim and travel many miles without a second thought. While Morgan was luckier than most, his world was still considerably smaller than it once was.

Having barely left the borders of Umatilla or Eustis, it was a mystery what was happening even in Orlando, let alone California or New York. The small radio was the only link to the outside world they had. And it opened the nation to them in the few broadcasts they picked up. News they had no idea of had found its way to them. And it was disturbing to say the least.

They may have bested the government in their immediate area, but across the country the war raged on. And now it

1

appeared the President had called for help from our former adversaries, who were all too willing to *help* in our time of need. But what would that help look like? And who, in the end, were they really looking to help?

While this was certainly a paramount concern, Morgan had more immediate issues to deal with. The farm was well under way, but gardening without the aid of fertilizers and pest control was daunting at best. And it appeared that with their plot being the only one for miles, every bug in the state was alerted to the buffet.

If this were his only concern, as difficult as it was, it wouldn't be so bad. But there was also the issue of governance. Morgan wasn't a politician and didn't want to be one. Nor was he a judge; and that particular issue was one he wanted to shed post haste. This latter duty was one of particular importance to him to delegate to others. But it required the right person. One with the temperament, personality and fortitude to do what must be done in such a situation.

While there were plenty of possibilities and even some volunteers, the right person for the job had yet to rise to the top. The ones that were most disturbing were those that wanted the position and the perceived power that came with it. These Morgan eyed with a great deal of suspicion. And none of them would be his choice.

The need for governance was another issue altogether. And here too there were issues again with those that wanted the position. One of those was becoming a real concern and would need to be dealt with soon. In one way or another. Earlier on, when he was trying to establish the rule of law, he had no issue with dealing with such problems in a less civilized manner.

And of course, there was always the unknown. As well as Mr. Murphy to keep an eye out for. Florida in the summer had its own issues to deal with. And now its full weight was upon them. Mother Nature could well decide at any moment to unleash her fury upon them with little or no warning at all. In the end, it came down to sheer chance and a whole lot of luck. There was no way to predict these things. Gone was the 24/7 weather coverage. The seven-day forecast was a thing of the past. Now, every day was a roll of the dice. And the house always wins.

CHAPTER 1

THE SUMMER HEAT WRAPPED ITS humid arms around us. The days were stifling and the nights offered limited relief. While the sun may not be overhead, the heat of the day was slowly released throughout the night. And God forbid it rained that day. The mosquito population meant doing anything outside near or shortly after sundown was an act of self-loathing. Every time I stood night watch at the bunker I'd say to myself, *they can't possibly get worse.* And every day or night, as the case may be, they seemed to become even more prolific. It was maddening.

And so, I lay in the bed, soaked in sweat and trying to sleep. But this too was a futile effort. In the Before, I loved a cold room. I was one of those people that turned the air down as low as it would go in a hotel room. And that's what I was thinking about now. Lying in one of those comfy beds, wrapped in a fluffy comforter that I so enjoyed about Hilton Hotels; and it cold enough to hang meat. But that was fantasy and useless.

Reaching over, I picked up my watch and checked the time, 3:47. Dropping it back to the nightstand, I hung my head off the side of the bed for a moment, taking in the breeze from the fan. A trickle of sweat ran down my neck and into my beard. I scratched at it and cussed the beard. It seemed everything was bugging me. Life was just out to get me.

Sensing the futility of trying to sleep, I got up and pulled on a pair of shorts and walked out to the kitchen. Opening the fridge, I stuck my head in. It was so cool. Such a relief. But it wasn't a solution; and admitting defeat, I took the glass water pitcher out and poured myself a glass before returning it to its shelf and closing the door.

Glass in hand, I walked out onto the front porch. The dogs weren't there, and I guessed they were probably out hunting, or doing whatever dogs do in the night. Taking a seat on the bench, I stretched my feet out and leaned back. The air outside hung like a suffocating cloak. There would be no relief out here. Raising the glass, I ran it across my forehead and the beads of condensation ran off onto my face. Glancing up, I was able to make out that the needle on the large round thermometer was slightly past eighty degrees. At four in the morning!

This is madness! I thought. *How did people live without air conditioning!* Then I thought about it. It wasn't necessary for survival. People lived all over the world in places hotter than this without it. But then, in many of those places the nighttime temps could drop to near freezing. Not here in Florida though. The nights could be just as uncomfortable as the days. The only relief being that giant ball of fire wasn't overhead to scorch you as well.

Draining the glass, I got up and went back inside. I may as well try and rest, even if I didn't sleep. There was a lot of work to do tomorrow or later today; as was the case. So I returned to bed to lie there, thinking of the wonder of central air conditioning and if there was any way I could resurrect it.

One of the things that this new life brought us was a tremendous improvement to our senses. At least as I saw it. I could smell better than before. I could hear better, though only in certain ranges, as I already had a serious case of tinnitus.

And as was the case now, I could see better. Not in the manner of more acute vision. Age played too big a role in that. But in sensing changes to light. I woke up, having drifted off into a delirious sleep at some point, when the rising sun began to lighten the sky, brightening the room ever so slightly.

Sitting up, I peeled the sheet from my legs and got up and went to the bathroom. I've always been a hot-shower guy; the hotter, the better. But now, the lack of a water heater was of no concern whatsoever. I turned on the water and climbed into the shower to soak myself in the seventy-two-degree water. That was one good thing about the well. The water was the same temp year-round. After washing off the funk from a fitful night's sleep, I came out and dressed in a clean pair of shorts and t-shirt.

I'd taken to wearing shorts recently as it was just too damn hot to wear long pants. Between the plate carrier I now wore in place of my vest and all the associated hardware, I sweated like a whore in church. Of course, Sarge gave me hell for it. Telling me if we got into a scrape of any kind I'd be scraped to shit. I told him I was willing to roll the dice.

Returning to the fridge, I poured myself a glass of tea and went back out to the porch again. The dogs were there this time, fast sleep. Apparently, whatever they were up to last night wore them out. They didn't even look up when I came out the door. I pushed Meathead out of the way with my foot so I could have a place for my feet. He groaned, but didn't stir.

This was my morning ritual. To come out and sit on the porch with my tea before anyone else was up. It was my time. And while it would have been a good time to think about the day ahead, I didn't. I'd made the conscious decision not to. Instead, I sat on the porch and watched as my yard came to life.

Since Little Bit had stopped shooting them, I'd discovered

where all the squirrels lived, and watched as they would wake to a new day. Some of them were very much creatures of habit like me. One fat male would emerge from his nest in a large oak and sit on a limb for some time. He would just sit there, occasionally scratching or otherwise grooming himself. But for the most part, he simply sat there. Others would come out with a mission in mind and get to work immediately. I could relate to that fat old male limb rat. I felt he and I were a kindred soul. But I also knew come the fall, he would wind up in the stew pot. After all, I knew where he'd be every morning.

With my tea done, I went back into the house. I had established a habit of making a round through the house to check on everyone. I'd open the girls' door and peak in on them, then go back to my room and give Mel a kiss before heading out for the day. When I kissed Mel, she stirred, kicking the sheet off her legs.

"Turn the fan this way," she mumbled.

I smiled, patted her ass and turned the fan. Picking up my carbine and pistol, I went out to the living room and put on all the junk I carried. We hadn't needed this crap in a while now. Not since the issue at the Elk's Camp was resolved. But Sarge insisted we wear it whenever we left the *hood,* as we now called our little place.

Sitting down, I pulled on a pair of socks and my Merrill hikers. I'd started wearing them again in place of the boots for the same reason as the shorts. That and they were way, way more comfortable. Finally dressed, I pulled my hat down over my head, let out a breath and headed out the door.

Thad was kneeling in the yard, petting Little Sister. Like me, he'd changed his wardrobe as well, taking to wearing a wife-beater in place of the long-sleeve Dickies shirts he favored. But that was as far as he was willing to go. Shorts were an anathema to the man. Saying, *only reason to wear short pants is if you is going swimmin'. And there ain't no reason to go swimmin'!*

He looked up when I came out and smiled. "I love these dogs."

I snorted. "Take them home with you. They're useless."

Rising to his feet, he said, "You ready to go? I want to get this out of the way before it gets too hot."

"Yeah. We need to stop by the plant on the way in. See how things are going. Terry and Baker said they might be ready to try a soft start on the plant today."

Thad's eyebrows shot up. "Really? That would be some good news."

I laughed and shook my head. "You have no idea how much work that will create."

We walked towards the old Suburban. I was amazed the old thing was still running. As we approached it, I stopped, holding my arm out to stop Thad. He looked at me and asked, "What?" I pointed at the truck. Sitting in the driver's seat was Dalton. He grinned at us with something of a cross between the Joker and Jack from the Shinning.

Thad saw him and started laughing. Shaking his head, he said, "Ain't right. He jus' ain't right."

"What day is it, Thad?" I asked.

He shrugged, then laughed. "I have no idea." Then, thinking for a minute said, "Damn! I don't know what day it is!"

Dalton stuck his head out the window and shouted, "It's Tuesday, you cheeky bastards! Now get in!"

Thad's enthusiasm quickly faded. "Is he driving?"

I couldn't help but laugh at him. As I opened the passenger door and tossed the keys to Dalton, I replied, "Sure. Life's an adventure."

Dalton quickly started the truck and revved the engine a

little. He worked his hands, gripping the wheel, then shouted, "Let's go, man!"

Thad dropped his head and climbed into the backseat. In that famous cockney voice, Dalton asked, "And where to this morning, Capt'n?"

Sitting back and putting my foot on the dash, I said, "The plant, Jeeves. And take us by the park this morning."

Smiling a twisted smile, he replied, "Of course, sir!" Then he dropped the truck into reverse and stomped the gas.

Now, there are a lot of trees in my yard. And this crazy fool never looked away as he executed a near perfect J turn, at speed! I was thankful when he dropped it into drive and floored it once again. We shot out my driveway, sliding sideways onto the dirt road. He raced down the road towards the bunker. I can't be certain, but I swore I heard Thad saying the Rosary or some sort of prayer from the backseat.

As we approached the bunker, I was surprised to see no one there. I was getting concerned as we slid to a stop beside it. Mike and Ted popped their heads over the top from the far side, weapons shouldered. They looked around for a moment as the dust from Dalton's wild ride was still hanging in the air. "What the hell's going on?" Ted asked with a look of concern.

I leaned back and pointed at Dalton. "Any other stupid questions?"

Mike dropped his carbine to hang from its sling. "You're a braver man than me! No way in hell I'd ride with his crazy ass."

With a lisp, Dalton asked, "But would you ride *me?*"

Ted snorted and laughed. "Like a rented mule!"

Straightening up, Dalton replied, "Ok, just checking."

"We'll be back in a little while." I said, then added. "Have to go by the plant and then to the farm to see what it looks like this morning."

Ted leaned over the top of the bunker and replied, "We'll be here."

We left them and headed to town. As we approached Altoona, Thad suggested we stop at the Kangaroo. "Good idea," I replied. "Give us a chance to wave the flag."

The little market, as we called it, came to life early each day. And things were actually improving to a degree, if you judged it by the offerings that were appearing. Milk, cheese, eggs, fish and the occasional meat products of various sources were now becoming common. There was even one older lady doing a bang-up business in chickens. She sold both adult birds and chicks. It had been a hobby of hers in the Before, that she'd turned into a productive enterprise.

We wandered around the tables and small booths that some of the more industrious folks had put together from what they could find. I stopped at one booth in particular. It was one of the most ingenious and sought-after services offered. One that I would have never thought of. And yet it was now one of the busiest services available. A cobbler. Kelly Christopher was a big guy with a white goatee. He didn't know anything about working on shoes, but necessity is the mother of invention.

When his boots wore out, he repaired them by resoling them with a slab of a tire. It wasn't long before he was repairing all manner of shoes. I was very happy to see this, as it was something I'd worried about. When you go to walking everywhere, footwear becomes very important. And at the moment, we had a distinct lack of shoe stores. But having someone around that could resurrect a worn pair was just about as good. The sad part is most shoes today aren't made to be repaired. Like most everything else in our world, they were designed to be disposable.

"Morning, Kelly," I said as I stepped up in front of his booth.

11

He looked up from the extremely worn engineer-style boot he was working on. "Morning, Morgan. How's the law and order business?"

I laughed, "Same as always. Only thing more reliable would be an undertaker."

Kelly pointed the small hammer he was using at me. "Now there's a business idea."

I shook my head. "Nah. I hear backyard burials are all the rage today."

He laughed. "Yeah, I guess it is. Hey, check this out." He reached back to the small bench in the rear of his booth and picked up a pair of gray canvas shoes and handed them to me. "What do you think of these?"

I looked them over. They were made from a heavy canvas and soled with a piece of heavy Berber carpet. "They look really nice. Like something some green weeny would have paid a lot of money for back in the day. But I don't think that carpet will last long."

He stuck his foot out to show the pair he was wearing. On his foot, they looked like moccasins. "I thought that too. But I've been wearing these for a week." He turned his foot up to inspect the sole. "They're holding up pretty good though. The key is trimming the edge to keep it from fraying."

Inspecting the trimming, I said, "Well I'll be damned. Not bad. What kind of canvas is this?"

Kelly smiled. "It's my boat cover. And the carpet came from the Florida room. Cost me nothing to make. I'll trade these to folks that don't have much, you know. They're better than nothing."

"You'll have everyone around here in new shoes in no time," I replied.

He nodded. "Yeah. That's part of the problem. Business is slowing down."

The statement gave me an idea. "You know; you should go to Eustis. I bet you'd be covered up with work there."

Kelly whistled. "I probably would be. But that's a hell of a walk."

"Hell, I'll give you a ride down there and get you back if you want. It would really help out the people down there. I've already noticed some folks going barefoot. I don't know if it's by choice or not, but I'm certain you'd be a popular man."

"You'd really do that for me, Morgan?"

I nodded. "Hell yeah I would! It'd be a service to the community."

Kelly thought for a minute. "I'm all for it. I've got a little work to do here today but I'd be free to go any time after that. I'll post a note here telling people to just leave their shoes for me."

"Sounds like a plan then," I said. "I'll have someone pick you up tomorrow and carry you to down there. We always have someone going."

Kelly came out of the small booth and wiped his hands on the canvas apron he wore when he worked. Offering his hand, he said, "I can't tell you how much I appreciate this."

Shaking his hand, I said, "We're all we have, my friend. We have to look out for one another."

He looked into his booth and said, "I'll fix me up a traveling kit and be ready to go. Thanks again."

I gave him a nod and went off to find the guys. Thad was making a trade with our resident dairy man. Once their business was done, we got back in the truck and onto the road. I told the guys about my talk with Kelly and what we were going to do. Both thought it was a good idea.

Thad reached up and grabbed my shoulder. "You see, Morgan. That's why you're the Sheriff. You're always thinking about other folks. Always looking for a way to help, any way to assist."

"I guess," I replied.

We made a quick stop at the Umatilla market as well. It may be good to get ole Kelly over here once a week too. After my talk with him, I found myself looking at people's feet. There were many more barefoot than I first thought. Again, this could be by choice. But I was certain it wasn't for everyone.

The Umatilla market had one major difference from Altoona. Every time we stopped in, there was some sort of bullshit to deal with. I don't know if it was because Umatilla was more of a town than Altoona, where most folks lived farther apart and were by necessity more self-reliant. Or if they were just plain nuttier.

Almost as soon as my feet hit the ground, I heard a familiar voice. "Sheriff Carter! Sheriff Carter!" I looked back to see a thin bandy-legged woman trotting my direction. I looked at Thad. The coward wouldn't make eye contact with me and went off into the market.

"Sheriff Carter," she said again, nearly out of breath when she got to me.

Exasperated, I asked, "What is it this time, Jean?"

Pointing, at what I had no idea, she said, "That Gail is at it again, Sheriff. She's been in my garden stealing my pole beans."

"Jean, I told you last time, I can't just take your word for it. If she's stealing your beans, you need to catch her doing it. If I come up here and find her hog-tied in your garden, I'll believe you."

She protested, "But Sheriff, she ain't got no garden! Where's she getting beans to trade?" She pointed at Gail, "Look at her. She's got a fistful of my beans!"

Shaking my head, I looked at Dalton. He asked, "Want me to call the crime lab?"

"Shut up," I replied, which just made him laugh. And that wasn't helping. At all.

"Alright. Come on, Jean." I walked over with Jean in tow to the other woman, who had watched the entire exchange.

Jean jabbed a bony finger at Gail, "I know you're sneaking into my garden. I know them are my beans!"

Gail looked at the pathetic handful of green beans in her grip. "No they ain't."

"Look. I'm tired of dealing with this crap between you two." Pointing at Gail, I said, "I promise you, if you are stealing from her garden and I catch you, you will pay the price."

Gail huffed up. "What are you going to do to an old woman for stealing food?" She then looked at Jean and added, "Which I ain't!"

I crossed my arms over my chest. "Well, if you were, and I catch you, since you like being in gardens I'll put you on the chain gang in town to work on the farm."

"Work you like a slave," Jean sneered.

Cocking my head, I said, "Shut up or you can go too. No more of this crap. You two understand me? This is done? I don't have time for your nonsense."

"So long as she stays out of my garden," Jean replied.

"Well, I ain't doing anything anyway," Gail said dismissively.

"You better hope not," I said as I turned and headed for the truck.

This is the kind of crap I had to deal with on a daily basis. It made me not want to even leave the house. Garden thieves, chicken thieves and general thievery filled my days. Oh, there were a few real crooks around. But they decided they didn't want to live around here too long. The first offense for such trivial crime was public shaming. And for most people that was enough. A second offense came with time on the chain. If there was a third, and there'd only been two, the stakes went up dramatically.

It was Dalton that came up with it and administered it. We had talked about it and decided that if shaming and hard labor didn't get it through their heads, we'd beat it into them. This too was done in public at the park. The only rule was we didn't let kids watch. But as kids will do, they always managed to find a way to peak in. We took the offenders and tied them between two trees, and the habit of stealing was beat out of them with a five-foot piece of garden hose. And the results were dramatic.

Both of the men that received the punishment left town the moment they were able to. But there was an added benefit. For a week or so after such punishment was administered, all forms of theft stopped. I mean, completely stopped. But desperate folks will do desperate things and it would start back up.

Not that we enjoyed this sort of thing. But what else could we do? We tried easier methods of discouraging their behavior. We made it clear there would be further consequences. But a couple of the local miscreants wanted to test our fortitude. In the end, it was a test of theirs against ours; and they quickly discovered ours was far stronger than theirs.

I met Thad and Dalton back at the truck. Thad was holding a handkerchief by the corners, its middle weighed down. "What'cha got in there, Thad?" I asked.

He smiled. "Eggs."

"We've got plenty of eggs at home," I replied.

"These are for Cecil. I told him I'd bring him some. He's so busy with the farm he's having a hard time getting to the market to trade for food to eat now. He works hard and needs to eat better. Cecil is an old man and he pushes himself too hard."

I thought about it for a minute. Nodding, I said, "Yeah. We need to make sure he's got plenty to eat. Tomorrow we'll bring him a load of groceries. How's his wife doing?"

Thad smiled again. "Oh, he says Miss May is just fine. He fusses about her. That's how I know she's okay."

We made the quick trip to the plant and pulled up beside the building containing all the motor-control systems. Terry was standing beside the large generator that was howling away. He had a set of earmuffs on and an instrument in his hands. Getting out, I walked over to him. Seeing me, he nodded. I leaned in and shouted, "Is everything alright?"

He gave a thumbs-up in reply, and left I him to whatever he was doing. Dalton was leaning against the front of the truck, arms folded over his chest and chewing on his fingernails. Glancing sideways at him, I asked, "What's with you?"

Without looking away from what had his attention, he grunted and replied, "It's that ginger-haired maiden. She does something to me."

I looked up to see he was staring at Doc Baker. She was in BDU pants and a t-shirt that was a little tight, revealing her shapely figure. Looking back at Dalton, I said, "Leave her alone."

Still chewing on his nails, he rocked his hips. With a quick jerk of his head, he replied, "I'll do me best, lad."

"Leave her alone," I said again as I started to walk towards them.

She, Scott and Eric were gathered around a large motor. As I walked up, I asked, "What's up?"

Baker, who was leaning over the motor, straightened up. She stretched her back, hands on her hips and leaning back as far as he could. I glanced over my shoulder at Dalton. He was stomping the ground with one foot. It made me laugh.

"We're testing the motors. This is the last one," Baker said. "It'll be another hour and this will be done."

"Then you'll be ready to try and fire this thing up?" I asked.

Wiping his hands on a rag, Scott replied, "Yep. Everything else already checked out. I'm surprised we didn't find any real issues."

"Good. Good deal. If this will run, then we're going to have a ton of work to do." I replied. Eric was looking around nervously. I laughed and said, "Don't worry, Eric, the old man isn't here."

The relief on his face was obvious, but he replied, "Oh, I'm not worried about him."

I laughed at him. "You say because he isn't here."

Thad walked up and looked at the instrument connected to the large motor. "What is that thing?"

"It's called a High Pot, or high potential machine." Baker said. "It induces high voltage into the motor to check for faults. Right now we're running 14,400 volts through it."

Thad's eyebrows went up. "I don't do electricity. Anything you can't see, hear or smell that could still kill you, I don't want anything to do with."

With a chuckle, I replied, "Oh, you can see, hear and smell it sometimes."

Scott smiled. "Yeah, but when you do, it's never a good thing."

"Indeed," I replied. Then, looking over at the large yellow gas line, I asked, "is the gas pressure still up?"

"I check it every day. It's still good," Eric replied.

I shook my head. "I'm really curious why we still have gas pressure."

Baker brushed hair from her face. "I've wondered myself. I mean, it's strange that it's still pressurized."

Scratching at my beard, I thought about it for a minute,

then said, "I'd like to know where it comes from. Someone, somewhere is keeping it going."

"Keeping what going?" Terry asked as he walked up.

"Gas," Baker replied.

Terry smiled. "Oh that. MREs."

I was confused. "What do MREs have to with the gas?" I asked.

Baker rolled her eyes. "Because he shits himself all day long. Blames it on the MREs. Personally, I think it's because he's rotten inside."

Terry patted his stomach. "I have a sensitive pallet."

"You're a garbage disposal," Baker shot back.

Looking at Baker, I said, "I'll leave you and the disposal to your work. We've got to run to town and will stop by on our way back. I'd like to be here to see if this thing will start."

"It'll start, Sheriff." Scott said with a smile. "Have faith."

"We'll find out in a couple of hours," I replied with considerable skepticism.

Thad and I walked back to the truck. On our way, he asked, "You really think this will run?"

Shrugging, I replied, "We'll see."

Dalton was still leaning against the front of the truck as I passed him on my way to the passenger side. I said, "Wipe your chin."

Dalton let out a low grunt. "She does something to me."

Opening the door, I said, "A goat would do something to you right now."

Dalton looked down. "I'm wearing the wrong boots for that."

Thad started to laugh heartily. "That's just wrong, Dalton."

Dalton pulled out of the plant headed towards Eustis. Since I wasn't driving, I was afforded the opportunity to really look at things. I'd noticed the trash and leaf debris before. But now that I was able to just observe it, it really stood out.

The road was covered with windblown trash. Papers, wrappers and the like seemed to be everywhere. For some strange reason, potato chip bags seemed to be prolific. Maybe it was what they were made of and the fact it would take them a very long time to break down. Add that to how light they are and it's easy to understand how they are easily carried by the breeze far and wide.

Of course, there was the usual natural detritus. Leaves, small twigs and dirt littered the road. With no traffic on the roads, this really built up. I could see in a couple of years there would begin to be a natural layer of compost beginning to form that would allow the growth of grass. It wouldn't take long for long black strips of asphalt to become long green strips of grass. The Florida Bahia grass was already encroaching from the sides of the road. Someday, it would conquer the blacktop.

We sped down the road as trash swirled in little vortexes created by the passing of the old Suburban. We arrived at the farm quickly. The field was crowded with people, much to my surprise. Dalton pulled to a stop near the tents used by the Guardsmen that provided security for the farm. The fields were now full of quickly growing crops. The curse of daily rain showers was also a blessing for the production here at the farm.

Work here was concentrated on the morning and late afternoon. It was just too hot during the day, not to mention unnecessary. If people came out in the morning, the rows could be weeded and the bugs abated some. There was no sense in being out here in the heat of the day.

And those bugs. Worse even that the persistent grass were the bugs. But Cecil handled it in a way I would never have imagined. As I looked out across the field, I saw many of the kids from town working their way through the crops. He made it a game and offered small rewards for the kids that removed the most pests from the plants.

All across the field were young kids, mason jars in hand, picking the insects from the plants and dropping them in the jars. At the end of the morning shift they would gather around Cecil who would inspect the jars and shower the kids with praise. The Guardsmen had agreed to giving all the candy from their MREs to Cecil for the rewards for the *best buggers* as Cecil called them. And while back in the day most kids would probably turn their noses up at a roll of Charms candy, today they were highly coveted prizes.

As a result of this little bit of motivation, the bugs were being kept in check. The war raged everyday against the army of invading pests, but for the moment at least, we were winning. If we kept things up as they were, we would have a bumper crop. There would be an incredible harvest of veggies of all sorts. And it couldn't come soon enough.

Shielding my eyes from the sun, I surveyed the field, looking for Cecil. Thad pointed him out on the far side of the field. "There he is."

I squinted even harder in the glare. "How the hell can you see that far?" I asked.

Thad smiled and replied, "Good vision runs in the family."

We walked through the rows, passing both adults and kids hard at work. An older woman stopped grubbing in the dirt with a hoe as Thad and I approached. She wore a broad-brimmed straw hat. Standing up, she wiped sweat from her flushed face. "Morning, Sheriff. Morning, Thad."

"Morning, ma'am," Thad replied.

"How's it looking?" I asked.

The old woman leaned the hoe against her shoulder and

looked around the field. "I think it's looking pretty good. Everything is growing really nice."

"You folks are doing a fine job," Thad replied.

The woman pulled a cloth from the pocket of the dress she wore. Looking up, she wiped her face and said, "It's getting hot though. I hope the rains keep up or we'll lose it all."

Looking up into the searing blue sky, I replied, "Let's hope Mother Nature takes pity on us."

Thad gave the woman a nod as we continued across the field to where Cecil was talking with a small group of people. As we walked up, he offered his hand. "Morning, fellers."

Shaking his hand, I replied, "Morning, Cecil." Then I nodded at the others, "Guys. How's it going today."

One of the men looked around the busy field. "We're getting it done, Sheriff."

"Honestly, it's coming along better than I thought it would," Cecil added.

I took a long leaf of a corn plant that was already chest high. "It's looking good out here. I hope it all makes it to harvest."

One of the other men in the group nodded. "We need it. My youngins are hungry."

Cecil took off his hat and wiped his forehead. "We have another issue, Morgan."

"What's that?" I asked.

"Salt. We're running very low on salt."

"We're not just running low, Cecil. Most people don't have any salt at all." Another of the men said.

"I don't know anybody that has any," another man said.

"That's not good in this heat," Thad said. Looking at me, he asked, "Is there anything we can do about it?"

I thought about it for a minute, remembering an old book I'd once read. Nodding, I replied, "There is a way to get salt. If we lived near the coast it would a lot easier. But can get salt from hickory wood."

Cecil bunched his eyebrows. "Hickory?"

"Yeah, the roots are best. You chip up the wood and boil it. When the water turns dark, and that won't take long, keep boiling until it starts to thicken a bit. Then strain out the wood and keep boiling. You'll end up with a thick black sludge. Take it off the heat before it burns and spread it out to dry. Then pound it into a powder. It's mostly salt with some other minerals."

Thad shook his head. "How in the world do you know all this stuff?"

Shrugging, I replied, "Like I say, I used to read a lot."

One of the men in the group rubbed his chin. With more than a little skepticism, he said, "Does that really work? Sounds like a lot of work to me."

I laughed, "You got a better idea? I know this works. I've never done it, but it is real."

"So just put some hickory into a pot and boil it?" Cecil asked.

"There's a little more to it than that. You need to chip it up, the smaller the better. But too small and it's hard to strain. And the roots are better than the timber. But the that will yield results too."

One of the men said, "I'm up for it. These hot days are killing me. My legs cramp real bad at night." Looking at another man, he said, "Darrell, you want to help me? I know where there's several hickory trees right here in town."

Darrell nodded. "I'm willing to try anything at this point."

The other man looked back at me and offered his hand. "I'm Hank Johnson."

Shaking his hand, I replied, "Good to meet you guys. Let me know how the salt production goes."

My radio suddenly crackled to life. "Morgan, you there? It's Livingston."

Rolling my eyes, I keyed my mic and replied, "I'm here. What's up?"

"We need you and Linus down here at the armory. We need to talk."

"About what?" I asked.

"We'll talk in person. You two need to come here."

Looking at Cecil, I asked, "What do these guys think? I'm just sitting around with my thumb up my ass?"

Keying the mic, I replied, "I'm at the farm. The old man is back at the ranch. I'm not going back to get him and then drive all the way back down there. You guys have more fuel than I do, why don't you come to us for a change?"

Sarge's voice rattled over the radio. "I agree with the Sheriff. You guys come up here for a change. I'm busy right now."

Thad cocked his head to the side and asked, "What's he doing?"

I laughed, "Probably sitting on the porch drinking a cup of coffee."

There was a long pause before Livingston replied. "We'll meet you guys around noon. Make sure you're not busy then."

I shook my head. "Whatever," I replied to no one.

"Hey, Cecil. I have something for you. Come over to the truck," Thad said.

Hank and Darrell said goodbye and got back to work on the hoes they had. Thad, Cecil and I walked back to the truck.

"What'cha got, Thad?" Cecil asked.

Thad took out the eggs and milk he had traded for in Altoona and gave them to him. "These are for you. We need to make sure you're strong enough to keep up with all you're doing."

Cecil smiled. "I really appreciate it. But you guys don't have to go out of your way for me."

I put my hand on his shoulder. "You are an important part of things around here, Cecil. We need you, buddy."

Cecil was a man that did things because they needed doing. Not for atta-boys or recognition. And someone taking a minute to actually put it to words made him uncomfortable.

With a slight jerk of his head, Cecil replied, "I'm just doing what needs done. Same as you boys."

"How bad is this salt thing?" I asked.

"It's pretty bad, Morgan. There isn't much at all in town now. The folks out working in this heat is getting cramps an such in their legs and arms. We need to get some in a bad way."

"How about you? You have any?" I asked.

He nodded. "I have a shaker full that I use very sparingly."

Looking at Thad, I said, "Let's bring him some next time we come down." Then looking back at Cecil, I said, "We have some. Not enough for the whole town, but I can get you some."

Cecil smiled broadly. "That'd be fine. I'll share it around."

I nodded, "I knew you would. Just go sparingly. There isn't much."

"Morgan, if you're going to meet Livingston at noon you won't be able to go to the plant on the way home." Thad said.

"Yeah. I thought about that. We'll just have to go home and then check on them tomorrow. Maybe we can stop by real fast on the way." Shaking Cecil's hand, I said, "Keep up the good work, my friend. Hopefully this will turn things around for the folks here in town."

He nodded. "All we got to do is let it grow. It'll get there."

We said our goodbyes and got back in the truck. I told Dalton about the change in plans, but that I still wanted to stop by real quick. We dropped in on the plant for a brief visit. Baker said it would be some time this afternoon before they would be ready to begin start-up. I told them we had a meeting and would try and come back.

With that taken care of, we headed back towards the house. On the ride back, I was thinking about what Sheffield could possibly want. It wasn't like we had enough to do as it was. He had a tendency to get on my nerves. They had plenty of people at the armory. More than enough to take care of whatever they needed done. So why mess with us?

We were just passing the Altoona fire station when a blur came off the right side of the road. Before I could say anything, it was in front of the truck. Dalton slammed on the brakes but we still hit the deer.

"What the hell?" Dalton asked.

"I think you just hit a deer," I said.

Before we could get out, a pack of dogs emerged from the same path the deer had been running. They immediately jumped on the stricken animal. There was no way I was letting them have the deer though, and I quickly got out. There were four dogs. They all looked mangy, with tangled and matted fur and were dirty. When they saw me, they started to growl and bark.

"Get!" I shouted. But they weren't about to back off.

"You're going to have to shoot them," Thad said over my shoulder.

Keeping my eye on the mutts, I replied, "That's what I was thinking. They look like crap. And if they're out running deer down, then they could attack people too."

Thad stepped around me as they continued to bark and snarl, keeping themselves between the deer and us. Thad reached back and pulled the shotgun from its scabbard and said, "I'll take the two on the right. You get the two on the left."

Raising my carbine to my shoulder, I nodded. It was over in a couple of seconds. The dogs were all dead. Thad was reloading his shotgun when another shot rang out that startled both us. I looked up to see Dalton standing beside the deer with his Glock in his hand.

Dalton looked at us and said, "What?" Pointing with the muzzle of the pistol, he said, "The deer wasn't dead."

"Is now," Thad replied.

The doe was fat and healthy. She would be good meat for sure. Looking down at her, I said, "I wouldn't have believed this if I wasn't here when it happened." Then I laughed and added, "What are the odds of a car hitting a deer now? I mean, we're the only car on this road."

Dalton holstered his pistol and looked at the doe, adding, "Hmm. I think it committed suicide. Better to be run over by a truck than torn apart by a pack of dogs."

I looked at the front of the truck. It wasn't good. "Oh, man! It broke a headlight. Look at the bumper!" I said. Then I looked at Dalton, "How fast were you going?"

He wagged a finger at me. "Don't blame me for this. You said yourself you wouldn't believe it if you weren't here. I mean, what are the odds?"

"My poor truck. It's like the world is out to get it."

Thad grabbed the deer by the back legs. "Come on. Let's get this loaded up. No sense wasting it."

Slinging my rifle over my back, I replied, "Hell no! I'm going to make Biltong out of it. We've got plenty of meat right now. Some of this is going to dry."

As we carried the animal to the back of the truck, Thad asked, "What's Biltong?"

Dalton dropped the tailgate and he hefted the carcass up

into the truck. "It's a kind of jerky made in South Africa. It's really good."

Once it was loaded, I went back to the front of the truck to take another look. With a sigh, I shook my head. *Maybe I can find another headlight,* I thought. Unlikely, but maybe.

"Come on, Morgan! Get in!" Dalton shouted.

"I'm coming, I'm coming!"

We stopped at the bunker where Aric, Fred and Jess were taking their turn on watch. Jess came up to the truck and leaned on Dalton's window. "Where you guys been so early?" She asked.

In a deep Johnny Cash voice, Dalton replied, "Hello, darlin'." Jess palmed his face and pushed it to the side.

From the back seat, Thad added. "We been out deer hunting."

Confused, she replied, "Huh?"

Jabbing my thumb at Dalton, I said, "Richard Petty here hit a deer a minute ago."

She stretched to look into the back of the truck. "Really? Did you get it?"

Thad reached over the back seat and patted the animal. "Oh, we got it."

"Just for you," Dalton added with a smile. Jess looked at him. He was still smiling at her. She shook her head without saying anything.

"Where's the old man?" I asked.

"I think he's at Danny's house."

"Alright. Livingston and Sheffield are on their way here. Just send them to Danny's when they get here," I replied.

"Will do." She turned back towards the bunker and shouted, "They got a deer!"

"Woohoo, fresh meat!" Aric shouted.

We left them and went to Danny's house. And sure enough, Sarge was sitting on the porch with Miss Kay drinking a cup of coffee. Dalton stopped the truck near Danny's sheds, where all butchering took place. As I got out, Thad said he'd take care of the deer and Dalton said he'd help.

"Cut the hams out whole for me. I want to use those for Biltong. The rest we can use for whatever," I said.

"Right oh!" Dalton shouted as he dropped the gate on the truck.

As I walked up to the porch, Sarge barked, "Where the hell have you been?"

Stopping, I eyed him, "Some of us have shit to do."

He held up his cup and replied, "Some of us have important shit to do!"

Shaking my head, I replied, "Like sitting on the porch drinking coffee?"

He took a noisy sip from the cup and gave a quick nod. "Nothing is more important than coffee. What's that booger-eater Livingston want?"

Walking up on the porch, I sat in one of the rockers. Shrugging, I replied, "I have no idea. He wouldn't say."

Holding the cup up, he said, "Some sort of bullshit, I'm sure." Then he took another sip.

"Morgan, are you hungry?" Kay asked.

"Always."

Getting up from her chair, she said, "Mel and Bobbie are inside. We'll get you something."

"You ain't got to fuss over him, Kay." Sarge said.

She looked back and swatted at him. "Oh you stop, Linus."

With a broad smile, I added, "Yeah, Linus."

His right boot flew out and connected with my knee. "You know damn good and well not to call me that."

"Oww, shit that hurt!" Rubbing my knee, I added, "What? Call you by your name?"

He nodded. "Exactly."

"How about I just call you asshole?"

Sarge cackled. "You can't be first, but you can be next."

"I would imagine that line is long as hell!" I replied.

"How's things up at the farm?" Sarge asked.

Rocking back in the chair, trying to forget about the pain in my knee, I replied, "Looks good. That field is full. Everything looks like it's growing fast."

"Let's hope so." Sarge stabbed a thumb in the direction of Thad's little garden. "If it's growing anything like Thad's little patch of dirt, we should be covered up in veggies."

"Let's hope." I said and added, "Oh, we got a deer this morning."

Sarge cocked his head to the side. "A deer? What'd you get it with?"

I pointed at the Suburban. "That truck."

Sarge's head rocked back in his chair as he started to laugh. "You hit it with the truck? What are the odds of that today? Only damn thing on the road and that crazy-ass deer manages to run out in front of it!" He slapped his knee as he roared with laughter.

"Yeah, Dalton said it committed suicide." The old man laughed even harder. "It was being chased by a pack of dogs and ran out into the road."

Getting himself under control, Sarge asked, "A pack of dogs?"

"Yeah. Mangy looking things. We had to shoot them. They were really aggressive. They wanted that deer."

Taking another sip from his cup, Sarge said, "Guess I'd jump in front of a truck too if a pack of crazy dogs was after me."

I pointed over towards the shed where Thad was working on the deer. "They're over there now, dressing it out."

"Fresh meat. That'll be good."

Taylor came out on the porch with a plate in her hand. "Here, dad," she said as she handed it to me.

"Thanks, kiddo." There was a pile of fluffy scrambled eggs on the plate.

"I made them for you." She replied.

"They look great!" I said, then took a bite. "And they taste even better!" She grinned ear to ear and went back into the house. I was happy to see her out and about. She was getting around now without issue. She'd taken some time to get back on her feet, but now she was back to normal.

"That's a good girl," Sarge said.

Nodding as I scooped up a forkful of eggs, I replied, "They all are. I'm just glad she's back up and at it again."

Sarge rose to his feet. Looking into his cup, he said, "Time for a refill. But first, I'm going over there. Want them boys to do something for me."

I sat on the porch and finished my eggs. The sun was getting high and the lack of any kind of breeze made the air feel heavy, almost oppressive. But it was a nice morning even if it was hotter than the hinges of hell already.

Mel came out on the porch and sat down beside me. "Wow, it's hot out here," she said.

"Yeah. I hate the summer."

"It's not much better inside. We've got every fan we could find running in there."

I looked at her. "You didn't take our fan did you?"

She looked at me like I was nuts. "Hell no! I wouldn't be able to sleep without it."

I snorted. "I can barely sleep with it!"

She started to rock in her chair. "I don't have any issues sleeping. But if we didn't have the fan, I would for sure."

I looked sideways at her. "You never have an issue sleeping.

I wish I could sleep like you. You lie down and you're asleep. That' doesn't happen for me."

She got up and took my plate, then leaned down and kissed me. "That's because you worry too much."

"It's not like I want to." I replied, then looked around. "Where's Little Bit?"

She nodded her head towards the house. "She's out back with the kids and Danny."

I chuckled. "It's funny how much time she spends outside now. Even on a day as hot as this. Remember how she used to fuss about playing outside?"

Mel looked out from the porch. "Well, things are different now. And some things for the better."

Sarge walked over to where Thad was working on the deer. He was just hoisting it up into the air when the old man walked up. "Hey, Thad, do me a favor. Don't cut that thing open yet."

Thad looked at him. "Okay. What's up?"

"Let me find a jar."

Thad looked at him cautiously. "A jar for what?"

Coming out of Danny's shed with a quart jar in his hand, he said, "I want to catch the blood."

Twisting his face, Thad asked, "For what?"

Sarge knelt down beside the hanging deer and pulled his knife out. He quickly and smoothly cut the deer's throat. As the blood began to flow, he held the jar out to catch it. "The Maasai tribe in Africa use it as a food."

Thad looked disgusted. "I ain't about to drink no blood."

Sarge laughed. "I know you ain't. I'm just doing this to see how they did it." When the blood stopped flowing, Sarge stood up and set the jar on one of the sawhorses. Taking his knife, he opened the animal up. There was a lot of bruising on the left flank. He cut the chest open and reached in and removed the heart. Taking it over to the jar, he drained it into the container as well.

Thad watched the macabre scene in complete revulsion. He shook his head. "That's just nasty."

When the heart was empty, Sarge set it on the sawhorse. "It's all yours now." Looking around, he picked up a stick and started to stir the blood.

"Now what are you doing?"

"This removes all the platelets and coagulants," Sarge replied.

He continued to stir the jar. As he did, a buildup started to cling to the stick. Thad stepped over and looked at it. "That just ain't right."

Sarge chuckled. "You should watch a little Maasai kid do this." He removed the stick from the jar and held it up. It had a pink glob on it. "Then pull this out and eat it."

Thad turned his head to the side and closed his eyes. One hand went to his mouth and other to his stomach. "Get rid of that before I puke. Swear to God. I'm gonna be sick."

Sarge laughed even harder. Getting control of himself, he whistled. It didn't take long for one of the dogs to show up. Drake was there in no time. He sat politely in front of Sarge and licked his chops. "Look. He wants it," Sarge said with a chuckle.

Without looking over, Thad waved a hand at him. Sarge asked Drake, "You want this?" Drake licked his chops again. "Yes you do, don't you?" Thad made a gagging sound. Sarge laughed again and held the stick down to Drake who eagerly licked the substance from it. It was gone in an instant and Drake looked at him as if to say, *that was good. Where's the rest?*

Sarge patted him on the head. "That's it, boy. That's all you get." Drake seemed to get the message and walked over and lay down at the base of one of the large oak trees. After all, there was still a whole deer hanging there.

Sarge picked up the jar and said, "I guess if you don't want this, I'll take it."

Thad wouldn't look over, but replied, "Get that jar of nastiness out of here."

Chuckling to himself, Sarge took it over to his Hummer and set it in the passenger seat.

CHAPTER 2

SHEFFIELD AND LIVINGSTON SHOWED UP shortly after noon. We were all out at the shed where the deer was being finished up. We'd cut every piece of usable meat we could from the carcass. Even the bones were going to be used. Miss Kay already had them in the kitchen boiling away in a large pot. Nothing would go to waste. The heart and liver were set aside for stews and the rest of the entrails would be fed to the dogs.

"Where'd you guys get a deer? Nobody has seen one in a while now," Livingston said.

Dalton was cutting sinew from one of the front quarters. He looked up and said, "They aren't hard to find." Pointing at it with his knife, he added, "This one came to us."

Livingston was obviously confused, so I saved him the headache of sorting out Dalton's riddle. "We hit it with the truck. It was running from some dogs and ran right out in front of us."

Dalton smiled. "Committed suicide."

"Damn," Sheffield said. "What are the odds of that today?"

"That's what everyone says. We were probably the only truck on the road for a hundred miles. And yet it managed to run out in front of us."

"What's so important to bring you fellers all the way out here?" Sarge asked.

Sheffield was looking at the meat on the table. Sarge's comment brought him around. "Oh, uh, yeah. General Fawcett called. He needs us to take a look at something for him."

"And just what does the good General need us to look at?"

"They've lost contact with some Army Corps of Engineers that have been maintaining the Crystal River nuclear plant." Livingston said. "They haven't been able to reach them for a couple of days and have asked that we send someone over there to check on it."

"What?" Sarge barked. "They've got far more assets than we do. Why don't they use some of their damn people?"

Livingston crossed his arms and pushed the dirt with the toe of his boot. "Well, we said the same thing to them. They told us they were utilizing their assets. They see us as one of their assets."

"Bullshit!" Sarge barked.

"Look, Linus, we don't like it any more than you do. But they are pretty tied up right now. He said they are chasing Russian advance units all over the state. They can't spare anyone at the moment and we're the closest people they have."

"Russian advance units?" I asked.

Livingston nodded. "It looks like they have some pathfinders on the ground."

Sarge's spine stiffened. "So, who are you sending? You've got plenty of people."

Sheffield took a deep breath to brace himself for what he knew was coming. "That's why we're here. We want you guys to go."

Sarge ripped his hat from his head and threw it. "You sum bitches! Why the hell are you asking us to do something like that? You've got ten times as many people as we do! Use your people. Morgan is the local Sheriff." He pointed an accusatory finger at Sheffield, "And you damn well know I'm retired!"

"You and I both know that retired shit went out the window when all this started. *And* you know I wouldn't ask for your help. Fawcett has specifically requested you and your people do this. You and these idiots you have are better suited for this kind of thing than our guys. Our people are National Guard. They aren't trained for this sort of thing. Mike and Ted are. It's what they live for."

Dalton was still cutting meat. He looked up and said, "Fuck it. I'll do it. I could use a walk-about." Sheffield looked at him but didn't reply.

With his hands on his hips, Sarge was shaking his head. "This is bullshit."

"Bullshit or not, you've been tasked with it. It's out of my hands. Fawcett needs you to go over and see what's going on. They're afraid the Russians have moved on the facility. He needs to know what the situation on the ground is."

"And what if the Russians have taken the plant?" Dalton asked.

"You're to simply observe and report. Do not take any action if there are Russians at the plant. We can't risk damage to the facility. A meltdown is the last thing we need right now." Livingston replied.

Dalton looked at Sarge and winked. Sarge rocked on his heels as he glared at Sheffield. After a moment, he asked, "Fawcett really wants us to do this?" Sheffield nodded. "He asked for us personally?"

Sheffield nodded again. "You know this wasn't my idea."

"When?" Sarge asked.

"He said as soon as you can. We'll provide you with fuel and ammo. Whatever you need." Livingston added.

"I'm not going." I said. "I've got too much to do here. Fawcett can kiss my ass."

Sarge looked at me. "That's fine, Morgan. You need to stay here. This isn't your job anyway."

Dalton jabbed his knife into the table. "Well, I'm going. I want in on this."

Sarge nodded. "I'd like you to go. Mikey, Doc and Ted. That'll be enough."

Thad cleared his throat. "You know Jamie is going to want to go."

Sarge shook his head. "She ain't a hundred percent yet. I know she thinks she is, but she ain't. She'll have to sit this one out."

"I don't care who you take. We just need you to get over there and put eyes on the plant." Sheffield said. "They're really worried about this. The fear is that the Russians have moved in on it and may try and cause a meltdown. It'd be a giant dirty bomb."

"Why though?" Thad asked. "What would be the point of doing something like that? We're already down."

Livingston shrugged. "Who knows. And that may not even be what they're up to. But we need to make sure the plant is secure."

"We'll handle it," Sarge said.

I was watching Sheffield. He was still staring at the venison being cut up on the table. I picked some up and asked, "You want to take some of this with you?"

Sheffield looked surprised. "Uh, yeah. I mean, if you can spare it."

"We've got plenty. I'll go get you something to put it in."

Livingston smiled. "Fresh meat. Man, that's going to be good."

I went to the house and asked Bobbie for a plastic bag. These crappy little shopping bags that people used to bitch so loud about were now very useful. Not to mention becoming a rarity. People used to throw them away. And in the early stages of the event they seemed to be everywhere. Being blown around by the wind. Now they weren't seen at all.

Coming back out to the table, I loaded some of the cut-up venison into the sack and handed it to Sheffield. "Here, don't say I never gave you anything."

Holding the bag up, he smiled. "Thanks, Morgan. I appreciate it."

Livingston rubbed his chin. "You know, maybe we should come out here more often. Every time we do, we either get fed or get something to take back with us."

"Don't get used to the idea," Sarge barked back. "It's only 'cause we take pity on you."

Sheffield opened the bag and looked in. "Call it what you want. I'll take it." He looked at Sarge and asked, "When do you think you guys will head out?"

Sarge scratched his head. "I don't know. We got to get some things together. I'll need another truck though. I want to take two."

Sheffield nodded. "Not a problem. Like I said, whatever you need."

"When we're ready here, we'll come to town. I'll also need plenty of fuel for the truck, as well as lots of ammo." Sarge replied.

"We'll have it ready," Livingston said.

Sarge nodded. "alright. We'll see you when we're ready."

"Oh, one more thing," Livingston said. "Shane wants to

know how much longer he's going to have to deal with that prisoner, Dave, I think his name is."

I nodded. "Dave Rosa. The one that killed his girlfriend. I guess we need to address his execution."

With a look of mild contempt, Sheffield asked, "And just how do you plan on carrying that out?"

Not giving him the fight he may have been looking for, I replied, "That's a civilian matter. We'll sort it out."

Sheffield held the bag of venison up. "Thanks for the meat. We've got to be getting back."

"Thanks for coming out, Captain," I replied.

"We'll be in touch," Sarge added.

Sheffield and Livingston got back into their Hummer and headed back to town. We watched them as they left. As they were passing in front of Danny's place, I said, "Well, they were just full of good news."

Sarge waved the comment off. "This ain't no big deal. We'll go over and have a looksee."

"And what if you find it full of Russian Spetsnaz?" Dalton asked.

"Sheffield said we were supposed to observe and report." Sarge said with a smile. "But Fawcett knows me better than that. If the place is full of commies, we'll deal with it. At the least, we'll cause them some heartburn."

Slightly concerned, I said, "I don't think a nuclear power plant is the right place for your type of mayhem."

Sarge laughed and slapped me on the shoulder. "Don't worry, Morgan ole buddy! You forget, I'm a professional!"

Thad laughed. "I think that's what he's worried about."

"At least I ain't got to go. You boys have fun and stay safe," I replied.

Sarge nodded. "We'll set up a comms protocol before we leave. We'll stay in touch with you."

"You want to take Hummers and not the smaller buggies?" Dalton asked.

Sarge thought about it for a minute. "The war wagon is good. But for a trip this far from home, I'd rather have the Hummers. We can carry more fuel and ammo in those."

"We're going to need to get you guys some food as well," I said.

"Don't worry about grub. We'll get some MREs from Sheffield."

"Morgan, how do you want this cut up for that Biltong you talked about?" Thad asked.

I held my fingers up, "Just about three quarters of an inch thick. This can be thicker than jerky."

Sarge clapped his hands. "You making Biltong?"

Surprised he knew what it was, I asked, "Yeah. What do you know about Biltong?"

"Shit. I've been eating Biltong since you were shittin' yella! You sure you know how to make it?"

Nodding, I replied, "Hell yes. I've made it before. I just need some vinegar, salt and coriander."

Sarge smiled his toothy grin. "That's what I wanted to hear. I worked in South Africa for a while and was introduced to it there by some Afrikaners. Good people."

"Is there any place you haven't been?" Thad asked.

Sarge shook his head. "Nope. At least no place worth going to." Sarge let out a long breath. "I guess I'll leave you boys to it. I've got to go get Mutt and Jeff ready."

"I think it's BS you're even going. Why don't they use some of their own people?" I asked.

Sarge shrugged. "Don't know. But my guess is they are

pretty busy. And if that is the case, that they're so busy they can't spare anyone, then we need to keep an eye out around here."

"Have you heard anything recently on that radio?" Dalton asked.

Shaking my head, I replied, "No. Nothing new. But I'll be sure to catch the next broadcast."

"I'll come check in with you before we leave," Sarge said with a wave as he headed off.

"I'll get my gear together and meet at your place," Dalton said as he headed off as well.

Thad watched as Sarge disappeared. Once he was out of sight, he said, "I'm worried about them on this one. Crystal River is a long way from home."

With a nod, I replied, "Yeah. But if anyone can get there and back, it's them." I pointed at Dalton, who we could still see. "That's a formidable group of men. I wouldn't want to come up against them in a dark alley."

Thad added, "I wouldn't want to come up against them in broad daylight in an open field!"

I slapped him on the shoulder. "Me neither, buddy. Let's go make some Biltong."

We carried the meat into the house. Miss Kay smiled when she saw it, "Oh, what do you have there?" She said as she reached out for the big bowl containing the lean venison.

I pulled it back, saying, "I'm going to make something with this. You get what Thad has there."

She cocked her head to the side. "What are you thinking of making?"

"Biltong".

"Oh no. Not that again?" Mel moaned.

Miss Kay looked at her. "What is it?"

Mel pointed at me. "The last time he made that, it hung in my kitchen for weeks."

Kay looked at me. "You hung it in the kitchen?"

"Yeah." I replied. "Biltong is a kind of jerky made in South Africa. You treat the meat then hang it up and let it dry for a couple of weeks."

Kay scrunched her nose. "That doesn't sound safe to me."

"It's one of the oldest methods of storing meat there is. It's perfectly safe. I ate the last batch I made and I'm still here."

"You aren't hanging it in my kitchen!" Bobbie called from the sink where she was washing dishes.

"I'll do it at my house," I replied.

"Good!" Bobbie called back.

"Miss Kay, I need some apple cider vinegar, coarse salt and coriander."

"Well, we have all that. Let me get it," she said as she went into the kitchen to find what I asked for. She returned with the spices and handed them to me. "Here you go. Just bring them back."

I took them and said I was going to my house to prepare it. Thad said he was going to work on his garden and asked Mary to join him, which she did. Mel told me not to make a mess and have it done before she came home. I had to laugh, she really didn't like it when I made Biltong. It bugged her to see it hanging in her kitchen.

As I headed for the door, I looked at Mel. "Where's Lee Ann?"

"She's out with Jess and Fred some place."

"Mmm. Keep an eye on them," I said as I went out the door.

Danny was sitting on the porch when I came out, watching the kids play in the front yard. Seeing me, he peered over the side of the bowl. "What's that?"

I lowered it so he could see in it. "We hit a deer this morning with the truck. I'm going to make some Biltong out of this. Miss Kay has the rest of it inside."

Danny laughed. "Only thing moving on the road and you still managed to hit a deer."

"Yeah. Dalton said it committed suicide. It was being chased by a pack of dogs. We had to shoot all the dogs. They were pretty aggressive."

Danny rocked in the chair. "That's not good. At least they're not an issue anymore. Where was it?"

I pointed towards Altoona. "Just up the road near the fire department."

"Hmm, that's kind of close."

"Yeah. But like you said. They're gone now."

"How was the trip to town?" Danny asked.

"It was alright. Typical shit at the Umatilla store though. Oh, and that General Fawcett has asked Sarge to go over to the Crystal River power plant. They say they can't reach the engineers there and are worried there could be some Russians or Chinese troops."

Danny looked surprised. "No shit? Why are they asking him to go? Don't they have people they could send?"

I snorted. "I asked the same thing. Sarge thinks that since they're asking him to go they must be pretty busy. Looks like this whole Russian thing could be real."

"Let's hope they don't show up here."

I looked around. "What the hell would they want here? There isn't anything, any reason to come here."

"Let's hope," Danny replied.

I looked at the bowl of meat. "Well, I'm going to take care of this. I'll see you later."

Setting the bowl on the counter in the kitchen, I sprinkled the vinegar over it and mixed it around. Now, it would sit in the fridge overnight. But for now, this was done, and I went to find Sarge and the guys. I wasn't comfortable with them leaving like they were. I didn't like the idea of so many of our people being so far from home.

I found them at their house. The Hummer was pulled up into the yard near the door as they carried out various gear and loaded it into the truck. As I walked up, Mike came out the door with the Gustav slung over his shoulder.

"Hey, Morg. You're not going on our road trip with us?" He asked.

I shook my head. "No. I'm going to stay here. I don't even think you guys should be going."

Mike dropped the weapon into the back of the Hummer. "Ah, ain't no big deal. We'll just ride over there and take a look. No biggie."

"Let's hope," I replied. "Where's the old man?"

He nodded towards the house. "He's in there."

I went into the house and found him in the kitchen filling a thermos with coffee. Seeing me, he said, "Hey, Morgan. You come to beg your way into this cluster fuck?"

"Hell no. If anything, I'd try and get you guys to not go."

He screwed the lid on the thermos. "Don't worry about us. This isn't a big deal. We'll only be gone a couple of days."

"Provided everything goes smoothly. It's a long way over there."

He nodded. "It is. But things are a lot calmer now than they used to be. We shouldn't have to worry about any bandits or anything like that. Besides, those guys at the plant are probably just having equipment issues. We'll probably get there and find everything is just fine and turn around and come home."

"Yeah. Well, you guys need to call and check in with us every four or five hours. I'd also like to know the route you're taking so if we need to come looking for you we'll know where to search."

Sarge pointed at a map on the kitchen table. "Way ahead of you, and I'm glad you're thinking. That's your map. I marked our route on it along with waypoints. We'll let you know when we reach each one."

I sat down and looked at the map. The waypoint names were written on the map in marker. They were names like Disney World, Six Flags and Universal Studios. I laughed, "Theme parks. Nice."

Sarge grunted. "Had Mikey do this. He was going to use other names but I had to correct him."

Knowing Mike, I had to ask. "What was he going to use?"

Sarge pointed at the map. "Disney was going to be dildo, if that gives you any idea."

I rolled my eyes. "Of course he would."

As we sat talking in the kitchen, Ian came through the door with a pack over his shoulder and weapon in his hand. Sarge looked at him and asked, "Where the hell are you going?"

"With you."

Sarge shook his head. "No you're not. You're staying here with Morgan."

That didn't sit well with him. "This is bullshit! Me and Jamie are just as capable as you guys."

Sarge stood up. "Which is why you're staying here. First, Jamie isn't a hundred percent yet and you both know it. I know she'd go regardless, but I can't let her. And I'm not going to let you go without her." He paused and pointed at me. "Besides, he's going to need help as well."

Ian looked at me. "He's got plenty of people. We're not cops. We're warriors!"

Sarge put his hand on Ian's shoulder. "I know you are. And

don't think for a minute I don't think you're up to it. I know you are. But I'm not going to ask you to leave Jamie here. She needs you right now. Plus, and this is the main reason, I need a QRF, and you're it. If we run into trouble, you, Jamie and Perez are going to have to bail our asses out."

I laughed. "You're relying on Perez to save your ass if you get in trouble?"

"I heard that, pendejo," Perez said as he pushed past Ian into the kitchen. Jamie followed him. Both of them carried their gear with them.

Jamie leaned against the wall and crossed her arms over her chest. "So why can't we go?"

Sarge looked at her for a long minute. Then he said, "You know why. I know you want to go. And I know you would without hesitation. But you're not totally back on your feet."

She looked down at her feet. "Looks like I'm standing on them."

Sarge jabbed a finger at her. "Don't be a smartass! You know what I mean. Mike, Ted, Doc and Dalton are going." He pointed at the group in front of him. "You three are the QRF. If something happens, I'm relying on you guys to come get us. Now sit your asses down so we can go over the route."

They could tell he was serious and none of them commented. They all took seats at the table as he went over the route to the plant.

"What's the deal with this plant? How have they been running it this long if the power has been out?" Ian asked.

"The plant was shut down in 2009 for an upgrade. All kinds of shit happened during that process and it was never brought back online. Now it's used to store old fuel rods." Sarge replied. "That's the real concern. There's a lot of old fuel there and they're concerned that the Russians may have moved in on it and could be setting up as a massive dirty bomb. So they want us to go in and take look at it."

Jamie shook her head. "What sense would that make? Setting something like that off at this point?"

Sarge shrugged. "It doesn't. Not now with all the people that have died off. But they can't reach the engineers working there. We're just going to go have a look. I imagine they're just having radio issues. We'll probably get there and find everything is fine and turn around and come home."

"It's only a two-hour ride over there," I said.

"Should be a milk run," Mike said from the hallway.

Sarge looked at me. "I need a chainsaw, Morgan."

"I'll get you one. Good call, in case the roads are blocked."

"Exactly."

"I'll run get one." I said, and left the group to continue to discuss the mission.

Instead of walking, I hopped into one of the buggies and rode it over to the house, parking it in the backyard by the shop. Getting the Stihl saw out, I checked the gas. It was full, so I set the choke and gave it a couple of pulls. It coughed on the third one. Turning the choke off, I pulled again and it started right up. I ran it for a few minutes before shutting it off.

Taking the saw back, I set into the back of the old man's Hummer. Mike came out with his gear and tossed it into the truck. Seeing a jar with something in it, he picked it up.

"What the hell is this?" He asked.

Doc was standing at the back of the truck and looked over. "Looks like blood."

Sarge came out of the house and piled his kit into the truck as well. Seeing Mike, he replied, "It is blood."

"What the fuck? What are you doing with a jar of blood?"

Sarge shrugged. "I don't know. Was just trying something out."

Mike's face twisted. "I knew you would be into some sort of voodoo shit!"

Sarge snorted, "Voodoo! What the hell are you talking about?"

Pointing at the jar of dark liquid, Mike shouted, "That! You gonna start cutting off chicken feet now too?"

"Oh dry up, Nancy! You afraid of a little blood in a jar?" Sarge shouted.

Pointing at it, Mike shouted, "I don't mess with voodoo, witches or ghosts! Some shit ain't supposed to be trifled with!"

Sarge doubled over laughing and looked back at Ted, who had been observing the show. Pointing at Mike, he said, "Can you believe Mikey is afraid of ghosts? The same idjit that will run into gunfire, take on too many people at one time. Plays with explosives and snakes! Snakes! Is afraid of shit that ain't even real!"

Ted cocked his head. "I'm with Mikey on the ghost thing. Voodoo too. I've been to Haiti. Some thing's just aren't meant to be messed with."

Doc shook his head, "Voodoo is no Bueno."

Feeling justified, Mike pointed at Ted, "See! They agree with me!"

Sarge straightened up. "That's just because you're all a bunch of panty-waisted twats!"

"Whatever. I ain't riding with that in the truck," Mike shot back.

Sarge snorted. "I wasn't taking it. But now that you think you're going to tell me what I can and can't do, it's going!" He walked over and grabbed the jar and set it on the console of the Hummer.

Mike glared at him. "When we get to town and pick up the other truck, I'll ride in that one. You can have the blood mobile all to yourself!"

Sarge laughed again. "Whatever works for you girls."

Ted walked over and set his gear into the truck. "Top. How are we going to do this with only five of us? It seems a little light."

Sarge glanced over at Ian. In a low whisper, he replied, "We're not. We're going to take a couple of Sheffield's people with us. Jamie isn't ready for this kind of thing yet, and I don't want to take Ian away from her just now."

Ted nodded. "Agreed."

Dalton arrived with his gear. Looking around, he asked, "What's all the hubbub?"

"We got us a voodoo priest," Mike said, nodding at Sarge.

"Mmmm, yes. I've dabbled in the dark arts a bit myself."

Mike looked at him wide-eyed, "You have got to be the weirdest fucker I've ever met!"

Dalton looked at him sternly and nodded. Reaching into his shirt, he pulled a small leather medicine bag out. Mike eyed him suspiciously. Dalton reached out and deftly plucked a hair from Mike's beard.

Grabbing his chin, Mike said, "Ow, what the hell?" Dalton loosed the tie on the pouch and tucked the hair into it before dropping it back into his shirt. "What are you doing?" Mike asked.

Dalton smiled and pointed at him. "Careful now." He patted his chest. "I own you now."

Mike went into a fit. "This is what I'm talking about! This shit is crazy! What the hell is this shit!"

Dalton patted Mike's shoulder. "Don't worry. I won't use

it unless I have to." He walked to the truck and dropped his pack in.

Mike stood there with his mouth hanging open. "What the hell is happening around here?"

Sarge walked past him and pushed his jaw shut. "Close yer mouth. Yer drawing flies." He paused and eyed Dalton for a moment, saying, "He's right though. You are one of the weirdest fuckers I've ever come across. Think I'll start calling you Baba Yaga."

Dalton howled and started to laugh. Holding a clenched fist up, he shouted, "Yes! Baba Yaga takes on *his* true form!"

"What the hell is Babet Yeager?" Mike asked.

Dalton turned to face him. With a near psychotic look on his face, he said, "Baba Yaga is the Russian boogieman. Usually, it's a woman, or three sisters." He stepped back and waved his hands in front of him, "but behold! The true form of *Baba Yaga!*"

Doc shook his head as he walked around the truck. "Things just get stranger and stranger."

Mike shook his head and muttered. "This shit is crazy." And he went over to the Hummer and climbed up into the turret. He pulled on a radio headset and checked the SAW. Sarge looked up at him and smiled. Nudging Ted, he asked, "Think he's had enough?"

Ted smiled. "Oh, he's done. You can take the fork out."

I shook my head and said, "You're worse than a bunch of high school kids."

Sarge smiled. "I know," and he cackled as he went around to the passenger side of the truck and got in.

Ted, Doc and Dalton got in and I walked over to the driver's side. "You guys be careful. Stay in touch."

"Just keep someone at the radio. We'll be in touch," Sarge replied. Then he looked at Ted, "Roll out, Teddy."

I looked at Ted and smiled. "Vaya con Dios, amigo."

He squinted as he looked out at me. "I hope it's not that eventful of a trip and he can take the day off." With that, the truck backed out into the road and headed out.

As the dust from the truck settled, Ian asked, "Now what?"

"Doesn't change what we have to do." I looked back at him. "Nothing changes here. I need to run over to the plant. You guys want to get out of here for a while?"

Perez stepped out of the door of the house and lit a smoke. "Yes I do. But I'm driving."

Jamie looked at him. "Dame uno cigarro, poppie."

Perez smiled and shook one out for her. She took it and he lit it. "You know these are bad for you, chica."

Taking a drag, she replied, "No te preocupes por eso. You don't have that many left."

"Let's take one of the buggies." Ian said as he looked up into the blazing sky. "I could use the air."

Perez climbed in behind the wheel of the old man's war wagon and started it up. Ian, Jamie and I all took a seat. I asked Perez to run by the house before we left. He nodded and started out. We stopped at Danny's real fast so I could let everyone know we were going to be off the reservation for a bit.

"When are you going to be back?" Mel asked.

"We shouldn't be long. The engineers are going to try to start the power plant today. It's just a test to see if it'll actually run. I just want to drop in and see."

"Well, I hope it does. Having the power back on would be wonderful," Kay said from the kitchen.

With a little laugh, I said, "Even if it runs, it could be a long time before we see power here. If at all."

"Hurry up so you can be home before dark. We're going to have some of that venison for dinner tonight," Mel said.

I kissed her and promised to be home soon. Back in the buggy, we headed out and stopped by the bunker. The girls were there with Aric. I told them what we were doing. Lee Ann asked if she could go.

I looked in the buggy. "There's an empty seat. Hop in if you want to go."

She climbed in and looked at Jamie. "How are you feeling?"

Jamie patted her stomach. "Good as new."

Looking at Jess, I said, "We'll be back in a little while."

She waved as she stepped back under the tarp at the back of the bunker. Perez pulled off and left the neighborhood behind us. This time, we didn't stop at the markets in Altoona or Umatilla. I wanted this to be a quick trip. But the sight of the unusual ride passing through town drew some curious looks.

When we arrived at the plant, Cecil was there going over a drawing with Scott, Terry and Doc Baker. Getting out, I asked, "How's it going?"

Scott shook his head. "Hard to say. Some of the systems are running, some aren't."

Cecil added. "It ain't nothing. We'll sort it out in no time."

Ian and Jamie climbed out of the war wagon and up onto the hood and sat down. Perez put his feet into the passenger seat and pulled his hat down over his eyes. Lee Ann walked up beside me and looked at the drawing and said, "That looks like hieroglyphics to me."

I put my arm around her. "I guess it does to you. But it all makes sense if you know what you're looking at."

"Didn't you used to work on these plants?" She asked.

Nodding, I said, "Yeah. A long time ago." Then, looking at Cecil, I asked, "So what's the holdup?"

Baker pointed at the drawing. "It's the fuel-forwarding skid. The gas isn't getting past it. I think there's a bad valve there."

I asked Cecil, "Are there any spares around here?"

Shaking his head, he replied, "No. But I know which valve is the problem. If they pull it out, I can rebuild it. It's been sitting a long time and is probably just seized up. I've had to do it before."

"How about the rest of the plant? Any of it been tested yet?" I asked.

Scott ran his finger over the drawing. "We've decoupled every motor and run them. They all run. We've tested all the valves; they all operate. All the thermocouples read properly. I think once we get this valve sorted out, we can start it up." Looking up, he added, "I think this old heap will actually run."

"So, when are you going to pull the valve?" I asked.

Terry nodded his head in the direction of the plant. "Eric is over there now pulling it out."

"I'll tear it down and get it working. We should be ready to try again tomorrow," Cecil added.

With a sigh, I replied, "Well then, we'll just try again tomorrow."

I took Lee Ann's hand. "Come on. I'll show you how power is made."

We walked over to the turbine. She looked at the complex machine for a minute, then said, "How do people come up with this? I mean, look at it. It's so complex." She pointed at a pipe running alongside the turbine housing. "What's that do?"

I patted her shoulder. "It's an electrical conduit. I would imagine it's carrying instrumentation wiring."

She shook her head. "It's crazy. To think we used to have all this stuff. All these complex machines that we felt were so necessary. And here we are with none of them and we're doing just fine."

Rocking my head back and forth, I said, "That may be true.

But a lot of people have died since all this went south. All these complex machines, as you say, kept a lot of people alive. It made our lives easier." With a chuckle, I added, "Remember sleeping with air conditioning?"

She rolled her eyes. "It is *so* hot at night." She smiled and added, "I put my sheets in the freezer before I go to bed. They feel so good when you get in them. I did it for Ashley too. She thought that was the coolest thing. Now I have to do it every night."

I gave her a hug. "It's really sweet you're looking out for her."

She shrugged. "She's my little sister. I have to look out for her."

Giving her a skeptical look, I replied, "I remember a day when you didn't think that way."

She starred at the ground for a moment. Looking back at me, she replied, "That was before. Now I know what really matters." She looked at the turbine again and added, "I kind of hope it doesn't come back on."

Shocked, I said, "What? It wasn't that long ago you were pretty upset about everything being lost forever. You said your life was over."

She nodded. "Like I said. That was before I knew what was really important. I'm very happy now. I like my new life." She plucked the silver star from her chest. "I like being a part of something. I like standing up for people who can't do it for themselves." She pinned the star back on her chest and looked at me. "I like being with my family and my friends. That's what's really important."

It was a profound statement from my daughter. When all the trappings of the *modern* world were stripped away, the essence of life was able to shine through. It's what we all strive for. It's why we work our lives away trying to *buy* time and comfort for our families. Time with our friends. Time to pursue those activities that bring us joy. The problem with that is, you can't buy time. You can only spend it. And once spent, it's gone forever. The entire paradigm the modern world was built on was a sham. If only we could have stepped back and seen it for what it was.

Taking her hand, I said, "I cannot tell you how happy hearing that makes me. Just knowing you're happy where you are. With who you are. There's nothing more I could ask for."

She blushed a little and said, "It's no big deal, dad."

I looked up at the plant. "Well, I guess we'll come back tomorrow."

Lee Ann cheerfully replied. "Okay."

We walked back to Baker and her crew. "Guess we'll come back tomorrow sometime."

"I'll get that valve sorted out by noon tomorrow," Cecil replied.

Waving, I said, "Alright, guys. See y'all tomorrow."

Walking back to our ride, I kicked Perez's feet out of my seat. "Wake up, old man. Let's head back."

Everyone got in and we started back towards the house. On the way, Lee Ann leaned forward and asked if we could stop at the Umatilla market. "What for?" I asked.

She shrugged. "I don't know. I've never been to it is all. Just want to look around." I looked at Perez and he nodded.

We pulled up to the Umatilla Kangaroo and stopped. As usually happened, when we were out in this thing, a number of people stared at it. We got out and I leaned against the front of the buggy. Jamie and Lee Ann wandered out into the market under the canopy of the old gas pumps. I for one, didn't want to get out in the crowd. I just hoped those two crazy old women weren't around.

Ian came up beside and leaned back over the hood of the wagon, resting on his elbows. "Anything out there worth looking at?" He asked.

I shook my head. "Nah. I was up here earlier today. We've got everything we need. The Altoona market is a little better, I think."

As I watched the crowd, two men suddenly stood out. I hit Ian on the arm. "Hey, man." Nodding my head, I said, "Look at those two guys right there." He looked where I indicated. "Notice anything funny about them?"

He shrugged. "Besides the tacky track suits?"

Nodding, I replied. "There's the tacky track suits. What looks like new shoes. They're clean shaven and their hair is short."

"They look like some eastern European douchebags." Perez added as he took a drag on his smoke.

"They do, don't they." Ian and Perez suddenly caught onto what I was thinking.

Ian straightened up. "They're trading for food too."

"Yeah. Lots of it from the looks of those bags," Perez replied.

Standing up, I said, "Let's go see what they're trading with. I'm curious."

The two men wandered around the stalls looking at the offerings of produce, eggs and the occasional fish or other meat. It appeared to me they were very deliberately not paying attention to us. I walked over to a small table where a bearded man in overalls and nothing else was trying to barter eggs. He was looking at something in his hand. "Howdy," I said.

He looked up. "Howdy, yerself. Lookin' for some eggs?"

I picked up one of the brown eggs and inspected it before replacing it in the bowl. "No. I'm curious. What did those guys over there trade for your eggs?"

The man smiled and held up a small gold coin. "He traded me this."

"Can I see it?"

Eyeing me suspiciously, he said, "You going to give it back to me, Sheriff?"

I laughed. "Yeah, I'll give it back. Just curious what it is."

He dropped it into my hand. "It's an African gold coin."

I saw he was indeed right. It was a tenth ounce Kruggerand. I handed it back to him. "Nice swap for some eggs."

He looked at the coin in his palm. "Yeah it was. I give 'em three dozen."

With a nod, I said, "Thanks."

We took a couple of steps away and I told the guys, "We need to have a word with those two."

Ian was looking around. "You think they're alone?"

I shrugged. "Hell if I know."

"We should wait until they leave the market. If there's any shooting, we don't want any civilians getting killed," Perez said.

"Good idea. Go over there and get Jamie and Lee Ann. Let them know what's up. Keep an eye on those guys. When they leave, we'll follow them." I said.

"Keep an eye out for anyone else," Ian said, and added, "I bet they have an over-watch someplace."

Considering the statement, I said, "I'm going to wander over to the wagon and call Sheffield and get them to send some folks down here."

"Good idea," Perez said as we parted ways.

I made my way back to the buggy and keyed my radio. "Hey, Eustis, you guys listening?"

"Go ahead, Morgan," Livingston replied.

"I need you guys to get some people up to the Umatilla Kangaroo as quick as you can."

"What's up?" He asked.

"I think we may have some Russian visitors in town."

His reply was less than assuring. "What?"

A little irritated, I said, "Just get some people up here. Now!"

With that done, I walked back over to Ian. The two men that we were watching were at the edge of the market. There was nothing else for them to look at, but they were delaying leaving, or so it appeared. I maneuvered us away from them, to give them some space. It didn't take long for them to take the opportunity to leave the market.

They headed west down 450, away from the market. I told Ian and Perez to get the wagon and bring it around. Catching Jamie's eye, I motioned for her to follow them. We met at the corner of the Kangaroo lot. The two men were about a block away when I heard the wagon start up. Ian was smart and didn't just drive through the lot. He went through the parking lot of the post office and came out on Kentucky Ave.

When the two men saw the wagon moving towards them, they started to run. Quickly, they had a whole block lead on us. But Ian was behind the wheel and raced towards them as we started to run. One of the men pulled out a pistol and fired at Ian. Jamie and I both fired back, dropping him in the street. The other one tried to get away on foot.

But it was futile. Ian came up close to him and Perez swung his rifle like a ball bat, knocking him down. We got to them just as Ian was rolling him over. The man was shouting and wrestling with Ian. I ran up and kicked him in the head, taking the fight out of him. We were all on the side of the buggy when a shot rang out. I immediately grabbed Lee Ann and pulled her to the ground.

The first shot was followed by an intense barrage of fully automatic fire. From where I was lying on the ground, I could see a truck of some kind on 450 to our west. It was obviously military, but small. We all began to return fire from under the wagon. Our return fire slowed the advance of the truck, but the machinegun fire continued. The incoming rounds snapped as they passed us and splattered the hot asphalt in front of us that burned our skin. Bullets were hammering into the armored panels on the side of Sarge's war wagon. Combined with our return fire, the sound was hellish.

Suddenly, there was the sound of a heavier weapon firing from behind us. I looked over my shoulder to see one of the new MRAPs we'd confiscated from the DHS, its Ma Duce machinegun working away. The gunner was holding the trigger down on the joystick and the old Browning was working hard.

Looking back under the bug, I saw the small truck start to back away. The large fifty-cal rounds skipped off the road in front of it as well as slammed into it. I could clearly see large holes in the windshield. The truck continued to back up but veered off the road and rammed into a house. There was more fire now pouring into the truck as another MRAP had joined the first, along with a couple of Hummers.

Someone called a ceasefire and it was suddenly quiet, though my ears were ringing ridiculously loud. I looked at Lee Ann. She was reloading her H&K, and two empty mags lay on the road beside her. "You OK?" I asked.

She nodded. "Yeah, my elbows are burned from the road. Are you ok?"

I looked around and replied. "Yeah. I think so." And I stood up.

Ian was sitting on the one man we'd caught. He wasn't saying anything. It wasn't until I took a second look I realized he wasn't conscious. "Is he alive?" I asked.

Ian looked down at him, then rolled him over. A large

section of his forehead was missing above his left eye. "Uh, that'd be a negative."

"No shit," I replied.

I heard the unmistakable voice of Sarge barking, "I can't leave you fucktards alone for a damn minute, can I?"

He and the guys got out of one of the Hummers and walked up to us. Dalton looked down at the man on the ground. "Hmm. Ain't getting much out of him."

Doc quickly knelt beside the man, but it was obvious there was nothing to be done for him.

Sarge nodded before replying, "Let's go check out the truck and see what's in there."

A line of men had formed in the street and we slowly approached the truck. Knowing that MRAP was right behind us with its large weapon was reassuring. Coming closer to the truck, I could see blood dripping out from the passenger door. The driver had reversed when the heavy rounds started slamming into it. It had veered off the road and come to rest on the front steps of a small house. The truck sat askew with the left rear tire nearly onto the front porch.

Once at the truck, Dalton pulled the passenger door open and stepped back, his rifle to his shoulder. But it was obvious these men were no longer a threat. The two men inside were dead. Really dead. Fifty caliber bullets do horrible things to a human body. Not to mention the small truck. Steam poured form under the hood with a hissing sizzling sound. Coolant, motor oil and other fluids leaked from under the vehicle onto the painted concrete walkway.

Dalton leaned into the truck and retrieved an AK-74 and slung it over his shoulder. "I'm keeping this." He then grabbed what was left of the man in the passenger seat and pulled it out into the yard.

Mike walked around to the driver side and yanked that door open. "Holy shit!" He shouted. "Check it out. He lost his head!"

The windshield was shattered and I couldn't really see through it, so I stepped up behind him. "Oh damn," I said. "That's fuckin' gross." It looked like the driver took one of those huge fifty-cal rounds right in the grape. It busted like an over-ripe melon.

But I was more interested in the truck and asked, "What is this thing?"

"It's a Gaz Tigr," Dalton replied as he pulled a pistol from a holster on the body he knelt beside. Looking at the pistol, he added, "I've never seen one of these for real. Only read about them. Think I'll keep it too."

"What is it?" I asked.

Standing up, he replied, "It's a Russian 9mm Grach."

"Let's see what else is in this thing," Sarge said.

The truck was full of weapons and ammo. Not to mention the assorted gear men need to conduct combat missions. There were radios, GPS units. Personal kits that disturbingly held family photos and the like. I was sorting through one of the packs. It was kind of interesting to get a glimpse into the life of a man I didn't know by seeing what he carried.

The one thing that we found extremely odd was that each of the men, even the ones killed back at the market, carried a cell phone. I collected them all. "What are you going to do with those?" Livingston asked.

"There's a shitload of information in these. I'll go through them and see what I find."

As we went through the equipment, laying it out in the street, a larger crowd began to form. They peppered us with questions to the point they got on Sarge's nerves. He pointed at a couple of the Guardsmen and told them to push the crowd back. The men did as instructed, and we were again able to focus on the task at hand.

Perez wandered over with the ever-present cigarette in his lips. He walked straight to the bodies and began searching the pockets. After a moment, he smiled and stood, "I knew they would have some!" He held a pack of Russian-made cigarettes in his hand.

"Is that all you're worried about?" Ian asked.

Stuffing the pack into a pocket, he said, "Priorities, my man." Looking at me, he added, "We have another problem. Two tires are flat on that wagon over there."

I looked back at Sarge's buggy. "Oh, you're shittin' me."

Perez shook his head. "I wouldn't shit you; you're my favorite turd."

I looked at Sarge. He was shaking his head. "Good job, dipshit."

"It ain't my fault!" I shot back.

From the crowd, a man said, "I can fix them tires for you."

I looked back to see who was talking. He was a skinny bearded man, like most are today. I waved him over and asked, "How can you do that?"

He jabbed a thumb over his shoulder. "I got everything I need back at the shop. I can break them off and patch them." His eyes darted back and forth before adding, "But it'll cost you."

Of course it will, I thought. "And what's it going to cost me?"

The man nodded at Perez, "A pack of them commie smokes." He licked his lips as he rubbed his chin. "I haven't had a smoke in a long, long time."

Perez looked back, "No."

I held my hand out, "Give 'em up."

Perez got indignant. "Hell no! Give him something else!"

"I don't want nuthin' else." The man replied.

Jamie stepped around from the back of the truck. She'd been back there digging through the equipment and said, "Here, you can have one of mine." She tossed a pack of cigarettes to the man. Seeing them, he reached out as if he were being offered something from heaven.

I reached out and snatched the pack out of the air. "Fix the tires," I said, waving the pack at him. "Then you can have these."

The man looked as though he was just told there was no Santa Clause. Licking his lips again, he said, "Give me one. Just one."

I opened the pack and shook a smoke out and handed it over. He took it and closed his eyes and ran it under his nose as he took in the aroma of the tobacco. Placing it in his lips, he reached to his pocket where any smoker would keep a lighter. But he patted his pocket and looked up desperately. "Anyone got a light?"

Perez stepped over and lit the man's cigarette. He inhaled deeply, savoring the taste and smell of the tobacco for real this time. After holding it in for a long moment, he blew the smoke out. A smile crossed his face and he muttered, "Whew, head rush. Damn that's good."

I held the pack up. "Get on those tires and these are yours."

With a look of determination and the fag clenched in his teeth, the man nodded at me and quickly departed. My attention was turned back to Sarge, who I could hear hollering about something.

"What in the hell are you bunch of booger-eatin' knuckle draggers thinking?" He shouted.

Mike's arms were full of things from the truck. He looked at Sarge confused. "What?"

"You ain't takin' none of that shit! All of that goes with

Morgan back to the ranch so we can go through it all very carefully!" Sarge replied.

Mike looked at his haul of loot. "What do you think you're going to find in this stuff?"

"Well, I don't know," Sarge replied quietly. Then shouted, "That's why I want to go through it all, you numbskull! Take that shit and dump it into the wagon."

Mike looked at Dalton. "Why's he gets to keep that AK and pistol?"

Sarge crossed his arms over his chest. "You really going to screw with that big man? He'd pull yer arms outta their sockets."

Mike looked back at Dalton. Dalton held his arms out in front of him, then jerked them out to his sides while making a popping sound. Mike's head went back and he asked, "You wouldn't?"

Dalton nodded. "Oh yeah. I've seen me do it."

"Put that shit in the wagon, Mikey," Sarge said.

Butt hurt, Mike started towards the wagon, "This is bullshit."

As he passed me, I said, "Don't worry, you'll get it back."

Mike smiled. "Thanks, Morg. You're all right." He looked back at Sarge and added, "Not like these other assholes."

"You'll get it back after I take what I want from it," I said with a laugh.

Mike looked back at me. His lips were curled into a sneer. "You're a dickhead. You know that?" I flipped the collar of my shirt up and pulled my head down to my shoulders. Sarge started laughing as Mike stomped off towards the buggy.

Sheffield walked up and said, "This is all very entertaining. But what are we going to do about this?"

Confused, Sarge asked, "About what?"

Annoyed, Sheffield held his hands out, "This! We've got dead Russians in town!"

Sarge rubbed his chin and looked thoughtful for a second. "I see what you mean." Looking at Sheffield, he said, "I think we should kill 'em. Oh wait. We already did that!"

Sheffield shook his head. "Would you stop being an asshole for just a minute? We've heard rumors that there were Russians. But now we know there are. What are we going to do?"

"Calm down, Captain." Sarge said. "We'll deal with them as they show up. There isn't much we can do." Sarge looked at me and asked, "What exactly happened here?" I took a few minutes to lay out what happened. Sarge, Sheffield and Livingston listened carefully until I finished.

"Where are the two you saw in the market?" Livingston asked.

I pointed back down the road towards the buggy. "They're back there."

"Let's go have a look at them," Sarge said.

We walked back up the road to the buggy. The man I'd given the smoke to was there, jacking the buggy up. The Russian we'd caught was still there on the far side of it. I rolled him over so they could see him. Sarge studied the man for a minute before speaking.

"What is with these Russians and their fetish with track suits?"

Sheffield looked at him and asked, "That's what you're wondering about?"

Sarge pointed at the body. "Look at him. They were obviously trying to get some food. Maybe a little intel at the same time." Sarge looked at me and asked, "You said they were trading for food?"

I nodded. "Yeah. They traded one guy a tenth ounce gold coin for a few dozen eggs."

"Did you hear 'em talk?" Sarge asked.

Shaking my head, I replied, "No. But we could go back to the market and find the folks they traded with."

"Let's go do that," Sarge said.

As we walked back to the market just down the road, we passed the body of the first man we shot. There were two Guardsmen there keeping people away from it. Sarge stopped and asked, "Did he have anything on him?"

One of the men shook his head. "Not really. A wallet and the pistol was about it."

"I already got the phone he had," I said.

Sheffield shook his head. "I don't get why they had phones. There's no service here."

Sarge held out his hand, "Let me see one of those phones." I handed it to him and he looked at it. "Their cell systems are different than ours here. Most of the world uses a different type that actually provides better service."

I laughed and said, "That was a long time ago, old man. There are only two kinds of systems used today, and Russia uses the same ones we do. I turned the phones off because they had signal bars. I don't know if they've put up portable towers or what and I don't want someone to be able to find these things, so leave them off."

Sarge glared at me. "You think your smart, don't you?"

I shrugged and replied, "I worked in technology, you forget."

"How could they have a signal? How far can that thing send a signal?" Sheffield asked.

I thought about it before replying. But Sarge was getting impatient and snapped, "Well? Come on, smartass. Spit it out!"

Shaking my head, I replied, "The max distance is around forty-five miles."

"So all they need is a tower within a forty-five-mile radius?" Livingston asked. I nodded.

Sarge took on a serious tone. "Crystal River is probably sixtyish miles as the crow flies."

"I was thinking the same thing," I replied.

Sheffield looked even more worried. "That's too far though."

"Not if they've put one up in the middle. Someplace between here and there," Sarge said.

Livingston shook his head. "This doesn't make any sense. Why would they be using cell phones? The Russians have secure communication equipment just like we do."

"I'm sure they do," I replied. "But they've also come up with a secure cell system that they claimed at the time was un-hackable. They showed it off at some conference in Shanghai. They know that we're all royally screwed, but maybe they think the old NSA is still up and operating. Just a thought."

"Any radio signal can be tracked." Sarge said. Pointing at the phone, he added, "Even if the NSA couldn't figure out what was being said, it wouldn't be hard to figure out where the signal is coming from. As soon as that thing starts transmitting, they can determine range and bearing, if the equipment is near enough."

We made it back to the market, which was now empty of people except for the few at their booths. They weren't willing to leave their wares to watch the action on the road. Many of the customers at the market ran off when the shooting started. But they returned when it stopped, curious to see what was going on. Entertainment today was at a premium. This was the biggest thing to happen in Umatilla in a very long time.

We went to the table of the man that sold the eggs. He was looking concerned at our approach and asked, "What the hell is going on?"

Sarge held out his hand, "Let me see the coin that boy gave you."

The man stepped back. "It's my money. You can't take it from me."

Sarge smiled. "Actually, I can if I want to. But I don't want to. Just let me see it. I'll give it back to you." He emphasized his words by motioning with his hand.

The man hesitantly reached into his pocket and removed the coin. He paused for a moment to look it over, as though he'd never see it again. He finally handed it over with a little sigh. Sarge took the coin and inspected it before handing it back, much to the relief of the trader.

"Those guys have any accent?" Sarge asked.

The man shrugged. "Not that I noticed."

"Ever seen them before?" I asked.

The man nodded. "A couple of times. They've been here buying food. They had real money and didn't bother anyone."

"How long they been here?" Sarge asked.

Again, the man shrugged. "I really don't know." He paused and pointed to a young woman standing on the curb looking back in the direction of the shooting. Even from this distance, it was obvious she was crying. "That girl there knows 'em."

We looked over at her. She was tall and thin, as were most people today. She had long red hair that wasn't knotted and looked to be very well kept. The man then added, "I think she had a thing for one of them."

Sarge smiled. "Is that so?" He started walking. "Let's go have a word with her then."

We followed him to where the young woman stood with another woman that was older. Sarge walked up behind the two women and stopped, and we did as well. They were talking about the two men lying in the road.

The red-haired girl wiped her eyes and said, "I can't believe they shot him. He wasn't doing anything. They were just buying food." She sobbed and added, "He was going to make us dinner tonight."

The older woman wrapped her arms around her. "I'm so sorry, honey. I can't believe they killed them like that. In cold blood. Right in the middle of the street."

The young girls seemed to stiffen. "I'll get that Sheriff." She sobbed harder. "I can't believe he's gone."

Why, why did people always want to *get* me? Why was it every time some asshole did something wrong, in this case *shooting* at me, did people want to take a shot at my ass as a result? This, above all other things, really, really, pissed me off. Stepping to the side of Sarge, I said, "Well, there's no time like the present."

The two women, startled and turned to face me. The older woman's face was clearly painted in fear. The younger one though, had a much different look about her. She glared defiantly at me. Sarge stepped between us. "Easy there, yougin'. Be careful just what you say and do. We just want to ask you a few questions."

The young woman still glared at me as though I was the only one involved in what just happened. The older woman was growing more concerned and asked, "About what? We haven't done anything."

Sarge smiled. "Of course not, we know that. We'd just like to know who these men were. Where they came from and how long they've been here."

Still defiant, the young woman said, "I've got nothing to say to you."

Sarge looked at the older woman. "What about you? What can you tell us?"

She was very obviously nervous. "I don't know what to tell you."

"Don't tell them anything, Mom." The young woman replied.

I was getting annoyed. "Look. We didn't start this shit. They did. All we wanted to do was talk to them. They started shooting first. They did it to themselves." Looking at the older woman, I said, "Now answer the damn questions."

The young woman looked at her mother. "Don't tell them anything."

I shook my head. Looking at Sarge, I asked, "Why does it always have to be the hard way?" As I pulled a set of cuffs from my vest, I looked at the young girl and said, "You can talk to us here, politely, or we can go to Eustis and talk there. The choice is yours."

The girl's mother became even more afraid and appealed to her daughter. "Britney, just tell them what they want to know." Tears welled up in her eyes as she continued. "I don't want you to get arrested. Just tell them."

Looking at the mother, I said, "I don't care which one of you answers the questions, but some-damn-body is going to."

"How long have they been here?" Sarge asked the mother.

She shrugged. "I don't know. A week maybe."

The young woman grabbed her mother's arm and pulled her. "Don't tell them anything! Come on! Let's go!"

I stepped in and grabbed the girl's wrist. She looked at my hand for a moment, then looked at me. I said, "It doesn't work that way," and snapped a cuff onto her wrist. And as they say, *that's when the fight started!*

The girl went crazy trying to get away from me. She screamed and screeched as she spun and fought. I had ahold of the other cuff and that was all I had. I thought Sarge or Livingston would step in. But in one of her twirling passes past Sarge, I clearly saw him laughing at me. But she didn't just fight with her arms and legs. Her mouth was going a mile a minute as she cussed me like a drunk sailor.

I finally managed to pull her out and get the palm of my right hand against the back of her elbow. Once I had control of her arm, it wasn't a big deal to take her to the ground. She couldn't weigh more than ninety pounds, so pulling her other arm back and cuffing it was easy. But that didn't stop her mouth. She continued to cuss me. Screaming she would kill me, and anything else that came to her mind. To silence her, I pulled my bandanna from my pocket and shoved it into her mouth.

"Shit!" I shouted as I stood up to her muffled complaints.

"What?" Sarge asked.

I shook my hand and looked at my finger. "She bit me." Sarge grabbed his stomach as he belly-laughed.

Sheffield didn't look happy and asked, "Is that really necessary?"

I looked down at the girl, then back at him. "Yes, it is."

Sarge looked at the older woman, who was pleading for me to let the girl go. "Just tell us what we need to know and we'll let her go. We don't want to take her anywhere."

The woman's hand trembled as she held it to her mouth. "What do you want to know?"

"How long they been here?"

The woman looked at her daughter before replying. "About two weeks. They started coming into town for food. They hung out with some of the younger people. Britney became friends with one of them and they spent a lot of time together."

"Did they have an accent?" Sarge asked.

The woman shook her head. "No. Well, sometimes they sounded a little funny. Like when they got drunk."

"And how did they manage to get drunk?" I asked. "There hasn't been any alcohol around for a long time."

"They brought a bottle of vodka to our house one night. They had food and we had a kind of party. They were really nice."

Sarge and I were looking at one another. "Vodka, huh?" Sarge asked.

She nodded. "Yeah."

"What were they doing here? What did they do all day?" I asked.

"They just hung out. They liked to go over to the old juice plant."

"Did you ever see them with any guns?" Sarge asked.

She nodded. "Sure. But everyone has guns now."

Sarge pointed down the road at the Tigr sitting against the house. "Did you ever see that truck before?"

She nodded. "Yeah. They said it was an old army truck."

Shaking my head, I asked, "You didn't think it was kind of odd they had a running truck with fuel?"

She looked at me. "No I didn't. What we thought was they were nice guys. They brought us food and other things no one has anymore. They didn't bother anyone and helped people out. Then you killed them."

With a sarcastic laugh, I replied, "You didn't notice they started shooting at us first? If they were such nice guys, why did they do that? We just wanted to talk to them. But they started shooting. They killed themselves."

The woman didn't reply. She looked down at her daughter lying on the ground, and at her feet. She glanced up and asked, "Are you going to let her go?"

"Where were they staying?" Sarge asked.

The woman shrugged. "I don't know. We only saw them when they came to town."

I nodded towards the guys lying on the road. "Did she ever go to *their place?*"

The woman shook her head. "No. I wouldn't let her leave with them."

Looking at Sarge, I asked, "You satisfied?"

The old man nodded. "Yep. I reckon they told us everything they know."

I knelt down beside the girl and grabbed her shoulder. "I'm going to take these cuffs off you now." She cut her eyes up at me. Pointing, I continued. "You behave yourself when I do or you won't like the outcome. Got it?" She didn't respond, just stared at me. "Got it?" I asked again a little louder.

This time she nodded, so I unlocked the cuffs and removed them. She quickly ripped the bandana from her mouth and threw it on the ground and tried to swallow. I could imagine how dry her throat was with that cloth being jammed in there, so I pulled a canteen out and uncapped it. Holding it out, I said, "Here, have a drink."

She took it and took a long gulp. Wiping her mouth with the back of her hand, she threw the canteen at me, sloshing some water on me. Without saying a word, she got to her feet and quickly walked off. I looked at her mother and said, "You should go with her. I know she's in a bad way right now. But what happened wasn't my fault and I take no satisfaction from it. Make sure she doesn't do anything stupid."

The woman nodded and followed the girl. We watched as she disappeared behind the store. Once she was gone, Livingston spoke. "Well, we don't know any more now than we did."

Sarge leaned forward and pinched off one side of his nose. Taking a deep breath, he fired a snot rocket into the sand. I smiled when I saw Sheffield grimace and shake his head. I wondered what he was in the Before. He damn sure seemed a little odd to me.

Sarge wiped his hand on his pants, getting another queer

look from Sheffield, before replying. "Actually, if you were listening, we learned a lot. We know the Ruskies are here. We know they're throwing money around, real money. We know they're playing the hearts and minds game, trying to show folks they're the good guys." He paused and looked around our small group. "And now we know it's working. They've been coming in and out of town here and we didn't even know about it." Sarge looked at me, "You didn't know they were here, did ya?"

I shook my head. "No, this was the first time I've seen them. But we don't spend a lot of time here. Not as much as we do in Altoona."

"Looks like that needs to change, Sheriff," Sarge replied.

I nodded. "Was already thinking that."

We walked back over to the vehicles. Everything had been removed from the Russian's truck. The war wagon was now sitting on all fours again. The man that repaired the tire was leaned over it with one foot up on the bumper with a very expectant look on his face. Sarge walked over and kicked the tire.

"It'll hold," the man said.

Sarge nodded. "I reckon it will. Good work." He looked at Jamie and said, "Pay the man."

Jamie tossed him a pack of smokes, which he nearly knocked out of the air in his exuberance. He tore the pack open and quickly shook one out, pinching it in his lips. Then, like a man lost at sea with water, water everywhere and not a drop to drink, he realized he didn't have a lighter.

Patting his pockets, he muttered, "Aw shit."

I smiled and gave Jamie a nod. She tossed him a Bic lighter, which he quickly used to light up. I walked over to Jamie and took another pack from the carton she held under her arm. Walking back over to the man, I handed it to him. He smiled broadly, "Hot damn! Thanks, Sheriff."

"No problem. I appreciate the effort on the tire. If we ever need another one fixed, you'll be our man."

With his smoke dangling from his lips, he smiled and said, "Good doing business with you. Any time you fellers need something fixed, just let me know." He collected his tools and started back towards his shop. He didn't get far before a crowd descended upon him. It was very obvious, and rather comical, that they all wanted a smoke. It was obvious the men in the crowd were shit out of luck. But it looked as though one woman just might get her nicotine fix.

It was funny and sad at the same time to see what people were reduced to. Here was a woman willing to trade her body for a cigarette. Of course it was a luxury today. And for all I knew, they could be together. But it was still disturbing to me.

CHAPTER 3

S ARGE STOOD ON THE SEAT of the Hummer, looking over the roof. "Let's make like an asshole and get the shit outta here! We're burning daylight!"

Mike was talking with the Guardsmen that were going with them on the patrol over to Crystal River. They were taking one of the MRAPs and one Hummer. Sarge, Dalton and one of the Guardsmen were going to ride in the Hummer. The other guys would take the MRAP. As one of the Guardsmen approached the truck, Dalton nodded at the driver's seat. "You drive; I'll take the turret."

The man nodded and held out his hand. "Kevin Harris, good to meet you."

Dalton took his hand and shook it. "Nice to meet you too, Kevin."

"Harris!" Sarge barked. "Get yer ass in here and let's get on the damn road!"

Dalton smiled and winked at Kevin. "Good luck."

"You too, Dalton! Get yer Sasquatch-lookin' ass up in that turret!" Sarge barked again.

Dalton moved immediately. "Yas'sah, boss! Shakin' the bush, boss! Shakin' the bush!"

Harris got in behind the wheel and closed the door. He

looked over at Sarge, who was giving him the stink eye. "Can you drive?" Sarge asked.

Kevin nodded. "Yes sir."

Sarge's face twisted into a sneer before screaming back. "That'll be enough of that sir shit! You see any fucking jewelry on my fucking collar?"

Kevin shook his head vigorously. "No, no s…" Sarge cut him off. His finger was touching Kevin's nose. "Don't you fucking say it!"

Kevin hesitated and shook his head. His mind was searching for the right word. Dalton was sitting in the sling seat of the turret, smiling to himself. He leaned down and looked at Kevin. He could see the panic on the man's face. Coming to his aid, he looked at Sarge and asked, "We ready, Top?"

Sarge never took his eyes off Kevin when he replied. "I don't know. Are we, Harris?"

Kevin nodded. "Ready if you are, Top."

"You ain't fucking waiting on me! Get moving!" Sarge barked.

Kevin dropped the truck into gear and pulled off. His eyes stayed fixed out the windshield. Sarge glared at him for a long minute until he was certain Kevin wasn't going to look over. Then he smiled and sat back in his seat. He pointed at the windshield and said, "Take 450 here all the way to forty-two and turn west." Kevin didn't reply, only nodded.

Dalton spun around in the turret, checking to make sure the MRAP was there. Satisfied everything was as it should be, he settled into the ride. He liked it up in the turret. The air, though hot, was at least moving. As the trucks wound their way down 450, they passed the Elk's Camp. Dalton looked over at the gate as they passed. The makeshift roadblock was still partly there and Kevin maneuvered around what was left of it. Sarge also watched as the camp passed. He glanced up, half expecting to see the sky full of buzzards. They'd left a lot of bodies lying out there and he wondered what became of them. He'd like to stop and look around, but they had a mission and time was an issue. He wanted to get it over with as fast as he could.

While he knew this needed to be done, he wasn't a fan of running around anymore. He was quite happy to sit on the porch in a rocking chair with Miss Kay at his side. For the first time in his life, he felt as though he had a home. Not in a physical sense, because if that were the case, he wanted to be back on the river. But the grubby little collection of houses and idjits living in them was his home now. And he couldn't ask for anything more. Not that he'd say it to anyone there. They'd just get all dew – eyed and make it into something it wasn't. Bunch of booger-eaters.

Mike was driving the MRAP. As the camp came into view, he looked at Ted. "Hey, ask the old man if we can go in there and look around."

Ted's head rolled to the side to look at him. "You ask him."

Mike's lip curled and he replied, "You're right. We ain't got time."

Ted smiled. "That's what I thought you'd say."

Mike looked over at him. "You think the old man is getting weird?"

Ted snorted. "How could you tell?"

Mike's head rocked back and forth. "I know what you mean. But he seems different. I don't know," Mike got a sour look on his face, "meaner, if that's possible."

Ted laughed. "Yeah. I don't think that's possible. I think he's just getting older. He's had a long hard run at it and done more shit than you an me put together." Rolling his head over to look at Mike again, he added, "And that's saying something."

"Yeah. Maybe," Mike replied. "I think that old woman's getting to him."

"*Miss Kay,*" Ted replied, making a point out of emphasizing her name, "is the best thing to happen to him. He needs someone in his life. Shit, I, for one, am happy for him. Gives him something else to focus on besides us."

Mike smiled and licked his lips. "I guess you're right. It's kinda good, really. I'll be taking over this outfit soon."

Ted laughed and slapped his knee. "You? You think you're going to take over from the Old Man?"

Mike's eyebrows narrowed. "Yeah. Why not?"

Still laughing, Ted replied, "You couldn't organize a troop of Cub Scouts! Let alone this outfit!"

"Whatever, dickhead. You were probably in the damn Girl Scouts."

"I was. But they kicked me out," Ted replied. Then he sat up and pointed his hands like pistols at Mike, "when I ate all the Brownies."

Mike shook his head. "That's just fucked up!"

Ted sat back in his seat. "Whatever, Scrub Scout."

We watched as the two trucks disappeared down the road. Turning to head back to the buggy, Jamie asked, "What do you want to do with the bodies?"

I shrugged. "Someone will sort them out when they start to stink. I want to hook a strap to that truck of theirs and drag it home though."

Perez grunted, "What do you want that wreck for?"

"I don't know," I replied. "Just want to take it with us."

My radio crackled. "Hey, Morgan, it's Baker. We're not

going to be ready today. Cecil is installing that valve now, but we still need to test it."

Keying my mic, I replied, "That's fine. We've got our hands full as it is."

"What was all the shooting? We saw the column haul ass your way."

"We found a couple of Russians and tried to have a word with them. They didn't want to talk to us though."

"Already, huh?" Baker said. "Thought it would take longer."

"Me too," I replied. "We'll see you guys tomorrow."

"We'll be ready in the morning," Baker replied.

I looked at Perez, "Let's get that rig hooked up and get the hell out of here."

We got a strap hooked to the truck and Perez and I watched as Jamie got in the war wagon and pulled it off the porch. It had a flat tire on the front, but it should make it back with us. Watching it as Jamie pulled it out onto the road, I glanced at Perez, "Hey, man, you're going to need to get in to steer that thing."

Perez cocked his head to the side and pointed at it. "Have you seen the fucking blood in there? I ain't about to sit in that shit."

Nodding, I replied, "I know it's nasty. But we can't just drag it."

Perez snorted. "You get in it." Then he crossed his arms and shook his head. "I ain't doing it."

I was shaking my head when I looked back at Jamie. She wagged a finger at me, "Don't even think about it, Sheriff."

I had to laugh about it. Not that I could blame them for not wanting to sit in that shit. I walked over and opened the driver's door. It was a disgusting mess. There was blood, tissue and bone all over the interior. I shook my head as I pulled the poncho out of its pocket on my vest. I laid it out over the seat. As I was tucking it in, Lee Ann walked up and looked in. "You really going to sit in that?" She asked.

"Looks that way. Hop in and let's head home."

She pointed back at the buggy, "I think I'll ride in that one."

Everyone got in the buggy and gave Jamie a wave and she pulled off. Perez decided it was siesta time and pulled his hat down over his eyes in the passenger seat. As we headed home, I looked around the cab of the truck. I really wished it hadn't been shot up so bad as it was a pretty cool ride. But it had been. One thing I hadn't noticed upon first inspection was the large piece of the steering wheel that had been shot away. It made steering a real adventure.

As we passed the Altoona market, we drew some serious looks. Not that I blame them. No doubt, the folks here heard all the gunfire. And to now see the shot-up remains of a foreign truck being towed surely piqued their curiosity.

But it was the girls and Aric at the bunker that were really surprised. Jamie stopped by the side of the fortification and stepped out. Jess, Fred and Aric all came over to inspect the truck.

"Is everyone Ok?" Aric asked. "We heard the radio call."

"And the shooting," Jess added.

"We're alright," Fred replied.

Aric had his head in the window of the truck. With a whistle, he said, "Doesn't look like these guys are though."

I looked around the cab of the truck. "You could say that."

Jess walked over and looked in. Her face twisted in disgust. "Oh, that's so gross!" "How can you sit in that? That's so disgusting!"

I shrugged. "It's not so bad once you get used to the smell."

She jerked her head back, covering her nose. "Oh God, that's gross."

Jamie asked Perez to drive back to my house; she and Lee Ann were going to stay at the bunker. So Perez towed me the rest of the way to my place. Danny and Thad were both there when we pulled in. I indicated where I wanted to park the heap, and Perez pulled around to the side of the house where we unhooked the truck.

Thad looked inside and shook his head and muttered, "Damn."

"What the hell happened?" Danny asked.

Perez and I relayed the story to them as they looked the truck over. Thad listened as he opened the hood of the truck. He was inspecting the engine as we wrapped up our story. He peered under the hood at a couple of large holes in the radiator and said, "Shame this thing's so shot up."

"Yeah, I felt the same way," I replied.

"It's an interesting truck for sure," Danny said.

"The stuff in the buggy is the real interesting part," Perez said.

"Oh yeah, we got all their stuff," I replied as I stepped over to the buggy.

We set the packs and bags out on the ground, then laid the weapons out along with the ammo. When everything was laid out, Danny stepped back and looked at it. "That's quite the haul."

Thad knelt down and picked up a radio. Inspecting it, he asked, "Have you tried this thing yet?"

I shook my head. "No. You speak Russian?"

Thad smiled and shook his head. "Nope."

Danny nodded at the small radio, "Turn it on. Let's see if we can hear anything."

Thad looked the device over for a moment before finding the power switch. A short burst of static let us know it was on, but that was the only sound it made. Danny asked for the radio and Thad handed it over. Danny fumbled with the knobs and buttons which all had more markings we couldn't decipher.

"Well, this is useless," Danny announced.

I laughed. "Wish someone knew Russian."

"Doesn't Dalton know it?" Thad asked.

Nodding, I replied, "He knows some, I think. Maybe he can make sense of this thing."

Danny was looking at the gear and asked, "How many guys did you say there were?"

"Four." I replied.

"There's only three radios. I would think they'd all have one."

Thad knelt and opened one of the bags. "Maybe there's another one here."

But there wasn't another one. But just like going through the pockets of the men at the scene, it was interesting here to see what was in all the packs and bags. Danny started to laugh as he pulled a magazine out of one of the bags.

"Check this out," he said, holding it up.

He handed it to me and I too had to laugh too. "I had no idea Penthouse printed a Russian edition. That's too funny."

"What's the date on it?" Thad asked.

I flipped it over and looked at the cover. "It's from last month."

"Nice to know the porn industry wasn't affected," Thad replied with a smile.

"Really? Really?" I looked up to see Mel standing over me with her hands on her hips. "This is what you're out doing, getting porn magazines?"

I looked at the magazine and back at her. "What? No. This was just in this stuff we're going through."

"Mmm, hmm," she replied in snarky tone. Then she waved a finger at the truck and the gear on the ground. "And the one thing you pull out is a porn mag?"

"What?" I asked again and looked at Thad. He held his hands up and shook his head. "Not me." He looked at Mel, "I ain't touched it."

I couldn't help but laugh at him. "Coward," I said.

Little Bit came running out of the house. I saw her coming and stuffed the magazine back into one of the bags. Looking at Mel, I said, "Don't let her near that truck. It's a bit of a mess."

Mel looked at it, then back at me. "Why did you bring it here?"

Shrugging, I replied, "I don't know. We took everything they had."

Mel looked at the equipment laid out on the ground, then back at the truck again. Then, looking at me, she asked, "Do I want to know what happened?"

I shook my head. "Probably not."

Her eyes narrowed and she started to turn away, then stopped and pointed at me. "I better not find that thing in my house."

I smiled. "Does that mean the bathroom too?"

With her head cocked to the side, she said, "Oh, you think you need that? Is that it? Then I suggest you keep it. Because I can promise that you *will* need it." With that, she spun around and headed for the house. She intercepted Little Bit on her way and took her back to the house.

Thad was laughing at me and pulled the bag over to him. Pulling the magazine out, he folded it and tucked it into my vest. "You better take that with you; sounds like you may need it."

I snatched it out and tossed it back at him. "Keep it for Mikey, smartass."

Danny was laughing at me as well. "You're an idiot."

I cocked my head to the side. "Can't help it. I like to mess with her."

Thad slapped his leg. "Don't sound to me like he be messin' with her any time soon."

"Nope," Danny added with a laugh.

"Everyone's got jokes, huh?" I asked.

They both laughed ad replied, "Yep."

Grabbing a couple of the bags, I said, "Well, you jokers, let's take all this gear and put it in the shed out back."

We stowed all the gear in the shed and headed over to Danny's place. One of Sarge's Big Green Monster radios was set up there as there was usually someone around his place. That way, if they called at any time, someone would be around. It was getting late in the day and supper would be on soon. Mel was in the kitchen with Kay and Bobbie when we came in.

Looking at Mel, I smiled and said, "Hey, babe."

She narrowed her eyes but didn't reply. Danny nudged me from behind. "Gonna be a while."

I laughed. "No it ain't. Watch."

Walking into the kitchen, I slapped her ass. She looked over her shoulder and said, "Hands off, magazine boy."

I smiled and kissed her cheek. "Love you too."

"Whatever," she replied.

"What's for supper? It smells good in here." Thad asked.

Kay smiled. She loved to feed people, getting genuine joy from it. "We're having meatloaf with gravy and greens."

"You cooking those sweet potato greens tonight, Miss Kay?" Thad asked.

"Yes I am, Thad. Thank you for bringing them in. I think you're going to really like them."

"I had no idea you could eat the leaves of sweet potatoes," Bobbie said.

"We're lucky we've got Thad's garden," Kay said.

"I got a surprise for you guys," Thad said. "It'll take a little while, but we're going to have some potatoes in the fall."

Kay looked at him. "What kind of potatoes?"

"That I don't know," Thad replied. "I found the plant in what was someone's compost pile. I dug it up and brought it back and planted it in the garden."

"Does that mean we can have French fries?" Little Bit asked.

"French fries!" Little Edie shouted.

"Yes we can!" Kay shouted.

"It's only one plant and we'll have to see how it grows. We'll probably have to use most of the first ones for seed so we can get more plants." Thad said.

Kay rested her elbow on the counter. "I don't care how long they take. It's probably the only potato around here. If we can get more plants out of it, that's a good thing."

"Makes me wonder what other vegetables we won't see anymore." Mel said.

"Like broccoli," Bobbie replied.

"Yeah! No broccoli!" Little Bit shouted.

Thad smiled. "Sorry, Little Bit. I'm growing some in the garden now."

"Really?" Mel asked. Thad nodded and Mel continued. "I wish we had some garlic. I love sautéing it with garlic."

"Sorry, Miss Mel, I don't have any garlic in the garden." Thad said.

"Thad, you and I should probably eat so we can go take our turn at the bunker," I said.

"Oh, Morgan. You're just trying to get your supper early," Kay said.

Looking at my watch, I said, "No, we really do have to be down there to let those girls and Aric take a break. But we can wait till we get off later."

Kay swatted at me with a dish towel. "No, no. I don't want Thad going down there hungry."

Smiling, Thad thanked her. I shook my head, "Hey! What about me?"

Kay smiled at me. "You'll get yours too."

"Well, Thad, I'm glad folks around here like you," I said.

He sat down at the bar and smiled. "Don't worry, Morgan. I'll make sure they feed you too."

Mounting a stool beside him, I slapped him on the back and laughed. "Don't go out of your way or anything."

Kay and Bobbie had prepared a meatloaf of bear and pork. It was the first time for this particular dish and I was impressed. Though I did inspect it closely, getting the stink eye from Kay.

"Just what are you looking for?" Kay asked as she wiped her hands on a dish towel.

"I'm just making sure it's cooked all the way."

"You think I don't know how to cook meatloaf?" Kay asked.

"It's not that. It's just that bear meat is notorious for carrying Trichinosis. It's so bad in fact that about ninety percent of all cases in the US come from eating under-cooked bear meat," I replied.

Thad looked down at the nice thick slab of steaming meatloaf on his plate and said, "Why do you always come up with this kind of thing at just the wrong time?" He looked at me and appeared he was about to cry. "Why now? I'm so hungry and it smells so good."

I laughed and looked at Kay. "Did you check it with a meat thermometer?"

She crossed her arms over chest and leaned against the counter. "Of course I did. But not for the bear meat. Pork is where you get Trichinosis."

I pointed at her. "Used to. But when the government made it illegal to feed domestic pigs uncooked garbage, the Trichinosis disappeared from the domestic population. You can still get it in wild hogs though."

"So what temp does the meat need to reach, Mr. Science?" Kay asked.

She pursed her lips. "To a hundred and forty-five degrees, if you don't trust me!"

Smiling, I said, "Come on now, Kay. You know that's not it."

Thad looked at his plate again, then at me. "You gonna eat it?" He asked.

I nodded. "It's safe. I was just saying we need to be careful. Even if you get it, it's not that bad in normal times. But as we all know, these ain't normal times."

Thad looked at my plate and nodded. "You first."

I cut a big piece out with my fork and held it up so Kay and Thad both could see it and shoved it in my mouth and started chewing. With my mouth full, I mumbled, "Wow, Kay, this is really good."

She waved her hand at me. "Too late, mister." She turned to the sink, muttering to herself, *undercook my meatloaf.*

I had to laugh about it, but it was a real concern. Thad watched me as I took another bite before taking a tentative bite himself. But a broad smile quickly spread across his face, and he said, "This is really good, Miss Kay. Wow."

She turned from the sink and smiled warmly at Thad.

"Thank you, Thad. You know I enjoy cooking for you." Then she looked at me and scowled before turning back to the sink.

With sweet potato greens dangling from my fork, I pleaded, "Oh come on, Miss Kay. Don't be like that."

Leaning over his plate, Thad cut his eyes at me, "You might as well give up."

Mopping gravy up with the last bite of the meatloaf, I nodded. "Guess you're right. I'll have to figure out some way to make it up to her."

Thad chuckled. "Good luck with that."

With our supper done, I collected our plates and walked to the sink to wash them. Kay was still there and took them from me, shooing me out of her kitchen. I started to say something about it being Bobbie's kitchen, but better sense prevailed and I kept my mouth shut. Just as I was walking out of the kitchen, the radio set up in the corner on a folding table crackled.

"Stumpknocker is at Universal."

I walked over to the radio and picked up the mic. "Roger that. Buy the express pass so you can beat the wait."

"Keep the dumbass chatter off the radio, dipshit." Came Sarge's terse reply.

I shook my head as I set the mic down. Turning around, I asked, "Did someone sneak in and steal everyone's sense of humor."

Bobbie was wiping the counter where Thad and I just ate. Her back was to me when she replied, "You're just not nearly as funny as you think you are."

I looked at Mel, but she held a hand up. "Don't talk to me. Go see what the girls in that magazine think about it."

"Oh, for cryin' out loud," I replied. Looking at Thad, I asked, "You ready? I gotta get out of the crazy here before I catch it."

"Ha!" Kay barked from the kitchen.

Thad came up and pushed me towards the door. "Come on. Let's get you outta here before you get yourself in any more trouble."

As we went out the door, I said, "Let's take Sarge's buggy. My truck is starting to get rough."

"Fine by me," Thad replied as we walked to the small vehicle.

We arrived at the bunker as the sun was beginning its descent. The oppressive heat of the day was starting to wane, though it was still hot. Jess started clapping when she saw us.

"I'm so ready to go," Jess said.

"I'm hungry," Lee Ann added.

"We're going to take this back to the house." Aric said as he headed to the buggy.

"Go for it," Thad replied.

As she passed, Lee Ann gave me a hug and asked, "How long are you going to be down here?"

"Until morning, I guess."

"Yeah, Danny and I will be back early in the morning," Aric replied.

"Being shorthanded sucks," I replied. "But we'll get through it."

Fred waved as she got in the buggy. "See you guys later. I'm starving!"

They quickly departed, leaving Thad and me alone. Thad looked down at my legs and said, "You're going to be sorry you didn't put on long pants."

Looking down, I said, "Oh shit. I forgot to change."

Thad smiled, "Bet you won't again."

And he would be proved right. As the sun started to set, the blood sucking masses emerged from their daytime hiding places to drive us mad. To aid our sanity a little, I suggested we build a smudge fire. Thad said it was too hot for a fire. And while he was certainly right, I needed some relief, so I dug a small fire pit under the tarp at the rear of the bunker.

The fire would be kept small, as I was more interested in the smoke than any heat. It didn't take long to get a decent fire going. To encourage the smoke, and discourage the bugs, I threw on the green leaves of Beauty Berry. The smoke did its job and ran most of the tiny terrors out from under the tarp.

Checking the time, I set the small radio up on top of the bunker and extended its antenna. It was almost time to catch JJ Schmidt tonight. I wish I knew what frequency they used on the radio and when they used it, so I could pass along to them the fact we found those Russians. But at least getting info from them was a benefit. It was strange in a sense. As if the darkness were pulled back a bit. The information vacuum let up just a little each time I caught his broadcast.

This was the one thing I really fell short in. I hadn't considered the effect of being in a near total void of information. The not knowing what was happening even a county over, let alone across the nation, was a real shortfall. If I had the opportunity to go back and change things, this is the one I certainly would. Of course, more power would be nice. But we'd adapted to that just fine. But news. Real news of what was happening or could be coming our way, that I wish I had.

The radio gave nothing but static, so I turned it down and left it sitting. While we waited to see if there would be any news tonight, I busied myself with the fire while Thad used the NVGs to scan the area. The evenings were so quiet now. As the sun set, most critters went to their dens or roosts. The air felt heavy and a haze fell onto the earth. It was an odd time to be out. The mid-summer evenings in Florida, following the height of the sweltering daytime heat, had a very ominous feel to them. As though it were the opening scene to some horror movie.

But there never was any horror. The sun would continue to drift toward the horizon. The temps would ease ever so slightly. And some days when the east and west coast sea breezes collided at the right time, thunder would roll in the distance. Tonight was one of those nights.

Thad and I stood under the tarp as the little radio hissed and popped, the volume so low it was just barely audible. Out to our west, straight down the street, heat lightning lit up the sky in fantastic patterns. The thunder would come rolling across the fields a short time later as a low roiling rumble. The flashes would light up the thunderheads for an instant. Like the flash of a camera, we'd catch a momentary image that seemed to be burned into our eyes.

Thad stepped out from under the tarp and looked up into the sky with the NVG. He spun in a circle as he said, "I think we might get wet tonight."

I walked away from the reprieve the smoke offered to look up as well. The sky overhead was dark and growing darker. The sun, now set, was nothing more than a faint line of color on the distant horizon. "You could be right." I replied. "We could use it, though. The farm needs the rain and it'll run these damn skeeters off," I added.

We stepped back under the tarp, and I dropped a couple pieces of wood on the small fire and another handful of leaves. As I stood up, the first raindrops hit the tarp. It was a dull thud of a large drop. The lightning intensified and the thunder came quicker. No longer simply heat lightning, the flashes came in brilliant bursts of light that lit up the world, followed nearly immediately by fierce thunderclaps.

The rainfall grew more and more powerful, until it was

pounding on the tarp over our heads. The sound of the rain battering the sheet overhead became so loud, we had to nearly shout at one another to be heard.

"It's a frog strangler!" Thad shouted.

I nodded. "Looks like we should have been building an ark!"

The road was soon a running torrent of water, carrying sand, sticks and leaves. The small fire was quickly washed away and we had to step close to the bunker to keep from getting our feet soaked. I picked up the radio and held it to my ear. It sounded like a voice, so I turned the volume to near full before I could make it out. It was JJ Schmidt alright and he'd already started the broadcast.

...ut it would appear the Chinese are not heeding the warnings. These are dangerous times, folks. If the Chinese do not turn their fleet away from the California coast, they risk annihilation. It would be the first time a nuclear weapon has been used in the modern era. The potential side effects are tremendous, not the least of which could be a retaliatory strike against us. But officials from NORAD believe an invasion of the mainland by Chinese troops would be catastrophic. Reports coming out of the Hawaiian Islands paint a grim picture of what could be in store for all of us. We, of course, will keep you up to date as the situation develops further.

As if this weren't bad enough, it now appears there are Russian pathfinders in Florida. Several reports emerged from the Florida Keys about Russian and Cuban forces landing there, as well as in other less populated areas of the state. The DOD, operating out of Patrick Air Force base, is tracking these forces down and eliminating them. While it does not appear to be a full-on landing, the presence of any foreign forces is troublesome.

Both the Russian and Cuban governments claim to have abandoned their planned humanitarian assistance operations, as they called them, after warnings that any attempts to land forces on the Continental United States would be met with extreme force. But reports emerging from the area indicate that appears to not be the case.

We are down. But we are not out. And any nation that thinks they are going to take advantage of us in our time of distress is going to learn a hard lesson. God bless the men and women of our armed forces. Pray for them and the nation as a whole.

Then a woman's voice came on the air.

Good evening, patriots. The moon is full. The moon is full.

With that, the transmission ended. I hadn't noticed the passing of the storm as I listened. The radio's static was suddenly very loud in my ear, and I turned it off. I was closing the antenna when Thad spoke.

"Don't sound good. Them talking about nukes."

I shook my head. "No. I hate to say this, but thankfully they're talking about the California coast."

"Anyone in their right mind would be thankful not to be in the way of that fight. But as the man said, if we nuke them, they might hit back. And they could be anywhere."

Tucking the radio into its pocket, I said, "I know, and that's what worries me. Like we don't have enough shit to worry about."

"Yeah. Like Russian and Cubans running around here."

I looked at Thad. "We already know there are Russians. But from the sound of it, there may not be many of them."

Thad held his hand into a stream of water running off the tarp. It collected in his hand before spilling out of his palm. He quickly brought his hand to his mouth and sucked up the water. "That may be true. But how many is too many?"

"Well. There's four less than there were."

Putting his hand back into the rivulet of water, Thad sighed. "All I want to do is grow a garden. Work the land." He drank the water again. "I want to be left the hell alone so I can grow old in peace."

"I'm right there with you," I replied.

With a slight tilt to his head, Thad half smiled. "No you ain't, either." He paused and stared at me for a moment. "You like the fight." He held his hand up to squash the protest I was about to respond with. "I know you won't admit it. Hell, you may not even know it yourself. But you is all about this. You'll carry the fight to anyone that is bringing the pain." He paused again and pointed at me. "And you is good at it. It's in your bones. You couldn't not fight."

I thought about what he said. Turning, I rested on the top of the bunker and looked out into the clean black night. The rain had washed the air and it smelt clean and fresh, mixing with the smell of the wet earth rising up.

There was no malice in Thad's words. And one thing I knew well and sure, he had an insight into people, and me in particular. Our chance encounter on the side of the road may not have been so random. People come into our lives for a reason. I believed that now more than ever. Every person in my life today was there for a reason, and many, hell most, of them came about through a series of events that would surely have to be by design.

After thinking about it for a minute, I said, "Like you said, I don't really agree with that. But I also see where you're coming from."

Thad smiled. "I know."

I turned and leaned back on the bunker. The river of water that had been flowing down the road was gone now. That was one of the good things about Florida's sandy soil. Water didn't hang around and we didn't get the flash floods other places in the country saw. That and the fact it was flat as a pool table.

With a nod I said, "But you know there's some of that love of the game in you too. Otherwise you wouldn't be here either."

Thad laughed. "You could be right about that. I don't like to see good folks suffer none either."

I patted the pocket where the little radio was. "But this. This isn't the kind of fight I want a part of."

Thad's smile faded. "Me neither. That's that kind of thing that is out of our control. The effects are just too big and there's so little we can do about it."

"That's what I'm worried about," I said as I stepped from under the tarp. It was still raining, though nothing like it was before. Looking up into the sky, I added, "I hope this drizzle keeps up. It'll keep the skeeters away."

His smile was back now. "You and them skeeters."

"I hate 'em!" I said.

Laughing, Thad replied, "I'd never guess."

We spent the rest of the night listening to the light rain as it dappled on the tarp. It went on for a long time. Another benefit of the quick and violent storm was that it cooled things off and made it more comfortable. We would still scan the area from time to time. But that sort of storm would drive people to seek cover. Except for the professionals. A storm like that simply created opportunity for them.

The storm worked in Sarge's favor. The two trucks were able to make it through the potentially more populated areas without incident. The pounding rain drove people inside. Well, most people. Sane people. Sarge had to shake his head at Dalton who stayed in the sling seat of the turret howling like Lieutenant

Dan from Forest Gump. The turret was his ship's mast as he cursed *at the gods,* using the plural purposely.

His antics unnerved Kevin, causing him to grip the wheel a little tighter. But the old man was no comfort. He'd heard the stories of the guys in this group. They were often talked about around the armory. Some despised them. Some liked them. But everyone respected them. They were known for taking on insane tasks and coming out the other side while causing a very, very bad day for whoever they were up against.

But this. Nothing could prepare him for this madness. The stories damn sure didn't live up to the reality of actually running with them. As Dalton howled and wailed in a driving rain that caused the trucks to slow to a near crawl, the old man sat there as though it was normal. He was certainly second guessing volunteering for this madness.

"Stop," Sarge barked.

Kevin slammed on the brakes, hard. Causing the old man to spill his coffee. A red dome light illuminated the cab of the truck and Kevin swallowed hard when the old man looked over at him as hot coffee ran down his hand into his lap.

Sarge shook the hot brew off his hand and looked at Kevin. "Harris. There is one thing you better learn, ricky tick." He held the cup up before him. "This is one of the most important things on this ride. You do not fuck with it. In any manner. Got it?" Kevin nodded and Sarge continued. "I know this is your first trip with us, so I'll overlook it, this time."

The radio crackled. It was Mike. "What's the holdup?"

"Stay off the radio, puss nuts," Sarge calmly replied.

Dalton ducked down into the truck and wiping water off his face, he asked, "Oi. You fookers know something I don't? Anything you'd like to share with me?"

"Shit for brains here spilled my coffee," Sarge said and held the cup up to emphasize his point.

Dalton snatched the cup from the old man and quickly gulped the little bit of steaming coffee that remained. Sarge immediately went off, cussing and screaming. Dalton held the old man back with one arm as he drank. He was doing a good job of it until the old man grabbed his pinky finger and bent it back. Dalton cursed as he did.

"Ow dammit! Ok, ok, here's your cup!" He spun the cup around on his finger.

Sarge snatched it from him and pointed an accusatory finger at him. "That's the last time you try that shit! I know you're a big bastard, and there's only one way to deal with a big bastard! You shoot 'em in the fucking nuts! You tracking me?"

Dalton patted his chest. "I'm hurt you'd begrudge me a hot brew when I been riding in the rain as I have. Providing security for you to ride comfortably here in the truck."

"Cut the shit, sasquatch! I can forgive a lot of things. But fucking with my coffee ain't one of em!"

Dalton again wiped the water dripping from his face away. He nodded and asked, "What else is on that list? Just so I know in the future."

Sarge began to sputter and curse again and drew his pistol from its holster. He jammed the muzzle into Dalton's crotch and screamed. "Left or right? Which one is it going to be? Take your pick!"

Dalton leaned in a little closer and grabbed the muzzle of the pistol and pressed it firmly against his forehead. In a calm, even tone, he said, "Right here. Do it. Go ahead, pull the trigger."

Kevin was in near shock and didn't know what to hell was

happening. He watched the scene unfold before him, unsure what to do. Or more importantly, what not to do.

Sarge jerked the Colt away and looked at Kevin. "See. That's the problem when you're dealing with crazy bastards. You just can't do shit with them." Sarge holstered the pistol and pointed out the window. "Turn down here." Looking back over his shoulder, he said, "Get your ass back up there Gigantor."

Dalton saluted. "Right oh!"

Sarge picked up the radio mic and keyed it. "Mikey. Pull around us. This bridge is the perfect place for a bad surprise and I don't want to find it with this un-armored heap."

"Roger that." Mike replied.

Sarge leaned back and shouted up at Dalton. "Keep your eyes open up there, Gulliver."

"Aye Aye, Chief!" Dalton replied.

Sarge turned back and slapped Dalton's thigh. "I ain't a fucking squid, you jackass!"

But Sarge had to pull back when Dalton started kicking at him with his enormous boot. He smiled to himself as he listened to the old man bitch and moan. He liked the old shit because he was so easy to spin up. Life was kind of boring today and needed something to break the monotony.

The MRAP pulled around the Hummer and started up the Ocklawaha Bridge. Dalton scanned the area around and behind them. He was looking at the Sunny Hill Restoration sign when Mike called over the radio.

"We have company on the other side."

"What is it?" Sarge asked.

"Hard to tell from here. There's bodies down there with weapons."

"Well, dispshit, what are they doing?" Sarge barked back.

"Right now, they're looking at us."

Sarge pointed up the bridge, "Pull up there, Harris."

Kevin nodded and started up the bridge. He stopped behind the MRAP and Sarge got out. He banged on the rear door of the of the large truck. "Open up, dammit!"

The rear door opened and Sarge climbed in. The interior was illuminated by red light. "Make a hole!" He shouted as he worked his way up to the front.

Once there, he looked at Mike and said, "Give me your NODs." Mike handed him the PVS-14. Looking out the windshield, he could see what Mike was talking about. At the bottom of the bridge were a couple of makeshift barricades with armed men around them. They were all looking at the armored truck and talking amongst themselves nervously.

"This thing got a PA on it?" Sarge asked.

Mike picked up a mic and handed it to him. Sarge keyed it and said, "I don't know what you booger-eaters are thinking. But you better rethink it. We're coming down this bridge and if any one of you so much as looks at us sideways we'll smoke all yer asses. Are we clear on that?" There was no reply from the group as they talked and gestured towards the truck. "I said, are we clear on this? I can see your dumbasses down there." Sarge shouted. "Someone better fucking respond or we're going to start shooting now!" One of the men stood up and waved at them.

Sarge looked at Ted, "Let me get back to my truck. If you see any of these morons do anything hinky, light their asses up."

"Roger that, boss." Ted replied.

Sarge turned and made his way back through the truck and out the rear door. Getting back in the Hummer, he keyed his mic and said, "Roll out." Then he looked up at Dalton, "Eyes up. You see any fuckery, kill it."

Dalton swung the turret around as he replied. "With pleasure!"

The MRAP started over the bridge. Sarge had Kevin wait until there was about fifty feet between the two trucks before telling him to go. Dalton was watching the top edge of the bridge intently as the horizon of pavement rose up and then began to fall away, revealing what was on the other side. A quick glance at the MRAP confirmed the gun mounted on top was pointing to the left side of the road. Seeing that, he swung his turret around to cover the right. But he kept an eye on the left side as well.

The men standing at the bottom of the bridge all stepped back as the trucks moved down. They obviously wanted no part of the two trucks and were very careful not to provoke a fight they certainly wouldn't win.

Dalton however hoped for a fight. As the Hummer made its way past the group, he leaned over and shouted, "Don't you fookers be here when we come back!" The men looked at one another but made no moves. He watched them through the NVG mounted to the helmet he wore. He switched the IR laser on the SAW on and swung it from man to man, whispering *pow*, each time the muzzle swept one of them.

"What the hell are you hollering about, Gulliver?" Sarge asked.

Dalton ducked down into the truck. "Told 'em not to be here when we come back."

Sarge laughed. "Yeah. I was thinking on the way back we should stop and see what this is about."

"I say we raid them on the way back. Rape their livestock and pillage their women." Dalton replied with a smile.

Sarge turned in his seat to look at him. "Would you get that enormous head of yours out of here? Don't you have somewhere to be?" Dalton saluted and disappeared.

Kevin looked over at Sarge and asked, "What do you think that was about?"

Sarge shrugged. "Only a couple of things it could be. Either they're just working security for their area or they're a bunch of bandits looking to bushwhack folks. The former is fine," Sarge looked over at him and added, "the latter has to be dealt with."

Kevin nodded in a knowing way, then asked, "How will you know the difference?"

Sarge looked at him and smiled. "We'll ask."

Picking up his mic, Sarge said, "When we get to 441, turn right. Take it up to the bypass and turn left."

"Roger that, boss," Ted replied.

The two trucks made their way into Summerfield, where they turned north on highway 441 for a short distance before turning back to the west on 484. Kevin drove as Sarge stayed hunch over the atlas.

It was dark and the trucks were driving blacked out. The drivers and gunners were all wearing NVGs. Kevin studied the road ahead of him, paying attention to the green glow laid out before him. *Driving with these is certainly a little demanding. Depth perception is a real challenge. But with attention to detail and a little slower speed, it was easy enough.*

The group was passing through the Marion Oaks area of Ocala. It was one of those large pre-planned neighborhoods designed for perceived comfort and convenience. The lots were advertised as *wooded,* though those woods would have to be cleared to build a house on the small lots. When people came out to view the perspective lots, they would see all these trees and imagine living in the wilderness.

But as the lots around them would be bought up and

built on, that wilderness would disappear. And that's just what happened on the eastern side of the Oaks. It was working its way to the west, but as the economy slowed and the bottom fell out of the housing market, the construction slowed. So now the west end of the project was largely undeveloped. This is the part Sarge would take the trucks through.

Sarge was looking at the map when he suddenly blurted, "Who the hell names these damn roads?"

Without looking over, Kevin muttered, "Huh?"

Sarge looked at him. "Huh? Huh hell! Up ahead, you're going to take a left onto SW 67th Avenue Road. Avenue road? That's the dumbest shit I've ever heard."

"Well," Kevin said, "an avenue usually runs north-south with a median in the middle. A road has no special designation. It just connects point A to point B."

Sarge looked at him, his eyebrows coming together. After a moment of silence, Kevin looked over. The green hue the NVG put on him looked appropriate. "What?" He asked.

Sarge smiled. "Thank you for the geography lesson. Now pay attention and don't miss the damn turn."

Once on the avenue road, they continued for a short way before Sarge had him turn once again onto a small side street. This took them back onto a small road with few houses on it. Those that were there were mostly mobile homes, something that wouldn't be allowed in the east end of the development. But while these people may have been poorer in the Before, it was that very lack of resources that made them more resilient in the now. These people back here were probably doing better than those with the manicured lawns and *open spaces* back east.

The road came to a power line right-of-way. Sarge pointed and told Kevin to turn onto the small dirt two-track just past it. "This will take us straight to the plant. I want to stay off the roads as we approach because they'll surely be watching them," Sarge said.

Kevin turned onto the sandy track and asked, "You don't think they'll be watching this too?"

"Probably. But we're not going to just drive up to the damn gate."

The old man picked up his mic, "Teddy. Keep someone on that thermal camera. These power lines run all the way to the plant. We're going to follow them for a while. Just keep an eye out for any OPs."

"Roger that, boss."

As they moved down the dirt track, the MRAP pushed through the pine trees lining each side, tearing branches and limbs from the trees. The Hummer, being substantially smaller, made it through without incident.

The rain stopped and Dalton pulled his poncho over his head and dropped it into the truck. Putting his helmet back on, he adjusted the NVG and looked back at the big armored truck behind him. There were several pine limbs hanging from the top of it. Spinning back around, he focused on the road ahead. Though the term *road* was a bit of a stretch. It was just a sandy trail through the scrub growing under the transmission lines overhead.

The white sand of this part of Florida glowed brightly in the monocular, allowing the men to clearly see the route. But it would be a slow ride towards the plant. The roads would be mush faster, but also much more dangerous.

It wasn't long before they ran into an obstacle that was a real issue. A narrow but deep creek cut across the right-of-way. Sarge studied it for a moment, then looked back down at his map. "We're going to have to backtrack to find a way around this," he said.

Picking up his mic, Sarge told Ted to turn around and find a way around the water. "Roger that," Ted replied.

They found a trail out from under the power lines. It wound a short way through the woods before coming to Highway 200. This is a major artery for Ocala and not something Sarge wanted to drive on very long. The MRAP pulled out onto the paved road and Sarge told Kevin to go around them and take the lead. 200 paralleled the power lines at this point. Sarge had Kevin take a right on Withlacoochee Trail, which brought them back to the relative safety of the power lines. For the rest of the trip, the only obstacles they encountered were gates, and those were easy to overcome.

Once they passed Central Ridge Park, they had to find their way through an RV park. A four-board fence blocked the way, forcing them to reroute through the rows of abandoned RVs. Dalton eyed each of the now-empty recreational vehicles as they passed by. It brought him back to a time in his single days when he lived in one on top of a mountain in north Georgia. It didn't have electricity or running water, but it was one of the happiest times of his life.

Not this though. He shook his head at the sight of these things sitting so close to one another. The spaces were just wide enough to fit the trailer sitting on the slab. Hell, if he stood between them and stretched his arms out he could probably touch either side. This was horrible. But it was empty now.

A short time later, they came to the last way point before the plant. Sarge stopped the trucks and called in to the ranch. Picking up his mic, he said, "Stumpknocker is at the Magic Kingdom."

Jess was lying on the sofa in Danny's living room. The radio call woke her up and she walked over to the Green Monster and sat down. She listened for a moment and Sarge repeated his call. She smiled and keyed the mic, "Roger that. Watch out for Mickey Mouse."

Hearing Jess's voice, the old man smiled to himself. He keyed the mic one more time and replied, "Will do, Cinderella."

Smiling a little harder, Jess laid the mic down and returned to the sofa. Closing her eyes, she dreamt of Disney World.

Dropping his mic, Sarge said, "We're going to sit here for a bit and watch this road. We need to move to the south from here." He opened a folder and took out an aerial photo of the plant and oriented it. "The reactor is on the south side. I want to get out into the woods over there and approach on foot."

Kevin didn't reply. He simply nodded his head.

Sarge reached back and yanked on Dalton's pants leg. "Hey, Gulliver. Get out there and take a look at that road. See if there's any commie assholes out there."

Dalton dropped back into the truck and climbed out through the door with his carbine in his hand. Sarge called the guys in the MRAP and told them what was going on. Ted acknowledged him and Mike hopped out to go with Dalton. The two men moved silently towards the road lying before them. It was Highway 19, which ran north to south between them and the power plant. The trucks were stopped a couple hundred yards from the road in a stand of trees that split the right-of-way. Dalton and Mike made their way through this same stand to a vantage point where they could watch the road.

Taking up a spot inside the tree line where they would overwatch, the two men went prone on the wet ground. Mike grumbled, "This is bullshit!" He spat in a whisper. "Lying in the fucking water!"

Dalton snorted. "Says the guy that rode here inside the truck."

The two men scanned the road for a while. Before Mike asked, "You seen anything?"

"Nothing," Dalton replied.

"I say we give it another fifteen minutes. If we don't see anything, I say we move." Mike said.

"Roger," Dalton replied.

They continued to watch, scanning the length of the road before them with the NVGs mounted on their helmets. This was boring and tedious, but most definitely necessary. They were about to call it when, in a low whisper, Mike said, "Contact at ten o'clock."

Dalton looked over. He couldn't see a person but could see a small light that looked much larger through the intensifier. "What do you think that is? Cigarette?"

"Uh huh." Mike replied. "It's moving."

"Looks like he's on the shoulder of the road."

They watched the small light move out onto the road. It wasn't thirty meters from them when it stopped. Now they could see the man as well. He carried a Kalashnikov rifle, slung over his shoulder. He stood in the middle of the road and unzipped his trousers and proceeded to urinate.

"Well, that takes balls," Mike said.

"Obviously, he's been here a while and is comfortable. That's in our favor." Dalton replied.

"Notice he's wearing a set of NODs. We need to be careful with these guys."

"Agreed," Dalton said. "Let's watch him and see where he goes."

The man in the road finished his business and zipped up. He took a minute to light another smoke, without trying to conceal it, before turning and heading back the way he'd come. As he moved away from them, Dalton motioned to Mike that he wanted to follow him. They paralleled him on their side of the road to the edge of the stand of trees. Here, they stopped and watched. It was too risky to head out into the open ground under the power lines.

The man disappeared into the woods on the southwest corner. Mike and Dalton watched for a while longer and were able to see at least one other person. Mike tapped Dalton and motioned for the two of them to pull back from the road. Mike led the way and Dalton followed. Once they were far enough away from the two potential hostiles, Mike started to talk.

"We need to find a way around them to the south. We need more distance between us and them."

"Agreed." Dalton said. "We're going to have to backtrack a bit. Leaving the trucks here and going in on foot is a bad idea too."

"Yeah. I've got a feeling they probably patrol this. We need to didi mao from here."

When they got back to the trucks, the old man was standing off to the side of the truck in the woods. As they came up, he asked, "What's the word?"

"We saw a couple of guys out there on the southwest corner." Mike said. "We're going to have to backtrack a bit and put some space between us and them."

"That's not good," Sarge replied as he rubbed his chin.

"True. But they are also real comfortable here. One of them walked out to the middle of the road while smoking to take a piss. Then stood there and lit another one without trying to conceal it." Dalton said.

Sarge nodded. "Alright. That's some good news then. If these commie assholes think they've got this place locked down, then we can use that to our advantage. Let's mount up and find a way around them."

It took about an hour of driving around, checking the numerous roads in the area. The did manage to find a road nearly a mile from where the power lines crossed the highway where they had crossed over, putting them on the same side as the plant. Through a little more trial and error, they made their way west while trying to keep that mile between them and the plant.

While the Crystal River plant did indeed have a nuclear reactor, it also had coal-burning steam boiler units. The reactor had been shut down, but the steam units were running the day the balloon went up. Coal was brought in by barge through a canal cut out to the Gulf of Mexico. It was piled up and fed into the plant through a series of conveyors. And it just happens that this coal pile sits to the south of the reactor across the canal.

After finding a place to leave the trucks, Sarge, Dalton, Mike, Ted and Doc set out on foot. The Guardsmen would stay behind to provide security. The five men ended up lying on the top of the coal pile where they had an unobstructed view of the reactor. It was still dark as they took up positions in the pile. Doc and Mike stayed about thirty yards from the others to provide security. Sarge, Ted and Dalton crawled up to the edge of the pile and looked out at the plant for the first time.

"That's an awful lot of light down there," Ted said.

CHAPTER 4

JAMIE AND IAN SHOWED UP early in the morning to relieve me and Thad. I told them what we heard on the radio about the possibility of a nuke being used on the Chinese fleet. The consensus was, *at least it's not on the east coast.* Sadly, that was where we were. Better them than us.

"California is a beautiful state. Be a shame to lose it," Ian said.

"Yeah, but it's full of fruits and nuts. And I'm not talking about the valley either. That place was always screwed up. The laws they passed. Taxes were just stupid. Why one of the most beautiful parts of the country got that screwed up is beyond me," I said.

"It ain't going to matter none now," Thad added. Looking at me, he said, "You ready to go? I'm tired."

I nodded. "Yeah. Let's go."

Thad and I left and I dropped him at his place and headed for the house. I was tired and could still get a few hours sleep before the sun came up. At the house, I stepped over the dogs lying on the porch and went in. The rain had cooled the night enough that I didn't feel gross, so I was going to skip a shower, until I pulled my shirt off. The smudge fire had done its job and I could smell the smoke in my clothes. A quick shower, then to bed.

After taking a very short shower, I slipped on shorts and a t-shirt and made a pass through the house, checking on everyone. Little Bit and Lee Ann were sound asleep. Checking on Taylor, she'd fallen asleep reading, and the book was sitting on her chest. I picked it up and set it on her nightstand. She rolled over, but didn't wake. I smiled and left her room.

Mel was under the sheet when I climbed into bed. She didn't move, and I tucked a pillow under my head and closed my eyes. The last thing I remember was thinking about a trip I took a couple years ago to Long Beach. I'd taken Taylor with me then. We'd gone down to the beach so she could stick her feet in the water of the Pacific Ocean. I was picturing that day. But we were watching a large mushroom cloud rise into the sky out over the horizon.

I woke up in the morning when the room lightened from the rising sun. Mel was already gone. I guess she thought I needed the sleep. Getting up, I went out to the living room. The house was empty and quiet, so I took advantage of the rare moment of solitude and poured myself a glass of tea and fell onto the sofa. The only thing that could have made the moment better was being able to watch an old movie on TV. But I settled for the peace.

Back in the Before, we were losing our attention span. Everyone had to have some sort of a device in their hands, either a phone, tablet, laptop or just the TV remote. Many, hell most, were not comfortable to just *be* for a moment. Content to sit with themselves and their thoughts. They had to have some sort of constant stimulation. It made me wonder how those people were managing today. Of course it would be worse for the younger generations that never knew a world without internet and cell phones.

This very affliction affected my older girls. They had come

to an age where they had their own phone. Little Bit, however, hadn't made it to that age, and therefore didn't suffer as much from the loss of the internet. She was still a kid in a purer sense, one I could relate my youth to. But I would guess that those still alive today had gotten over it by now.

Sitting there contemplating the lack of technology made me think of the phones we took off the Russians. I went to the bedroom and grabbed my pack and carried it back out to the sofa. Sitting back and propping my feet up, I dumped them out in my lap.

They were all quality phones. Two of them were Iphones, two were Samsung and one was Motorola. The Motorola caught my eye. It was a little different than the others. More rugged, Mil-Spec you might say. I looked it over and powered it up. It was kind of strange seeing the screen light up as the Motorola emblem rolled across it. Once it was on, I quickly went to the settings. Even though all the commands were in Cyrillic, the symbols were universal. I found the little airplane icon and set the phone to airplane mode, killing all signals.

Once I knew no one could hear the thing, I started going through it. First thing I did was look at the photos in the gallery. There were hundreds of pics. Some of them bothered me a bit. Pictures of a smiling man holding a small, blonde-haired smiling girl. Other pictures of a woman, several of her, and more with her and the little girl. You had to think it was the man's family.

But I was more interested in the photos of the uniformed men. Farther back in the phone, the pics were obviously from Russia. But there was a change in them. The last one that I guessed was in Russia showed a line of smiling men standing at the back of a large transport plane. They were standing in the open ramp of the plane. In the background was a truck secured in the cargo bay. The same one, it appeared, now sitting in my front yard. There was a symbol on the bumper. It looked kind of like a E, Z and an A. But obviously Cyrillic. Seeing that, I went outside and compared it to the truck. The same symbol was there; so it was very likely the same truck.

Back inside, I sat down and looked carefully at the following pictures. The next picture I saw showed four men standing with their arms over each other's shoulders. The truck was in the background, but it was sitting on a pallet and what must have been parachute lines trailing from a series of straps. They'd obviously just parachuted in.

Looking at the geo-tagging data on the phone, there was a location, but I couldn't read it because it was in Russian. I needed to find a way to change the language on the phone. This was going to take some trial and error. But if I figured it out, I'd know where they landed and maybe get an idea of where they are, or were.

But that could wait. I finished my tea while going through the pics. The guys had been busy it appeared, and they really liked to take photos of what they were up to. It made me wonder about the other phones, so I turned on another. The status bar showed there was no signal, but for safety I set it to airplane mode as well. This phone, like the other, had many photos of the same guys, but this one had a picture of what must be the owners of the other phones as well.

I really wanted to figure out a way to reset the language on these things. Mainly, because there were numerous text messages that I wanted to read. These things could be a goldmine of information. But I'd wasted enough time for today. I needed to make a run to town. I was picking up Kelly today and taking him to Eustis to see what sort of business he could drum up. Not to mention, today was the day for the plant startup.

Getting dressed, I walked over to Danny's house. He was

out at the shed working on a small bicycle for the kids. The kids were all gathered around, *helping*. Despite that, he was oiling the chain and getting ready to put it back on its wheels.

"Looks like you've been busy this morning," I said.

Danny smiled. "Yeah. We were short one bike. Now they all have one." He flipped the bike over and set it on its wheels to several squeals and laughs. Little Edie jumped on the bike and the three kids were soon tearing across the yard. "What've you got planned for today?"

I sat on a stump beside the shed. "We're supposed to try and fire the plant up today. And I'm taking a guy from Altoona down to Eustis to see if he can drum up some work."

Danny was putting wrenches away and asked, "What's he do?"

"Makes shoes."

Danny looked at me. "Really? That's a pretty good idea."

"Yeah. They're pretty cool. He makes them from carpet and boat-cover canvas."

Danny laughed. "Carpet and boat canvas." He shook his head as he wiped his hands on a rag.

"What are you up to today?" I asked.

"Jamie said the water tower over there is leaking. Thad is going to the farm, so I'm going to work on that and see if we can get the leak stopped. Then I'll probably refill it too."

I looked towards the house. "Any breakfast in there this morning?"

He nodded. "Yeah, Mel made a big quiche this morning. She used some sausage and sweet potato greens in it. Came out really good."

"I wish we had more greens. Guess I need to get out in the woods and see what I can find."

Danny laughed. "Yeah. In your spare time."

With a chuckle, I replied, "Yeah. In my spare time. I'm going to go grab a bite."

I went up to the house where Kay, Bobby and Mel were sitting on the porch. As I came up, Mel smiled, "About time you got up."

Stepping up on the porch, I smiled back, "I've been up for a long time, actually."

"Are you hungry?" Kay asked, "Mel made a really tasty quiche this morning."

"I heard that," I said. "I'd love some."

Kay started to get up, Mel told her to stay in her seat. "I'll get it for him." Mel looked at me, "Come in and sit down."

I followed her into the kitchen and sat down at the bar. She puttered around the kitchen preparing my breakfast. These days, there was no more aluminum foil or plastic wrap. I looked at the large round dish sitting on the kitchen island. It was covered with a dish towel. It made me smile and I asked, "Did Bobbie eat any of this?"

Mel removed the towel and cut a piece. Setting it on a plate, she placed it in front of me. "Of course. Why?"

Taking a bite, I pointed at the dish with my fork. "Because it's just sitting on the counter, covered in a towel. Remember how she used to be? If anything sat out for more than an hour, as far as she was concerned, it was spoiled."

Mel laid the towel back over the dish and smiled. "Well. As they say; times, they are a changin'."

I laughed. "I guess they are." Holding a forkful up, I said, "This is really good."

She smiled and leaned over the bar for a quick kiss. "Thank you. It was really simple. What are you doing today?"

Finishing up the meal, I gave her the rundown on the plant and about taking Kelly to Eustis. She was just as surprised as

Danny about the idea of someone making shoes. It was one of the most overlooked things that everyone wore everyday. Even clothes. I would imagine there are people all over the country wearing clothes that were less than ideal. Probably ill-fitting. It made me think of people in third-world countries that we would see on TV. Some poor guy in Haiti walking the streets with no shoes but wearing a sports coat.

She took my plate and set it in the sink. Turning to me, she leaned against the counter and asked, "So no shootouts with Russians today?"

I shook my head. "I hope not."

She turned back to the sink to wash the dish. "Then you'll be home for dinner?"

I got up and walked around the island. Standing behind her, I wrapped my arms around her waist. "Should be."

"Just be careful today."

I kissed her neck and replied, "I will."

Slapping her ass, I said goodbye and headed out the door. Danny was on the porch talking to Thad and Mary. Mary held a basket full of green leaves. Looking into the basket, I was surprised to see a tomato. "Oh man. A tomato!" I said.

Thad smiled. "Yeah. Just the beginning. Them plants is full of them. We're going to have loads of them soon."

From her rocker, Kay chimed in. "Oh good! There is so much we can do with them. I'll make some sauce and we'll can it."

"That's good, Miss Kay." Thad said, "We have so many that we'll need to find a way to store them."

"We'll store them fresh," I said.

Kay and Thad both looked at me. "And just how will we do that?" Thad asked.

"Well, you're probably not going to believe me. But if we

store them in a bucket with wood ash, they'll last for many weeks." Thad didn't reply immediately. The look on his face told me he didn't believe me. "I'm serious. I've never done it, but I've read about it."

"I've certainly never heard of that," Kay said.

"Me neither." Thad replied. Giving me a suspicious look, he added, "But we'll try it and see if it works."

"It'll work. You'll see. Are there a bunch of green tomatoes hanging out there?" I asked.

Mary smiled. "Bunches."

I looked at Kay. "I love fried green tomatoes."

With a sudden look of shock, she replied, "I can't believe we haven't done that yet!"

With a laugh, I replied, "No time like the present!"

Kay rose to her feet. "We're having them for supper tonight!"

Mary took Kay's hand. "Come on, Miss Kay. I'll help."

Thad smiled at the two. "I'll be back later. We're headed to town."

Mary turned and looked back, waving at him. Thad and I walked out towards the old war wagon. It was becoming the primary transportation. In this summer heat, its open design made it more comfortable, unless it rained of course. Plus, it was more fuel efficient.

Looking at Thad, I asked, "You wanna drive?"

With that signature smile, he said, "Sure."

I climbed into the passenger side. We headed out the gate and down the road. Ian and Jamie were at the bunker. The morning was already getting hot and they were standing under the tarp when we stopped.

"How's it hanging?" I asked.

"It's friggin hot," Jamie complained.

Thad looked up into the blazing sky. "It's gonna get hotter too."

"Y'all be careful," Ian said.

I looked out towards the road. "This shouldn't be a big deal."

"We'll be here, trying to move as little as possible." Jamie said.

With a laugh, I said, "Good idea."

"You know what we should do?" Ian said. "We should go back to that park where we had the pig roast. I'd like to take a swim in the lake. Cool off."

I looked at Thad. He nodded and said, "I'd like that too."

"Sounds like a plan. Let's get a day set aside and do it," I said.

We told them we'd be back later and headed out. As we passed Thad's road, we saw Danny and the girls working on the water tower. He turned and drove down to them. Danny was on a ladder cutting a PVC pipe.

"You got that sorted out?" Thad asked.

Danny set the hacksaw on the top of the ladder. "Yeah. I think this will fix it."

I was happy to see Taylor there as well. While Thad and Danny talked, I was watching her and Lee Ann as they laughed with Jess and Fred. The girls were talking and carrying on while they sat on the top board of a fence. It made me feel good. Taylor was back to her old self now and even had her H&K slung over her shoulder. I was brought back to the present by Aric asking me a question.

"You headed to the plant?" He asked.

Shaking off the mental fog, I said, "Yeah. We're on our way there now. Got to swing through Eustis as well."

Aric stepped up on the buggy and climbed in. "I'll go with you."

"Cool," I said.

Aric looked over at Fred and shouted, "I'm going with Morgan!"

Fred looked over and waved. "Be careful! Bring him back in one piece, Morgan!"

I laughed and asked, "I gotta bring him back?"

"Yes, please!" Fred shouted back.

"Only cause you asked!" I replied.

Aric kicked the back of my seat. "I see how you are."

Danny came down off the ladder and leaned on the buggy and said, "Soon as we're done here, I'll refill it too."

"I appreciate that," Thad replied. "Wish we could find some way of keeping the water colder. It gets hot in that tank."

"At least you ain't got to take cold showers," I added to the conversation.

"I guess that's true. But some cool water would be nice."

"Well, we're going to go to the lake soon. You'll be able to cool off there."

"What?" Danny asked. "The lake?"

"Yeah. Ian and Jamie suggested we go to the lake for a swim. Thought it was a good idea."

"Lake Dorr?" Danny asked.

I nodded. "Yep."

"Oh, hell yeah. That would be fun. The kids would have a blast." Danny said.

"The little ones will have a ball," Thad said.

"I think we all will," I said. "We could use some fun."

"When are we going?" Danny asked.

"I think we should wait until Sarge and the guys get back."

Thad agreed with me. "That's probably a good idea. In case anything happens, we're here to help them."

"Not to mention, the old man would probably kick our ass if we went without them," I added.

Danny stepped back and clapped his hands. "Cool. This'll be a lot of fun."

"We'll be back later," I said and nodded at Thad.

He looked at Danny and smiled. "We'll see you later." Then he backed and turned us around and headed for town.

We pulled into the Kangaroo to pick up Kelly. Mario and Shelly were there with their table set up. When Thad stopped, I saw Kelly. He waved as he picked up the little box he'd built for his *mobile* work. He picked it up and started towards us. I turned to talk to Mario and Shelly.

"Morning, Mario, Shelly," I said as I walked up. "What's new?"

Shelly's eyes lit up. "Oh, I've got something for you." She said as she picked up a small jar. Spinning the lid off, she said, "You've got to try this."

"What is it?" I asked, peering into the jar of light brown stuff.

"Try it. You'll like it," Mario said with a broad smile. "It's our new product."

I stuck my finger into it and licked it. My eyes went wide when the sweet creamy flavor hit my tongue. "Is that honey butter?"

Shelly laughed. "Yep. What do you think?"

"It's delicious!" I replied.

Thad stepped up beside me. "Did I hear you say honey butter?"

I held the jar up. "Yes you did. But you don't want none. Tastes like soap."

"Soap my ass!" Shelly shouted.

Thad reached over. "Give me that jar." He took it and stuck his finger in and licked it. He closed his eyes and his head rocked back as he savored the flavor. After a moment, he said, "Oh my lord, Miss Shelly. That is so good." He looked at the jar again and brought it up to his nose. Closing his eyes, once again he inhaled deeply. "This smells just like the honey butter my Momma made." Spinning the lid back on the jar, he added, "That brings back some very good memories for me. Thank you." He held the jar out to Shelly.

She waved him off. "That's for you. Keep it."

Thad smiled broadly as he looked at the jar as a small child would a shiny quarter or surprise toy. "Thank you, Miss Shelly. Thank you very much."

"So you and the milkman over there got together and came up with this?" I asked.

Mario smiled and wagged a finger at me. "Oh no. This was all my idea."

Shelly rolled her eyes. "Yeah, yeah, yeah. He just won't stop with that, *it was my idea* thing."

Pleading his case, Mario said, "But it *was* my idea!"

"I don't care whose idea it was," I said as I reached for the jar, "it's delicious!"

Thad pulled the jar away. "Get your own. This one is mine."

"What? I had it first!"

Thad nodded at Shelly. "Miss Shelly gave it to me. Not you."

She laughed and picked up another jar. "Here, Morgan, this one's for you."

Taking the jar, I said, "Thank you, Shelly." Looking at Thad, I added, "That's very nice of you, unlike some people around here."

Mario pointed at me. "Hey. That's going on your tab."

"Whatever. I've got it!" I said. Looking at Thad, I said, "Come on there, princess, we got to get going." Giving Shelly and Mario a nod, I said, "Thanks for this, guys. You need anything?"

"Just some power," Mario said. "You done with my generator yet?"

"Not yet. We'll find out today about the plant."

"Good luck," Shelly said.

Waving, I said, "Thanks," as I turned and headed towards the buggy where Kelly was waiting. "You ready to go?" I asked.

He looked excited. When he spoke, it was obvious he was. He practically bounced as he spoke. "Yeah, man. Thanks a lot for doing this for me. I haven't been out of Altoona since this happened." He looked at the buggy and continued, "And look at this thing! It's awesome!"

"Well hop in," I said.

He quickly climbed in beside Aric and introduced himself. Thad got in behind the wheel and started off. As we got out onto nineteen, Aric stuck his head up between the front seats. "What's in the jar?"

I handed it to him, "Try it. You'll like it."

He spun the lid off the jar and dipped a finger in and tasted it. "Awe, man that is good!"

Thad looked over his shoulder and said, "Imagine how good it's going to be on a sweet potato!"

Aric took another taste. "Wow, that's going to be so good."

"Kelly, we've got to make a quick stop on the way south. Hopefully, it won't take long."

He was leaned out the side of the ride, letting the wind blow in his face. With his eyes closed, he replied, "You take as long as you need, man. Like I said, I ain't been out of Altoona since this shit started."

I asked Thad to slow when we passed through Umatilla. I looked down 450. The bodies were gone, thankfully. I waved Thad on, I didn't feel like stopping at the market there. It was active with a number of people engaged in their various endeavors. Thad wheeled into the plant and parked beside the generator. The crew was all there, even Cecil. It looked like today would be the day.

As we got out, Scott looked at his watch and said, "About time you got here."

"Whenever I arrive is exactly when I'm supposed to be here," I replied with a smile.

I introduced Aric and Kelly to the crew there. They all thought Kelly was onto something and were very impressed when he showed them his canvas shoes.

Baker was looking at a pair and asked, "These are pretty cool. What do you want for a pair?"

Kelly shrugged. "I don't know. What do you have?"

"How about a couple MREs?" She asked.

"Those Army meals?" Kelly asked. She nodded. He smiled broadly and said, "Yeah. I'd trade for that."

"Let me find a pair that fit," She said.

"Y'all take yer time. Ain't like we're doing anything today," Cecil said.

Baker smiled. "I guess we should get down to business." She looked at Kelly, "We'll finish this before you leave."

Cecil looked at the group. "Everyone know what they got to do, right?" He was answered with a round of nods. "Alright then. Morgan, you and Thad come with me. We'll go to the control room and see if this old bitch will fire up."

"I'll keep an eye on our ride," Aric said as he climbed in.

With a chuckle, I replied, "You gotta stay awake to do that."

He smiled at me as he fell into the seat and leaned back. "Don't worry. I got this."

Thad and I followed Cecil to the small control room. As we stepped in, I looked at the panels mounted to the wall with all the gauges, buttons and switches. "We're lucky," Cecil said.

"This thing is still analog controls. If it was like all the newer ones that run off a touch screen, we wouldn't be here."

Thad nodded at the wall of controls and asked, "You know what all that does?"

With his hands on his hips, Cecil nodded. "Yeah. It's been a couple years, but it's like riding a bike, and came right back to me."

Thad looked around and saw a chair. Pulling it into a corner out of the way, he sat down, saying, "I'm going to stay over here. Out of the way."

Cecil stepped up to the controls and keyed his radio, "You all in position?"

"Waiting on you," Scott replied.

"Here goes nothing. I'm turning on the lube pump." Cecil said as he raised a cover on a button on the wall and pressed it. It turned green, and in a moment, the radio crackled.

"Got flow," Terry said.

Cecil looked at a gauge and replied, "We've got steady pressure. Starting diesel crank engine." Raising another cover, he pressed the button beneath it. After a moment, a green indicator light came on.

"Crank engine is running!" Terry shouted into the radio over the roar of an engine.

I was impressed. "I can't believe this is actually starting."

"We ain't there yet," Cecil said.

It was getting louder in the control room. The big generator we borrowed from Mario was screaming just outside the door. This new motor Cecil had started added to the roar.

"Initiating purge," Cecil called over the radio.

"What's that for?" I asked.

"It's blowing out all the fuel nozzles to make sure there's nothing in them before the turbine fires."

"Synchronous clutch just engaged," Baker called over the radio.

"Roger that. Green light on the SSS," Cecil replied.

"Turbine is spinning!" Eric called.

"Roger that," Cecil replied. "Beginning warm-up." Cecil watched the gauges on the wall. The needles were bouncing all over. Lights were flashing. It looked like chaos. "Thermocouples are reading," Cecil said.

"Turbine just fired!" Baker called excitedly.

"Roger that. Green light on turbine start," Cecil replied.

"So, it's running?" Thad asked.

Without looking away from the controls, Cecil shook his head. "Not yet." He pointed to a gauge on the wall. "When this gets to sixty percent, that diesel motor will drop out and the turbine will be running on its own. Then it has to reach speed."

I watched the dial as the numbers increased. Twenty percent. Thirty, forty, fifty. It hovered there for several minutes. "Is something wrong?" I asked.

"Nothing to be worried about yet."

The dial rolled over to sixty percent. Several lights on the board changed colors.

"Synchronous clutch disengaged. It's running under its own power!" Baker shouted.

"Roger that. Green light on clutch disengage. Starter motor shutting down."

"Starter engine just shut down!" Eric called.

"Turbine is accelerating," Cecil called.

The one diesel engine dropped out. But now there was another, much louder noise taking its place. It was a combination of a high pitched whine and a roar. The turbine was running.

"We're at eighty percent." Cecil called.

Baker called, she was laughing. "It's running! It's actually running!"

"Stand by, Baker. We ain't there yet," Cecil replied.

The dial continued to rise. There was a mark on it at ninety-five percent. When the needle moved past it, lights on the board again started changing colors.

"Lube oil shut-down. We're at ninety-five percent," Cecil said over the radio.

"Lube oil shut down!" Terry called.

"Roger that. Lube oil shut down. Turbine is at one hundred percent."

A series of shouts came back over the radio. Cecil stepped back and smiled. Looking over at me, he said, "Now, it's running."

Thad rose to his feet. "It's making power?"

Cecil nodded. "Indeed it is," he smiled broadly, then laughed, slapping his knees. "I can't believe we did it!" He tapped a digital gauge on the wall and said, "She's producing fourteen thousand four hundred volts. Right where she should be."

"Amazing," I muttered as I looked at the flashing lights, gauges and buttons. Looking at Cecil, I said, "But now, the real work starts."

Cecil whistled. "Boy, you got that right. Let's walk outside."

The three of us walked out. Baker, Scott, Terry and Eric were gathered around beside the turbine. The sound was intense. They were all wearing hearing protection, I didn't have any, nor did Thad. The engineers were all high-fiving one another and laughing.

Walking up to Baker, I grabbed her arm, "Hey, can we go someplace quieter?"

She smiled and nodded and motioned for the others to follow us. We walked over to the buggy where Aric was now sitting on the hood. He was shaking his head as we walked up, "I can't believe you guys pulled it off."

I looked back at the exhaust coming out of the stack over the plant. "Me neither." Looking back at him, I added, "Now the real work begins."

He looked curiously at me. "How?"

Laughing, I said, "The power is here. If we want it to go anywhere, we have a shit-ton of work to get it out."

"Oh, like wires and stuff?"

"Yeah, wire, transformers, poles. You name it, we're going to have to do it," I replied.

"We'll worry about that tomorrow," Cecil said with a big smile. "Today, we celebrate this success."

Smiling and nodding my head, I replied, "Good idea. This," I pointed at the plant again, "is a huge success. I still can't believe that thing is running."

"What? You doubt our skills?" Scott asked.

"Uh. In a word. No," I replied with a laugh.

"Well," Baker said, "thank you for your support, good Sheriff."

Cutting my eyes at her, I replied, "It's not so much you. It's that maybe I didn't want the extra shit to deal with."

Thad slapped me on the back. "Come on, Morg. I got faith in you. If anyone can bring the lights back on, you can."

Looking sideways at him, I corrected him. "*We* can, big man. We can."

Thad laughed. "I don't climb poles."

"I will." Aric volunteered.

I nodded at him, "Duly noted, my friend."

The young engineer Eric raised his hand as well, "I will too. I used to work for the phone company back home. I can climb."

I looked at Cecil and smiled, "Looks like we have our first two linemen."

He nodded back. "It's a start."

Cecil looked at the plant, then at Baker. "Go ahead and shut it down, Doc."

She looked at the crew, "Let's go, guys."

The engineers all headed back for the plant. I hopped up onto the hood of the buggy beside Aric and leaned on my knees. "Well, this should be interesting."

Cecil Leaned back against the buggy and reached into his shirt pocket. He removed a tin of Cohiba Penquenos. Seeing them, I grinned. "Oh man. Where did you find those?"

"I've been saving these for a special occasion." He opened the tin. There were three cigars. He removed one and took it out of the wrapper and smelled the tobacco deeply. "Man, that smells good."

"I bet it does," I said. He handed it to me. I ran it under my nose, taking in the rich aroma of the tobacco. "It's not even dried out," I said as I handed it back to him.

"No. I kept them in a humidor I have. Made sure I kept it tight. These are the last ones."

"Damn," I whispered as I watched him cut the tip and light it with a match.

With the cigar clenched between his teeth, Cecil glanced sideways at me. "Want one?"

It was very tempting. I did want one, bad. "I'd love one, Cecil. But give it to one of those guys." I said as I nodded towards the plant. "They've worked hard for it."

"I like cigars," Aric said.

"Me too," Kelly said.

Cecil smiled and reached back into his hip pocket. Extracting another tin. "I had a feeling you'd say that." He waved the still-wrapped tin as he spoke. Cecil gave both Aric and me a cigar as the sound of the turbine faded. Looking at Kelly, he said, "Sorry. You're out of luck." The diesel engine fired up again and Cecil explained it was to allow the shaft to cool without warping. It would keep spinning the turbine as it cooled.

Aric and I lit our cigars. I leaned back and inhaled the smoke deeply. I know, I know, you're not supposed to inhale cigar smoke. But it wasn't like I could make a habit out of it. Kelly was watching the three of us smoke. I smiled and handed him mine. He took a deep drag from it, closing his eyes as he handed it back to me. He held the smoke for a long time before letting it out.

With a little goofy look, he said, "Ooh, head rush."

I laughed, "Yeah. Me too."

Aric started to laugh. Obviously, the tobacco was affecting him too. Cecil smiled and said, "Good, ain't it?"

With the plant now cooling down, the engineers walked back over. Scott pointed as he got closer, I could see him saying, *what the fuck?* Cecil must have seen it too. He smiled as they walked up and asked Scott, "What?"

He was still pointing, "Where the hell did you get that?"

Cecil unwrapped the second tin and opened it, peeling back the gold paper. "You want one?"

Scott delicately removed one and, just like the rest of us, sniffed the cigar. Cecil offered the others one as well. I was surprised when Baker took one. She noticed and asked, "What? You don't think women smoke cigars?"

Aric was still feeling the effect of the smoke and blurted out, "That's not what I was thinking."

I elbowed him in the side. "No, Doc. I expected you would."

She used a folding knife to expertly cut the tip of her cigar. Cecil handed her a small box of matches and she lit up, passing the matches to Scott. We all stood gathered around the front of the buggy as we savored our prize. Well, most of us. The young kid Eric obviously wasn't a smoker. He coughed and hacked.

Terry stuck his hand out, "Give me that thing before you kill yourself."

Eric jerked it away. "No! It's mine and I'm going to smoke it!"

We all got a laugh out of him. And many more as he continued to work his way through the rest of it. Fortunately for him, and unfortunately for us, they aren't very big. Cecil looked into the tin, there was one left. He snapped the lid closed and dropped it into his pocket. "One left for me."

The old man stretched his neck out to see over the edge of the coal pile. We were using a pair of binoculars instead of the NVGs as the area around the reactor was very well lit by a number of diesel-powered light towers. The exhaust hung thick in the bright lights like a chemical fog. They were about three hundred fifty yards from the reactor building. The coal pile they were in had several conveyors running through it. One of them crossed the small lagoon to the two coal-fired units to the west side of the reactor.

"I don't see anything over there at those two. Whatever is going on down there is happening at the reactor only," Sarge said.

Ted grunted in agreement. "You see anyone armed down there?"

"I see lots of folks in coveralls," Sarge replied.

Dalton was lying beside Ted. He looked back to where Doc was keeping an eye on the back door. Doc saw him through his NVGs and gave a thumbs up. Dalton replied in kind and turned his attention to the reactor. He'd brought the old man's M1 with him and was using the scope to observe the action.

"There's plenty of guns on those two boats," Dalton said.

Sarge swung his binos towards the lagoon. "Sure are. Notice what's missing though?"

Dalton studied the two boats moored to the north side of the lagoon. After a minute, he spotted it. "No flag."

"Yeah," Sarge replied. "And the name's been painted over too."

"Well now, that just stinks of pirates, now don't it," Ted added.

Mike looked down at the two boats and clucked his tongue. "Prepare to be boarded, fuckers."

Without moving the optics from his eyes, Sarge reached over and palmed Mike's head, pushing him down. "Not yet."

Mike flattened himself a little closer to the ground and said, "You just say when."

Sarge quietly replied, "You'll know when I take yer chain off."

Ted was back to looking at the reactor. "You see anything down there with an emblem on it?"

"No," Sarge replied. "And we're too far away to hear them."

There were several people visible at the reactor where what looked like a set of train tracks ran into the building.

"I still don't see anyone with a weapon. Or anything that tells us who is down there," Ted said.

"I do," Dalton said. "There's two men on top of the reactor. You can see them now."

Sarge and Ted both watched the two men. They were armed and in a uniform of some kind. But in the darkness, it was hard to make out. "Can you tell anything about them?" Sarge asked.

"They're armed with AKs," Dalton replied. Then, in a Russian accent, added, "The Kalashnikov is very good rifle."

"And who carries AKs?" Ted asked.

Dalton laughed, "Fuckin' everybody. One in every five rifles found on a battlefield worldwide is an AK."

"He was looking for a different answer there, Gulliver," Sarge said. "Russians carry AKs."

Dalton looked up from scope. "So do Hadji. Somali pirates, Hamas, Boko Haram. You name it."

"I don't think the PLO is here finger-fucking a nuclear power plant in Crystal River," Sarge shot back.

Dalton settled back behind the rifle. "I'm just saying, don't find an answer before the question's been asked. Two more on top of that white tank at our eleven o'clock, other side of the lagoon."

Ted and Sarge both looked to where he said he saw the two men. They were standing on a large tank and had a perfect view of both the back of the reactor and the two boats.

After a moment, Dalton said, "You know who else carries AKs?"

"According to you, everyone does," Ted replied.

"And has an interest in nuclear shit?" Dalton continued. Before they could say anything, he answered his own question. "The Iranians."

Sarge dropped the binos from his face and looked at Dalton. "You see anything to make you think it's Iranians down there?"

"Not yet."

Sarge looked around the area. "We need to find a place to lay up and watch the proceedings during the day. We're too exposed here."

"That tower over there," Dalton said. "The one with the metal siding on it. If we got into that, we could see everything."

"It's enclosed, so we'd have some cover," Ted said.

Mike sat up and took the binoculars from Ted. He looked at the tower they were talking about. "If we're going over there, I want to go back to the trucks for some dry goods."

Sarge looked at him, then back at the scene before them. "Good call, Mikey. We might need it."

"We ain't got much. But I'll get what we have."

"I'll go with you," Dalton said as he scooted himself back from the edge of the pile.

Once the two men were gone, Ted asked, "You think that's a good idea? Introducing explosives into the mix with nuclear fuel?"

"I'm not a dumbass, Teddy. But if we move out there, we're there. Going back to get something at that point ain't going to happen. So I'd rather have it and not need it."

"I wonder what those boats brought in here?" Ted mused.

Sarge rolled over on his back, putting his hands behind his head. Letting out a sigh, he said, "I'm more worried about what it may be taking out."

Ted looked at him. "The fuel? You can't do shit with it. It's practically useless. Just a hazard to be buried someplace for millennia or two."

"That's what I thought too. But someone is going through an awful lot of effort down there; and the only thing down there is fuel rods."

Ted kept an occasional eye on the activity at the plant. While they waited for Dalton and Mike to return, he wanted to keep an eye on everything. After a while, the old man fell asleep. Ted smiled as Sarge quietly snored beside him, remembering the threats of severe bodily harm the old man had issued over the years for falling asleep. But the smile faded when he took a longer look at his old friend. His mentor. He was getting older.

134

Not that he'd ever dare say it to him, but time wears on a man's body as a river does a canyon. The smile returned. The ornery ole bastard wasn't done yet. He went back to observing the area.

"What do you think?" Jess asked.

"I'm in," Lee Ann said.

Fred looked around tentatively. "Will we get in trouble?"

"Trouble from who?" Lee Ann asked.

Jess laughed and lifted the silver star from her chest. "We're Deputy Sheriffs." Leaning closer to Fred, she added, "It's our job!"

Fred shrugged. "Hell, since you say it that way." Smiling over her shoulder as she walked towards the smaller buggy, she said, "I'm driving."

Jess ran towards the now-running buggy and shouted, "Shotgun!" She and Lee Ann giggled with excitement as they scrambled aboard.

Fred quickly spun the small vehicle around and tore out from the house, racing down the road. Ian stepped out from behind the bunker. Fred skidded to a stop in front of it as he took a quick step back. Fanning the dust from his face, he asked, "Where are y'all headed?"

Fred shrugged. "To town."

Spitting our dust, Ian asked, "For what?"

Jess stood up in her seat and looked over the roll bar. "We're going to take care of some deputy stuff." She dropped back in her seat and laughed. Fred laughed as he stomped on the gas, throwing sand and dust everywhere.

Jamie walked out and stood beside Ian. After watching the buggy speed away, she asked, "What the hell was that about?"

Ian started to reply but paused. Gagging, he spat at his feet. Looking up, he ran his tongue around his mouth for a moment, spat at his feet once again, and replied, "I have no fucking idea."

Jamie shrugged and looked up at the blistering sun. Shading her eyes, she said, "It's hot as hell. Let's get in the shade."

Ian nodded. "Yeah. Let's do that."

The girls laughed as they raced down the road towards Altoona. They were enjoying the wind in their hair and the freedom of totally open road. Lee Ann leaned up between Jess and Fred. "This is awesome!" Jess looked over her shoulder and nodded as she held her hair out of her face. The ride to Altoona didn't take long when you drove as fast as the little buggy would go. It wasn't long before it was in sight. Fred pulled into the market and shut the buggy off. The girls quickly headed towards the traders set up under the gas canopy.

They wandered among the offerings of the traders there for a bit and then agreed to move on to Umatilla. Jess was going to drive the next section. She started it up and was just beginning to move when Lee Ann tapped her on the shoulder. Jess looked over to see her pointing at a woman on a bike on the west side of nineteen coming up highway forty-two. She was waving a white cloth and shouting something.

Jess pulled out of the parking lot headed towards her. She stopped in the street as the woman made it to them. She slumped from the seat, straddling the bike. She breathed hard, unable to speak. "You ok?" Jess asked.

The woman tried to speak, but still couldn't. She looked at Jess with red swollen eyes and held a finger up. After another moment, she managed to say, "My daughter."

"Is she hurt?" Jess asked.

The woman managed to catch her breath enough to speak. "She's being raped."

"She was raped?" Jess asked.

The woman shook her head. "No. She's *being* raped right now!"

A rage began to rise in Jess. Her eyes narrowed and she could feel the heat rising up her neck. With gritted teeth, she said, "Get in and show us where."

"We need the Sheriff." The woman said.

Jess pulled the star up, "We are. Get in." The woman looked at the star in disbelief. "Get in," Jess said with more authority.

The woman nodded and dropped the bike in the road. She managed to get in with Lee Ann's help. The woman directed them down forty-two as they quickly sped away. The woman told them they needed to go about ten miles down the road. Lee Ann was looking at the woman. She was older, and looked older than she probably was. She looked tired and Lee Ann wondered how she managed to ride that far.

Jess looked over her shoulder. "What's happening?"

The woman tried to shout over the rush of air. "She was taken by a man. I know he's got her in his house. We need to get her back! She's only seventeen!" She started to sob.

Jess pushed the little cart as fast as it would go. After what seemed like an eternity, the woman told Jess to turn left. They drove down the narrow road until they came to a trailer park. She indicated for them to turn in. Jess slowed down in the park. She was surprised at the number of people. The sign at the entrance announced Sun Lake Estates was a community for *active adults*. That means no kids. But there were many kids running around and playing in the street as adults sat under the carport or porch of the many small homes.

The woman directed them to a small house on Sun Lake Blvd, right across from the pool. She quickly got out, showing much more vigor than she did going in. Once the girls were out, she pointed to a house two doors down. "She's in there." She looked at Jess and grabbed her shoulders. Pleading, she said, "Please go get her. Will you go get her?"

Jess looked at the house and asked, "What's her name?"

Holding her hands over her the mouth, the woman replied, "April. Her name's April."

With no discussion, the girls started towards the house. They stopped in the yard in front of the door. Jess stepped up on the porch and knocked on the door. Then stepped back with Fred and Lee Ann. After a moment, the door opened wide. A tall man stepped into the door and leaned on the jam. He wore only black jeans with no shirt. A large oval buckle swung from the belt hanging loosely from the loops. He was hairy. In a Wookie kind of way.

He looked down at the girls and smiled as he picked his teeth with a small nail. After a moment, he smiled and pointed at Jess with the nail. "Well now. Look at this." He leaned out the door and looked up and down the street. "You girls lost or something." Then laughed.

"Where's April?" Jess asked.

He glanced over his shoulder and replied. "She's alright. The real question is, who are you?"

"We're here to get April. Is she in there?" Jess asked.

He smiled back and pointed at her again with the nail. "You know, it's kind of funny."

"What is?" Jess asked.

"I usually have to look for it. It's kind of strange it just walks up to my door."

Jess's ears were getting even hotter. "And just what is *it*?"

He smiled broadly this time. Running his tongue over his bottom lip, he leaned forward slightly and replied, "Pussy."

Jess quickly drew her pistol and fired one round. Fred

jumped at the report of the .45 going off right beside her. The man in the door however, growled in pain as he fell to the floor, holding his left leg.

Looking up, he shouted, "You bitch! You shot my leg!"

"I was aiming for your little pecker!" Jess shouted back.

He reached back into the house and swung out a shotgun as he screamed, *bitch* in one long shriek. Jess quickly fired again as Fred drew her pistol. Then Lee Ann walked between them. As soon as she was just in front of the two women, she evenly pressed the trigger on her MP5. The small German weapon spewed gleaming brass into an arch in the hot sun. The man's body flinched with every impact. The shotgun fell from his hands onto the porch. After a couple seconds, Lee Ann was replacing the mag in her weapon.

He fell forward onto his face with a thud. Lee Ann stowed the mag and looked back at Jess and Fred, "You going in?"

The reality of what just happened came to Jess. Fear crept into her and she said, "Oh God. I hope she's in there."

Lee Ann looked at the body slumped on the weathered porch. "Doesn't matter. He needed killing."

She looked back at the other two and headed for the open door. Stepping over the body, she entered the house. It was dark and hot, really hot, inside the trailer. As she crossed the small living room, she glanced back and saw Jess and Fred behind her. The trailer was small and it was only a few steps until she was standing before a closed door. Steeling herself, she opened the door. What she saw made her sick and she had to cover her mouth with her hand.

A young woman was tied face down on the bed with several pillows under her hips. The evidence of her numerous assaults was plainly visible. Jess rushed into the room and quickly cut her free. She rolled the girl over. She was unconscious. Her skin was dry and hot. The hair matted to her face where the sweat dried it.

"Oh my God. She is so hot!" Jess shouted.

Fred was looking at the girl. "We need to get her outside."

Jess ripped the pillows from the bed and pulled the corners of the sheet out. "Grab a corner. Let's carry her outside."

The girls carried her outside. As Jess was passing through the door, she drew her pistol again and fired a round into the top of the guy's head. The unannounced shot scared Lee Ann and Fred and they dropped the girl onto the porch with a thud.

"What the hell!" Fred shouted. "Would you let us know when you're going to shoot something!" Fred shouted.

"Oops," Jess replied as she holstered the Colt. "Sorry."

"We need to take her to town. The clinic is the only place that can help her," Fred said.

They picked the girl up and carried her out to the buggy. The problem was, it was only a four-seater and there was no way to lay her down. Working together, they managed to get her in. Fred got into the backseat to hold her. As they were doing this, the older woman, who had been hiding behind a large oak, came running up.

"Is she ok?" She cried as she leaned in.

"She's alive. But we need to take her to Eustis. There's a clinic there and she really needs some help," Jess replied.

"Oh! Poor April. I told you to stay away from him!" She looked at Jess and cried, "I told her to stay away! It wasn't my fault!" Her guilt was now laid bare.

Jess grabbed her hands. "It's not your fault!" She pointed back to the body on the porch and said, "It was *his* fault! No one else's! We're taking her to Eustis and we're leaving now!"

The woman stepped back and nodded her head. Jess quickly

got in behind the wheel and took off as fast as the little buggy would go.

We were about to leave the plant when the sound of a vehicle surprised everyone. The security detail at the plant quickly moved towards the road. I was shocked to see the smaller of our two buggies come racing down the road. I saw Jess, Fred and Lee Ann were in it, along with someone else who looked slumped over. They didn't see us and continued on towards Eustis.

"Let's go!" I Shouted as I jumped in behind the wheel and started the war wagon.

Everyone quickly got in and I took off to try and catch them. But they had a good head start on us. "Was that Fred?" Aric asked.

Thad nodded. "Jess and Lee Ann were there too."

"Who was the other person?" Aric asked.

Thad shook his head. "I couldn't tell. But they didn't look good."

We followed them into town and saw the little buggy wheel up in front of the clinic where the girls quickly got out. I pulled up behind them and stopped quickly as staff from the clinic came running out. Jess was shouting for help as the nurses and medics pulled a girl from the back of the buggy.

"What the hell is going on?" I asked.

"We found her tied to a bed in a trailer," Jess replied as the medics carried the girl into the clinic as they shouted orders.

Confused, I asked, "What? Where?"

Jess stopped and brushed her hair from her face. "Down forty-two. We were at the market in Altoona when this woman came up. She said...," she paused as she broke down and began to cry. "She said this girl was being raped. We found her tied to a bed in a little trailer." She looked me in the eyes and added, "It was awful."

I felt for her. I knew her pain. But what could I say? I wrapped my arms around her. She hugged me and wept. Looking at Lee Ann, I asked, "Where was this? We need to find him."

Lee Ann was leaning against the buggy with her H&K slung over her shoulder. She produced a mag and held it so I could see it was empty. "He's already been dealt with."

It was a sobering sight to realize how casually she said it, as though she just told me she had taken the trash out. Which, in a way, she did. "You alright?" I asked.

She nodded and smiled. "Yeah. I'm fine."

Jess pulled away and wiped her face, feeling a little embarrassed. "I'm going to go in and check on her." She was looking at the entrance to the clinic. "I'm probably going to stay here with her."

Nodding, I gripped her shoulder. "That would be good."

She disappeared into the tent. I looked at Lee Ann and said, "Go with her. Keep an eye on her." She nodded and headed inside.

Aric was talking to Fred. She was upset, but not nearly as much as Jess. She was giving him the rundown on what happened. As I stepped over to them, Kelly stopped me. "Thanks for getting me up here. I'll hang out a couple of days if you don't mind."

Nodding, I replied, "That'd be good. When you're ready to go back, just go to the armory and let them know."

He waved as he walked towards the park, "Will do! Thanks again."

"Is Jess staying here?" Fred asked. I nodded.

"We'll take this one back, if you want to take the other." Aric said, pointing to the small buggy.

"That'd be good." Thad replied. Aric and Fred climbed into the small buggy and pulled away. Thad watched them for a moment then said, "They some brave girls."

"Yeah. But I wonder why they were out."

Thad walked over to our ride. Stuffing his hands into his pockets, he leaned back against the fender. "They was just doing what they thought they needed to. Same as you."

"You're right about that. It's actually good that they're getting out and riding around. We can't be everywhere. And it's obvious they can handle themselves."

Thad added, "Obviously."

Letting out a long breath, I said, "I'd like to go see where this all happened."

Thad nodded. "Me too."

Shane came trotting up as we talked. "Hey, Morgan, Thad."

"Hey, Shane. How's the law and order business?"

He stopped and scratched his head. "Well. What are you planning on doing with Dave Rosa?"

Shaking my head, I looked down at the ground. "Hell. I don't know." Looking back up at him, I added, "He's guilty of murder. There's no doubt about that. But a judge should decide what to do with him."

"He's starting to be trouble. Says he wants to go home. Says he's spent enough time on the chain."

I laughed. "Well, he damn sure ain't going home."

"Can you come talk to him?"

I looked at Thad. He smiled. "Go on, Sheriff."

"In that case, let's go talk to the prisoner, Deputy."

Thad stood up off the buggy, and we walked with Shane towards the Eustis PD. "Where's Sean?" Thad asked.

Shane pointed off towards the park. "Oh, he's over there. This heat is getting to people. They want to fight for some damn reason." With wide eyes, he asked, "Who the hell wants to roll around on the ground and fight in this miserable shit?"

Thad opined. "Not me!"

"Yeah. Me neither." I said, "All I want to do is sit in a cool pool somewhere."

"When you find one, let me know where it is," Shane said. "I wish the city pool still worked. That would be awesome."

"After what happened today, it could happen," Thad replied.

Shane got excited. "Really? You got the plant running?"

"We didn't do shit." I replied. "The engineers did all the work. And yes, the plant fired and ran. But there's a crap-ton of work to do to get power here."

"Oh man. Power again." Shane said, shaking his head. "That would be awesome. Having AC again. Being able to sleep comfortably. Man, I can't wait!"

"You won't have power at your house, buddy," I said. "Sorry to piss on your parade. We'll be lucky to get a couple of buildings here in town lit back up."

Shane thought about that for a moment. Then asked, "What about the water plant? Can we get that back up? Bringing treated water back to town would make a huge difference. People having running water would be a big relief. The clinic stays packed with people sick from water-related issues."

"It ain't that simple, my friend. We'd have to get the pumps running as well as the treatment plant. There probably aren't enough chemicals around to treat much water. Then, we'd have to get the sanitary plant up as well. The waste would have to go somewhere. I don't know if we can do all that."

"I'll look into it. I'll see what we have for chemicals and

stuff. One of the plant operators lives here in town. I'll get with him and see what it would take."

I stopped at the door of the PD. "See if you can find the plant operator. We'll look at it then."

Shane opened the door and Thad and I followed him through. He led us back to the holding cells. "Rosa!" He shouted.

Dave Rosa lifted himself from his bunk and rested on the bars of the cell. "What?" He asked. He looked rough. His hands and clothes were dirty and he hadn't shaved in some time. He looked homeless. Or what we would associate with homelessness in the Before.

"Sheriff wants to talk to you," Shane said.

Hearing that, Dave perked up a bit. "How long you going to keep me chained up? You're working me like a slave. Every day is the same thing and I'm getting tired of it."

I looked at Thad, he shrugged and I looked back at Rosa. "Think we're being a little hard on you?" I asked.

He scratched at his nappy head. "Well, yeah. I mean, this falls under cruel and unusual punishment." He paused and looked up at me, half squinting. "It's unconstitutional."

I looked at Shane and asked, "You still have volunteers going out to the farm every day?"

Shane shrugged. "Some days more than others. But yeah, we still have people going out every day."

"Sounds like your neighbors don't think it's cruel and unusual."

Rosa kicked the cell door. "But they ain't on a damn chain! They ain't worked like a fucking slave in that blazing sun!"

I stepped closer to the bars. "And they haven't killed anyone either."

Rosa snapped. "It was an accident!"

I laughed at him. "Yeah. You accidentally killed that poor

girl. You can say what you want. But your sorry ass will stay on that chain." I stepped a little closer to the cell door, "You'll die on that chain. That or we can get it done today. Your choice."

Rosa's eyes went wide. His hands shot out of the bars and wrapped around my throat. I was stunned for a moment. He was strong and had a hell of a grip. He was screaming as Thad and Shane grabbed his arms. But I had another idea. I calmly drew my Springfield and stuck it through the bars. When I felt it push against him I squeezed the trigger.

The blast from the .45 was deafening inside the holding area. Thad and Shane both jumped back. Rosa released my neck and stepped back holding his stomach. Looking at his blood covered hand, he said, "You shot me."

When he looked back up at me, I had the pistol leveled at his face and pulled the trigger again. He collapsed in a heap in the cell. And while he was certainly dead, he was still breathing, kind of. The sound coming from his throat was disturbing. His chest would heave as that part of his brain still tried to fulfill its task, and a sucking gargling sound rose from his throat. Thad and Shane stood silently beside me. I looked at them each and asked, "Anyone have a problem with this?"

Thad shook his head. When I looked at Shane, he said, "I do." I turned to face him. He was still looking into the cell when he added, "I have to clean that shit up."

I looked at Rosa's body lying a very large pool of blood. The sucking sound had stopped and he was lying motionless. As I examined the body, something caught my eye. Turning my head to the side, I looked at one of his hands. It was lying out in front of him and looked normal, except for the pinky. It was twisted out at ninety-degree angle from the palm.

"Damn, bet that hurt." I said.

"Must not have hurt too much," Thad said. "I figured he'd let go of your neck when it broke, but he didn't."

I looked at Thad, "You broke it?"

He nodded and pointed at Rosa. "Yeah. When he grabbed you round the neck, I took hold of his little finger and bent it back. He didn't let go, so I broke it. But he didn't even flinch."

I looked back at Rosa. "Didn't flinch when I shot his ass either."

Shane walked out of the holding area and returned, pushing a mop bucket and mop. Leaning the mop handle in the corner, he asked, "Will you two help me get him out of here?"

"That's going to make a hell of a mess," Thad said.

"I'll go get a body bag from the clinic," I said.

I left them there and walked back towards the clinic. Crossing the parking lot, I noticed that my neck hurt. I rubbed it as I ran through what happened in my mind. It seemed it happened in slow motion at the time. Though I know that certainly wasn't the case. As the scene went through my mind, I drew my pistol and dropped the mag, replacing it with a full one and tucked the other mag into my dump pouch.

It was odd to be walking through the parking lot of the police department replacing the mag in my pistol. But then, I guess it wasn't nearly as strange as shooting an inmate in a holding cell inside the jail. But it was a new world we lived in. I was brought out of my stupor by the sound of an engine. Livingston and Sheffield pulled up beside me.

"Hey, Morg," Livingston said. "Heard the test went well. So when can we expect power in town?"

I shrugged. "It's going to take a while. We've still got a lot of work to do. One thing I need you guys to do is find out what size transformer the armory has. We'll probably have to replace it when the time comes."

"I'll sort it out," Livingston replied. He looked out the window of the truck and asked, "Where are you going?"

"I need a body bag."

Sheffield leaned forward and asked, "For what?"

Cocking my head to the side, I asked, "Really?"

Sheffield now looked around and asked, "Where? Who?"

I jabbed my thumb over my shoulder towards the jail. "In the jail. Dave Rosa is dead."

"What happened?" Livingston asked.

I told them the tale of Dave's death. When I finished, Sheffield asked a ridiculous question. One I would have expected in the Before. "You couldn't stop him without killing him? Was that really necessary?"

I leaned towards the window so I could see his face. "How about I walk around there and throttle you by the neck? Let's see what you think about it. Besides, we did try. Thad broke one of his fingers trying to get him off me. Dude had a grip. Not to mention, he *was* going to die one way or another. Just happened sooner than I planned."

"How's your search for a judge coming?" Sheffield asked.

Running my hand through my hair, I replied, "I don't know. Haven't found anyone yet. Now, if you don't mind, I need to find a bag for that sack of shit bleeding out in the jail." Turning back towards the clinic, I walked off. I'm sure Sheffield was grumbling, but I didn't give a shit.

I found a body bag at the clinic, having to answer the same stupid question once more. Bag in hand, I went back to the jail where Shane and Thad had moved Dave's body out to the vehicle sally port. A rivulet of blood ran across the floor and into a drain. I unfolded the bag and dropped it on the ground. Looking at the body, I said, "Looks like you guys were busy."

Thad nodded at Shane. "He wanted to clean that cell."

I looked at the mop bucket, now full of red water, and added. "I guess in this heat you don't want to waste any time."

Shane stepped up and grabbed Dave's feet. "No, you don't; now let's get him in this bag."

We quickly loaded Dave into the bag and zipped it up. With that part of the task done, the question now was, what do we do with him?

"I guess we'll take him out to the farm and bury him there," Thad said. "I'll have Cecil bring his tractor out."

"Alright. You ready to head home?" I asked Thad.

Pulling a small cloth from his hip pocket, he wiped sweat from his forehead. "Yeah. Let's head back. I say we go to the lake tomorrow. I could really use a dip in the lake to cool off."

"Alright, Shane. Cecil will collect this sack of trash in the morning," I said.

He nodded. "Sounds good. Catch you guys later."

I gave him a wave as we walked out the roll-up door. As we headed back to the clinic, Thad said, "I want to check on Jess before we go."

"Good idea."

We stepped into the clinic and found Jess and Lee Ann sitting in a couple of folding chairs. The girl they'd brought in was now in a bed. She was wearing one of those little gowns that shows everyone your ass. But that wasn't an issue as she was lying in bed and mostly covered with a sheet.

I put my hand on Lee Ann's shoulder. She looked up and smiled and I asked, "How's it going?"

"They said she should be alright. She was really dehydrated. They put an IV in and gave her a bunch of stuff. She has injuries though, you know, inside."

As I was talking to her, Thad knelt down beside Jess. She

was looking at the girl and he stayed quiet for a moment before asking, "You ok, Miss Jess?"

She didn't reply. Just stared at the girl. Thad placed his hand on her arm and gave it a gentle squeeze. When she looked at him, he said, "You saved her, Jess."

She looked at him for a moment, then back at the girl, then back to him. "It doesn't feel like it. Someone should have been there sooner."

Thad nodded as he looked at the young girl. Getting up, he stepped to the bed and pushed her hair behind her ears. Looking back at Jess, he said, "But if you hadn't gotten there when you did, she wouldn't be here now. You saved her. You did a really good thing." Jess gave a little shrug in reply. Thad walked over to her and held his big arms out, "Now give me a hug so I can head home."

She reluctantly stood up and leaned into the big man. Thad wrapped his arms around her and lifted her off the ground. She smiled and then laughed. "Uhg, you're squeezing me in half!"

He smiled and said, "I knew I'd get you to smile."

Jess smiled in an exaggerated manner, "There, you did. Happy now?"

He set her back on the floor and replied, "Yes ma'am."

"You two going to stay here tonight?" I asked.

Jess nodded. "I am."

"Me too," Lee Ann added.

"Alight then. I'll come check on you guys, and her, tomorrow."

"We're going swimming tomorrow," Thad said, grinning.

Jess stabbed her finger at me, "You better come get us before you go!"

Holding my hands up, I replied, "I will, I will. Well, someone will."

Jess crossed her arms over her chest. "You better."

"I'll make sure you get home," Thad said.

"Alright. We're out." I said and leaned over and kissed Lee Ann on the head. "See you two in the morning."

As we walked out, Thad said, "I'm driving."

Walking around to the passenger side, I replied, "Fine by me."

Thad started the buggy up and was pulling out of the parking lot when a man came running up, waving a piece of paper and shouting. I dropped my head back against the seat and moaned, "Now what?"

CHAPTER 5

"**S**ETTLE DOWN, GULLIVER," SARGE SAID from under his hat.

Dalton was restless. The men had moved out to the small structure at the juncture of two conveyors. They made the move in early morning hours while it was still dark. The sun was now up and activity was picking back up around the reactor.

Dalton rolled his neck and settled back in behind the scope. He was resting behind the old man's M1A. But all he was doing was looking through it. He wanted to be on the trigger. Not just staring through the scope's twenty-five power magnification. After a moment, he asked, "Are we just going to sit here or are we going to dance?"

Sarge was lying on his back with his feet stretched out and propped up on the conveyor belt. His hands were folded on his chest and he was trying to sleep. Rocking his feet back and forth, he said, "The dance don't start till tonight. Simmer down."

"I think ole no-neck down there is the jefe," Mike said.

"That's one big-ass Russian," Doc said.

Dalton clicked his tongue and said, "You think he's a religious man?"

Doc was looking through a compact pair of Steiner

binoculars. He studied the large man for a moment and replied, "I don't know. Why?"

Dalton smiled. "Because he's about to have an out-of-body experience." He clicked the safety off on the M1. "In three, two…"

"You pull that trigger and I'll stuff that rifle up your ass sideways," Sarge said without moving. Dalton clicked the safety back on and Sarge added, "Good man."

"You seeing our guys down there?" Ted said.

Sarge sat up, "You see those Corps guys?"

Doc handed Sarge his binos. "Yeah. They're down there at the door to the reactor."

Sarge looked down at the plant and saw several men in multi-cam uniforms. They were surrounded by armed men in green fleck camo pattern. The man they called no-neck was talking to them and gesturing with his hands. A couple of the engineers were obviously wounded, the bandages clearly visible.

"We got to get those guys out of here," Dalton said.

"Where'd they come from?" Sarge asked.

"They came out of the reactor building." Ted said. "Probably walked them through from the other side."

Sarge shook his head. "We don't have enough people."

Dalton looked over at the old man. "We can't leave them here. We've got to get them out."

"Look son, I know how you feel. But there's four of us." He pointed down at the reactor. "Look at how many are down there." Then he pointed to the tall steam plant to the west of the reactor, "Look how many guys are up there. They've even got armor down there. This is a fight we can't win."

Dalton turned his attention back to the scope. "There's got to be something we can do."

Doc leaned forward and looked at the boat tied up in the

lagoon. "I still don't get what they're doing with the old fuel rods. I mean, it's hazardous waste. You can't do anything with it. Why in the hell are they hauling it out of here."

Sarge looked down at the boat. "They've got two of those casks loaded, and looks like there's room for one more. My guess is when that third one is loaded, they'll pull out."

"Think they'll leave those engineers?" Ted asked.

Sarge shook his head. "I don't know."

"Well, whatever they're planning with that shit, we can throw a wrench in the works," Mike said. "I've got enough plastic to sink that boat."

"If that boat were to sink right there, they wouldn't be able to get another one in here," Dalton said.

Sarge was watching the boat as he thought about it. After a moment, he said, "You feel like going for a swim tonight, Mikey?"

"You know it, boss."

"I'll go too," Dalton added.

Sarge handed the binos back to Doc. "Alright. Get some rest. You two go over there tonight and send that thing to Davey Jone's locker."

Mike pulled his pack over and smiled, "With pleasure."

They spent the rest of the day observing the activity at the reactor and trying to get a hard count on the number of Russians. There were soldiers obviously, but there were others as well. These people may have been in uniform, but their mannerisms gave them away. They obviously weren't military. Ted had a running tally on a small notepad. Currently, the count was twenty-nine armed men and eleven *others*.

"Damn this fucking dust," Dalton growled.

Sarge raised the brim of his hat to see him. "What's the matter? Little coal dust bothering you?"

"A little?" Dalton asked, holding his blackened hands up. "The shit is everywhere."

Sarge chuckled. "It's a coal conveyor. What the hell did you expect?"

Mike slapped Dalton's shoulder, causing a small cloud of black dust to rise. "Don't sweat it, man. It'll come off when we take our swim later." Dalton looked at Mike and couldn't help himself. He started to laugh. "What?" Mike asked.

Dalton was laughing so hard while muffling the sound with his hands that he could barely talk. He pointed at Mike and managed to mutter, "Your face!" And he ran a finger around his mouth.

"What?" Mike asked.

Sarge looked at Mike and stifled a laugh as well. "What the hell, Mikey. You look like you been sucking on a dirty asshole."

Mike's face was covered in black dust. But, like little kids that play in the dirt, they always seem to develop a really dark ring around their mouths. And Mike had a thick black ring of coal dust around his mouth. He pulled his pack over again and took a small signal mirror out and looked at himself.

"How in the hell do you get so damn filthy?" Ted asked.

Looking in the mirror, Mike muttered, "Holy shit." He pulled a bandanna from his pocket and started wiping at the black ring. "This shit isn't coming off!"

"Hang on," Doc said. He opened his bag and took out a bottle of saline. Handing it to Mike, he said, "Use this."

Mike used the saline to wet the cloth and managed to scrub most of the dust from around his mouth, though his face was a couple shades darker than normal. But then, so was everyone else up there.

"You might want to lay off those dirty assholes, Mikey," Sarge said with a laugh.

Annoyed, Mike shot back, "I got your dirty asshole."

Sarge blurted out a stifled laugh. "I bet you do! Dumbass!"

Ted dropped his head onto the deck, rocking it back and forth. "Mikey, you really need to think before you speak."

"Fuck off, Ted. You half-eared freak!" Mike snorted.

Ted sat up and said, "What have I told you about that shit?"

But his warning was useless. Mike grabbed his belly and pointed at Ted as he started a stifled uproarious laugh. "Holy hell!" He said in a loud whisper as he fell back.

Confused, Ted asked, "What?"

Dalton was still lying behind the rifle. He picked up Mike's signal mirror and handed it to Ted. Ted took a look and realized when he'd dropped his head, he'd rolled it back and forth in coal dust as though he were inking a stamp. Even the tip of his nose was black. He leaned forward and snatched the bandanna from Mike's hand and wiped his face off.

"You booger-eaters need to quiet down. Them commies find out were up here and the shit's going to get kinetic in a hurry," Sarge said. As he lay back and pulled his hat down over his eyes, he added, "Shut the hell up."

Mike leaned over and pinched off the side of his nose and fired a black snot rocket into a pile of coal dust. Ted shook his head and commented, "You really are disgusting."

Sarge kicked Ted in the hip, "Already told you to shut up."

Ted rolled his eyes and turned his attention back to the group of Americans standing in the open door of the reactor enclosure. While some of them certainly were wounded, it appeared as though they were being treated decently. The thought was confirmed when a man walked up and started to check the wounds on one of them.

"You seeing this?" Dalton asked.

"I'm tracking," Ted replied.

From under his hat, Sarge asked, "What is it?"

"Looks like they've got a medic down there taking care of our boys," Dalton replied.

Sarge shuffled his feet and said, "They're soldiers too. We'd take care of theirs, so it only makes sense."

"Not what I'd expect from 'em," Mike said.

"How you think they'll feel if we off a couple of theirs? Think they'd take it out on those guys?" Dalton asked.

Ted looked over at him, "What would you do?"

Dalton's head rocked back and forth. "I'd probably flay one of 'em alive."

Ted's face contorted. "For fuck sake. Let's hope they're not like you."

Dalton shrugged. "I tend to be direct and to the point."

"Saves time," Sarge mumbled from under his hat.

"I need a break off this glass," Dalton said.

Mike offered to relieve him from the observation duty and took up position on the rifle. Dalton found a place big enough for him to stretch out in and laid a shemagh over his eyes, crossed his arms over his chest and dozed.

"Do I need to have you give me the mag out of that rifle, or can you keep your social finger off the bang switch?" Sarge asked.

Mike looked over at the old man and silently mocked him while tapping the trigger with his finger, then said, "No, you don't. I'm not fucking stupid."

Sarge snorted. "Huh. Must be a recent thing." Mike gave him the finger in an exaggerated manner. Sarge, without lifting his hat, said, "Keep it up and I'll break it off and feed it to Gulliver."

"And I like finger food," Dalton replied.

Mike looked at Ted and mouthed, *what the fuck?* Ted

shrugged in reply. Holding his hands up and working his fingers in the air, he said, "Mystery."

"No it ain't." Sarge replied. "He's as predictable as a damn clock."

Mike shook his head as Ted stifled a laugh, and began observing the reactor area. The rest of the afternoon was spent watching the activity at the reactor. A third cask was moved out on a special trolley and loaded onto the boat in the lagoon with a crane. The men from the Army Corps of Engineers were kept in the area for the day. It was noted that they were regularly given water and even fed. It seemed the Russians down there were taking good care of them.

Doc had replaced Ted on the binos and he moved to the rifle so Mike could get a little combat nap in before his swim. Doc was most interested in the condition of the Corpsmen and commented on the treatment they were receiving from the Russians. He made a mental note about the fact. If they were treating his wounded and prisoners well, he would do the same if the opportunity presented itself.

As the sun began to set, the Americans were rounded up and led off. Ted watched, trying to determine where they were being held. But they were taken back into the reactor building and he quickly lost sight of them. They were probably being moved to the structure on the other side, though they had no way of figuring out where. Ted roused Mike and Dalton and the two started to get ready for the task at hand.

When Sarge woke up, he sat up rubbing his eyes and asked, "What's up?"

Dalton was wrapping a bundle of C4 blocks with duct tape. He quickly replied, "My dick and your interest."

Mike started to laugh, tilting his head back with his mouth wide open. Sarge looked around and scooped up a handful of coal dust and dropped it into his gaping maw. This served to stop Mike from laughing. He started cussing and spitting, trying to get the black grit out of his mouth.

"Calm down, Nancy. I was just trying to help you cover your face," Sarge said as he rubbed coal dust in his hand. "This stuff makes good camo for night ops."

Mike spit a black slug out. "That was really fucked up. I mean, really."

Ted smiled and shook his head, saying, "Never going to learn."

Sarge turned his attention to Dalton. Dalton never looked over, just kept working on the explosives. The old man scooted closer to him and said, "You know, that could be." He rubbed his chin as he looked down at Dalton's crotch. This gave Dalton pause. Sarge licked his lips and said, "I've always wondered what the backside of one looked like." He drew his knife from its sheath and added. "Whip that bad boy out and we'll find out together."

Dalton thought for a moment before replying. "While your offer is tempting, I have to swim in that filthy lagoon in a moment." He shook his head, "The risk of infection is too high. We'll have to wait."

Sarge held the blade up. "That's fine. I always have it." He sheathed the knife and added, "And I'm a patient man."

Dalton scooped a handful of dust off the conveyor and began rubbing it on his face and neck, covering his arms as well. He removed his blouse top, keeping his t-shirt on. He was going to take his pistol and kukri with him and nothing else. Mike was likewise stripping down and getting ready. He was also carrying his pistol and the explosives in a pack.

"How you going to initiate that charge?" Sarge asked.

Mike held up a small green tube. "I've got two waterproof

fuse igniters. There's about forty-five minutes of slow burn fuse on each one. That should give us plenty of time to get away from the boat and back on this side."

Sarge nodded. "We're going to pull out of here and go back to the coal pile. If you get spotted, we'll put fire on them to try and cover you. But you'll be totally exposed when you come out of the water."

"Only if they're looking for us. But they won't be," Dalton replied. "Because we're ninjas and won't be seen."

"Well, you nidiots get ready to head to the boat." Looking back at Doc, he said, "You and Ted move down the conveyor and get set to move to the top of the coal pile. I'm going to stay here and cover these clowns while they swim over. Once they've set the charge and head back, I'll hook up with you guys on the pile." He looked around at the men and asked, "We clear on this?"

They all nodded and Mike slapped Dalton on the shoulder. "Come on, big boy. Let's get our frogman on."

As they collected the gear they would take, Sarge asked, "You got that charge set right?"

Mike looked at the bag and nodded. "We've got two ten-pound charges of C4. One of them will surely go off."

The old man nodded. "Good. Two is one. One is none." He wagged a finger at them. "You two get yer asses over there and back in one piece. If you get spotted, we'll lay down covering fire, but we'll all probably get our asses shot off, so don't get spotted."

"Wasn't this supposed to be a recon-only mission?" Ted asked.

Sarge looked at him. "We've made a tactical decision. I don't want that old fuel leaving here. Don't know what they're doing with it, but we're gonna fuck that plan up. You got a problem with that?"

Ted shook his head. "Me? No. I love blowing up radioactive material that's surrounded by Russian Spetsnaz troops with a slim chance of success and a near certain death sentence."

Sarge smiled and nodded. "Good to know you're on board."

Doc and Ted made their way down the conveyor. They had to go slow so as not to knock coal dust off the structure. It would potentially draw unwanted attention. Plus, they were carrying Mike and Dalton's gear with them. Sarge maintained his position as overwatch while Mike and Dalton climbed down the support of the conveyor.

The old man chewed his fingernails as the two men made their way very slowly down the steel supports to the ground. It seemed to take forever for them to make it down. The two men crawled on their bellies to the water and carefully entered it, trying to minimize the disturbance to the water as they slid in. Here, there was considerable coal at the water's edge, which was a blessing as they weren't trying to navigate through muck.

Once in the water, they cautiously made their way towards the boat, swimming very slowly. Sarge cursed them under his breath, wishing they would hurry the hell up. But he also knew that if they did, it would create more disturbance in the water and increase the chance of them being spotted. So he counted his blessings, aggravating as they were.

It seemed to take forever for them to make it to the boat. Sarge watched them through the binos as they paused beside the boat, getting their plan together. After a moment, Mike disappeared under the water. Dalton remained at the surface with just the top of his head visible. Sarge's pulse quickened as he kept an eye on his watch.

This part of the mission was without a doubt the hardest. They had to swim down under the boat, in total darkness and set the charges by feel alone. After about two minutes, Mike's head appeared. Sarge watched as they two men discussed their options. After a moment, Dalton disappeared and Mike bobbed in the water with his head barely visible.

Again, Sarge kept an eye on his watch. He started to get nervous at three minutes when there was no sign of Dalton. The minutes ticking by seemed like hours. Four, five. At five minutes and twenty-seven seconds Dalton's head reappeared. The old man let out a breath he didn't know he was holding. He actually felt a physical strain lift when he saw him. *Sum bitch,* Sarge muttered. He watched as Dalton wiped his face and took a couple deep breaths. He and Mike talked and suddenly Dalton disappeared again. *Sum bitch!* Sarge spat.

But Dalton wasn't gone as long this time. After a couple of minutes, he reappeared and the two started the slow swim back towards the coal pile. Again, the old man let out a suppressed breath. His head dropped onto his arms as he got control over his breathing before turning his attention back to watching them as they made their way back.

Sarge maintained his position until the two men slipped out of the water. Once they were on the shore, he collected his gear and started down the conveyor towards Ted and Doc. It took him longer to navigate the conveyor than it did for Dalton and Mike to cover the distance to the top of the coal pile and they were there when he arrived.

Mike was wiping his face with a shemagh and asked, "Your hip acting up? You took long enough."

Sarge ignored him and looked at Dalton. "What the hell? You got gills or something?"

Dalton was pulling a dry shirt on when he replied. "No. Just years of various martial arts. Meditation is a big part of it. Learning to control your breathing. How long was I down?"

"Almost five and a half minutes! That ain't human!"

"Damn," Dalton said. "I could have stayed down another minute."

"How long we got until that boat goes up?" Sarge asked.

Dalton looked at his watch. "Twenty-three minutes."

Sarge looked around. "Alright. Let's make our way down to the tree line. Soon as that boat goes up, we head for the trucks and get the hell out of here."

"You don't want to make sure it goes down?" Mike asked.

"You guys go down there. I'll stay here and give you a BDA," Dalton said.

Sarge hesitated. "This place is probably going to come alive like a kicked-over anthill."

"It'll be alright. I'll make it down there. We just need to know what happens to that tub."

The old man agreed. "Ok. As soon as it goes off, you get your ass down the hill. I'll leave Teddy in the tree line. The rest of us will be at the trucks. If you get your ass in a sling, we'll be able to come in with some heavy weapons and get you out."

Dalton smiled and replied, "You won't need to come get us. We'll be there shortly."

Sarge looked at Doc and Mike, "Alright, minions, move out." Then he looked at Dalton, "Don't fuck around. Get out as soon as it goes off." Dalton smiled and nodded.

Everyone moved out to their assigned positions. Ted took up a spot just inside the tree line as the others moved back towards the trucks. Dalton kept the M1A with him, reasoning he could use the scope to better assess the results of the blast. But he had another reason. Once everyone was gone he settled in behind the rifle and began looking for targets. There were several people on the dock near the boat, and he examined each of them in turn.

The M1A was suppressed and the explosion would certainly

mask the supersonic crack of the bullet. He figured taking out the boat was a good thing, but why not use the situation to eliminate some of the more important looking personnel on the dock. He checked his watch, three minutes.

Had anyone near the boat been paying attention, they may have seen the trail of bubbles coming up on the port-side stern of the boat. The waterproof fuse burning under the boat was emitting a steady string of small cloudy bubbles as it slowly inched its way towards the charges secured to the wheel shafts. The charges were placed there with the intent that even if they didn't breach the hull, they would blow the packing out around the shafts.

When there was one minute left, Dalton settled the scope on a man with a beard. He wore glasses and a white lab coat type garment. He determined the guy was some sort of scientist or nuke specialist. Not only from the way he looked, but from the way the others deferred to him. Just as he flipped off the safety on the rifle, there was a muffled *wump* under water at the back of the boat. Initially, there was a rising of the water and the stern of the boat, but that was immediately followed by an enormous geyser of water erupting into the air from either side, soaking those on the dock.

The people on the dock were momentarily stunned, and while they ducked, they didn't move. Dalton settled the crosshair on the man's head and squeezed the trigger just as the second charge detonated under the boat. The man's head exploded and Dalton quickly engaged others in rapid succession, using the chaos on the dock to his advantage. When the mag was empty, he took a quick look at the boat. The stern was already under, and water was rushing up the deck. More people were running to the scene. Dalton quietly folded the bipod and slipped away from the lip of the coal pile, leaving a sinking boat and seven dead and several others wounded on the dock.

Ted stood up when he saw Dalton sliding down the coal pile. When they were together, Ted motioned with his head and with a knowing smile, asked, "What were you shooting at?"

Dalton looked at the rifle and replied, "Oh. Just fish in a barrel."

Ted laughed and the two headed into the woods towards the waiting trucks. As they came out of the brush at the trucks, Sarge was standing in front of them with his hands on his hips. Shaking his head, he asked, "What the hell took so long?"

"Just enjoying the show," Dalton replied as he walked past him.

Enjoying the show, the old man muttered as he turned and headed for his truck.

CHAPTER 6

T HAD STOPPED AS THE MAN came running up. I recognized him from our meeting at the farm. "Mitchell, isn't it?" I asked.

He nodded and held out the piece of paper. "I thought you should see this."

I took it, and for a moment didn't recognize what I was looking at. "Is this a weather radar image?"

"Satellite. It's from a NOAA weather satellite." Mitchell replied.

Looking at the image in disbelief, I asked, "How the hell did you get it? Is it recent?"

He pointed to a time/date stamp on the upper corner. "Yeah, this was two hours ago." He handed me several other images. "You can see the track of this thing. It's going to roll right over us."

The image was a very large tropical storm. It was working its way up through the Bahamas at the moment. On one of the images there was an arch drawn in red ink. Mitchell pointed to it and said, "This is the possible track if it stays on this course."

"How the hell did you get these?" I asked.

"The satellites are still up and working. I built an antenna that could receive the signal and connected it to my laptop. It was just something to play with before. But now, I can keep an eye on the weather with it."

There was obviously more to this guy that met the eye. "Can I see your setup?" I asked.

Without hesitation, he replied, "Sure. We'll go to my house and you can see the latest images. Just follow me." He walked over and got into a side-by-side UTV that I hadn't noticed.

As he pulled away, Thad said, "This should be interesting". Looking at the printed images in my hand, I said, "Very."

We followed him down Orange Ave, which is also highway 44. We went a fairly long way down 44 before he turned left onto a dirt road and immediately into a driveway. I recognized the house because Mel and I had looked at it when it was on the market a couple of years ago. It was without a doubt the perfect place to live today. Most of the place was underground. There was a large section above ground that gave a very good view of the surrounding area. But most of it was either underground or covered with an earth berm. There was also a very large Quonset hut behind the house that made for a great shop.

We pulled in behind Mitch and stopped. As he was getting out of the UTV, he pulled a handheld radio from his hip and made a call. Looking at us, he smiled and said, "Just letting Michelle know I'm back and you're with me so she doesn't shoot you."

With a little laugh, I said, "I appreciate that."

He smiled and nodded, saying, "Come inside and I'll show you the setup."

We followed him into the garage of the house, which was already cooler that the outside temp. Going through a door into the house proper, the temp was even cooler.

"Wow, this feels great in here," Thad said.

Mitch smiled. "It's one of the reasons we bought it. It's not in the best location, but the house is perfect." As he was talking, a woman came down the stairs. Mitch looked at her and smiled. "This is my wife, Michelle."

I held out my hand and introduced myself and Thad did likewise. She smiled warmly and welcomed us into her home. "Would you like something to drink? Tea, maybe lemonade?"

Thad smiled broadly. "I'd love a lemonade, ma'am."

"Sweet tea would be great," I replied. She excused herself and disappeared into the kitchen just off the room we were standing in.

"Come back here to my war room and I'll show you the setup," Mitch said.

We followed him to a small room and stepped in. It looked like a vault with a very heavy door. The room was lined with shelves and racks. Several long guns sat in the racks and numerous ammo cans lined the wall all the way around the room. A work bench that occupied most of one wall was covered with various electronic equipment.

"You have Ham radio?" I asked.

Mitch nodded. "Oh yeah. I monitor it all day. Been listening to the broadcasts from the Radio Free Redoubt."

Surprised, I said, "Me too. He's got some interesting news."

"To say the least," Mitch replied. He patted a laptop sitting on the bench. "This is the machine that receives the signals from the NOAA satellites. Every time it passes over, I get a new image. I've been watching it very closely since the storm formed."

"Where's the antenna?" I asked.

He pointed at the ceiling. "All the antennas are mounted on the roof."

Michelle came into the room with two glasses full of ice and drinks. I thanked her and looked at the glass. "Ice?"

Mitch smiled and nodded. "Yeah. We have an ice maker.

There's a well inside the house. It was drilled during construction, so we can get water with the electric pump or the hand pump. It's good water too," he added with a nod.

I sampled the tea and it was refreshing. "Indeed it is," I replied.

Thad tried the lemonade. It must have been very good because in no time he was looking at an empty glass. He smiled and said, "That was very good, thank you."

Michelle smiled and took his glass, "I'll get you another."

"Thank you, ma'am, but don't go to no trouble for me. It was very good though. Ain't had lemonade in a long time."

She waved him off. "It's nothing. We have plenty. I'll get you some more."

Thad smiled and nodded, "Yes ma'am. Thank you."

Sipping on the tea, I said, "You've got quite the setup here, Mitch."

"We've been prepping for a long time. I knew it would happen someday. So we put a lot into it. We have power, radios, food, everything really."

"I did too. Wish I had this house though," I replied.

He smiled. "It really is perfect."

"You have any trouble with the neighbors?" Thad asked.

Mitch shrugged. "There's been a couple of little things. But nothing major. We're out of sight and keep it that way. Plus, I have this." He tapped a couple of keys on the computer and camera images of the outside of the property came up. "I can watch everything from in here."

Michelle returned with another glass of lemonade and handed it to Thad. He smiled and thanked her, saying, "I'll try to make this one last."

She smiled. "It really is good. We have two lemon trees and

I dehydrate them when there's a surplus. The dry ones aren't quite as good as the fresh, but it's not bad."

We spent some time talking and Mitch and Michelle showed us around the house. I was actually surprised that they opened everything up the way they did, and I asked him about it. He shrugged and said, "You're the Sheriff. If you can't be trusted, no one can. Besides, we try to help people all the time."

"We've helped a lot of people around here. We do it quietly though so no one thinks we have a lot," Michelle added.

I looked at the laptop and said, "Well, I appreciate the heads-up on the weather. I'll let the armory in town know so they can start spreading the word."

"We'll help in any way we can," Mitch said.

Something about the way he said that struck me. "Really? You want to help the community?"

"Of course I do. We all need to do our part."

I looked down at my vest and lifted the gold star. "You know this wasn't my idea." I looked back up at him. "It's actually a real pain in the ass. It's a burden. But someone needed to do it and it fell on me."

Mitch nodded. "Service to your community shouldn't be a burden. That's what George Washington said."

I smiled and pointed at him. "It's funny you should say that." I looked at Thad and smiled, as he crossed his arms over his chest.

"What?" Mitch asked.

I reached out and grabbed his shoulder. "Your community needs you, Mitch. I realize I don't know much about you, nor you me, but I've got a feeling you're just the guy we're looking for."

"I think so too," Thad said.

"What for? I'll help any way I can," Mitch replied.

"Careful now. You don't even know what we're talking about," I cautioned.

Mitch shook his head. "I mean it. As a nation, we were so divided before this happened. It's bringing us closer together now. You know your neighbors now. You offer a hand when you can and take one when you need it." He swung his arm out in front of him. "All of the people around here, we work together."

"We knew most of our neighbors before," Michelle said. "But we know them *all* now. We've helped them, they've helped us. We work together, and only by doing so can we all succeed."

"I knew I was right," I said with a smile.

"So. What do you need?" Mitch asked.

I leaned back against the workbench. "We need a judge."

"A what?" Mitch asked, surprised.

"A judge," Thad repeated. "We need an impartial person to deal out justice. Up to now, Morgan here has been doing it. But that isn't right. He's the law, but there needs to be someone else to sit in judgment."

Mitch was obviously surprised, and he stood there silently for a moment before looking at Michelle. She stepped closer to him and said, "You said you would help. And I think something like this would bring us even closer to restoring a sense of community."

Mitch nodded. He was thinking. "It adds legitimacy." He looked at me. "I don't know anything about being a judge, but if that's what you need, I'll do my best."

Finally, I thought. Giving him a nod, I said, "You'll do fine. You'll have plenty of help. Why don't you meet us at the police department tomorrow at noon. I'll introduce you to some people you'll be working with."

He offered his hand, saying, "We'll be there."

I took his hand and replied, "Great. See you there."

Thad and I said our goodbyes to Michelle, thanking her again for the drinks. She surprised Thad with a half-gallon Mason jar of lemonade. He smiled. "Thank you very much, Miss Michelle." "I don't think it will make it home though."

I laughed and added, "I know it won't."

As we made our way to the war wagon, Thad was already spinning the top off the jar. I laughed and said, "You're going to ruin your dinner."

He took a big drink and looked at me smiling with a lemonade mustache. "No I won't." And handed me the jar.

I took a drink and looked at the jar as I swallowed it. "Damn! That is good." I said as I took another gulp before handing it back to Thad.

"I'll keep this. You shouldn't drink and drive," he said with a smile.

We stopped at the jail to let Shane and Sean know there was now a judge in town. I felt as though I'd just taken a long nap in a hammock on some beautiful beach somewhere. Relaxed, relieved, these words just didn't do the feeling justice. Such a weight was lifted off my shoulders. I was happy.

At the jail, the guys were sitting in rocking chairs out front. Like something out of an old western. There was even a shotgun leaned against the wall behind them. We both took a seat in chairs as well. I inspected the chair, it looked new.

"Where'd these come from?" I asked.

"I kind of restored them," Sean said.

Thad rocked his back and forth and replied, "You did a good job. These are real nice."

"Too damn hot to sit inside that damn building in the afternoon," Shane added. "We like to sit out here instead."

"Modern construction is totally dependent on air conditioning." Sean interjected. "Take it away and the buildings are just hot and miserable. There's no air flow. We're starting to have issues with mold in a couple of places. But I think we got a handle on it."

"That mold ain't no good." Thad said. Then he smiled and got up, saying, "I got something for you guys." He went back to the wagon and grabbed the jar of lemonade and brought it back. Spinning the top off, he took a drink and offered it to Sean.

Sean took it and didn't hesitate to turn it up and take a swig. Wiping his mouth, he said, "Damn that's good!" As he handed the jar to Shane, "It's almost cold too!"

Shane took a pull on the jar and his eyes rolled back in his head. He swished the sweet and sour mixture in his mouth for a moment before swallowing it. Looking at the jar, he said, "Wow. It's been a long time since I've tasted anything like that. Lemons aren't too hard to come by, but sugar is nearly nonexistent."

He offered me the jar and I waved him off. "You guys drink it. We had some already."

Shane smiled and replied, "I ain't going to argue with you." And he turned the jar up again before handing it to Sean.

As Sean drained the last from the jar, he asked, "Where did you get this?"

Thad smiled and said, "From the Missus of the new judge. She's a real nice lady."

"Awwwww," Shane moaned. "Wonder if we can get her to make us some?"

I laughed. "I'm sure she will."

We chatted a little longer before Thad said he wanted to get home. We said our goodbyes and they walked us back to the buggy.

We left the jail, telling the guys we'd be back tomorrow to meet with the new judge. As we got into the war wagon and headed home, Thad asked if I wanted to stop by the armory. "Hell no!" I replied. He smiled and continued past it towards Altoona.

As we passed the farm, I looked over. There were a few people in the field working. That was good. "Let's stop by the farm in the morning on the way in," I said.

Thad nodded. "That'd be good."

We made it back to the ranch and stopped at the bunker. Danny and Perez were there. Perez was stretched out on the top of the bunker asleep. I had to shake my head. The guy was Army all the way for sure. He'd rigged a poncho from the tarp to shade him.

"How'd the test go?" Danny asked.

"It ran," I replied.

He looked surprised. "No shit? Now what?"

Sighing, I replied, "Now the real work starts."

"How's Jess and Lee Ann?" Perez asked from under his hat. "Fred told us what happened."

"They're good. Staying the night at the clinic." Thad replied.

"That was a hell of thing." Danny said. "Fred said Lee Ann just dumped a mag into the guy. You see her? Is she alright?"

I nodded. "Yeah. It's a little unsettling how comfortable she is with it all."

"Don't worry about her," Thad said. "She talks to me. She's going to be fine."

"I hope so. Any word from the old man?" I asked.

"Yeah, he called earlier and said they were headed for Thunder Mountain. They're on their way home," Danny replied.

"That's good," Thad said with a bug smile. "I knew they'd do it."

"I'll feel better when they are back here," I said. "I'm tired and I'm going home."

"You want a ride?" Thad asked.

I shook my head. "No. The walk will do me good. Thanks, ole friend."

He smiled and waved as he pulled away. I told Danny and Perez I'd see them later and headed down the road to the house. Drake met me on the road before I got to the house. He nosed my hand until I patted his head and scratched his ears. I remember reading somewhere that people with pets lived longer. Maybe this is why. He must have known I was in a weird place and stayed with me all the way to the house.

We passed Meat Head lying in the driveway as we came up to the house, but all he did was lift his head before dropping it back into the pine needles. He wasn't the kind of dog to extend anyone's life. As a matter of fact, he was the kind that shorten it through aggravation. But I still liked having his annoying ass around, but had no idea why.

The house was empty when I walked in. Going straight to the fridge, I poured myself a glass of tea as I soaked up the cool air falling out of the open door. After downing the first one, I poured another and headed for the couch. Stripping off my gear, I dropped it all onto the cushions and fell back onto it. I was exhausted. Laying my head back, I closed my eyes and fell asleep almost immediately.

Sarge had Kevin take a different route on the way home. Driving the same route was an invitation to ambush. And they'd certainly drawn some attention to the fact *someone* was in the area. They were heading down highway 200 in Dunnellon when Mike came over the radio.

"Holy shit! Do you see that?"

"See what?" Sarge asked as he looked around.

"That sign. Stumpknocker's on the River. You got your own bar and grill out here!"

"Stay off the radio, shit for brains." The old man replied. As he looked over at the sign. Sure as shit, Stumpknocker's on the River. He smiled.

While this part of the route was altered, there were only so many places to cross I-75, and they would have to go under the same overpass taken on the ride over here. Sarge reached back and tugged on Dalton's pants. "Pay attention up there, Gulliver. That overpass is coming up. If those shitbags are still there, encourage them to move on."

"Right-O!" Dalton shouted back. He was already looking forward to seeing them again. He'd told them not to be there when he came back. Sarge's order was moot, he was ready.

But it was unnecessary. As they approached the overpass, it was quickly obvious it was abandoned. As Kevin drove under it, Dalton scanned the abutments. But there was no one there. Dalton was let down. He wanted to waste these assholes worse than he did the Russians. He had respect for the Russians.

They made the rest of the trip to the ranch without incident. In this new world, not much happened after dark. And that which did was never good. The only reliable source of light most people had was fire, as batteries, candles, lamp oil and other sources of temporary light were long exhausted.

It was the rare individual or small group that planned properly and stored away batteries and the like in sufficient numbers that could push back the veil of the night. But they had to use these precious resources carefully, as there was no way to replace them.

Danny nudged Perez, who was still asleep, when the Hummer turned onto the road. For a moment, his pulse quickened as he remembered other such encounters. But when the headlights flashed a couple of times, he relaxed. As the trucks approached, he knew for certain who it was when Dalton began to shout.

"Hale to the victorious! We have returned triumphantly!" Dalton called out.

Perez leaned against the bunker and lit a smoke. Taking a drag, he said, "That dude is crazy as a caged rat."

Danny laughed. "You ain't shittin'."

The truck rolled to a stop, but Dalton was just getting started. With his hands raised into the night sky, in a deep baritone, he belted out:

"Widely is flung, the warning of slaughter,
the weaver's-beam-web tis wet with blood;
is spread now, grey, the spear-things before,
the woof-of-the-warriors, which Valkyries fill…"

Sarge cut him off. Turning in his seat, he punched him in the thigh, hard. "Knock that caterwauling off, Gulliver! Next one's in the nards! Can't hear myself think!"

Dalton looked down through the turret and shouted, "Bollocks! You uncivilized heathens!"

Sarge balled a fist and reached back. Dalton cocked his hips to the side and stuck one of his giant boots out to block the punch. Every time Sarge tried to maneuver around his foot, Dalton would parry, he wasn't going to take a shot to the nards.

Sarge ripped the door open and stepped out. Looking up, he said, "You're almost as fucking annoying as the waterhead in that truck!" He pointed at Mike, who knowing something was being said about him, held his hands up as he shrugged in a *what* motion.

Dalton leaned back against the turret and folded his hands

on his chest. In a calm and even voice, he replied, "And here I thought we were friends. That was just uncalled for."

Perez distracted the old man when he asked, "Well, what's the word about the plant?"

Sarge turned to look at him. "Oh, it's crawling with Commies."

"There's less now though," Dalton added.

Sarge looked up at him and asked, "What?"

Dalton shrugged. "That rifle was heavy. I left all the brass on the coal pile and gave the bullets to the Russians."

Sarge's brow narrowed as he pondered the statement. After a moment, he asked, "How many?"

"Seven dead for sure. Several others wishing they were."

Sarge nodded and replied, "Alright. I take back what I said."

"Did you see the Army Corps guys?" Perez asked.

Sarge nodded. "We did. But there wasn't anything we could do about it. There was way too many of them to try and get them out."

"But they're being cared for," Doc said. He'd walked up, unnoticed. "I saw their medics treating the wounded. No way to know if any of them were killed or not."

Sarge leaned into the open door of the Hummer and shouted, "Harris!" Kevin was sitting behind the wheel and had dozed off. The shout startled him and he jumped.

Trying to get his bearing, he asked, "What, what?"

"Why don't you guys go with Teddy and Mike and rack out at our place tonight. It's too late to go back to the armory and I know you guys are tired."

Kevin rubbed his face. He was definitely tired. "Alright. Sounds good to me."

Doc climbed into the passenger seat, "I'll show you how to get there."

The two trucks turned around in the road and headed for house. Sarge stayed at the bunker. Looking at Danny, he asked, "Miss Kay still up?"

Danny shrugged. "I don't know. Maybe. Morgan came back earlier and fell asleep at his place. He came over late for supper."

Sarge snorted. "Figures. Lazy ass."

Perez took a drag and blew the smoke out through his nose as he said, "He's had a hell of a day. Lot of shit went down today. Jess and Lee Ann are at the clinic sitting with some poor girl they found being raped. Morgan found someone to be a judge, then got into some shit with Porky, whoever the hell that is, in town."

Sarge's ears perked up. "No shit? Who'd he find for a judge?"

Perez shrugged. "Hell if I know. Ask him."

"I'll do jus that," Sarge said as he pushed his carbine around to his back and started towards Danny's house.

Perez held his hand up, "Bye." And he shook his head before turning back to the bunker. Looking at Danny, he said, "That guy has no people skills."

Danny laughed. "Yeah, he's special alright."

When my eyes opened, it took a moment for my brain to register what I was seeing. Little Bit's face was inches from mine. Her chin was resting on the sofa and she was smiling. "You're awake!" Sitting up, I rubbed my face. She climbed up onto the sofa and squished herself up against me. She looked up and smiled, saying, "I've been watching you sleep."

I rubbed my eyes and looked around. "Guess I slept on the couch, huh?"

"Yeah. Mommy said you were tired and to leave you alone. But it's morning now and you're awake!"

I wrapped my arm around her and hugged her tight. "And seeing you first thing in the morning is a perfect way to wake up, too."

A subtle smell filtered through the house and I asked, "What's that smell?"

Little Bit jumped up shouting, "Mommy is cooking breakfast!" She headed for the kitchen.

I got up and stumbled towards the kitchen. Mel was standing at the island behind the Butterfly stove with a sizzling skillet sitting on top. Looking up from the skillet, she smiled, "Morning, babe."

I stepped up behind her and wrapped my arms around her, slipping one hand into her robe while kissing her cheek. "Morning, beautiful. What's this?" I asked.

Smacking my hand, she pulled it out of her robe and replied, "I just felt like making breakfast here this morning. Burritos sounded good."

Then I noticed the tortilla press sitting on the counter as well. "Oh, that sounds awesome. Just wish we had some cheese."

Mel walked over to the fridge and pulled it open, taking out a small plastic container. "We have the farmers cheese from the market. Kay took it and pressed it so it's kind of like fresco."

Looking into the pan, I said, "Oh, and there's sausage too."

"Sure is. Get yourself a glass of tea and sit down. I'll bring you a burrito in a minute."

"I want one too!" Little Bit shouted.

Mel bent over slightly and said, "Then go get your sister and tell her breakfast is ready." Little Bit took off through the house yelling, *breakfast is ready!* "Speaking of sisters," Mel said, "Is Lee Ann coming home today?"

She walked over and set a plate down in front of me. I smiled and replied, "Yeah, I think so. Jess just wanted to stay with that girl and I asked Lee Ann to stay with her."

Mel fixed two more plates and set them out on the table as well before sitting down with her own. She adjusted her robe and said. "Good. But what they were they doing out there?"

Taking a bite of my burrito, I said, "I don't know. I think they're getting restless and just wanted to get out. But they can handle themselves pretty good from what it looks like."

To my surprised, she agreed. "I believe so. They've been taught by some of the best. I think they'll be ok."

Little Bit came running out to the table and slammed into her chair, bouncing the table. She smiled and said, "Oops," as she climbed up into it. Her sister came out right behind her and we sat and had breakfast together, as a family. We were missing Lee Ann, but I wasn't worried about her. I knew she was safe.

Working on my burrito, I said, "I think we found us a judge."

Mel was trying to refold hers, with little result, and replied, "Really, who?"

"His name's Mitch Williams. He's a good guy. He and his wife have that underground house over on forty-four."

"I remember that house." Taylor said. "I wanted to live there so bad. We would have had the whole upstairs all to ourselves."

"You girls were always quick to try and claim your space in any house we looked at," Mel replied.

"Anyway," I said. "I think he'll do a good job."

Mel wiped her mouth with a towel and smiled. "You're just glad someone else has the job now."

Looking at the last bite of my burrito, I said, "There's always that." Then I popped it into my mouth and chewed it while grinning ear to ear. With my breakfast done, I rose from the table and said, "Guess I'll go over and see if they made it back last night."

Little Bit was working through her burrito, and with a mouthful, said, "Mister Sarge is back."

I couldn't help but smile at her as she picked up a glass of water in front of her and took a big swig, in the manner of small kids. She swallowed hard to get the liquid and the burrito down. Wiping the wet mustache from her face with the back of her hand, she said, "Can I come?"

Nodding, I replied, "Sure. Go get dressed."

She jumped from her chair and ran towards her room. I helped Mel collect the plates and carried them to the sink. Setting them down, she asked, "What are you doing today?"

"Got to go back to town to meet with Mitch and introduce him to everyone. We'll have to sort out some place for a courtroom."

"The city building in Eustis used to be the courthouse. Bet there's a meeting room or something like that in there that could be used."

Kissing her cheek, I said, "Good idea. We'll check it out."

She turned from the sink and asked, "When are you going to spend some time around here?"

Stepping over, I wrapped my arms around her waist. "It's not that I don't want to. There's just so much to do."

She leaned out and gave me a quick kiss before pushing past and walking towards the bedroom. "I know. I'd just like to see you more."

"Me too," I said.

Little Bit came running out dressed and announced, "I'm ready!"

Looking towards the bedroom as I walked towards the door with Little Bit in tow, I said, "I'll be back in a bit." I stopped at the door and looked at the vest and carbine leaning in the corner. Only pausing a second before I said screw it and left them behind for the short walk to Danny's.

The dogs were taking most of the front porch, and we had to step over the lazy beasts. Little Sister was the only one to even look up. Taking Little Bit's hand, we headed across the yard to Danny's. As we rounded the shed we could hear the kids playing out back. Little Bit quickly ran around the porch to join in on whatever sort of fun was being had back there. I saw the old man sitting on the porch, coffee cup in hand. When he saw me, he looked at his watch and shook his head.

Pointing at me with his cup, he said, "You are the laziest Sheriff I've ever seen."

"It's good to be king," I replied.

"Right!" He spat. "King of dumb folks island maybe."

"I think we've got us a judge," I said.

He leaned back in the chair and rocked it a couple of times. "Good. That's good."

Walking up on the porch, I sat in one of the chairs. The old man refilled his cup and we told each other our news. He filled me in on what went down at the plant in Crystal River and I told him of the judge and run-in with Porky. When I told him about the plant, he almost smiled.

"That's going to be a hell of a lot of work," he said.

"Yeah. And it's hotter'n two hells right now," I replied.

"Yeah, but getting power into town would be a really good thing."

Rocking back in my chair, I said, "I guess. I have to run to town in a bit and introduce the new judge to everyone."

"I'll go with you," Sarge replied as he lifted himself out of the chair and headed for the house. "Let me get some more coffee."

"We got time," I replied.

As he went inside, Perez and Thad came up onto the porch. Naturally, Perez was smoking a cigarette and Thad was trying to keep out of the smoke. "What've you been up to?" I asked Perez.

Thad smiled and replied for him. Jabbing a thumb in Perez's direction, he said, "Oh he's been out bed shopping."

Perez stopped and stretched his back out. "I've spent the last two days checking every bed in this place. Trying to find one that wouldn't kill me!"

"Really? That's what you've been doing for two days?" Sarge asked as he walked out onto the porch.

Perez waved his cigarette at him. "I don't want to hear no shit from you. My back is killing me."

Sarge laughed. "Gettin' old ain't for pussies."

Perez fell into one of the chairs. "Tell me about it."

I told Sarge I would meet him at the Hummer. I had to go home and grab my gear. Of course he gave me shit for that, that he had to wait on me. I laughed and told him to suck it up. Stepping in the door, I hefted the gear and shouted that I was headed to town. From somewhere back in the house, Mel called back that she'd see me later. As I was turning to go out the door, Taylor came running out of her room.

"Dad, can I go?" She asked.

"Sure. Just tell your mom." I said. I was happy to see her wanting to go out. It'd been a while since she'd been anywhere.

"I already did. She said it was up to you."

Holding the door open, I said, "Come on."

She smiled and ran past me. I slipped my vest over my head as we walked and secured it. Walking next door without it was one thing, but that wasn't an option when heading out beyond our little neighborhood. I was muttering to myself about how much I hated the vest. It was heavy and hot. And right now, I didn't need any more heat!

She heard me and laughed, saying. "I wouldn't want to wear that all day."

"Trust me, you don't"

Sarge was sitting in the running Hummer when we got there. In the passenger seat of course. Getting in the driver's seat, I said, "Don't worry about it. I'll drive."

The old man snorted, "No shit, you'll drive!"

Taylor opened the door and climbed in the back. He looked back at her and smiled, saying, "You going with us?" She smiled back, nodding her head. "Good!" Sarge shouted. "You need to get out of the house."

We pulled out and headed to town. Doc and Thad were at the bunker when we went by and we waved at them. I felt for them. It was only about 10:30 and already hot. Today was going to be brutal. We didn't have any way of telling the weather, but there was certainly something going on. It felt like low pressure and it was sucking in moisture. The temp in the upper nineties was bad enough. But add in eighty or eighty-five percent humidity and it was disgusting.

As we passed Gina and Dillon's place, I told Sarge I wanted to stop by on the way back. He nodded but didn't reply. Taylor scooted up between the seats and asked, "Are we going swimming? I heard we were going to the lake or something."

"If we get back in time," I said over my shoulder.

"We'll get back in time, sweetie." Sarge said. Looking at me, he said, "I'll keep your daddy in line today."

"Whatever," I replied with a grunt.

We rolled through Altoona without stopping at the market. I Saw Mario and waved. He had a large umbrella set up by his tables and was sitting under it. He had a Yeti cooler sitting in the back of his UTV. I made a mental note of that, remembering he had a large commercial ice maker in the honey house. I'd have to drop by and fill up all the coolers we had. It would be nice to have a bunch of ice. We made some, but it went quickly during the day as hot as it is now.

Passing the market in Umatilla, everything looked calm. That was probably the only good thing about the heat. It made people slow and lethargic. Like big lizards, they collected in shady places and moved as little as possible during the heat of the day. It was only the early morning and evening that they came to life for a while to tend to the necessities of life.

Hot air rushed into the windows as we rolled down nineteen out of Umatilla. It was like being in front of a big oven with turkey or something in it. That hot moist air that hits you when you open the door. Only this was everywhere and you couldn't just shut the door and make it go away.

Passing the plant, I noticed Baker and crew were out in the switch yard. I had to laugh to myself because they looked just like typical municipal workers. There were standing in a circle looking up. Eric just happened to be scratching his head. It was like something out of a damn skit.

Laughing, I looked at Sarge and asked, "You see that?"

He nodded. "You mean them damn engineers over there with their thumbs up their asses?"

Laughing again, I replied, "I guess you did."

"I see everything," the old man replied.

Rolling up to the armory, I waved at Mitch and Michelle. They were standing out in front of the armory on Bay Street. Rolling to a stop on the curb, we got out.

"Morning, Mitch," I said.

He stuck his hand out, "Morning, Morgan. How's it going?"

Taking his hand, I replied, "Good, buddy. How about you two?"

Michelle smiled. "We're good. Little nervous."

Sarge walked up and asked, "This your judge, Morgan?"

I nodded. "Indeed it is. Sarge, meet Mitch and Michelle."

Sarge shook their hands, nodding to Michelle. Shaking his hand, Mitch asked, "Sarge?"

The old man straightened up and replied, "First Sargent Linus Mitchell, 101st airborne."

I smiled and added, "Retired."

Sarge's head slowly turned towards me. Shaking his head, he said, "Shut up. The grown-ups are talking."

Looking at Mitch, I nodded my head at the old man and said, "See what I've got to deal with?"

Mitch laughed and Sarge growled, "What you've got to deal with? What the hell are you talking about?" He stopped and jabbed his finger at me, "You're lucky to have me! You have no idea the amount of raw talent standing in front you! You ungrateful little shit!"

He was still going on when I leaned over to Mitch and said, "He still thinks he's in the Army."

Sarge stopped, finger in mid-air and glared at me. "You snot-nosed little runt," he said in a low voice, "I'll kick your ass up onto your shoulders!" His voice began to rise. "I'll stomp a mudhole in your ass and stomp it dry! I will put my boot so far up your ass you'll choke on my laces!"

I couldn't tell if he was really mad or not and started to laugh. "Make up your mind. You seem to have a real ass fetish today. You're going to kick it, stomp it and put your boot up it." I folded my arms and looked down my nose at him. "You having any trouble? I know you old guys like your prune juice. You got something you want to tell me?"

And as they say, that's when the fight started. Apparently, he was serious. He ripped his hat from his head and started to beat me while he shouted an unending, single-syllable string of curses. I turned to avoid the hat; the old shit was hitting me in the eyes with that ratty-ass hat, big mistake. He decided to act on his fetish. Grabbing me by the shoulder, the old bastard kicked me in the ass, hard. Not just once either. I had no idea the old man was still so spry.

Breaking away from him, I ran towards the truck to get away, still laughing. Getting some distance between us, I turned and pointed at him, "Knock it off, damn it!"

He stopped and started jabbing that finger at me again. "You son of a bitch! I'll whip your ass!"

I leaned against the truck and smiled. Looking at Michelle, I said, "This is no way to act in front of our judge." Pausing for a moment, I added, "And his wife."

He stopped and looked down at his hat and punched it out with a fist before putting it back on. Looking at Michelle, he said, "I'm sorry, ma'am." Looking back at me, he continued, "It's just hard when you're dealing with this kind of paste-eating, window-licking, water-headed idjits!"

Michelle smiled. "It's alright. I've heard worse."

I smiled and said, "If it's the last thing I do, I'm going to find you some prune juice."

I was laughing inside, watching the old man try to maintain his composure. He was about to explode. But Mitch saved the day when he reached into his back pocket and pulled out a folded piece of paper. Looking at me, he said, "I've got an update on that storm."

Sarge said, "What?"

Mitch unfolded the paper and held it out. The old man took it and gave it a quick glance before looking at Mitch and asking, "Where did you get this?"

"I printed it at home."

Sarge paused for a moment before asking, "How in the hell did you do that?"

"I made an antenna that picks up the signal of the weather satellites as they pass."

"I forgot to tell you about that," I said to Sarge.

The old man barked back, "No shit, numb nuts. Don't you think this is kind of important?"

"Well yeah. I was going to tell you. Just forgot."

Sarge looked at Mitch and shook his head. "See what I mean. Now you understand?"

Mitch smiled and nodded. "I get these each time it passes over. It's a GOES bird and I get images every thirty minutes."

"That's damn impressive, Mitch." Sarge looked at me and added, "You may be a total shithead, but sometimes, just sometimes, you screw up and do something right."

"This storm," Mitch said, "it's going to hit Florida. What do we need to do?"

Sarge examined the black and white image for a moment. "Well, the good news is there's no defined eye. This isn't a hurricane. It's only a tropical storm. But depending on where it comes in, that could still make some real trouble." He looked at Mitch, "You need to keep an eye on this thing. As it gets closer, we'll have a better idea of where it's going."

Mitch pointed at the drawing. "It's just east of the Bahamas now. By tomorrow evening, we should have a better idea."

I walked over to them. "We'll tell Sheffield about it when we introduce Mitch."

As we walked towards the armory, Sarge talked to Mitch and Michelle. Taylor walked beside me in silence for a moment before asking, "Is he mad at you? I've never seen him like that before."

I laughed. "No baby, he isn't mad at me. That's just how he

is. You know how you can tell when that grumpy old bastard is mad at you?" She looked at me, waiting for the answer, "It's when he's not giving you shit."

She smiled. "That doesn't make sense."

I put my arm around her shoulder. "To you. But you remember when I traveled for work for all those years?"

"Yeah. That's when we got to go to New York and watch the Macy's parade."

"Yeah. Those guys I worked with were just like him. We were always messing with one another. If no one was screwing with you, you didn't have any friends."

She laughed. "Guys are weird. Girls don't do that."

I hugged her a little tighter and said, "That's 'cause y'all are weird. Guys, we're normal. I think it's because you have to sit to pee. I think it cuts off circulation to your brain or something." I looked at her and smiled, "Girls, are really weird. And a mystery."

She smiled and pulled away, slapping my shoulder. "That's just not right, Dad. Sitting to pee. Where do you come up with this stuff?"

I put my arm around her again and pulled her in close. "Observation baby. Just a lifetime of observation. Remember, I'm married to your mother."

"I'm gonna tell her you said that," she replied with a smirk.

Smiling, I said, "No you won't."

Looking up at me squinting, she asked, "And why wouldn't I?"

I leaned over and kissed her head, "Because you love me." She leaned her head on my shoulder as we walked through the door of the armory.

CHAPTER 7

T HAD FOUND MARY SITTING ON the back porch of the house. She was looking out across the pond, seemingly content in the moment.

"Miss Mary," he said quietly.

She looked at him and smiled. "Hi, Thad."

That big warm smile spread across his face. "I was going to take a ride up to the farm in town. Would you like to go with me?"

Mary's smile faded as she considered the offer. "I don't know," she said, looking back out at the pond. "I haven't been anywhere since getting here. I feel safe here."

The statement surprised Thad. There'd been plenty of encounters around here to give anyone pause. He smiled again. "It's safe up there. I promise. I just thought you would like to take a ride." He paused for a moment before adding, "with me."

Mary smiled, "OK. I'd like that." Whatever trepidation she was experiencing, she managed to overcome it. Thad smiled even broader, if that was possible, and held out his hand. She took it and rose to her feet. "Thank you."

Thad nodded and replied, "Yes ma'am." They went inside and told Miss Kay they were going into town.

Kay smiled knowingly. "That's good. You two need to get out."

"We'll be back in time for supper," Thad replied.

"Sounds good," Kay replied. Then, taking the dish towel from her shoulder, she shooed the two out of the kitchen. "Go on, you two, git!"

With delight in their faces, Mary and Thad headed for the door. Once outside, Mary asked, "What are we going to drive?" The war wagon was sitting in the yard and Mary eyed it nervously. It looked dangerous and made her feel uneasy.

Thad pointed to a small red truck sitting in the road in front of the house. "I thought we'd take that."

Seeing a *normal* vehicle, she relaxed. "That's nice. Where did it come from? I don't remember seeing it before."

Thad thought back to where the truck came from. He saw Reggie's face in his mind's eye and the badly decomposed body of a once young and beautiful girl. Not wanting to share any of that with Mary, he replied, "Oh, it's been around here for a long time. We just don't use it much."

Thad led her out the gate and towards the truck. Little Bit, Jace and Edie were in the back of it playing. It didn't take the kids long to notice changes in their environment, and to them, this was nothing more than a jungle gym. Thad laughed as he reached into the bed and caught a squealing Jace.

"Come on, little man, I gotta go to town," he said as he set him down on the ground.

"Can we come?" Little Bit shouted the question.

Reaching in and grabbing the two girls, holding one under each arm, Thad replied, "Not today, little ones. Mr. Morgan ain't here for me to ask, and we're going to be awhile." The girls laughed and screeched as Thad walked to the side of the road with them. The fun little kids exude is contagious, and before he knew it, Thad was spinning the two girls around, getting even more volume out of them.

Jace didn't want to be left out, and he rushed Thad, wrapping his arms around one of Thad's legs. He looked like a giant in a world of little people, and they were trying to take him down. Jace stood on Thad's foot as he walked stiff-legged, making monster sounds. The kids laughed and squealed.

Mary watched all this. She couldn't help but smile at the sight. It warmed her heart to see such a touching moment. She'd told Thad moments ago that she felt safe here, and this was just another reason why. Everyone here was part of one big family, a tribe really, but just as close. She laughed as Thad piled the kids into one heap and tickled their bellies as they squirmed and shrieked with delight.

When Thad turned to go to the truck, Little Bit and Edie jumped up and quickly seized a leg each. Thad looked back and laughed at them. "Alright, girls. I have to go now. We'll play later." They didn't want to let go, so he looked at Mary and shrugged as he walked to the truck, dragging the girls as he did.

Once at the truck, Mary helped him extricate himself from the kids. They just wanted to play and were caught up in the excitement; but they eventually gave up and took off across the yard towards the house. Watching the kids with joy in their hearts as they ran off, Thad looked at Mary and asked, "You want to drive?"

The question surprised her and she quickly said, "Oh no!" Catching herself, she smiled and said, "No, thank you."

Thad walked around the truck and opened the door for Mary. She climbed in and he shut the door before walking around and getting in. He quickly started the truck and headed out towards the road. Mike and Ted were at the bunker now, and as the little red truck passed, Mike elbowed Ted and nodded at the truck.

"Looks like Thad and Mary are getting closer," Mike commented.

Ted nodded. "Good for him."

Mike started to shake his ass as he danced in a circle. "Looks like there's going to be a little *brown chicken, brown cow.*"

Ted slapped Mike's hat from his head. "Would you grow up?"

Thad saw Ted knock Mike's hat off and smiled as they rode past. He had no idea exactly what was being said.

As they turned out onto the paved road, Thad looked at Mary and said, "Let's stop by and see Miss Gena and Dillon."

Mary smiled back. "Ok."

Sheffield sat at the head of the table with his hands in front of his face and his fingers pressed together. He listened as I introduced Mitch and told him he was going to be our new judge. He said nothing as I spoke. When I finished, I sat there looking at him, waiting for a response. But it didn't come immediately. I looked at Sarge, but he only shrugged. He was going to wait him out.

Looking at Mitch, Sheffield said, "No offense to you, Mister Williams," and he looked at me before continuing. "What makes him qualified?" Looking back at Mitch, he asked, "Do you have a legal degree?"

Mitch shook his head, "No."

"That doesn't matter," I said. "We don't need someone educated in the laws as they used to be. We need someone with a level head and common sense." Looking around the table, I added, "Something that seems to be in short supply today."

Sheffield cut his eyes at me but didn't respond directly to the jab. "I'm just concerned that people won't see it as legitimate."

"It'll be as legitimate as we make it." Sarge said. "If we recognize him, if *you* recognize him, then it will be legitimate."

"And it will be legitimate." I added. "I don't give shit about the way it was done before, where some fast-talking shyster could get a guilty bastard off. Times are different now. If you commit a crime, you will pay for it. Period."

"Not to mention," Sarge said, "this is just a courtesy introduction. This is a civilian matter and Morgan is the top civilian authority at the moment. This adds another layer. It's good for everyone."

Sheffield shrugged and said, "Sounds like it's a done deal then." Looking at Mitch, he said, "Good to meet you, judge." Mitch was a little nervous but managed to smile and nod.

"Good." Sarge said, slapping the table. "Now that that's done, let's move on to other business." He looked at Mitch and held his hand out. "You got that paper?"

Mitch produced it from a shirt pocket and slid it across the table to Sheffield. He picked it up and unfolded it. Livingston leaned over to see it as well. Both of them studied it for a moment. Livingston was the first to speak.

"Where the hell did this come from?"

Mitch explained the antenna he made and the rest of the setup. Sheffield seemed surprised that satellites were still in orbit, but Mitch assured him they were and that these images were updated every thirty minutes.

"This is amazing," Sheffield said, looking at the paper. I laughed and he looked up at me, asking, "What?"

I shrugged. "It's just kind of funny when you think about it. You know, in the Before we had all this in the palm of our hand. Our phone could see this in near real time. Just kind of humorous how we took it all for granted. I acted the same way you did, amazed at a black and white image on a piece of paper."

Sheffield nodded. "I'm with you. But right now, this is amazing." He shook the paper as he spoke.

"This could get really ugly," Livingston said. "What do we do?"

"There ain't shit you can do," Sarge interjected. "If it's coming this way, it's going to come. I'd suggest letting folks know. But the impact won't be as bad as in the past. There's no power to knock out. We might have some roofs damaged and trees down, but that's about it."

Livingston was examining the image. "Doesn't look like a hurricane yet. I don't see an eye."

Sheffield tapped the sheet and said, "Yeah, but they often strengthen as they cross that warm Florida Straight. The water is shallower there and it'll probably get worse."

I rose to my feet. "We'll just have to wait and see." Looking at Mitch, I asked, "Can you bring us a new image each day so we can stay on top of this?"

He nodded. "Of course. If I see any real change, I'll let you know."

"On that note," Sarge interrupted, "you obviously have ham gear. We need to get you on with our protocol so we can talk to you. The armory here has radios as well. That way, you're not coming to town everyday unnecessarily. You only need to come to town if there is a need. Don't want you wasting fuel and such."

Sheffield looked at Livingston and said, "Get him up to speed and let's make sure we can talk to him at his place."

Livingston nodded and stood up. "Come on, Mitch. Let's go to the commo hooch."

"Mitch, I'm going to the clinic." I said, "Can you meet me there when you're done? I want to go take a look at the city building and see if we can find a suitable courtroom for you."

He nodded, "Sure."

I left the conference room and found Taylor sitting in a chair just outside the door. She jumped up when I came out. I smiled and took her hand as we headed for the door.

"What's the damn rush?" Sarge barked.

I looked over my shoulder and saw him coming up behind us. "Didn't know you were coming," I replied.

He looked at me as he came up and shook his head. "Where the hell did you think I was going?"

I snorted and replied, "Hell, if you don't change your ways."

He shook his head again and spat at his feet. Looking up, he said, "It's your hell. You burn it in. Come on, let's go check on them girls."

Taylor looked at me, nor sure what to think. I smiled and shook my head as we fell in behind grumpy. We wandered over to the clinic and found Lee Ann and Jess sitting on a couple of big green crates out front. Lee Ann looked up and smiled when she saw her sister. Getting up, she ran over and wrapped her arms around Taylor. Taylor brightened up. The girls chatted as I went over to Jess and sat down on the crate beside her.

She didn't look up and I sat there for a moment before leaning over and bumping her with my shoulder. She looked over, squinting against the morning sun.

"Sup?" I asked.

She shrugged. "Nuttin'."

"How's the girl?" I asked.

Her head rocked back and forth before replying. "She's better. She's awake now."

Nodding, I said, "That's good. What's she saying?"

Jess shook her head. "I don't know. She's acting like it's no big deal really. She said, *it's not like it was the first time.*"

I thought about it for a minute before replying. "Still doesn't make it right."

Jess shook her head. "No, it doesn't. It was a horrible thing done to her and she acts like it's nothing." She motioned towards the clinic tent and added, "She's sitting in there eating breakfast right now. Said she was just happy to be somewhere she could eat." Jess looked as though she was about to cry.

I shook my head. "It's a hard world out there. Times are a lot different now. I'm not saying that makes it right, just the way it is."

She sat silently for a minute before letting out a long breath. "It doesn't matter. We did what we could about it. He won't do it to anyone else."

"That's right." Tapping her shoulder, I said, "Come on. Let's go swimming."

She stood up quickly, a broad smile on her face. "That would be awesome!"

"Did you say swimming?" Lee Ann asked.

I turned to see her, grinning ear to ear. "You want to go?"

She clapped her hands, "Yeah!"

"Alright. Let's head home then."

Sarge came out of the clinic with a sour look on his face. He gave me a look that said he wanted a word, and we stepped around the side of the tent. I told the girls to get ready to go and followed him.

"What's up?" I asked.

The old man shook his head. "I've never heard anything the likes of it in my life."

"You mean the girl?" I asked.

He nodded. "I can't believe the way she's taking it. Like it's to be expected."

"That's what Jess said. Said she was just happy to have breakfast this morning."

He shook his head. "It's sad. Really sad. Says a lot about the state of the world."

I nodded. "Indeed it does. But for now, I'm not worrying about it. I'm going home and taking the girls swimming."

The old man looked up. "That sounds like a fine idea. I think everyone could use a break."

We walked back to the armory with the girls in tow. They were talking excitedly about going to the lake. It was kind of surprising how something as trivial as swimming in a lake could elicit such a reaction. It was just another testament to the change in our world.

Back in the truck, once again I drove as the old man drank coffee with his feet propped up on the dash. The girls were still yammering away in the back seat. For my part, I just relaxed as I drove and enjoyed the ride. We were leaving Eustis headed towards the farm when I decided to pull in and see what was going on. It was still early, but already hot, and it would only get hotter.

When I made the turn towards the farm, the old man looked over and asked, "Going to drop in on Cecil?" I nodded as the farm came into sight.

Pulling in, I looked the field over. There were some people out working the crops, but not as many as I expected. I stopped the truck in front of the tents the security detail occupied. A Guardsman was sitting in a camp chair in the shade of the big oak trees. Sarge got out and asked him where Cecil was and he pointed out toward the field. "Out there."

Sarge looked out over the field, then back at the soldier. "Well, no shit. You got a better idea than that?"

Rocking back in his chair, he replied, "Nope."

The girls got out of the truck and he noticed them. This got the guy's attention and he stood up, smiling. Sarge shook his head and started out towards the planted rows to find Cecil. As I passed the soldier, I paused for a moment and looked at the soldier. He was still looking at the girls. Glancing back at them, I said, "Keep an eye on my daughters." The soldier looked at me and I added, "know what I'm saying?" The man swallowed and nodded.

I caught up to Sarge as he walked through a row of head-high corn. I ran my hands along the stalks as I went. Inside the rows, it was even hotter, if that was possible. The ground beneath my feet was moist, if not wet. So far, we were being blessed with daily rains that were allowing the crops to grow big and fast. It was our saving grace as we didn't have irrigation here, unlike along the lake in town.

The small plots we'd planted there were the only thing keeping the folks in town going. Sheffield had to provide round-the-clock security for them as people were constantly trying to raid the small patches of food. Even those that worked the ground had to be searched every day for any vegetables they would try and sneak out. The same was having to be done here as well. People were getting desperate; and desperate people will do desperate things.

We finally found Cecil in a bean patch. He was with a couple of old women and the three of them were weeding around the stakes the beans were climbing. "Morning, Cecil," Sarge said as a greeting.

Cecil looked up. Standing, with some effort, he pulled a handkerchief from his pocket, removed his broad-brimmed hat and wiped the sweat from his face. "How you doing today, Linus?"

"Fair ta middlin," Sarge replied and looked around. "Starting to look like the garden of Eden out here."

Cecil looked around at the crops, some getting very close to being ready to harvest. "It is. We've been lucky so far. But we've got some problems."

"Like what?"

Cecil motioned for us to follow and started down one of the rows. The two women went back to their work. Cecil left the bean field and walked into an area dotted with small heads of cabbage. A group of men were working with spades between the rows, chains dragging in the dirt as they shuffled. There were seven of them chained together.

Cecil stopped and folded his arms and rubbed his chin. "Here's our problem."

"They stealing?" I asked. Cecil nodded.

Sarge shook his head. "Can't blame 'em really. They're hungry."

"True," Cecil agreed. "But if we don't get a handle on it," he waved an arm out over the field, "all this food will just dry up like it was never here to begin with."

"Agreed," I said. "We can't have this. I can relate to them. I get it. But we're trying to help these people out. The more we harvest at one time, the more there will be for them. Sure, they might get a little something today by sneaking it out, but there won't be anything tomorrow at the rate they are stealing it."

"Not to mention, if we don't do it right, we won't have seeds for next year." Cecil turned around to face us, "that's my concern. We have to manage this properly."

Sarge nodded. "And that's the real hook. Did you put them on the chain?"

Cecil shook his head. "No. The security folks did. We weren't sure what to do with them."

Sarge called to the men. They stopped work and turned to face him. "You fellas realize we can't have this stealing, don't you? You realize this food is for everyone and has to be handled properly or it won't make a difference?"

The men looked at the ground and one another. One of them spoke up. "Sure. But that ain't feeding my kids today. They're hungry. They're starving. What do you expect us to do?"

I walked past the old man. The men all stepped back a bit. "Look, guys. I get it. I really do. But we have to work together to make a change here. Look at all this," I said as I swept my hand over the field. "This will make a huge difference to everyone. And I know it's hard to see it here when you're hungry. But just a little longer and we'll be harvesting and there will be food every day."

One of the men in a grubby New York Yankees hat said, "We're not bad guys. We're just hungry. We can't just stand by and watch our wives and children starve to death."

"How can you take this from your friends and neighbors? Every vegetable taken is at least one less we'll have later. Surely, you realize that it's just as important to harvest seeds for future planting as it is to eat the produce. We've all got to look at the long-term picture, or we'll all starve."

It was a tough spot and I felt for them. But what they did was still wrong, if not understandable. We had to make the point that they couldn't do this, and yet, the punishment shouldn't be too severe. "Just don't try and steal from the farm again, guys. We can't allow that. If we did, there eventually wouldn't be anything for anyone."

"How long you going to keep us on this chain?" One of the men asked.

"How long you been on it?"

"Since yesterday," another answered.

I looked at Cecil and said, "Take them off it tonight." Then, looking back at the group, I said, "But if you get caught again, there will be consequences." The men all seemed relieved and nodded. I hoped they got it. While times are hard at the moment, stealing from the rest of the people in town isn't the way to do it.

Cecil looked at the group and said, "Go on back to work. This afternoon we'll cut you boys lose." The men nodded and went to back to work, their scuffle hoes casting small clouds of dust in the heat of the afternoon. Cecil turned to us and said, "Come on. I want to show you something."

"What?" Sarge asked.

With a nod, Cecil replied, "You'll see."

We followed him across the farm to the northeast corner. A row of low plants that turned out to be yellow squash were wilting in the midday sun. Cecil stopped and looked at the plants. "What do you think?" He asked.

Sarge and I looked at the plants. Sarge shrugged and said, "Looks like they need water."

Cecil nodded. "It looks that way. But look at those over there. They don't look like they need water." He pointed farther down the row at more plants that were standing tall and erect.

"How the hell does half a row of plants look like that?" I asked.

Cecil nodded and pointed at me. "Now that's the real question. Looking at these, it seems to me like they've been sprayed with something."

"What do you mean, sprayed with something?" I asked.

"Like weed killer?" Sarge asked.

"That's exactly what I mean," Cecil replied.

"Who the hell would do something like that? And why?" I asked.

Cecil shook his head. "I don't know. But it sure looks to me like someone sprayed it. It's the only thing that makes sense, and yet it doesn't make any sense why someone would do it!"

Thad's deep voice boomed behind us. "I'm with Cecil." We all turned to see him and Mary standing behind us. Greetings were exchanged and Thad stepped over to the plants and knelt down. He rubbed one of the wilting leaves between his fingers, then smelled them. Nodding his head, he said, "It's glyphosate."

"Round Up?" Cecil asked. "That shouldn't kill squash."

Thad stood up and brushed soil from his knees. "Not diluted. But sprayed on in its concentrated form, it will."

"Why would someone do that?" Mary asked. "This is food. Why would anyone kill our food?"

Sarge stretched his back and replied, "Well, Mary, that is the question."

I looked back across the farm. It was hot and a haze was settling over the broad open expanse. The Guardsmen that provided security for the farm were stationed at the opposite end. While they *were* here, I doubted seriously they made any real attempt at patrolling the land.

Looking at Sarge, I said, "I think you need to have those guys start patrolling. It may not be a bad idea to set up an LP over here too and keep it manned at night."

Sarge nodded. "I bet those lazy asses don't even leave their tents at night. I'll fix that shit today."

Looking at Thad, I asked, "What are you guys up to today?"

"I just wanted to come check on Cecil and see how the farm was doing." "Thought Mary would like to get out for a ride." She smiled, but said nothing. With a nod, I replied, "That's nice."

After Thad and Mary walked away, I took off my hat and wiped sweat from my forehead. "It's hotter'n two rats fucking in a wool sock. I think I'm going home and load everyone up and go to the lake."

"We're going swimming?" Taylor asked. I nodded and she clapped her hands, "I can't wait!"

"Let's go already!" Jess moaned. "It's hot!"

"That's a hell of an idea!" Sarge boomed. He looked at Cecil, "I'll get with those boys and address this shit here. Let me know if you see any more of this crap."

Cecil nodded. "Will do."

We walked back towards the truck. Sarge peeled over and headed towards the group of Guardsmen tasked with protecting the farm. His stride changed and I could tell he was in full NCO mode. I smiled and leaned against the hood of the truck. "This should be interesting," I said.

Thad was already at the truck, and he chuckled as he leaned over the hood beside me. "Looks like he's about to chew some ass."

Mary had joined the girls, and they were busy talking about the trip to the lake, oblivious to what was happening. It was funny in a way. The things people do and do not notice. "Here it comes," Thad said as the old man made it to the tents where the soldiers were lounging in camp chairs.

He stopped and stood there for a minute, looking at the four men who were sitting around the remnants of last night's fire. A few small wisps of smoke rose from the ash as they stared into it. They made only a cursory acknowledgement of the old man, giving him a nod. Thad and I watched as the old man flexed his hands, clenching and unclenching them.

The pressure was building and Thad and I started to laugh. Then it happened. Sarge wasn't a very big man. Kind of wiry and gnarly. But what he lacked in physical presence, he made up for with presence. Tearing his hat from his head, he began to shout and beat the nearest of the men to him with it.

"Get on your damn feet! You sum bitches got one job! One fucking job! And you can't even do that! You ain't doing shit sitting over here staring into the ashes of your circle-jerk bonfire from last night! On your damn feet!," I said. The men were all suddenly in motion, almost as one. The one Sarge was swatting with his hat tried to cover his head from the assault. He leaned forward to try and get out of the seat and away from the old man. The rear legs of his chair came off the ground and Sarge delivered a solid kick to it, sending him sprawling onto the ground.

They were surprised by the suddenness of the assault and were obviously confused about just what the hell was going on. They looked at one another and at the old man. "Where's the rest of your people?" Sarge barked.

One of the men pointed to a tent. Sarge cut his eyes to it and quickly disappeared through the flap. The tent started to bounce and shutter, as though there were a storm raging inside it. And I guess there was from the sounds coming from it. In a moment, a man came rolling out the front of the tent, sprawling into the dirt. Getting his feet under him, the man looked at his comrades.

The old man stomped out of the tent and stood in front of the group. "Do I have your attention now?" He asked. They all nodded quickly and he continued, "Well thank you very fucking much! You shiftless sacks of horse shit have been slacking, and that ends today!"

Thad and I were both laughing hard. It was always funny to see someone on the receiving end of the old man's admonitions. So long as it wasn't you. While Sarge laid out the new plan for securing the farm, Thad and I spoke about the afternoon's activity.

"I asked Miss Kay to get a pork shoulder ready to take to the lake this afternoon. I'm going to take it with us and cook it out there. Make it a bit of a picnic," Thad said.

That made me very happy. Of the many skills that make up this incredible friend, cooking pig parts over a fire is one of his finest. "Now that's the best damn thing I've heard in a long while, ole buddy."

He grinned when he replied, "I thought you'd like that."

I looked over at Mary. She was with the rest of the girls at the edge of the field. They were all on a row of celery, down on their knees, pulling weeds. For them, it was nothing more than busy work. Something to do while they waited. There was something that always needed to be done, and it made me feel good to see my family and friends take responsibility. It was good for others out there to see that they didn't feel as though they were above it. I elbowed Thad and nodded at the girls.

When he looked over his shoulder, I said, "You and Mary seem to be getting along pretty good."

He blushed, "It ain't like that."

I turned and leaned back against the Hummer. "Why not?" I asked. "She's an attractive girl." Seeing her smile and wave, I added, "She obviously likes you."

The smile faded from his face. "It's not that, Morgan. It's not that at all. She's very sweet and I care for her a lot. It's just…." He faded off without finishing the thought.

I put my hand on his shoulder. "Thad, old friend. Let me ask you something, and I know this is hard. If the shoe were on the other foot and something happened to you. Would you want Anita to spend the rest of her life pining over you? Or would you want her to find happiness, whatever that looks like?"

Without hesitation, he said, "I'd want her to find happiness. That would be the most important thing to me in life or death."

"Don't you think she'd want the same for you? In life, or death?" I asked. He looked at me without replying. I continued, "You've mourned for your loss. And I'm not saying it's diminished in any way or ever will be. But you have the right, shit, the need to be happy. You, of everyone I know, deserve it too."

Thad looked down at his feet as he pushed dirt around with the toe of his boot. After a moment, he looked up. His reply was short and simple. "Ok."

I leaned over and wrapped an arm around him, squeezing him tight. "That's my man."

Thad laughed and pushed me away. "You a mess, Morgan."

Sarge had finished his dressing down and was headed back in our direction. I called out to the girls and they came running towards the truck. They opted to ride in the back of Thad's truck, leaving me and the old man to get the Hummer back. And they chose wisely. Because all the way back, all he did was bitch and moan. But I got through it by thinking about Thad standing over some smoking oak wood as pig fat dripped into the coals.

"You think they'll catch whoever did the spraying on the crop?" I asked between tirades.

"They damn well better!" He bellowed.

Shaking my head, I said, "I still don't get why someone would do it. Just doesn't make sense."

"It's all about perspective, Morgan," Sarge replied. "From where you're sitting, it doesn't. But to whoever is doing it, it makes damn good sense. Someone it trying to keep the food stocks down. This is typical unconventional warfare shit."

"Alright," I replied. "Then who is *they?*"

He shook his head. "I don't know." Turning to look at me, he added, "Yet."

As we were approaching the ranch, I quickly wheeled off the paved road onto the dirt track that ran to Gina and Dylan's place. We hadn't seen them in some time and I wanted to check on them. As the house came into view, we could see Gina out front hanging the washing out on the fence to dry. She waved as I rolled to a stop.

"Hi, Morgan! Hi, Linus!" Gina shouted.

Stepping out, we waved back, "How's it going, Gina?" I asked.

She draped a wet towel over the fence and replied, "It's going pretty good. If it wasn't so damn hot, it would be better."

"Ain't that the truth," Sarge retorted.

Looking around, I asked, "Where's Dylan?"

"He's back in the greenhouse. We're covered up with string beans right now. We've had the canner running nearly nonstop."

I laughed. "Having more food than you know what to do with isn't a bad thing. You know, most folks around here would kill for that."

Gina smiled, "I guess we used to call that first-world problems."

"If you got more than you want to deal with, I know plenty of people that could use it," Sarge said.

"Well," Gina replied, "we have way more than we need, and I'm running out of jars. You thinking of taking it to town?"

Sarge nodded. "We could. The armory there could always use more food. Plus, they can give some out to the folks in town. The farm is getting close, but it ain't quite ready yet."

"I'll go get Batman and have him fill some baskets up for you. It'll make things a lot easier on us. I just can't stomach the thought of letting any of it go to waste," Gina replied.

"It'll be appreciated for sure," I said.

Gina disappeared behind the house, calling out as she went. She always made me smile. She was just a little thing but carried such a large presence. Always willing to help. And always in a good mood. As if she were from a different time and none of this affected her, it was just another normal day.

She soon returned with Dylan in tow. He was wearing cut-off jeans and no shirt. He was soaked in sweat. He smiled as he walked over, holding his hand out to Sarge. The old man grasped it tightly and they shook.

"How the hell are ya, Linus?" Dylan asked.

"Busy as a one-legged man in an ass-kicking contest." He nodded at Gina, "She keeps me hopping, day and night."

Gina swatted at him. "Oh stop it."

"She said you guys have more than you can use. Anything you want to give, we'd be glad to take to town," I said. "Lot of people there that could use it."

He nodded. "Not a problem. We got a God's plenty. It would take the load off us. You want to wait a minute; I'll get you loaded up."

Sarge waved him off. "Naw, don't worry about it right now, Dylan. We're not going back to town until tomorrow. Could we drop by in the morning and pick it up?"

"That'd be fine," Gina said. "It would give us some time to get it ready."

"We're going to the lake for a swim this afternoon," I said. "You two want to go? I think Thad is going to put a piece of pig on the fire too."

Gina looked at Dylan and smiled. "It is awful hot. A swim would be real nice."

But then Gina seemed to have a sudden change of heart and frowned a bit. "It would be nice. But with all this work we've been doing, I just don't feel up to it. But you can go."

Dylan retorted. "And leave you here alone?"

Gina's hands went to her hips. "I can take care of myself, mister!"

Dylan wrapped an arm around her. "I know you can. But who's going to take care of me?"

Sarge snorted. "Not me!"

Dylan nodded at the old man. "See? That's why I have to stay with you." He looked at me and said, "Appreciate the offer, but we'll pass this time."

"Not a problem, buddy. Maybe next time," I replied.

When we made it back to the ranch, the girls were already in their suits. It was kind of humorous to see them in bikinis with beach towels slung over their shoulders and even a couple of brightly colored inflatables. The kids, Little Bit, Jace and Edie were also in swimwear and unable to stand still. Jace had a small ring-float around his waist as he hopped up and down. Little Bit carried a boogie board slung over her back.

When we got out of the truck, Mel shouted at me to hurry up and change, they were all ready to go. Looking at Danny, I asked, "Who's going to keep an eye on the ranch?"

"Dalton and Perez are staying behind. Perez said he doesn't swim and Dalton didn't want to leave the place unsecured."

Miss Kay had prepared some food, and she and Bobbie were carrying it out to the vehicles. It didn't take long before all was ready and loaded into everything we had that rolled. With all but two of us going, we needed every set of wheels we had. I loaded Mel and the girls into the Suburban and we fell in line at the rear of our little convoy. As we passed the bunker, I stopped.

Perez was lazing in the shade of the tarp at the rear of the log structure. Dalton was leaned over the top of it looking down the road. "You two don't want to go?" I asked.

Without lifting his hat, Perez replied, "I ain't no wetback."

Dalton shook his head. "Nah. I'll hang around here. You guys go and relax." He placed his weapon on the top of the bunker and propped himself up on his elbows. "This is relaxing to me."

"Alright then," I replied. "I appreciate you guys hanging back."

"I feel bad leaving them here," Mel said.

I shrugged. "Someone has to stay behind, and they volunteered."

She reached over and grabbed my arm. "I'm glad you're going. It's going to be nice to just relax and pretend everything is normal. Even if it's only for an afternoon."

Lee Ann laughed. "Everything is normal, Mom. It's just that normal is different now."

Mel smiled. "I guess you're right."

We made it to the lake and pulled down to the edge of the water. It was mid-afternoon and getting hotter. As soon as we stopped, the kids bolted for the water. Lake Dorr had a small white sand beach and they wasted no time crashing into the warm water.

Likewise, most everyone else followed suit. Jess, Fred and my girls were quickly splashing one another as well. Then Ian and Jamie waded into it and soon the edge of the lake was a riot of laughter and splashing. Mel and Bobbie carried camp chairs down to the water's edge and set them up while Danny and I helped Thad with the pig parts he was going to roast. Sarge and Miss Kay took up position at one of the concrete picnic tables.

Once Thad had everything he needed, he told me and Danny to beat it. He was the king of his domain when it came to this, and he didn't like any meddling. So I left him to it and waded out into the lake, spreading my arms and falling backwards into the water. It was a little warm, but still refreshing.

It didn't take long before the kids set upon me like a bunch of water nymphs. I tussled with them as they shrieked and laughed. Danny quickly joined in, taking some of the heat off me, thankfully. But it was fun to be rolling around in the water with the kids. Someone, I think Mike, produced a football and an impromptu game started in the shallows.

It began friendly enough of course with the kids joining in and everyone being gentle. But Mike had the ball once and was making a dash up the edge of the water. He was running hard and fast and the kids didn't even try to catch him. Ted, on the other hand, had no problem with it. He slammed into Mike, knocking him from his feet and sending him flying into the air before crashing back into the lake. The ball popped free and landed with a splash right in front of Mary. Thad held his hands out, "Throw it to me!"

Mary picked the ball up with a big grin and tossed it to him. With ball in hand, he started towards the far end of the swimming area in knee-deep water. The kids were quickly on him. Like the Lilliputians trying to take down Gulliver. Then Jess, Fred and Aric jumped on. But the big man kept going. Ian and Jamie were lounging in the water's edge, watching the show. But even the addition of my girls couldn't bring the big man down.

Jamie slapped Ian's shoulder and nodded in the direction of Thad. Ian smiled and the two jumped up, running through the shallow water, sending up geysers each time their feet crashed into the lake. As they closed the distance, Jamie dove and wrapped her arms around Thad's knees. Ian came up from behind and slammed into Aric's back, who was the last one on Thad's back. This finally toppled the big man into the lake.

Mel and I sat watching all this. I'd taken a seat beside her in a folding chair. The laughter was infectious and we were both hee-hawing as we watched the show. It took Thad a minute to free himself from the tangle of bodies, but he did manage and made his way back to check on his roasting pig parts. He was smiling broadly as he left the lake, pausing to grab a towel to dry himself as he headed for the smoker we'd brought with us.

I got up and pulled my shirt off and dropped it into the chair. Mel looked up at me in a squint, "Going swimming?"

I nodded and looked up. "Yeah. It's hot, but I really need to cool off."

Little Bit saw me walking towards the water and threw the football. I caught it and ran right at her. She squealed and tried to run away, but the water made her slow and I dove and caught her, taking her into the water with me. We swam and played for a long time. Bobbie sat with Mel after swimming while Danny and I entertained the kids. Even Mike, Ted and Doc got in on it. We'd hoist the kids onto our shoulders and they'd jump in. Edie always held her nose, she was a cute little thing.

Sarge sat with Miss Kay in the shade and watched. He'd taken his boots off and rolled his pants up to reveal feet that were so white they appeared translucent. Miss Kay was full of smiles. She would wave from time to time and nudge the old man and point out some antic the kids were engaged it. It looked as though everyone was having a great time.

After spending time in the lake, I decided to get out and relax and returned to my chair. "I thought those kids were going to drown you," Mel said.

I laughed. "Wasn't for lack of trying."

Sitting in the chair, I dried my hair with a towel and hung it over the back of the chair. It was a funny feeling being here playing in the water as if everything were normal. But then, wasn't it? This was a normal thing to do, after all. It made me think of a line I used on guys when I worked industrial construction, *conditions are what you make 'em*. And we were making some fine conditions.

The activity in the lake died down a bit as everyone was getting worn out. The kids sat in the shallows, and with Danny's help, they set to making a sand castle, of sorts. We were sitting on the side of a lake on a beautiful summer afternoon. The smell of wood smoke and grilling meat drifted on the air. Fat dripped into the coals and snapped and popped. The two created an incredible aroma in the air. But this could also be a problem.

Reaching down, I pulled out the small radio from my vest lying beside the chair. Extending the antenna, I powered it up and started to go through the shortwave bands. Normally, I did this during the night, but I was relaxing and it seemed like something to do. Initially, there was nothing but static. But eventually, a faint signal came across. I tried to get it in clearer, but it just wasn't working out.

Pulling out my small survival kit, I took the small roll of brass snare wire. Wrapping one end around the tip of the antenna, I made a hook on the other and hung it up in a Myrtle tree. This improved the reception considerably. A British voice came clearly from the little speaker. It was some wanker from the BBC.

Hearing the voice got Mel's attention and she looked down at the radio. "You got a station? Are they playing music?"

I laughed. "No. It's the BBC. If they did, it would probably suck. Sounds like it's the news."

We listened as the talking head covered some domestic news. It was kind of interesting to hear someone talk about fuel prices and a shortage of potatoes due to some sort of strike. But the newscaster shifted to concerns on the international front. In particular, the good ole US of A.

I had to change my opinion of the guy reading the news. I

could hear the genuine concern in his voice. He covered the dire situation most of the USA was in now. Then he gave a statistic that shocked me.

In a thick British accent, he said, *Present estimates indicate that nearly seventy percent of the population of America are…dead.* You could hear the pain in his tone when he said it.

Mel looked at me wide-eyed. "Did he just say seventy percent?"

I nodded as the voice continued. *But as bad as things are for those that remain, it would appear they are about to become much worse. The United States Navy is currently engaged in a significant naval battle with the People's Liberation Navy. Reports we're receiving here in London indicate the Chinese have lost numerous vessels. But through weight of sheer numbers, their landings on the California coast continue. Threats of tactical nuclear weapons are being issued from both sides. Beijing has insisted that any such use would result in retaliation against the entire continent.*

The US Navy has likewise indicated that the use of any nuclear weapons would result in a full scale retaliatory launch. This, of course, has increased tensions around the globe, with Russia stating they would come to the aid of China should they be attacked. However, the Russians have been silent on their participation in the relief, as it was initially called. But reports coming out of the US via HAM radio indicate the Russians have already made landings there, using Cuba as a staging base. The southern peninsula of Florida is reportedly under the control of the Russian and Cuban forces at this time.

"What?" I practically shouted.

"Sounds like we've got some trouble coming our way." I looked over my shoulder to see Sarge standing there, coffee cup in hand.

"Do you believe this crap?" I asked.

He shrugged. "What would it benefit the Brits to make shit like that up? You could hear it in his voice that he was sincere."

"We're in a world of hurt," I said.

Sarge sipped his coffee. After a moment, he said, "Those commie bastards we've crossed paths with so far were probably just pathfinders. I'm guessing they're trying to consolidate Dade and Broward counties. Might even be up to Brevard by now, at the space center. Sooner or later, they'll start making their way into the more remote places."

"How the hell are we going to fight the Russian and Cuban armies?" I asked.

"Are we going to be alright?" Mel asked.

Sarge sniffed. "The Afghans kept them tied up for a long time. They never did settle that little conflict. Unconventional warfare can be hard on a conventional army. Against a dedicated and armed populace, they'll have a hell of a time."

I stood up and shook my head. "I don't want to fight a fucking war! I just want to make do. Try and live a peaceful life with my wife and kids. This is bullshit. Every time we make a little headway, something else comes up!"

Sarge patted my shoulder. "Anything worth having is worth fighting for. And, more importantly, the only easy day was yesterday. Now suck it up, buttercup. We got shit to do."

"Uh, Linus," I heard Thad say. It was odd to hear him use the old man's given name, so it got our attention. We both turned to see a group of people standing in the parking area. There were several men, women and even kids. All of them looked like shit. Their clothes were slick with filth. Their hands and faces grime-covered and their hair, all manner of ridiculous.

One of the little kids, maybe three years old, was wearing nothing but a t-shirt, from which his distended belly protruded. He, like many others of the group, scratched at their heads from what was probably a terrible lice infection. Several of the members of the group were armed with various types of weapons, including clubs. A girl, that I estimated was older than ten, stood staring at us as she picked her nose about two knuckles deep.

"They look like wild animals," Mel said.

Our visitors were not unnoticed; and now everyone was watching them, except the kids, who were always oblivious to such things. Sarge drew his knife as he walked over to Thad and cut a large piece of meat from the rear ham sitting over the coals. Taking a big bite, he stepped towards our visitors. With his lips slick with fat, he smiled and asked, "How y'all doing?"

The men and women of the group shared looks, most of them settling on one man in particular. He was bearded in the way most men were today. But his was unkempt and nappy, as was his hair. He was holding a single-shot shotgun by the receiver at his side.

"We smelled your meat. Came to see what it was." The man said.

Sarge took another bite and motioned at the man with the piece of meat. "You knew what it was. You said you smelled the meat. So, did you come to see what it was? Or see if could you take it, since you came with them guns?"

The man looked at the shotgun in his hand. "Hell, everyone carries guns." He licked his lips and continued. "We just smelled it and it was more than we could stand. Had to come see what it was. You don't smell that sort of thing now-a-days."

Sarge took another bite of the meat and asked, "When was the last time you folks ate?"

"Meat?" The man asked. "Hell, it's been a while. We kilt a possum last week, I think."

"What are you living on?" Sarge asked.

The man shrugged and scratched at his beard. "Whatever we can find. Game's getting hard to find. There's fish, but even that is getting harder."

Sarge nodded and stood there for a moment before looking back over his shoulder at Thad. "Thad, you think we could spare some of this fine pig for these folks?"

"I'm sure we can," Thad answered.

Sarge looked back to the group and motioned with the piece of meat dangling from his hand. "Lean your shootin' irons against that tree there and come over here and get yourselves something to eat. We got enough for all of you."

A murmur went through the small crowd and they all began to move. Most of them, in their rush, simply dropped their weapons where they stood. They rushed Thad, making me and the guys nervous. Mike and Ted ran up to get between them and Thad, weapons at the ready. The group slowed.

"Just line up, folks. You'll all get some," Sarge said. "Mind your manners."

Thad started cutting pieces of meat from the bone and handing it out. The members of the group took them greedily and immediately started to eat. Not like a hungry person. But like a hungry dog. Stuffing as much into their mouths as they could for fear someone would take it from them. It was sad and sickening.

As this was being done, I looked at Mel and told her to get the kids ready to go. While this was hospitable at the moment, it could turn at any time, and I wanted to be ready to bolt. Plus, our picnic was now officially over.

The people spread out from one another with their prize. I watched them as they eyed one another as they forced as much meat into their mouths as they could. Even the little kids did this. Though their primary defense was to run and hide. Like a small scavenger would when he manages to steal a piece of a large predator's kill. They would run into the underbrush, completely disappearing from sight.

Once they all had some food, Sarge walked over to the man that had spoken for the group. I wandered over to hear what was being said.

"Where you folks living?" Sarge asked.

The man jabbed a greasy finger in the direction of highway 19. "We been staying in the campground there."

Campground was a bit of a misnomer. In Florida a number of places called campgrounds became permanent resting places for all manner of travel trailers and campers and their residents. Maybe calling them a campground made it sound a little more fun than the reality.

"You folks need a doctor for anything? Some of them little ones look like they may have some issues."

He shook his head. "Naw. We're good. Everyone is healthy. We're just hungry is all."

"We got a doctor in town. I can bring them out here for you if you need." Sarge pointed at one of the little kids that emerged from the brush. "I'd hate to see them little ones get sick from something we could take care of."

Just as Sarge said that, the little guy stopped and grabbed his belly. An expression came over his face and he quickly dropped his pants, squatted and shit. As soon as he was done, he hitched his pants back up and walked back over to Thad and smiled, showing his rotted teeth. "Can I have some more?" He asked as he wiped his nose with his forearm.

Normally, Thad would smile at a child. He was good with kids and liked being around them. But he didn't smile. I could see the pain on his face as he carved another small piece off the bone and handed it to the little guy. He snatched it up and shoved it into his mouth as he walked away, where he was set upon by the other little ones.

Sarge watched this and looked the people over again. Then he looked back at Thad. Thad gave him a nod and Sarge looked back at the man who was sucking his dirty fingers. "Tell you what. We were about to leave. You folks can have this. We'll leave it with you."

The man sucked his teeth and looked at the meat. Without looking away from it, he asked, "You ain't going to eat?"

Sarge sniffed. "Naw. We already ate some earlier." Lying to the man.

The man looked back at him and asked, "Where'd you get the meat? Taste like pork. But it's been a while since I had any. Could be dog."

Sarge nodded. "It's a pig. We had one wander into our place and we killed it."

The man sucked his thumb again and pulled it out with a pop. "Didn't think there were any pigs left." He looked at Sarge and added, "That's pretty lucky."

"Lucky for all of us," Sarge replied with a smile. "We'll leave you folks to it. Good luck to you."

Thad collected his utensils and stepped away from the smoker. As soon as he cleared it, the group rushed it and a fight began. It was a brutal encounter. As the group fought, we got everyone headed to the trucks and loaded up. Little Bit got scared because of the shouts and screams coming from the brawl. Even the little kids among them were darting in and out of the fray. It reminded me of a documentary I watched once about a band of chimpanzees that killed a monkey and fought over the meat. Very primal and animal-like.

As everyone was loading up, I kept an eye on the melee. Mike walked over to Sarge and asked, "What the hell did you do that for? We could have smoked them. We didn't need to just give it to them."

Sarge stopped and looked back. "Look at them people. Look what they're doing to one another for a damn scrap of meat." He looked back at Mike and added, "You'll still get to eat tonight. If it wasn't for them youngins though, I wouldn't have."

"Yeah, but you gave it all away. And it smelled so good," Ted lamented.

Thad added, "Don't worry, Ted. We still have one at the house. I'll cook it tomorrow."

Ted rocked his head back and forth. "I guess I can wait till tomorrow."

"It'll be worth it. I promise," Thad replied.

"Come on, people. Load up. We got shit to talk about." Sarge said as he opened the passenger door for Miss Kay.

"That was a very thoughtful thing of you to do, Linus," Kay said as she took her seat. The old man just grinned and gently shut the door.

"Thoughtful, my ass," Mike muttered.

"You should try thinking about someone other than yourself from time to time," Sarge replied as he walked around the Hummer.

"What?" Mike asked. "I do all the time. I think about you every time I take a shit."

Sarge stopped and leaned over the hood of the truck. Glancing at Miss Kay to make sure she was out of earshot, he said, "That's gonna cost you. Maybe not today. Maybe not tomorrow. But it will cost you."

Mike thought about it for a minute. "No, no, no. Just do it now. I'm not going to wander around waiting for you to do whatever crazy ass shit is in that dried-up head of yours."

Sarge smiled as he opened the door. "Keep it up. It just gets better and better."

Ted shook his head, "You really should just shut your mouth."

"Why? I didn't do anything. I just have to live with a crazy man!"

Ted stepped right up in front of Mike. "You really are your own worst enemy. You do know that, don't you?"

The best Mike could muster in return was a sophomoric, "Shut up, Ted!"

Ted laughed and climbed into his ride. Mike of course followed him. I waited and watched until everyone was in their respective transports and moving before pulling out at the rear of the column. Looking in the rearview mirror, I could still see the people thrashing one another for the scraps. From what I could see, the only thing left were the bones. These, I imagined, would be picked clean and probably broken open and the marrow sucked out.

On the short ride home, I thought about how hungry they must be. But I was repulsed at their behavior. I wondered how many more people across the country were in the same condition. Most of the people I saw on a daily basis were indeed hungry. But none of them looked as desperate as these folks. It made me thankful for what we had.

I was relieved when we turned into the ranch. It felt good to be home. It felt safe. And not just in a physical security kind of way. It was more than that, this little collection of houses and people. Here, I knew there was food and water. There were good friends I knew I could depend on. I didn't have to look over my shoulder, wondering if they were going to try and steal my food or worse.

Pulling up to the house, Mel said, "I'm going in to change. Ashley, you need to go change too."

Little Bit hopped out of the truck and replied, "Ok." She stretched and yawned and started towards the house.

I smiled at her. What was it about swimming that made you so tired? I knew in no time she would be asleep on the couch. Taylor and Lee Ann passed me up the steps to the porch. I could see they too were tired. Their faces were red from the sun and their asses were dragging. It looked like it would be an early night for everyone this evening.

I dragged my gear into the bedroom and dropped it on the bed. Mel was in the bathroom changing and I caught sight of her through the partially open door. I whistled at her and smiled broadly. She was not amused and gave me a look of annoyance before closing the door.

"Your loss!" I said to the door.

Stripping down, I put on a clean pair of shorts and shirt before heading out to the kitchen. I stopped by the sofa to rub Little Bit's head. Just as I'd predicted, she was curled up, asleep. She didn't' stir, so I left her alone. After pouring a glass of tea, I was putting the pitcher back when Mel came in. She leaned against the island and looked at me, not saying anything.

"Having second thoughts?" I asked. "You had your chance." I said with a smile.

She rolled her eyes. "No. That's not it. I'm worried about what we heard on the radio."

I nodded. "Yeah. Me too. I can't imagine why anyone would want to nuke us now. There's nothing left hardly. It would be a total waste."

"But what are we going to do if they do?"

I shrugged. "I don't know." I wrapped my arms around her shoulders and said, "Honestly, it all comes down to where they hit. We can't really dig a shelter and stock it. There just isn't enough food around to do it. We'll just have to hope that it doesn't happen."

"That doesn't really make me feel any better," she replied.

Hugging her tightly, I said, "Don't worry about it. If it happens, it happens. There's nothing we can do about it." I didn't tell her I was far more worried about the thought of Cuban and Russian troops rolling into town. That was much more likely.

CHAPTER 8

MEL SAID SHE WAS GOING to relax with the girls. Everyone had changed their clothes and deposited themselves in a horizontal position somewhere in the house. I told Mel I was going over to Danny's to talk with Sarge. I wanted to get his take on things. Slipping on a pair of Crocs, I walked next door.

He was sitting on the porch with Miss Kay. Mike, Ted and Doc were there as well. I could hear Bobbie and Danny inside; and the kids were fussing, probably because they were tired. As I walked up on the porch, Mike shook his head.

"What the hell are those on your feet?" He asked.

I looked down at the shoes. "Uh. They're shoes."

"No. No they're not. They're gay. That's what they are. Fucking gay."

I shook my head, "What the hell do you care what I wear on my feet? Don't look at 'em if you don't like 'em."

Mike rolled his eyes and stretched out on the porch, putting his hands under his head. "Still gay," he muttered.

I pulled a chair over and sat down. Looking at Sarge, I asked, "So what do you think about that Russian and Cuban crap?"

He rocked his chair for a minute before replying. "The Ruskies working with the Cubans only makes sense. They've got a base of operation right in our backyard."

"But if they're headed this way, it could be a real issue for us," Ted said.

"Ain't much we can do about it. Just have to wait and see what happens. They may not even come up through here. I'd imagine Orlando and Tampa will see them. But little places like this, out in the woods, may never see them," Sarge replied.

"I doubt that," Ted said. "If they're making a push up the state, we'll see them eventually. It's just a matter of time."

"Have you told Sheffield yet?" I asked.

Sarge shook his head. "No. I figure we'll let him know tomorrow. I'll ride into town and have a talk with him."

"What do you think he's going to want to do?" I asked.

Sarge snorted. "Probably run and hide."

With a grunt, Ted replied, "Won't be no hiding from this."

I sat back in the chair and looked out at the field across the road. Thinking out loud, I said, "I guess time will tell. We'll just have to deal with it as it comes."

"Like we do everything," Sarge responded.

"Those people at the lake were so sad looking," Miss Kay interjected. Maybe she was trying to divert the conversation away from the military type of unpleasantness.

"Looked and acted like damn animals," Sarge acknowledged.

From under his hat, Mike said, "Did you see that little one just squat and shit, right in front of everyone?"

The old man kicked Mike's foot. "Watch your language." Mike didn't bother replying.

"I'm sure you noticed how swollen their bellies were," Doc said. "They're eat up with intestinal parasites."

"How do you know?" Sarge asked.

"I looked at the feces from that kid. It was crawling with worms."

Miss Kay fanned her face with her hand. "Oh, that is just vile, Ronnie."

He shrugged. "I was curious. Malnutrition can make the abdomen distend like that for a time. But I figured they were beyond that stage, and I was right. I saw round worms and tapeworms. So whatever food they are managing to find is being consumed by the parasites. Those kids will probably die of malnutrition later. Though it will take a while."

"That's just awful," Kay said. "We should do something."

Sarge patted her hand. "What could we do? They probably aren't going to come into town. We offered to bring them a doc out and they said no. Hard as it is to say, we just can't save everyone. People are going to die."

Kay looked visibly upset. "But to just let the children die. That's horrible."

"From what I saw out of them yesterday, I don't think they much care if the kids make it." I offered. "That band looked like it had one rule, every man for himself. Did you notice the kids would run off and hide when they got their piece of meat? I think that in their world you have to fight for every scrap."

"The world is a tough place," Sarge replied.

"Sounds like chili three-way from Steak and Shake," Mike said.

"What?" Doc asked.

"That kid's heap. Round worms and tapeworms covered in chili," Mike muttered from under his hat.

"That's disgusting, Mike!" Kay admonished.

Sarge shook his head. "Ignore him, Kay. He was shaken as a baby."

Kay was shocked. "Linus! You boys are so mean to one another!"

Mike was laughing under his hat and asked, "Imagine what it would be like if we didn't like one another."

Doc was picking at his fingernails. It looked like he was thinking about something. After a minute, he looked up. "Quieter. It'd be a lot quieter." Then, changing the subject, he asked, "You think we should build a fallout shelter?"

"For what?" Sarge asked.

"In case there's a chance we start swapping nukes."

"Wouldn't do us a bit of good." Sarge replied. "Sure, we might survive the initial blast and whatnot, if we're in it when it goes off. But we couldn't stock it with enough food to make a damn bit of difference."

"I had this same conversation with Mel a minute ago," I said. "Came to the same conclusion. We just have to hope they don't lob any in our direction if it happens."

"I don't think they would," another voice said. It was Dalton walking up to the porch. "The return wouldn't be worth the investment."

"How'd you hear about it?" I asked.

"Ian and Jamie came to take over at the bunker and told us about it." He replied. "If they nuke anything, it's going to be somewhere like DC or New York. Maybe even Colorado Springs, trying to take out some of NORAD's capability."

"Trying to hit Cheyenne Mountain would be a waste of time," Ted replied.

"Depends on what they dropped," Sarge said. "IF they dropped one of those Tsar bombs, it could probably take the mountain out."

"Mmmm, yes. Vanya could probably leave a hole where the mountain once was. But they only tested one of those, and that was in '61." Dalton said. "Plus, they'd have to get bombers through to do it, and that's unlikely."

Sarge looked at his empty coffee cup and stood up. "All this shit is theoretical. The most likely scenario is some of the commie bastards making their way up the turnpike and finding us here. They've already lost some boys this way and they may come looking for them."

"Or for revenge," Doc added.

"Potato, tater. It's all the same thing," Sarge said. "The end results would be the same. We'd be fighting the bastards. I need coffee." He said as he headed for the door.

"How much of that shit do you have left? You've got to be running out," Mike asked.

"Don't you worry about it! I've got enough for me!" Sarge shot back.

Mike laughed under his hat. "You'll run out one of these days. Then what are you going to do?"

Sarge turned towards him and stomped his feet on the porch. In a flash, Mike rolled off the porch and was running across the yard. Sarge laughed as Mike looked back over his shoulder and headed into the house. Ted and I were laughing at Mike when he finally stopped and headed back to the porch. "I thought that old man was going to stomp on my dick." He said as he snatched his hat from the ground.

"He didn't need to," Ted replied. "You nearly killed yourself."

Dalton looked at Miss Kay and asked, "Miss Kay, is there any chow ready? I'm kind of hungry."

She stood up. "Oh, you poor thing. I have a chowder on the stove. Let me get you some."

"You don't have to get up. I'll get it," he said.

She waved him off. "No sir! You come in and sit down and I'll fix you a bowl."

Looking at Kay, I asked, "Chowder? How in the world did you make chowder?"

She smiled. "You guys aren't the only ones full of tricks."

"Well, I got to try this," I said as I got up and headed into the house.

Several of the women were inside. Mary, Fred and Jess were clustered in the kitchen, talking while Thad and Aric sat at the bar with bowls in front of them. I walked up to the bar and looked at the empty bowls. "How is it?" I asked.

Thad looked down at his empty bowl. "What do you think?"

"Mmm. That bad, huh?" I asked. He smiled and nodded.

I sat down as the rest of the guys filtered in. Sarge was in the kitchen filling his stained mug. Once topped off, he stuck his head over the pot and inhaled deeply. "Damn, that smells good. You ladies never cease to amaze me. What you can do with so little to work with."

"We try," Bobbie said as she handed out bowls.

We sat and ate and discussed the watch rotation for the night. It turned out that I wouldn't have a shift tonight and could actually get a full night's sleep for a change, something to look forward to. Dalton was sitting at the table on the back porch, and I carried my bowl out there and sat down.

He paused, spoon in his mouth and raised his eyebrows in anticipation. I made a show of settling myself and looked at him. Rocking my head to the side, I asked, "Sup?"

He sucked the spoon as he pulled it out and chewed what was in his mouth. Stirring his bowl, he replied, "Worry and apprehension from the sounds of things."

I shrugged. "I guess so." Taking a bite of my chowder, I replied, "It's always something these days."

Dalton nodded. "It always has been. There's always something to worry about. The issues may be a little different. But there's always something. It may not be the mortgage and car payment now, but there is always something to be dealt with."

"True. But the things we worry about today are a little more severe. They can actually kill you. Missing a mortgage payment wouldn't kill you."

"No," Dalton replied as he scooped another spoonful. "But these issues are real. Unlike all the other bullshit we used to sweat over. These things make you feel alive. Keep you closer to your true self. Nothing makes you feel more alive than being closer to death."

"Maybe. But I'd like it better if we weren't so close to death. A little distance would be better."

Dalton nodded. "Distance from death breeds complacency. Living on the edge keeps you on your toes."

"Hopefully, we can keep a little distance. We're going to town tomorrow to talk to Sheffield and let them know what we heard." I said. "That, and I have some legal crap to deal with."

Dalton perked up when I said that. "What sort of legal issues?"

"Just some local BS to sort out. At least it ain't my problem anymore now that we have a judge."

Dalton laughed. "So you put it off on someone else?"

"Hell yeah!" I said. "Mitch seems like a good guy. We just need someone with a level head that can make these decisions."

"Other than you." Dalton said.

I nodded. "Other than me."

Dalton finished his meal and said, "I'll go with you in the morning. A trip to town would be good. Plus, I want to watch the circus in the morning."

"Oh, thanks for that," I replied.

I finished my dinner and bid everyone a good night. Sarge told me he'd see us in the morning for our trip to town. I reminded him we needed to swing by Gina and Dylan's to pick up the veggies they were giving to the town. He nodded and waved as I headed out the door. It wasn't dark yet, but it was close. The air was still and hot, heavy with humidity. It seemed to get the hottest right as the sun was beginning to set. It drove the humidity to the ground and gave everything a muggy feeling.

Even the animals were suffering. No birds sang. No squirrels scampered through the trees. It was as if everything was waiting for the relief the setting of the sun would bring. I crunched through the dry pine needles and fallen leaves as I passed through the fence to my place. Somewhere off in the distance I heard the rumble of thunder and hoped it would find its way here. A Florida rain shower was a double-edged sword. While it would cool things off for the moment, it would make the morning utterly miserable. You'd be able to see the steam rising from the ground as the sun heated it. But you gotta take what you can get.

The dogs were lying on the porch in their usual places, sprawled out and leaving me little room to get to the door. I just tip-toed around them. At the door, I paused for a moment to check them out. They looked thinner. Not really a concern yet; but if the weight loss continued, it would be. I made a mental note to try and find more for them to eat. They were still loyal, hanging around the houses all day. Not that they did a damn thing for us. But it was good having them around.

Inside, I found Little Bit still sleeping on the couch, and I left her there. The house was getting hot. God, I hated Florida summers. Even more so without the benefit of central air. Or any air for that matter. I checked on the other girls and found them in their beds, sprawled out with nothing over them. Leaving their doors open to encourage what airflow might happen, I adjusted their fans. Mel was in the bed with a sheet over her. The fan was at the foot of the bed, oscillating back and forth. These fans were a luxury. It reminded me of my youth. When I was a kid, we didn't have central air in the houses we lived in. We didn't even have window shakers. We had fans. And everyone had their own. I remember the day we moved into a house with central air. I thought we'd suddenly become rich!

I stripped down to my drawers. I wore wool underwear, which might sound counterintuitive in this heat. But they were much more comfortable. I'd pitched my cotton versions back in the Before. The wool wicked sweat and was naturally antimicrobial. Cotton is death cloth, and I avoided it at all costs. Hot or cold, it would kill you.

Pulling the sheet back, I lay down and pulled part of the sheet over my hips only, leaving my feet and upper body out. It helped regulate temperature, and everything you can do in these conditions helped. Reaching out to the nightstand, I made sure my pistol and flashlight were there. Feeling them in the dark, I relaxed and tried to go to sleep.

But sleep would be fleeting. My attempts to sleep were filled with dreams of troops rolling through Eustis. A very vivid image of the American flag being lowered at the armory was playing over and over in my head. The men who took it down simply wadded it up before attaching another. This one had even fields of white, red and blue. The flag of the Russian Federation. It kept replaying until it woke me up.

I looked around in the silent and dark room. Nothing was amiss, so I lay back down and rolled over towards Mel and put my hand on her hip. It was too damn hot to put my arm over her, so I settled on just the hand on her hip and tried to go back to sleep. I was just about to doze off when she grabbed my hand and tossed it off, saying, "You're hot, get off me."

It made me grin. She was right, after all. Maybe it was hearing her voice. Maybe it was just waking up. But I fell back asleep, and this time I wasn't haunted by dreams of marauding foreign troops. I woke up when the room started to lighten. Getting up, I was lightly covered in sweat and felt sticky. Sleeping when it's hot out is a miserable experience. Heading into the bathroom, I turned on the shower and got in. The water was warm to start, but cooled nicely in no time. I rinsed off and felt much better.

Getting out, I toweled off and dressed, Mel came in as I was pulling my shorts up. I stopped and looked at her with a squint. "Do I need to wait, or?"

She pushed me out of the way, yawning as she passed me. "No, don't stop, and get out. I need to use the bathroom."

I picked up my things. "Well, good morning to you too, Sunshine."

"Close the door on your way out," she replied as she took a seat on the throne.

I left and pulled the door shut. After dressing, I went to the kitchen for my morning tea. With my glass in hand, I went to the front door and looked out. It seemed darker than it should for the hour and I stepped out onto the porch. The morning was heavily overcast and it seemed I could smell rain in the air. It made me think about the storm brewing off the coast. *I need to talk to Mitch,* I thought and went back inside.

Even though it was early, I went to the radio and keyed the mic, "Hey, Mitch. You listening?" Setting the mic down, I sipped my tea. After a bit, I tried it again, but he never came back. "Looks like I'm going to town," I said as I headed back to the bedroom for some socks.

Mel was there making up the bed. "Why do you do that?" I asked. "We're just going to mess it up again later. And it's not like anyone is coming in here."

Fluffing a pillow, she replied, "Because it looks better and makes me feel better. I'm not doing it for anyone else."

Coming up behind her, I hugged her. "Well, if it makes you feel better."

She patted my hands. "It does. What are you doing?"

Releasing her, I went to the dresser and pulled out a pair of socks. "It looks like rain. It's really overcast. I'm going to go to town and talk to Mitch. He has a way to receive weather satellite images. There's a tropical storm brewing off the coast and I want to see if it's coming ashore."

"Who's Mitch?"

Sitting down on the bed, I updated her, "He's our new judge. Nice guy. You should meet him and his wife Michelle. They're really nice."

"Where do they live?" She asked.

"Remember that house we looked at that was partly underground?"

She thought for a moment. "Yeah. It had that big hut thing behind it. What'd you call it?"

"Quonset hut. Yeah, that's the one. They live there."

"How'd he become the judge?"

Standing up, I said, "I picked him. He seemed like a normal enough guy and we needed someone. I just wanted somebody other than me making some of these decisions."

"You going to be gone all day?"

"No. I'm going to make a quick trip. I'd like a day off," I said with a grin.

"I'd like that too. You're always gone. Be nice to have you around for a day. Plus, I'm still weirded out about those people from the lake."

"Well, they're not going to come here. I don't think you need to worry about them," I replied.

She shook her head. "It was just so sad to see people like that. Those poor kids."

"Yeah. Doc said they all had intestinal parasites really bad. Couldn't imagine living like that."

"We wouldn't. Even if we were grubbing around in the woods."

I'm gonna go," I said and leaned over and kissed her. "I'll be back later."

"Hurry home," she replied with a smile.

Stopping at the door, I put my shoes on and pulled my vest on over my head. Picking up my rifle, I went out the door and had to step over the dogs. Just as I was stepping into the yard, a voice called out, "You ready to go to town?"

I jumped and looked back to see Dalton sitting on the bench on the porch. "You scared the shit out of me. How long you been there?"

He reached down and rubbed Meathead's ear. "I was here when you came out earlier." He looked up at me. "You really should pay more attention."

"Why didn't you say anything?"

He shrugged. "You didn't have shoes on. I knew you weren't ready to leave."

I shook my head. "You're an odd duck."

Standing up and stretching, he said, "Quack, quack. Let's go to town."

Turning to head towards Danny's house, I said, "We got to get the old man."

Sarge was sitting on the porch with Aric. Seeing us, he looked at his watch and said, "You keeping banker's hours now, Sheriff?"

"I don't operate on anyone's schedule but my own," I replied.

"I been at his house for over an hour," Dalton said as he went into the house.

Sarge shook his head. "Must be nice. Having the world revolve around you like that."

I sighed and shook my head. "You ready to go?"

Standing up, Sarge replied, "Shit! I been ready! Been waiting on you all morning!"

Looking at Aric, I asked, "You coming with us?"

He looked around and shrugged. "What the hell. Why not. What's the plan?"

"Taking some food into town and meeting with the judge. Mister Personality here needs to talk to Sheffield," I replied.

He hopped off the porch. "Cool."

Dalton came out of the house with a large travel mug. Steam was rising from it and Sarge cocked his head to the side and asked, "What's in the cup?"

Taking a sip, Dalton replied, "Coffee."

Sarge's head jerked back. "My coffee? You drinking *my* coffee?"

Dalton pointed at the cup, "No, this coffee is mine." Then he pointed to the cup Sarge held and said, "That is your coffee. See the difference?"

Sarge's eyes narrowed and he turned to face Dalton. "Don't be a smartass!"

"You hush, Linus! I gave it to him," Kay said from the porch. "You aren't the only one around here that likes coffee."

Dalton grinned as he started towards the Hummer. "Yeah, Linus, you ain't the only one."

As Dalton passed the old man, Sarge slapped the hat from Dalton's head. "*You* don't call me that."

Dalton picked up his hat and replied, "Roger that, Top."

I looked at Aric and shook my head. "You'd think after this long, this kind of shit wouldn't happen anymore."

With a tilt of his head, Aric replied, "Shit, I think it's getting worse."

Opening the driver's door, I replied with a chuckle, "I think you're right."

"Let me drive," Aric said as he stepped past me into the open door.

"Fine by me," I said and opened the back door and climbed in.

Aric fired up the truck and headed out. We waved at Thad and Danny as we passed the bunker. When he pulled out onto the road, Sarge told him to go to Gina's house.

Dylan was sitting on the porch with a coffee mug in his hand when we pulled up. Sitting on the porch were several baskets filled to overflowing with various vegetables. He raised his cup in a salute when we stopped.

"That's a lot of groceries," Sarge said when he got out.

"Yeah it is. Glad to do it," Dylan replied.

We started loading up the baskets as they talked. When we had everything in the truck, I asked Dylan where Gina was.

"She's asleep. Had a rough night," he replied.

"Anything we can do for her?" Sarge asked.

Dylan shook his head. "No. She's got her medicine. Just needs some rest. But thank you."

"What are you drinking there?" Aric asked.

Dylan looked at the cup and said, "Chicory. We grow it and I roast the roots and grind them up. I like it."

Sarge's face twisted. "Better you than me. I can't stand that stuff. Went to New Orleans and ordered coffee. They gave me that stuff." He shook his head. "Ain't right."

Dylan laughed and sipped the brew. "More for me." Then he looked at Aric and asked, "You want some?"

Aric nodded. "Sure, thank you."

"You other guys want some?"

Dalton held his cup up and said, "I got the real stuff. Thanks though for offering."

"I'll take some for the road," I said.

Sarge shook his head as Dylan went into the house and said, "Y'all are just fuckin' with me, ain't you?"

Aric smiled, "I could just drink your coffee, I guess."

"Like hell you will!" Sarge barked.

"Just ask Miss Kay. She'll give you some," Dalton said as he loudly slurped from his cup.

"That's enough out of your ass, Sasquatch!"

Dylan returned with two Styrofoam cups and handed one to each of us. Picking a small bear-shaped bottle from the table beside his chair, he said, "I like it with honey."

Aric and I both added honey to our cups and stirred it in with a finger. Taking a sip, I was surprised how good it was. "Damn, Dylan, that's not bad at all."

"Yeah, that's good!" Aric added.

Sarge was shaking his head. "That's just nasty." Emphasizing his sentiments with a full body shiver. Dylan laughed at him.

"Thanks for the brew," I said. "And thanks for everything you're sending to town."

"Happy to do it," Dylan said with a wave.

We all loaded up and headed out. The clouds seemed to be getting thicker, if that was possible. Sarge looked up and scanned the sky. "It's about to rain like pouring piss out of a boot."

"I hope it ain't that damn disturbance rolling around out there," I replied.

"You going to get with Mitch?" Sarge asked.

"Yeah, I want to see the latest images."

Dalton looked up and said, "We need the rain though."

"This looks like it's going to hang around for a couple of days," Aric said.

As we came into town, we pulled into the armory and unloaded the baskets of veggies into the main hall and left to go find Mitch. I told Aric to head to the PD, thinking he'd probably be there. As we pulled up to it, I saw his side-by-side sitting out front. He was inside with Sean and Shane. They were sitting around the conference table talking when we walked in.

Spinning a chair around to take a seat, I said, "Morning, fellers." Dalton and Aric took seats as the guys greeted us. "What's up?"

"We were talking about your buddy back there," Sean said.

I nodded. "Guess you're going to deal with that?" I said, looking at Mitch.

"That's what we were talking about," Mitch replied. Pointing at Sean and Shane, he added, "They're going to go find some of the people that were there and bring them in. Then we'll hold court I guess."

"Just let me know when and I'll come in with Thad," I replied.

"You think we should do the whole, swearing in on the Bible thing?" Shane asked.

"I think you should," Aric said.

"Me too. It's always been done that way and adds a sense of necessity to tell the truth. That there is something more than man listening to your words," Dalton said.

"Looks like we're swearing folks in then," I said.

"I'll bring my Bible in," Mitch said.

We continued to talk about how the court proceedings would work for a time. Once the major points were worked out, I changed the subject.

"What's up with the storm?" I asked Mitch.

He slid a stack of papers across the table to me. "Doesn't look good."

I looked at the image. There still wasn't a defined eye, but going over the stack of images, I could clearly make out the rotation of the storm. And it looked as though it would come ashore near Melbourne or somewhere just to the south.

"Looks like the worst of it will stay to the south of us," I said.

Mitch nodded. "Looks that way. But we're probably going to get some pretty serious rain and wind out of it."

"I would have never guessed that from the way things looked this morning," Dalton quipped.

Shane laughed. "Yeah, but we're not getting the wind yet."

"No," Mitch replied, "But it's coming."

Looking at one of the images, I said, "So we're looking at a couple days of wind and rain probably." Mitch nodded. "Have you let the folks at the armory know so they can spread the word?"

"I have. They're supposed to be letting everyone know."

"Should make for an interesting couple of days," Dalton said.

Sarge sat across the table from Sheffield. He was waiting on the man to say something. He'd just given him everything he'd heard about the Russian and Cuban forces being in Florida. Sheffield was drumming his fingers on the table and staring at a point somewhere near the center of the table.

After a moment, he shrugged and shook his head. "I guess we have to wait and see what happens."

Sarge shook his head ever so slightly. "I think we need to be a little more proactive."

"And what would you do?"

"I think we should send out a long-range patrol. Send some folks down to the turnpike. I wouldn't go any further than that. Have them stop and talk to people, and see if anyone's seen or heard anything. At least we'd have an idea if they were up that far. If not, then we do it again in a week or so. I don't think it's a good idea to wait for them to drive into town before we know they're here."

Sheffield hesitated. "I don't know. Sending people out has a lot of risk."

"It's their fucking job," Sarge spat back. "It's what they're supposed to do."

Livingston looked at Sheffield. "We could send a couple trucks out the 429. They can hit the turnpike in less than an hour. It's a high-speed route. Shouldn't be too big a deal."

Sheffield thought for a moment. Then he nodded. "You're right. We need to have a look. As soon as there's a break in the weather, we'll send them out."

Sarge disagreed. "I say we send them soon, while the weather is shitty. If there are any commies in the area, they'll probably hunker down during the weather. It'll give our guys cover. We already know they were in Crystal River, so they are around. We just need to figure out where."

"And they know someone is around with capabilities too, thanks to your guys." Sheffield shot back.

Sarge snorted. "Good! They need to be worried. They got no idea who it was or where we are. That's an advantage for us."

Sheffield fidgeted. "I'm just nervous we could cause a confrontation. One we couldn't win."

Sarge leaned back in his chair and crossed his arms. "That's just the cost of doing business. If these fuckers are anywhere near, and it seems pretty sure they are, it's only a matter of time before they find their way here. And if they are anywhere close, they probably already know we're here. This place isn't a secret. So it's better we get out in front of it. I'd rather meet them someplace out there," Sarge pointed to the south, "than in the streets of Eustis."

Livingston was nodding his head. "I agree. If it comes to a fight, I'd rather we pick the spot."

"What about the Chinese. Heard anything on that?" Sheffield asked.

Sarge cocked his head to the side. "Don't you guys have a radio around here? You're not listening to what's going on?"

"We have AM/FM radios but we're not picking anything up."

"I'll get with Cecil. He's got a ham rig and can listen to the shortwave bands. That's where we're picking all this up. But as for the Chinese, if they don't pull that fleet out, the Navy is going to nuke it."

Sheffield's eyes nearly bugged out of his head. "What? They'll just launch against all of us!"

Sarge scrunched his face and shook his head. "I doubt it. Not a full exchange anyway. It'd be a waste of their weapons. What's left to nuke here? They may hit a few select places. I wouldn't want to be anywhere near DC or Colorado Springs. But the rest of us would probably be okay. Of course, they could hit Patrick and MacDill. Maybe even Eglin. That could cause us some trouble."

Sheffield sank back into his chair. "That's the last thing we need. There's no way we could even attempt to deal with fallout."

"We'll just have to hope it doesn't come to that," Livingston said.

"Alright then. I'm going to send some of the guys up in the morning. If you can have a couple of gun trucks ready, that would be good. Pick some solid people to ride with them.

I'll come up here and we'll monitor the mission together," Sarge said.

"I'll also put together a QRF of a couple more trucks." Livingston said. "Just in case."

Sarge smiled. "Now you're starting to think." He stood up and stretched. "I'll see you boys in the morning." And he turned and headed to the door.

Sarge walked out of the armory in a spitting rain. It was the kind of rain that made it hard to tell which way it was coming from. The wind was picking up and the drops seemed to come from everywhere. He pulled his hat down a little lower on his head and walked out towards the road. Looking around, he muttered to himself, *Where the hell are you, Morgan?*

We agreed to hold the hearing after the weather let up and left the PD. Walking outside, the weather had turned to windblown rain. Dalton and Aric ran for the truck as I looked up into the sky before walking out and climbing in.

"Gonna be a nasty few days," Aric said.

Shutting the door, I replied, "Looks that way. Let's go find the old man and head back to the ranch."

As I drove out of the parking lot, I saw Kelley running towards us, waving. I stopped and he quickly hopped into the back. "Thanks, Morgan. I didn't want to be stuck here during this storm. Looks like it's going to stick around."

"It's a tropical storm. Gonna get worse before it gets better," Aric said.

Driving towards the armory, I saw the old man standing in the rain at the curb. He was the only person outside. Everyone else, everyone with any sense, was inside somewhere. Pulling up, he opened the passenger door and looked at Aric. "Get your ass outta my seat." Dalton's head rocked back as he cackled.

Aric shook his head and got out, climbing in the back beside Dalton. Looking at him, Aric said, "That's why you didn't try to sit up front, isn't it?"

Sarge got in and slammed the door, brushing water off his arms. Holding my fingers about an inch apart, I said, "A Chicken's got a brain this big, and it knows to get out of the damn rain."

He swiped at my fingers but I moved my hand and sniggered. "If your ass had been on time, I wouldn't be out there in the damn rain!" Sarge shouted back at me.

I looked over my shoulder at Dalton and said, "I don't remember making a schedule of when we were coming back. Do you?"

Dalton started to reply but the old man cut him off. "Would you shut up and drive?" I pulled away and headed out of town. "Stop by the farm on your way by," Sarge said.

We drove through the rain towards the farm. The rain was growing in intensity and began washing the piles of leaves and debris down the sides of the road. I'd become so accustomed to seeing the trash in the road, I hardly noticed it anymore. But seeing stretches of clean road made me realize just how bad things had gotten.

"I'm getting soaked back here!" Aric shouted. Rain was pouring through the open turret.

"Oh dry up, you damn whiney baby!" Sarge shouted.

Aric shook his head as he tried to wad himself into the corner of the backseat, away from the rain. We pulled into the farm and stopped in front of the tents used by the security element. They'd strung a tarp over their fire pit and were standing around under it. The old man didn't hesitate. He immediately climbed out and stomped through the rain towards them.

"You going with him?" Dalton asked.

"Hell no. I'm not getting soaked," I replied.

"I'm just happy to have a ride," Kelley said from the back of the Hummer.

Dalton opened his door, saying, "I'm already wet."

He walked over to the tarp and had to stoop to get under it. Sarge was talking to the guys gathered there.

"No, no one around last night," One of the Guardsmen said.

Sarge looked out over the field and nodded. "That's good. I doubt anyone will be out in this crap today."

"We've still got a fire team out there." Another said.

Sarge nodded. "I wouldn't leave them out in this shit all day. Call 'em back in so they don't get drowned out there. Just keep your eyes open."

One of the Guardsmen laughed. "They'll like that. We drew straws to see who was going out."

"Alright. You fellers try and stay dry today," Sarge said and he turned and headed back to the truck with Dalton in tow.

Getting back in, Sarge shook the rain off his clothes and said, "Let's roll."

"Wonder where Cecil is?" I asked, looking around.

"He went home according to them," Sarge said with a nod towards the men under the tarp.

Rolling through Umatilla, the market was empty, as was the rest of town. Here, there was even more trash in the streets because there were more people. The garbage was being washed into the gutters and causing them to overflow. The truck sent off huge waves of water as we passed through them.

"At least the rain is cleaning some of the trash off the streets," Aric said, looking out his window.

"Just going to wash it into the lakes. Sad people can't take care of their garbage," Dalton lamented.

"World's full of shitheads," Sarge replied.

As we got closer to Altoona, I asked Kelley if he wanted me to drop him at home.

"That'd be great. Better than walking in the rain," he replied.

He directed me to his house and I stopped under a large oak tree in the front yard. Kelley got out and grabbed his things and carried them to the front porch. Running back to the truck, he shook my hand and said thanks for the ride.

"No problem. You going to want to go back?" I asked.

He nodded. "Yeah. I've got a couple pairs of boots to repair and I traded all the shoes I took with me."

"So it was a good trip then."

"Yeah it was," he replied and looked up at the rain. "When this mess stops, I'll go back."

"I'll find you after the rain," I said and started to back out.

Where the road went from paved to dirt near the bunker, there was a huge puddle. I slowed as the truck dropped into it and sent up a huge wake as we passed through it. Looking around, there was standing water in the pastures and a small river flowing down the road. We found Jess and Doc under the tarp at the rear of the bunker. They'd cut a small tree and used it to prop up the center of the tarp.

Stopping, I asked, "Y'all treading water?"

Doc had a poncho on and stepped out to the truck. "Yeah, it's really coming down now."

Sarge leaned forward and asked, "What's it look like inside that bunker?"

Doc looked over at him and replied, "A cesspool."

"Damn," Sarge muttered.

"We'll have to dry it out later," Doc replied.

Sarge shook his head and said, "Probably have to shovel it out too. Maybe even bring in new dirt."

Nodding, Doc replied, "Probably."

We headed for the house and parked the truck at Danny's. I was surprised to see the rocking chairs empty, and we went into the house. The kids were putting a large puzzle together with Bobbie in the living room while Danny snoozed on the sofa. Kay was sitting in a chair reading a book and looked up when we came in.

"Where's Mel?" I asked.

"Everyone is at home." Kay replied. Looking out the window, she added, "It's just a nasty day. Good time to nap."

"I guess that's about all it's good for," I replied. "Guess I'll join them."

I found the girls watching a movie on the laptop. Mel was taking a nap. "What are you guys watching?" I asked.

"Goonies!" Little Bit replied gleefully.

"Oh, that's a good one," I replied as I stripped off my gear.

"You going to watch it with us?" Taylor asked.

I thought about it for a minute. "I'm going to go find mom first."

"She's asleep," Little Bit replied, without looking away from the computer.

She made me smile. It was cool to see the girls so enthralled. A movie was a real treat today. Even if they had seen it a hundred times. "I might be back," I said.

"You're going to go to sleep too. You know it," Lee Ann chimed In.

"It could happen," I answered with a wink as I went through the bedroom door.

Falling onto the bed, I put my arm over Mel. She made

some unrecognizable noise, but didn't wake up. So I relaxed and quickly fell asleep.

Jess sat on an empty bucket and looked out at the rain. "This is ridiculous."

Doc was leaned against the bunker. Taking a deep breath, he said, "I kind of like it. It's cleaning the air. Washing the dust away. I always like it right after a rainstorm."

She looked up at him. "Yeah. It does smell better after it rains, doesn't it?" She looked out at the road again. "But it's going to be so muddy and messy."

Doc nodded. "You know when you start cleaning the house, you always make a little more mess. I see it like that."

Jess grinned and looked at him. "You always so positive?"

Doc shrugged and ducked into the bunker, stepping nearly knee deep into dank water. He grabbed an empty bucket floating in the putrid soup and exited. Setting the bucket down, he sat on it and leaned back against the logs. Looking around, he replied, "When given the choice to be happy or unhappy, which would you choose?"

"Happy of course."

"There you go. That's why I'm always upbeat. Given the choice, I'd rather be happy. There's so much in this world I can't control, so I don't worry about it."

Jess thought about that for a minute. "I don't know if I could do that. There's just so much going on. So much to worry about."

Doc sat quietly for a minute before replying. "That's true. There is a lot to think about. But does your worrying about it change any of it? You have the choice of how you spend your energy. You can sit around and fret about things you have no control over, or you can choose to roll with it and deal with what you have to when you have to. I guess it has a lot to do with living in the moment, kinda."

"That makes sense," Jess replied. Then she looked around at the rain and mud and said, "But what can you possibly take away from this moment?"

Doc laughed. "Well, I can't stop the rain, so there's no sense in giving it any of my energy. I'm just happy I'm sitting under this tarp and not having to be out there in it. There's almost always a worse alternative."

Jess laughed. "Okay, I get it now. Look on the bright side."

Doc nodded. "It can always be worse."

Jess watched him for a long while. Doc sat and watched the rain fall. He held his hand out and let the water running off the tarp fill his hand to overflowing before turning it over and letting it run off the back of his hand. He seemed content to be right where he was.

She stood up and pulled her bucket from the mud. Carrying it over to where Doc sat, she set it back down and sat on it, pushing it into the mud with a bubble, burping sound. Doc laughed at her when her face turned red.

"That wasn't me," Jess said, embarrassed.

Doc held his hands up and laughed, saying, "Hey, It's your lie, you tell it."

"Whatever," Jess replied as she leaned back against the logs. She fidgeted with her hands for a moment before saying, "You're right. I'm going to focus my energy on things that matter." With that, she reached over and took Doc's hand.

He looked down at his knee where their hands sat. Giving her hand a light squeeze he looked at her and said, "This is certainly worth our energy."

Jess smiled and looked down at her feet. She squished them in the mud as she played what he said over in her mind, *worth our energy.* She was giddy, then felt foolish. She wasn't a high school kid after all. But this still felt good. She looked up at him and smiled, saying, "Yes it is."

The two sat quietly for the rest of the afternoon. Jess never moved her hand, nor did Doc. They both were, for the time being, happy in the moment. This was more of an achievement for Jess than Doc, who could sit quietly for long periods of time, content to simply be. Whereas Jess was always on the move and had a hard time sitting still. But being around Ronnie had a calming effect on her, one which she enjoyed.

I don't know how long we slept. When Little Bit came in saying she was hungry, the room was just as gloomy as it was when I had lain down. Mel sat up and looked at her. Little Bit was standing at the door of our room, holding the door open.

"You're hungry?" Mel asked.

Little Bit nodded. "I want something to eat. Is there anything here?"

Mel sat up and stretched. "Yeah. I can make something."

"What?" Little Bit asked.

I rolled over and echoed the question, "Yeah, what do we have?"

Mel stood up and replied, "It's a surprise. But you'll like it."

Little Bit started to bounce up and down. "Can I help! Can I help!"

Mel walked to the door and put her hand on Little Bit's head. "Sure. You want to help cook?"

"I do, I do!"

"Alright. Come on," Mel said as she headed for the kitchen.

I pulled a pillow into a hug and said, "Call me when it's ready."

"Whatever, lazy ass!" Mel called over her shoulder. I heard Little Bit laugh. But I didn't care. I was comfortable. The rain lowered the temperature and made it very comfortable in the house. If it wasn't for the humidity, it'd be perfect. There was a lot of moisture in the air because of the rain. And the wind was picking up outside as well. It made me think about lighting a fire in the fireplace to drive some of the moisture out of the house. But that could wait. I was enjoying the cool day for a change.

Mel went out to the kitchen and took a big bowl out of the fridge. I could hear her talking to Little Bit.

"I put the basics together yesterday," she said.

"What is it?"

Mel placed a large cast iron skillet on the stove and said, "We're going to make fried mush!"

Little Bit clapped her hands. "I love fried mush!"

Mel placed the bread pan full of cooked cornmeal from the fridge on the counter. Using a knife, she began to cut slices. With Little Bit's help, they laid them out on a plate.

Hearing this, I got up. I liked fried mush too! Wandering into the kitchen, I said, "Did I hear something about fried mush?"

"Yeah!" Little Bit shouted. "Me and Mommy are making it!"

Mel took a large mason jar out and dug into it with a spoon and dropped the grease into the pan, saying, "I wish we had bacon fat."

"Me too. But that pig grease will work too," I replied. I looked over her shoulder and said, "I'll leave you ladies to it." And I wandered out to the living room where the older girls were watching another movie.

Plopping down on the couch, I asked, "What are you guys watching?"

"Transformers," Taylor replied.

I put my feet up and settled back onto the sofa to enjoy the movie. I enjoyed listening to Little Bit and Mel in the kitchen. The weather may suck, but it was making for a good day. While they cooked, we watched the movie and relaxed. It wasn't long before Little Bit came into the living room carrying a plate with slices of golden brown deliciousness in one hand and a jar of honey in the other.

The girls sat up, their excitement obvious. While fried mush wasn't exactly a culinary delight, it was something different. And more importantly, it was made at home. Most meals were made at Danny's where we ate communally. So it was nice to be eating at home with my family. Mel and Little Bit joined us and we snacked while the movie played.

Finishing my last bite, I leaned back on the sofa and put my hands behind my head. Sighing, I said, "As bad as I don't want to, I have to head to the bunker in a bit." I'd checked the board on Danny's porch earlier and he and I were scheduled to be there in about an hour.

Mel was drizzling honey onto a bite of the corn mush. "Why are you guys doing that? I mean, with this rain, there isn't going to be anyone out. Why don't you just stay home tonight?"

Standing up, I said, "I'd like to. But I gotta go for a couple of hours."

"You're going to get wet, Daddy!" Little Bit said.

I was at the door putting my gear on, trying to decide if I should wear my poncho or raingear. In the end, I decided to wear the poncho so my gear wouldn't get wet. Not that I was worried about the gear. Just that the vest would get heavier if it got wet.

As I pulled the poncho over my head, I looked at Little Bit and said, "No I won't!"

She laughed at me and said, "You like bush!"

I held my arms out and said, "I'm the swamp monster! Rhaaaaa!" And I started walking towards her like a bad monster-movie creature.

She squealed and ran for the kitchen. I kept up my monster walk until I was standing over Lee Ann on the sofa. "I'm the swamp monster!" I said.

She was watching the movie, lying on the sofa propped up on one elbow. "You don't scare me. Go away."

Looking down at her, I said, "I don't scare you?"

"Nope," she replied without looking away from the screen.

I studied her for a minute. Then I stuck my finger in my mouth, popped it out and stuck it in her ear. Lee Ann screamed and bolted from the sofa. "Ewww, dad. That's so gross!"

"Do I scare you now?" I asked, laughing.

Taylor quickly sat up and ran from the sofa. "You scare me! I don't want that nasty finger in my ear."

I leaned over Mel, who was still sitting on the sofa. "Don't even think about it," she said.

"What?" I asked, feigning innocence. "I was just going to give you a kiss."

She turned her head to the side and I kissed her cheek. "Now go away," she said.

"Well that wasn't very nice."

She turned and looked at me. "I just don't want you to do anything you'll regret."

I scratched my nose and asked, "Would I regret it?"

Mel laughed. "Oh, you'd regret it. Count on that."

"Alright. I'll see you guys later," I said as I headed for the door.

Outside, I looked up into the slate gray sky. The wind was already blowing and I thought about the solar panels. Walking around the house, I grabbed the little tool for separating the panel plugs and began to disconnect them from one another. Once separated, I took them into the shed and leaned them up against the wall. I could not afford for them to be damaged by this storm. Once they were all stored, I headed for the bunker.

Danny was already at the bunker when I got there. Jess and Doc were standing close to one another and looking a little weird. We chatted with them for a minute before they left. I watched them as they headed away, disappearing into the rain.

"Something seem a little weird with them?" I asked Danny.

"Yeah. I think they're up to something."

"Something?" I asked.

Danny laughed. "Yeah. *Something.*"

I got his drift. "Well, good for them. I hope they're happy and it works out."

The wind picked up even more and the tarp really started to snap. We worked to tighten it as much as possible, but I felt we would lose it tonight if the wind kept up. Once it was as tight as we could get it, I sat down on a bucket. Sitting with my back to the bunker kept me mostly out of the rain. Though with the wind, there was no place totally out of the rain.

I took out the little radio and hung the antenna on the pole in the center of the tarp. It wasn't very tall, but it would be better than the small collapsible antenna built into the radio. Turning it on, it was already tuned to the frequency for the Radio Free Redoubt. The signal was faint and hard to hear, but I could tell he was excited about something. I tried to fine tune the radio and managed to get it a little clearer. But with the wind, I still couldn't really hear it, so I pulled out my earbuds and put them in. Now I could hear it.

… retaliatory strike. The Chinese minister continued to say that the attack was unprovoked and the ships sunk off the California coast were delivering humanitarian aid. This of course is in direct conflict with what our military sources say. You don't deliver humanitarian aid with tanks and APCs.

But we are now facing a new and very perilous threat to the nation. Should the Chinese actually strike back with nuclear weapons it would be disastrous. But I take heart in the statements coming out of NORAD. They're saying the strike against the Chinese fleet was delivered by subs and not ballistic missiles. It was a limited strike aimed squarely at the invading vessels and not the Chinese mainland.

They go on to say that the use of ICBMs or even submarine-based weapons by the Chinese would yield little results. In other words, the return wouldn't be worth the investment considering the state of the country at the moment. When you add this to the statements coming from the President, it seems unlikely that they will retaliate in nuclear capacity. But they still could, if only to save face.

I fear a limited strike that would allow the Chinese to save face on the world stage while not being committed to a full launch and thereby squandering their arsenal. This is the real key. They cannot afford to leave themselves vulnerable to the Russians.

Now that we've mentioned the Russians, they have made it clear that any use of nuclear weapons on their personnel, no matter where they are located, would result in an immediate reply. The Russian Foreign Minister clearly stated they would meet force with force. Which was taken to mean they would launch in kind, however many weapons were used against them.

The only good news I have for you folks is that the Chinese invasion has been halted. Though it has stranded thousands of

Chinese personnel in California. But if the people will rise up, they can rid themselves of this Chinese scourge!

I was shocked at what I was hearing. To think that nukes were now at play was terrifying. Of course, they'd already been used against us as an EMP. But they were detonated high in the atmosphere and there was no risk of fallout. No worries of dying from radiation sickness or having your skin burned off. Or even worse.

The only saving grace to this was the thought that maybe the Chinese got a belly full and wouldn't try anything further. Of course, the Russians were still here; and while the Chinese weren't a direct threat to us here in Umatilla, the Russians damn sure were.

The wind was beginning to howl. The tarp was really whipping and we were being pelted with rain. Danny tapped my shoulder, and when I looked at him, he was gesturing for me to take the earbuds out.

He had to yell to be heard. "I been trying to talk to you! This is ridiculous! There's no reason to be out here. I'm going home!"

I nodded. "You're right! Let's get the hell out of here!"

We had to shield our faces as we walked back towards the house. The wind was fierce, and it forced us to lean into it to make any headway. Danny and I parted ways in the yard as he headed for his house. Limbs in the big oak trees were being thrashed and there were several large limbs lying scattered around the yard. I worried about the chickens, but there was nothing to be done now. Hopefully, someone thought about that ahead of time.

I made it to the house and stumbled in. I stumbled because the dogs were inside the house. Mel must have let them in because of the storm. Everyone was asleep. I was soaked. Even with the poncho. My boots would need drying, so I kicked them off and set them in front of the fireplace and headed into the bedroom to change clothes.

Mel woke up when I came in. "You back?" She asked.

"Yeah. The storm is pretty bad so we came home."

She rolled over, saying, "Good."

After changing, I went out to the living room and built a small fire. The house felt damp and this would help dry it out some, but I didn't want it to make the house too hot either. With my boots drying, I headed into the kitchen for a glass of tea and sat on the sofa and put my feet up. I would stay up while the storm raged in case something happened that needed immediate attention.

So I spent the night listening to the wind and rain pound the house. Occasionally, I would hear a crack followed by a dull thud as some large piece of a tree would come crashing down. Gusts would send debris slamming into the house as well. It was a long night to sit and think about what I'd heard on the radio. And as I sat there in the dark listening to the world outside being pummeled, anxiety began to build up inside me.

I'd always had a fear of nuclear war. It was kind of in the back of my mind. Not something I focused on daily. But it was there, nonetheless. When things changed, that fear faded from my mind with so much to worry about. Actually, I would never have imagined this threat returning. Who would want to nuke the US now? And for what? But here it was.

Something big hit the house. It rattled the windows and the bang woke up Little Bit. I heard her cry out in her room and I went to check on her. She was sitting up in her bed and I sat down beside her. It also woke up the dogs. They were all on their feet, whining. I stopped to pat their heads and rub their ears. It had the desired effect and they all lay back down.

"What was that?" She asked.

Putting my arm around her, I replied, "Probably just a limb or something. Nothing to worry about. Go back to sleep."

"Is the storm still going on?" She asked.

I laid her back in her bed and said, "It is. But I think it's slowing down now. I'll be up. Just go back to sleep."

She looked up and asked, "You're staying up?"

Leaning down and kissing her head, I said, "Yes. I'll be up."

"Okay," she replied as she pulled a stuffed bunny in tight and closed her eyes.

I rubbed her head for a minute before standing up and looking at her sister who was asleep on the upper bunk. Teenagers were blessed with the ability to sleep through anything, like work, school, chores and tropical storms it would seem. I smiled and shook my head as I left their room, pulling the door to. I checked on Taylor as well. She was sprawled out in her bed with a sleeping mask over her eyes. Again, I couldn't help but smile at her. *Must be nice,* I thought as I pulled her door to and headed back to the sofa.

Whatever hit the house did have one positive effect. It brought my mind out of the funk of nuclear annihilation. I settled back onto the sofa with my feet up. But instead of staying up as I told Little Bit I would, I fell asleep.

CHAPTER 9

I WOKE UP WITH HER STANDING in front of me, bunny under her arm.

She rubbed her nose and said, "You said you were going to stay up."

Blinking, I said, "I am up. I was just resting for a minute."

Little Bit wrinkled her nose and replied, "You were snoring."

I laughed and reached out and grabbed her. "I don't snore!" And I pulled her onto the sofa with me. She laughed and squealed as I tussled with her.

We played on the sofa for a minute before she asked if it was still raining. I told her I didn't know, but we would go find out, together. Picking her up, we went over to the window and I pulled the blind open. It was still raining, though only lightly and the sky was brighter than it had been the day before. It looked like the worst was over.

But all Little Bit saw was rain. A pout formed on her face as she moaned, "It's still raining?"

I set her down and replied, "Just a little. It'll probably stop soon."

She stood in front of the window with her hands on her hips, looking out. After a moment, she spun around and stomped off towards her room, saying, "I'm going back to bed till the rain stops!"

I shook my head and went to the kitchen. I needed some tea before going out in the soup. Mel came in as I closed the fridge. As she tied her robe, she said, "You're already up. I guess you're going somewhere?"

"Just going out to see what the storm did," I replied.

She looked surprised. "So you're going to be here today?"

"As far as I know," I replied and took a sip of tea.

"Something hit the house last night," she said as she placed a skillet on the stove. She opened the fridge and paused. "The light isn't very bright. What's wrong?" She asked.

I looked at the fridge. "I didn't notice anything when I was in there," I said as I stepped over. She was right though. The light was dim. Maybe because the compressor was running from when I opened it.

"I'll go out and check the system. We've had a lot of cloud cover the last couple of days so the batteries haven't been charging. Might need to run the generator today. I'll check it out."

Mel cracked an egg into a bowl and said, "Okay. Go check it and come back in. I'll have some eggs ready."

I patted her ass and kissed the side of her head. "Be back in a bit."

When I opened the door to go out, the dogs rushed for the door and pushed me aside. They were tired of being in the house. They were outside dogs and that's where they preferred to be. It was still drizzling a bit, so I reached back inside and grabbed my raincoat from the hook by the door and slipped it on.

First thing I did was set the panels back up. There was only a light breeze now, nothing that would knock them over. Once they were back up, I pushed a big pile of moss off the top of the trailer and opened it up. The meter on the system showed eleven

262

point six volts. Definitely needed a charge, so I dragged the generator out of the shed and brought it around. After checking the oil and fuel, I started it up and let it get up to speed while I dragged the big thirty-amp charger out.

With the generator warmed, I hooked up the charger. The generator changed pitch immediately, picking up the load. That was good, it meant the charger was working. With that task taken care of, I walked around the house, looking for whatever crashed last night. There were limbs down everywhere. Lots of moss as well. It was like a thick soft carpet covering large parts of the yard. I sat on the stump of a huge oak tree that had been cut probably two years ago from the look of it. Sitting there, I took in the scene.

The limbs and branches, the moss and the innumerable leaves mixed in created a scene out of some sort of fairytale movie. I half expected to see fairies or nymphs, maybe gnomes, moving about. It made me laugh to have such silly thoughts and I quickly got up and dismissed the notion and continued the search. Going up on the back porch, I climbed up onto the rail and looked on the roof.

There was a pretty good-size limb lying over the bathroom. I climbed up and dragged it to the edge and tossed it off. Going back over, I checked the shingles. There was some damage to two of them, but the tar paper hadn't been ripped below it. Nevertheless, I would need to find some way to patch it.

Just as Mel promised, there were eggs. She had a plate sitting on the table waiting for me. I sat down and she brought me a glass of tea as well. Eggs were plentiful. We usually had more than we could eat, even allowing for the ones that hatched. The chickens were prolific. Miss Kay made it a point to go out to the coop and check on the young roosters. They were kept in small cages to keep the fighting down. But the crowing could be obnoxious at times. As soon as two roosters were ready, she would have them butchered, always on a Sunday.

I'd made a chicken-plucker out of a four inch PVC cap and some of the black rubber bungee cords. A rod connected to the center of the cap was connected to a drill. Once the chicken was scalded, the drill was started and the bird rotated in front of the cap. The rubbers beat the feathers off the bird. It was crude but effective.

I looked at the plate of eggs, half a dozen from the looks of it. Picking up the salt shaker, I smiled. Breakfast was one of my favorite meals of the day. The only thing that could make it better would be some toast. I know you thought I would say bacon. But we have plenty of pork, having made sausage recently. And while that's not bacon, it's a close second.

But toast, preferably rye, and even Wonder Bread white would be good right now. That's something I haven't had in a long time, and there was little chance I could again any time soon. So I enjoyed my eggs like I do my whiskey, naked.

Mel joined me with a plate of her own, and together we commiserated the absence of toast.

"I could use a cup of coffee," Mel said.

"The old man has some next door."

She smiled. "That's true. But I couldn't ask him for it. It'd be like asking for one of his children."

"I think he'd give away his kids a lot easier," I replied with a smile.

She laughed and looked at me. "I like this. Having breakfast together. I miss this sort of thing."

"Me too. It's nice."

But then things changed. I saw Mel looking at the door. She pointed with her fork and said, "Well, you can ask him yourself."

I looked over my shoulder to see the old man standing at

the door. I waved him in and he opened the door. Mel greeted him, "Morning. Would you like some eggs?"

He smiled and waved her off. "No thank you, Miss Mel." Holding his cup up, he added, "I have mine already."

I looked at his thermos and said, "But Mel would love a cup coffee." Then I gave him a shit-eating grin.

He was right in front of her and couldn't reply in the manner I'm sure he wanted to. He glanced down at the thermos tucked under his arm, gave me a dirty look and smiled at Mel. "Of course!" He said, a little too happily.

As he came to the table, Mel retrieved herself a mug from the cabinet. Sarge opened his thermos and began to pour as he spoke. "We need to go to town this morning." He stopped pouring when the cup was just over half full and stole a look at Mel. He saw she was looking and let out a bit of a sigh as he topped it off. Stingy old fart.

"What for?" I asked.

Sipping his coffee, he replied, "We're going to send a patrol down south."

Mel was taking a sip from her mug. The old man was looking at me and I shook my head slightly and narrowed my eyes.

"What for?" Mel asked.

He smiled. The old prick liked these kinds of games. "Oh it's nothing, really. Just to see what sort of effect the storm had on things."

She looked at me and asked, "You're not going are you?"

"No. But I've got business in town too. Not to mention, we should take a look around the area here to see if there was any damage or if anyone is hurt."

Sarge smiled, "That's right, Sheriff. You should take a look."

Since my breakfast was finished anyway, I said, "We should probably get going then."

Grinning like ass-eating briars, the old bastard replied, "Indeed we should." I gave Mel a quick kiss as he got up. Sarge said he'd be in the truck waiting and headed for the door.

Just before he got to the door, Mel called out, "Thank you for the coffee!" She was holding the mug in both hands close to her nose.

He turned and waved, saying, "Any time."

I quickly gathered my gear and pulled some shoes on, without socks. I hate wearing shoes without socks. Told Mel I'd be back and hit the door. Coming out on the porch, I was surprised to see so many people in the yard, off to the side and out of view from where we were eating breakfast. It seemed like nearly everyone was there.

"What the hell's going on?" I asked.

Sarge was leaning on the hood of his Hummer. "We're just waiting on you to get your shit together. Take your time. The war can wait."

I looked at Thad and shook my head. Looking back at Sarge, I said, "I didn't even know we were doing this today. So don't give me any shit!"

"Some of us got a job to do!" Sarge barked back. "Must be nice to sit around all damn day!"

"Sounds like someone is a little pissed this morning," Aric muttered.

I laughed. "He's just pissed he had to give Mel a cup of coffee is all." Looking at Aric, I added, "He doesn't like to share."

"Aw, that's bullshit!" Sarge barked back. "I didn't mind giving your missus coffee! Stop running your cocksucker!"

I laughed. "Yeah. You filled her cup half and stopped. When you saw she was expecting a full cup, you looked like someone just told you the Easter Bunny wasn't real."

Mike was snickering under his breath. The old man glared at me. Finally, he replied, "You can kiss my ass."

Now he was aggravated and I laughed even harder. "Pick a stop, you ole prick. You're all ass!"

Mike let out a snort and Sarge looked over his shoulder at him. Not one to be outdone by anyone, the old man straightened up and quickly unhitched his pants and pulled them down to his knees, bent over and spread his cheeks and shouted, "Right here!"

A collective *Ohhh!* came out as everyone turned and started to walk in the opposite direction of him from wherever they were standing. Thad turned his back and started to laugh so hard tears were rolling down his face. Sarge was looking over his shoulder at me, but I wasn't going to let him get to me that easy.

I squinted and leaned forward a bit, as if I was straining to see. "I'm not kissing that. It don't look normal." I tapped Thad on the shoulder and nodded at the old man, "Thad, does that look normal to you?"

Still laughing, Thad replied, "I ain't looking! Ain't nothing natural about this!"

"What's it look like?" Mike shouted.

I shook my head and replied, "I don't know. But it don't look right." I asked, "Does it hurt?" That sent Thad over the edge and he lost it, belly-laughing so hard he nearly couldn't breathe.

Sarge straightened up and turned to face me, without pulling his pants up, and asked, "What the hell are you talking about?"

I nodded at him and said, "You may want to get a doctor to look at that. It just don't look right. I don't see how you can sit down." Sarge was unsure now. He couldn't tell if I was full of shit or not.

I looked at Doc and shouted, "Hey, Doc, you may want to come look at this!"

Doc replied by giving me the finger over his shoulder and saying, "Fuck you! If he ain't been shot, he don't need my help!"

I shook my head and said, "I don't know. Looks like he may have sat on a small explosive device."

Thad was already laughing again, and my last statement set Mike over the edge. He started to guffaw loudly. Bent over slapping his knees and making a real scene. Even Ted, who was usually a little harder to stir up, was now laughing. But all this was brought to an end when we heard Mel's voice from the porch.

"What the hell is going on out here?" She asked.

Sarge quickly hitched up his pants and turned several shades of red. Mike was still laughing and said, "He wanted to know if it looked funny? Does it look funny to you?"

Sarge glared at him as Mel replied, "There isn't anything funny about this." Then, looking at Sarge, she added, "You're lucky Ashley didn't see that."

Sarge was flustered and stammered when he spoke. "I'm real sorry, Mel. It's not what it looks like."

She folded her arms over her chest and leaned against a post on the porch, asking, "And just what does it look like?" I started to laugh as well. Mainly because I thought Thad was going to piss himself. He had his back to Mel and wouldn't look at her. But I probably should have kept quiet because she looked at me and asked, "What's so damn funny?"

That cut my laugh off and I shrugged, replying, "Well, you gotta admit, it did look funny." Mike let out a howl of laughter and ducked behind the truck.

She did not see the humor though. "There isn't anything funny about a bunch of grown men standing in my yard—" she paused looking for the right words. "with their junk hanging out."

From behind the truck, still laughing, Mike cried out, "It was just a little old junk!"

Sarge spun and headed around the truck. Mike defenseless as the old man set to him with his boot. Mike came stumbling out from behind the truck trying to run, but he was still laughing too hard and Sarge landed several hard blows to his thigh and ass.

Mel just shook her head. Checking over her shoulder as she turned back to the house, she replied, "You guys take your bullshit somewhere else!"

"Yes ma'am," Ted replied. "I'll get them out of here."

I looked at him, shaking my head. "You suck ass! You got tears in your eyes too!"

He smiled as he wiped his cheek. "True, but she ain't mad at me and I plan on keeping it that way."

Dalton's voice surprised me. I hadn't noticed him with all the crap going on. "Well, now that we've all seen the old man's pecker. Let's go to town."

Sarge shot Dalton a look, daring him to say more. Dalton raised his hands, "Hey, I'm not judging. It was a fine looking pecker if you ask me."

Mike had wandered out of earshot of Sarge and muttered, "In its day."

This brought Thad to tears again and he had to kneel down before he passed out. As I walked past him, I patted him on the back and said, "Come on, big boy. Let's go."

He stood up, wiping copious tears from his eyes. Shaking his head, he said, "Morgan. You boys are a mess. I swear! I've never seen anything like it!"

"Are we done now?" Sarge barked. "Everyone get a good laugh? Can we get to work now?"

Ted held a finger up and replied, "I did."

Sarge studied him for a minute, nodding his head slightly. In a calm voice, he said, "Go ahead, Teddy. Keep it up."

Ted shrugged. "You know I'm just playing with you."

"Does it look like I'm playing?" Sarge barked.

Ted didn't know what to say and blurted out the first thing that came to his mind. "You were the one pulling your fucking pants down!"

Sarge shook his head and looked around. Stopping on Aric, he asked, "You got anything to say? Some smartass comment to make?"

Aric shook his head and simply replied, "Nope."

"Well!" Sarge barked. "Someone around here's got some fucking brains! Load up, you assholes! The lot of you!"

Thad went to the little red truck and started it up. Dalton got in with him and Mike jumped in the back, he wasn't about to ride with the old man right now. I went over and climbed in the backseat of the Hummer. Ted was driving and Sarge was riding shotgun. Jamie was sitting in the back of the truck and scared the shit out of me because I didn't see her.

"You been back here the whole time?" I asked.

"The whole time," Jamie replied.

"Enjoy the show?"

"Shut up, Morgan," Sarge snapped. Ian just smiled and didn't say anything.

As we pulled out, we stopped by the bunker. Perez was there with Fred and Jess. He didn't seem to mind the mud and debris piled everywhere. But Jess and Fred were trying to free the tarp from a palm tree it was tangled in as Perez watched, smoking a cigarette.

Sarge motioned for Ted to stop, and he pulled up beside Perez. The old man stared at him as he sat there watching the girls struggle with the tarp. After a moment, he said, "Hey, Beaner! You gonna get off your lazy ass and help them?"

Perez looked over as smoke drifted out of his nose. "I'm Puerto Rican, cabron."

"Then get off your Puerto Rican ass and help them."

"Besa mi culo." Perez replied with a thick Spanish accent.

"No, no. We've seen enough culos for one day," Ted quickly replied. Getting a curious look from Perez.

Jess stopped and looked back at the truck. "Leave him alone, Sarge. We told him we'd get it out if he'd put it back up."

Sarge shook his head. "You should still be helping them, zurramato."

Perez smiled and pointed his smoke at the old man. "You do speak Spanish, don't you?"

Sarge smiled and replied, "Te meto la verga por el osico para que te calles el pinche puto osico hijo de perra!" Perez erupted into laughter, slapping his knee. Sarge smiled and added, "I know enough. Nos vemos mas tarde."

Perez waved at him and replied, "Anciano tarde."

Sarge waved back and nodded for Ted to go, and we pulled away. The paved road past the bunker was littered with leaves and branches. Everything was a mess. Even the yards of the houses on the street were a mess. Made me wonder what town was going to look like. But when we turned out onto Hwy 19, I saw something I would never have expected.

Ted stopped the truck and we all sat there staring. After a moment, Ian asked, "Should we shoot it?"

"It's got a rope hanging around its neck," Ted replied.

"I didn't think there were any left," Sarge said as he opened the door and stepped out.

The big black cow just stood there looking back at us. It

didn't move. Just stood there chewing its cud. I got out with Sarge and asked, "We got time to butcher that thing?"

"It wouldn't take that long. We could just quarter it without skinning it and take care of it when we get back," he replied.

"Wonder who it belongs too," I asked.

He shrugged. "Hard to say. We can't wrangle it."

Our discussion was cut short by the crack of a rifle. Both of us jumped at the sound and spun around to see Dalton sling his AK. "We're having steak tonight," he said as he walked past us, drawing that big-ass kukri.

The bullet hit the cow between the eyes. Its legs splayed out and it collapsed in a heap, blood gushing from the wound. Dalton stepped up to it and rolled its head to the side and cut its throat. A river of blood poured out.

Sarge looked at me and said, "Looks like we're butchering a cow," as he walked towards Dalton.

Thad came up beside me and said, "Someone is gonna be pissed off."

I grunted. "Yeah. Probably. When we get this thing cut up, can you take it home. I don't think we need to be driving through town with a truckload of beef."

Thad nodded. "That's a good idea." He slapped me on the back and said, "Come on. We got work to do."

Dalton was trying to roll the beast over when we walked up, and I told them what Thad and I discussed. Sarge agreed it was a good idea.

"Let's skin it out. I want the hide," Thad said.

"What in the hell for?" Sarge asked.

Thad looked at him like his head was on sideways. "I'll make leather out of it."

So we got to work butchering the bovine. After skinning it, we left the hide on the road to protect the meat. The quarters were cut off along with the ribs. The backstrap was cut out and the tenderloins removed from the bottom side. We also kept the liver, heart and kidneys. The neck was also salvaged. Once all the usable meat was removed, the quarters were picked up and Aric and I took the hide and laid it out in the bed of the truck and meat was piled on it.

But Thad wasn't done. I looked back to see him working on the head and walked back over. He had the head upside down and was cutting under the chin. "What are you doing?" I asked.

Without pausing his work, he replied, "I'm cutting the tongue out."

"Never had it," I replied.

"Oh, it's good," he said as he pulled it out through the hole he'd cut. He then sliced it off, holding it up. "Here, put this in the truck. I got one more thing to get."

I took the tongue and asked, "What? We've got everything."

Thad stepped around to the back of the animal and grabbed the tail. Looking up with a smile, he said, "Ox tail."

"But that's a cow," I said, pointing at it.

He started to laugh and Sarge, who'd walked up, said, "Ignore him, Thad. He don't know what's good. He's fucking ignorant."

Thad cut the tail off at the base of the spine and held it up. "I got some collards in the garden. I'll smoke this and we'll cook the collards with it."

"Damn good eatin'," Sarge said. "Get Miss Kay to make a cake of cornbread and I'll be in heaven."

Thad grinned. "Yeah, it is. Reminds me of my momma."

"Go on and take that home, Thad. Get Danny to help you with it," Sarge said.

"Oh I got this," Thad replied as he headed for the truck. "I was just going to town to check on the farm. This is more important."

I followed him to the back of the truck and looked at the mountain of meat. "What are we going to do with all this?"

Sarge snorted and barked, "We're going to eat it!", then added, "Dumbass."

"We got no way to store this much meat!" I replied.

Thad looked at me with a knowing smile and said, "Don't worry, Morgan. I'll take care of it."

"Let's take one of the quarters to town," Sarge said. "There's a lot of meat here and we can share it."

"Good idea," I replied as I grabbed one and started to pull it out.

Thad left and headed back home as we continued on towards Eustis. While I was concerned about how we were going to preserve all that beef, I was more caught up with the idea of a thick steak. A real beef steak. Grilled over an oak fire. My stomach started to rumble just thinking about it.

Jamie gave voice to my thoughts, kind of. "You guys better save us a steak."

"Yeah," Ian added. "Just the thought of having a huge ribeye is unbelievable."

"I wish we could have herded the thing home," I said.

"What in the hell for?" Sarge said over his shoulder. "It's not like you could get a calf out of it. There ain't no bulls around!"

"It'll be good," Dalton said. "If we hadn't killed it, someone else would have."

"And a lot of folks are going to be able to use this. We'll give this to the armory and give some to Gina and Dylan too," Sarge said.

"I guess you guys are right," I said.

"Of course we're right!" Sarge barked.

I rolled my eyes as I shook my head. Jamie laughed and slapped my shoulder. I looked back and she was grinning.

Rolling into town, we went straight to the armory. While the rest of the crew went into the armory to discuss the recon they were going on, I hung out long enough to bring the beef in. Which drew a lot of attention.

Dalton carried the slab of meat on his shoulder into the armory, like some kind of damn caveman. Livingston saw it and quickly came over, asking, "What the hell is that?"

Dalton looked at him, his eyes wild and a crazy grin on his face, replying, "It's meat, lad! Meat!"

"Where did you get it?" Livingston asked as Dalton dropped it onto a table. "And what is it?"

"It's beef," Sarge replied. "It was in the road on the way here." He motioned to Dalton and added, "This knuckle-dragging booger-eater shot it."

"Makes 'em a lot easier to butcher," Dalton said quite seriously.

I headed for the jail. Mike was sitting on the hood of the Hummer and I stopped, looking around. "Where the hell were you? Weren't you riding with Thad?"

"I was. But I was in the truck. Well, more correctly, I was on top of the truck."

Confused, I asked, "You rode all the way to town on the roof of the truck?"

Mike nodded. "It was too crowded inside. Smelt like feet and ass in there." He slapped the top of the truck and added, "Fresh air up here."

I laughed and shook my head. "You ain't right, man."

He smiled and nodded. "That's already been established."

With a wave, I left him and started walking towards the PD. Even here in town there was a lot of debris lying around. Leaves, limbs and palm fronds littered the ground. Unlike at home, there were also shingles and pieces of aluminum siding or fascia. I kicked a piece as I walked and wondered if the people in town would clean any of this up. I highly doubted it.

At the jail, I found Shane, Sean, Mitch and Michelle sitting in the rocking chairs out front. Two quart jars sat empty on the ground between the chairs. I said, "Looks like Miss Michelle brought you boys some lemonade."

Sean leaned back in his chair and patted his belly, "Yes, she did indeed."

"Well, I see you guys have met already," I said.

Shane nodded. "We've been talking for a while. Waiting on you."

"Good," I replied. "Saves me some time. You guys get things sorted out?"

Shane stood up. "Yeah. We showed him the courtroom."

"Looks good to me," Mitch said. "I don't think we need much room." He nodded at Michelle, "Michelle is going to be the clerk. You know, to help keep things organized."

"That's a great idea," I replied.

As we chatted, three MRAPs came rolling past us, headed south. "What's that about?" Sean asked.

Watching them drive away, I replied, "They're going to run a recon down south. We've heard the Russians and Cubans are working together and may be coming up from the south."

"What? Cubans?" Mitch asked.

I nodded and went on to tell them about the nuclear strike against the Chinese fleet off the coast of California. They were all stunned and listened intently as I told them all I knew. A couple of questions were asked and I answered them as best I could. When it was done, we all sat in silence for some time.

As we were all lost in our thoughts, Aric strolled up. He stopped and studied us for a moment before saying, "You all look like someone just killed your puppy."

Shane nodded at me and replied, "Mister good news here just told us about the Chinese fleet."

"Ah," Aric said. "Yeah, that could be a problem. Let's just hope they don't retaliate."

"What good would it do them?" Mitch asked.

Michelle looked particularly forlorn. She shook her head and said, "How much more suffering can we endure?"

I glanced over at her and warned, "Don't ask questions you don't want answers to."

She considered the reply for a moment before giving me a knowing nod. "I guess it could always be worse."

I stood up and said, "I guess we're going to head back to the armory. I want to go check on the farm on the way home."

Mitch stood up and said, "We've got this under control here. We're going to get things set up for the court to make it as efficient as we can."

"Good deal. But hopefully you won't have too much business."

Aric and I left them and headed back to the armory. We went up to Grove Street and headed north. There are several large old homes on the road and I was looking them over as we walked. At one, there was an older man in blue coveralls out cleaning the yard. He stopped and waved a gloved hand as we passed.

We were discussing the beef Thad was processing as we approached Orange Ave. Caught up in the thought of thick steaks, I wasn't paying attention to a group of people standing around a building on the corner. It was an old service station from years long gone by. In recent years, it had been a number of different failed businesses.

Most recently, it had become the hangout for Porky and his clan. And they were out in force today. By the time I noticed them, they were already well aware of our presence. I nudged Aric and nodded in their direction. "Got it," he replied.

As we got closer, a man stepped out into the road, crossing over to our side. "Mr. Hound would like to have a word with you," and he nodded towards the old service station.

I looked over to see Porky sitting in his barber chair. I laughed and said, "I ain't got time for his shit today."

Another of the men came running up and said, "We aren't asking."

I looked at Aric and shrugged. He half smiled and shrugged in reply. As quickly as I could, I drew my ASP, extended it and smacked the guy in the head as hard as I could. The other man was somewhat stunned and stood there. I squared off with him in the road, waiting to see what he would do. He looked at his friend on the ground, now holding his head, and stepped back, holding his hands up. I pointed the ASP at him and said, "Smartest thing you've done today."

He continued to back away as we crossed the street. Seeing he wasn't going to be an issue, I turned my attention to the rest of the group. They had all backed up to the shade of the service station, except for one. I figured we had the situation under control, until I heard a shotgun rack. I looked over to see Porky sitting in his barber chair smiling smugly, and a man with a shotgun leveled in our direction.

"Now, Mr. Carter, I will abide violence," Porky said as he heaved himself from his chair. "I politely asked you to stop and speak with me." He looked around at the people gathered and added, "Did I not? I simply asked you to stop and have a word and you resorted to violence against these men." Again, looking at the crowd and waving a finger in the air, he added, "Unarmed men! Unarmed men, mind you!"

"Well, Porky, I guess we see thing different. You had these

morons stand in the road in front of us and tell me you wanted to speak to me. I told them I didn't have time for your shit today and they told me they weren't asking. Now, does that sound friendly to you?" I pointed to the man with the shotgun and added, "not to mention you're the ones holding a gun on us."

He stamped his pudgy feet and screamed at me, "Do not call me that!" Jabbing a fat accusatory finger at me, he said, "You call yourself the Sheriff? You claim to be the law here and yet you mistreat innocent citizens in this manner? You, sir, are a Pharisee!"

I shook my head. "A what?" I knew what he was calling me. But I was hoping to annoy the shit outta the fat turd.

Porky stammered and stepped closer to me, close enough to poke me in the chest. "You know exactly what I mean!" He grabbed the gold star pinned to my vest and snatched it off. "You, sir, do not deserve to wear this!"

Now I was pissed. As he pulled his grubby fat arm back, I grabbed it and spun him around as I drew my pistol. I did it faster than even I thought I could. The group under the awning let out an audible gasp as I put the muzzle of my .45 to Porky's temple and looked at the man holding the shotgun. "I will only tell you once to lay that scatter gun on the ground!" Porky squealed as I held him around the neck. He was soft and squishy. His skin unnaturally clammy under the heat of the afternoon sun. It was like holding onto a giant frog.

The man hesitated for a moment, looking between me and Aric. Aric's response was to slowly raise his rifle until he was looking down the barrel at the man. The man hesitated as Porky began to croak. "Shoot him!" The man gripped the long-barreled shotgun a little tighter and I wasn't going to give him the chance. As soon as his eyes darted to Aric again, I swung the Springfield out and fired, hitting him in the chest.

The shot staggered the man, he stepped back and looked down in disbelief, still holding the shotgun. Aric made sure he didn't get to pull the trigger. Three rounds from his carbine dropped him in the street.

"Watch them," I said. Aric nodded and I took a step back, positioning my knee behind Porky's leg, and pulled him back and around. He crashed to the ground face down, his straw hat falling onto the road. He began to crawl away. I grabbed his belt and pulled him back as he clawed at the trash in the road and rolled him over.

"Get off me!" He squealed as he pawed at me with both hands.

I back-handed his face hard and it stunned him for a moment. When his fat mouth opened to protest, I stuck the muzzle of the pistol into it. "You're going to shut the fuck up and listen to me. I should kill you right here and now. But we don't do things that way anymore. So, for the rest of your life, however long that is, every day you wake up, you better thank me. Because every new day you see is a gift from me."

While Porky and I had our discussion, I glanced over at the people in front of the old service station. It was pretty obvious that none of them wanted any part of what was going on. Whatever bullshit Porky had sold them had obviously turned and they were no longer interested.

I removed my pistol from Porky's mouth. He stammered and it almost seemed he was about to cry. Standing up, I pulled him to his feet, with much effort on my part. I pushed him towards the old service station. Pulling his whale-like arms behind his back, I applied a cuff to one of his wrists. But it was obvious that short of dislocating one of his shoulders, which I wasn't against, there was no way I could get him into a single set. I had to get another set of cuffs and link them together before I would have him restrained. So I just held onto the one cuff for the moment.

Looking at the group standing to the side, I said, "Anyone else want to *talk*?" None of them made any sort of gestures. "Do you people see the issue with the way these men acted?" I surveyed them for a moment before shouting, "Do you!" Several of them nodded as I continued. "What in the world makes any of you think you can step out in the road and force a person to stop? And remember, they weren't asking! Not only that, but to pull a gun on the Sheriff? Are you fucking stupid?"

Porky was fidgeting and I tugged on the cuff, turning it into his wrist. He let out a yelp as the metal cut into him and he struggled harder. I pulled on his arm, spinning him around and it was in that moment I realized I had underestimated him.

I saw the flash of silver in his hand and felt it as he pressed into my left side. His eyes were wild as he said, "You, sir, are going to die!"

There was a pop and I felt a burning in the left side of my chest. My carbine was hanging from its sling and I'd holstered the pistol. Porky and I were face to face and neither of them were going to help me now. A smile spread over his face as the pain set in. I heard the clicking of a revolver cylinder rolling over. He was cocking it for another shot. But I wasn't about to let this sack of shit kill me. Not before he died anyway.

I pulled the ESEE from its sheath and jammed it into his neck at an upward angle, just under his jaw. The smile evaporated. With my left hand, I grabbed his pistol and pushed it away from me as I withdrew the knife. Turning it over in my grip, I stabbed it into the lower left side of his back, aiming for his kidneys. I stabbed it into him over and over. At some point I heard several loud shots, but ignored it. I was intent on seeing this man finished.

Porky's grip on the pistol weakened and I stripped it from his hand as he collapsed, gasping for breath as blood poured from his neck. He reached up in a feeble attempt to stem the flow of his life that was gushing out with every beat of his heart. He was sitting on the ground. His hands falling limp into his lap. He looked down at the crimson that covered him and the road.

The pain in my side was growing in intensity. But I had on armor, it couldn't be that bad. I took a step towards him and felt short of breath. I rapped him on the head with the little silver revolver. He didn't react other than to look up. I looked at the revolver and said, "You thought you were going to kill me with this." More shots rang out around me, but I ignored them and raised the little pocket gun and pulled the hammer back. "But I'm going to kill you with it."

He started to say something, but all that came out was a gurgle. I settled the muzzle of the gun on his forehead. It felt so heavy and it slowly began to lower. I pulled the trigger. The .32 caliber bullet hit Porky at the base of his throat. His eyes went wide for a moment and he gurgled again, before collapsing in the street.

My chest started to hurt and I reached back where the shot hit me. Looking at my hand, I was shocked to see blood. *How can that be?* I asked myself. *I'm wearing armor.* Then I heard the shouting and saw Shane, Sean and Mitch. Looking around, I saw several bodies lying in the street. Aric was bent over one, searching them.

I looked back at my hand. "You alright?" A voice asked.

I looked up to see Mitch. "I think he shot me," I replied and held my hand out.

Mitch's eyes went wide. He grabbed me, saying, "You need to sit down!"

As I tried to lower myself to the ground, I coughed and my mouth filled with the familiar taste of iron, or like sucking on a penny. I spat at the road, it was blood. Mitch helped get me to the road and rolled me over and started taking my body armor off. He ripped open my shirt and pulled the IFAK from the plate carrier as he shouted.

"I can't breathe," I managed to say.

Aric was on his knees beside me. "Don't worry, man. We've got help coming. Just hang on."

It was getting harder and harder to breathe. I could do that math even in my current state. Somehow, that pudgy piece of shit managed to put a bullet in my lung. *He wanted to kill me,* I thought. *At least he didn't get to see it.*

I heard tires crunching the storm debris. It stopped nearby and I heard people shouting. Then I saw the old man standing over me, looking down. Seeing him boosted me. If only for a moment. The look on his face took away any hope seeing him had brought me. Then he slowly faded away.

Three trucks were used for the recon trip. The plan was to run down to the Florida Turnpike. Construction was ongoing on the system and there was a connector that came as close as Sorrento. The convoy would leave Eustis and take the Orange Blossom Trail where they would hop on the 429 and head south. From there, it would be all interstate travel. Wide open roads with little chance of obstruction. They would have long views of the road ahead.

Mike, Ted and Dalton were in the lead truck with two Guardsmen. Jamie, Ian and Doc were bringing up the rear with two Guardsmen thrown in to round out the crew. The middle truck was all Guardsmen. A total of fifteen were on the trip. The trucks were loaded with as much weaponry as they could reasonably carry.

The DHS had fine gear. The confiscated MRAPs were fully functional and very well equipped. Since they weren't sure what, if any, forces they would encounter, the trucks were very well armed. The lead truck had an M2 fifty-cal mounted to the turret. The middle truck had an M240B. For extra firepower, the rear truck, with Jamie at the wheel, had a MK 19 automatic grenade launcher. While it couldn't do anything against armor, they just had to hope they didn't encounter any.

Mike was driving with Ted, acting as the navigator. Dalton insisted he man the Ma Duce. Which was fine with the other guys. Mike liked to drive and Ted liked to sit on his ass and let him. Radio traffic was being kept to a minimum. Chatter in the truck though, that was another story.

"Damn, I'm glad to get the hell out of there for a while!" Mike shouted as he pounded his fist on the roof of the truck over his head.

Ted sat back in his seat and put his feet up on the dash. "Tell me about it. I was starting to get a little fidgety."

"Yes, lads!" Dalton shouted as he watched the screen displaying his weapons sight picture. "It's a fine day for a ride through the country!"

They were on OBT passing under the old railroad bridge just outside Mount Dora. It was long out of use, except for the Orange Blossom Cannonball you could ride during holidays. The route was lightly populated even before. There were few houses and nearly no businesses. But just ahead was one of those cookie cutter subdivisions the country was so fond of. In front of it, right on OBT was a shopping plaza called Stoneybrook Hills. It had a Publix and assorted operations you'd expect in a neighborhood shopping plaza, grocery store, Chinese takeout, maybe a salon and a nail place. Everything the modern American wants and needs, conveniently located right at the entrance of the community.

But it didn't look like that now. The decorative canvas awnings hung in tatters. The grocery store and restaurants were long since looted. Even the nail salon and insurance office were looted. Store fronts lay smashed. The parking lot was littered with trash of all kinds.

But this was our new world. The relatively clean and maintained one was gone. This new one was dirty, litter-strewn and falling apart. And it happened right before our eyes and no one really took notice. Who cares if the corner grocery store was falling in on itself. It was useless to us now. The well-stocked shelves of overpriced and in many cases, totally unhealthy, and in many more, mere food-like substances, were no longer there. We were pushed back over a hundred years. Now, if you want to eat, you have to find it, kill it or dig it up, collect it or grow it. Now, as it should be in the natural scheme, calories required a substantial investment of the same to acquire.

But Dalton wasn't thinking about any of this as they rolled down the road. He was too busy playing with the controls of the fifty-cal mounted on top. It was like a video game and he was having fun. In a way, he hoped he'd have the opportunity to try it out. But at the same time, he knew better than to really want it. Maybe just a little.

They'd left Stonrybrook Hills behind them and passed through Tangerine and were coming into Zellwood. One of the Guardsmen had told them in the briefing to pay attention to this area. He said it was the home to a large migrant population. Not as big as it had been when the Zellwood farms were operating, but there was still a large number of people very likely to be desperate.

"Coming up on Zellwood," Ted called out. "Keep your eyes open back there, Gulliver."

"Right oh!" Dalton called back. Then he added, "But you call me that again and I'll have to cut your other ear off."

Ted looked at Mike, his eyebrows raised. Mike glanced over his shoulder at Dalton. Dalton stared back straight-faced. Mike looked back at Ted and said, "I think he means it."

Ted sat up and turned in his seat. Dalton's expression didn't change and Ted didn't say anything. He turned back around and looked at Mike, saying, "I think he means it."

"Oh I mean it," Dalton called back, his attention returned to the monitor.

"I wish El Corita was open," Mike said as they passed the small Mexican restaurant on Magnolia Street. "I could use a huge burrito covered in queso and jalapenos."

"Screw the burrito. I could use about a dozen ice cold Coronas with a bowl of limes."

"I'll take both of those and a bottle of Cazadores Blanco!" Dalton shouted.

"Oh man that sounds good," one of the soldiers riding with them added.

"I try to stay away from that poison," Ted said with a shiver.

Mike laughed. "What? Why? You still ain't got over Boys Town yet?"

Ted didn't look over. He dropped his head and rubbed his temples with one hand while he pointed at Mike with the other. "Don't say another word. Or *I'll* cut one of *your* ears off!"

Dalton sat back in his chair and looked forward. "Come on, lads! It's not nice to keep secrets!"

Mike started to laugh. "Oh it was awesome!"

"Shut up!" Ted commanded.

Mike laughed even harder, enjoying Ted's discomfort. "We were down in Boys Town for four or five days. I can't remember." He looked at Ted and asked, "Was it five?"

"It was an eternity."

Mike laughed and continued. "Five days in Boys Town! That's right. Anyway. No one needs to be in Boys Town for five days." He looked over his shoulder at Dalton and added, "No body." He turned back to the road and continued. "So we'd heard this story about this bar there. The beers were ridiculously expensive. But it's the only place to see this show."

"Would you please shut up!" Ted shouted.

Naturally, Mike ignored his pleas. "So we're shit-faced, right. And we'd said we weren't going to go to this place. But shit, after three days down there, you forget all about common sense. So we pay our cover at the door and go in. It was expensive is all I remember, and we get a table. This hot little Latina comes out on stage and the place goes crazy. Ted here is getting into it and hops up on his chair for a better look. He was really into it. Then this little dude leads this little donkey out, and—"

"That's enough!" Dalton shouted as he turned back to his monitor. "Don't say another word about it or you'll be listening out of one side of your head for the rest of your life!"

Mike laughed and looked back over his shoulder. "Oh! You've seen it!" He turned and howled with laughter.

Ted looked as though he'd be sick. He pointed ahead and said, "Your turn is coming up."

Mike nodded. "I got it." Then he looked at Ted and, in an over-exaggerated manner, he brayed like an ass. Ted shook his head and tried to ignore his companion. Dalton, however, took a different approach.

"Left or right?" He called from the back of the truck.

"Huh?" Mike replied.

Ted's head rolled over to face Mike. With a smile on his face, he said, "I think he's asking which ear you want to give up."

The smile faded from Mike's face as his hand subconsciously went to his ear. Suddenly, it wasn't so funny. It was Ted's turn to laugh.

The two Guardsmen had sat silently through all of this. Finally, one of them keyed the mic to his headset and asked, "He wouldn't really do that would he?"

Dalton spun around to face the man. Leaning in close, he said, "I'd have no problem doing it *again*," and spun back around and left him to think that over.

"Did you guys see any people on that drive?" Jamie asked.

"I saw two under a carport just outside Zellwood," Ian replied.

"I didn't see anyone and I was looking," a Guardsman said.

"Where the hell are all the people?" Jamie asked.

"There seems to be a distinct lack of people lately." Another soldier replied. "We even noticed fewer people in town. Not a big difference. Just some faces missing from the crowd."

"Did you guys tell anyone?" Ian asked.

"No. Didn't think much of it at the time."

Jamie looked back over her shoulder and asked, "Think much about it now?"

The soldier looked back out the window and said, "Maybe. A little."

The trucks took the ramp up and around onto the 414 connector. It was an elevated roadway with decent views of the surrounding area. The trucks extended the distance between them on the highway to about a hundred meters. The open road provided both the ability to see for great distances, as well as to be seen.

"Alright, guys," Ted broke radio silence. "Everyone keep your eyes peeled. We do not want to make contact. This is a recon only." Ted clicked the mic for the internal intercom and said, "Dalton, keep an eye out with that thermal camera."

"Roger," came the terse reply.

In the rear truck, Ian spoke over the intercom. "Everyone keep your eyes open for people. Any people."

Everyone onboard agreed to keep an eye out. The convoy rolled along, passing cookie-cutter housing developments set back off the road. Most of these were obscured by fences or stands of bush, and no people were seen.

The 429 is a toll road. Florida may not have state income taxes, but it does, or did, have toll roads. Being one of the newer tollways in the state, the tollbooths were built off the main road. The driver had to take an exit ramp of sorts to get to them. The best way to pay tolls was to have a small RFID tag in your vehicle that would allow you to remain on the travel lane and be charged your extortion as you passed under the device hung overhead.

As they approached the first tollbooth, Mike asked, "Should we go through the booth and throw something in the basket?"

"Fuck em!" Dalton shouted. "I dare a state trooper to try and pull us over. I got something for his ass! I'd love to wreck one of those black and tan bastards!"

But the ride was uneventful. They saw absolutely no one. Not on the road, not at any of the subdivisions they passed. But it wasn't only people. There were no cattle in the few pastures they saw. No dogs, cats or anything. It was as if the land were devoid of life.

"You guys feeling like we're the only ones on the planet right now?" Jamie asked over the radio.

"We haven't seen shit," Mike replied.

As the Central Florida Auto Auction was passing them on the left, the upper fly-over that would put you on the Turnpike south began to come into view, as if it were rising out of the road before them. Dalton broke the radio, "Contact front! BMP and BTR sitting on that overpass!"

Mike immediately slowed the truck, and the others did likewise. "See any bodies?" Ted asked.

"Oh yeah. We got bodies. BMP turret is moving. We better move before he gets that hundred-millimeter cannon pointed this way!" Dalton shouted.

"We're going to cross over to the other side," Ted said on the radio. "I don't want to try and back out, staring down the barrel of that thing!"

Jamie immediately began cranking the wheel as she started her turn. They were fortunate that in this section the only thing separating the two sides was a median of very overgrown grass.

"BTR is moving!" Dalton shouted as the road erupted in an explosion thirty meters to the left front of the truck.

Ted pointed to the left side of the road and started swiping his hand at Mike, shouting, "Go! Go! Go!"

"I can't do shit to those damn things!" Dalton shouted.

The Soviet BTR was a rubber-tired amphibious assault vehicle. Its counterpart, the BMP, had amphibious capability as well, but was tracked. They were also very well armed to deal with infantry and light armor, which the MRAP was. Mounting a one hundred-millimeter cannon on the BMP gave it the ability to fire a conventional shell as well as an ATGM, or Anti-Tank Guided Missile. The BTR was equipped with a thirty-millimeter cannon. Either of these weapons would penetrate the armor of the MRAP.

The BTR stopped and began to fire. The cannon didn't fire very fast, but the projectiles were lethal. The explosive rounds began to impact the road seventy-five or so meters away. Blasting chunks of asphalt into the air. The gunner adjusted his fire and they began to land closer as the trucks cut across the median.

As they turned and headed away from the armor pursuing them, the order of trucks was reversed, putting Mike's rig in the back of the pack. One of the Guardsmen made his way to the rear doors and looked out the window. He was shouting for Mike to hurry as he felt as though he was staring directly down the thirty-millimeter cannon. The trucks swerved back and forth so as not to offer nearly stationary targets driving directly away.

Mike looked back over his shoulder at Dalton and shouted, "Why isn't the fifty-cal firing?"

"It's not going to do any fucking good!" Dalton shouted back.

"Like hell!" Mike shouted in return. "I loaded it with SLAP rounds! We don't have many, so make them count!"

Dalton looked back at the monitor as he shouted his reply, "Why didn't you fucking say so!" He adjusted the crosshairs on the screen and began firing three round bursts. Since the truck was weaving back and forth none of them hit the target. It did seem to slow the beast down a bit, but had no effect on the gunner. He was still hard at work.

The soldier at the rear door looked forward and shouted at Mike again, "Hurry the fuck up!"

"I'm giving this piece of shit everything I can! This isn't exactly a high performance vehicle!"

As the wild-eyed soldier turned back to the window, there was a bang and the truck filled with sparks and smoke. Everyone began shouting at once as near panic set in.

"What the fuck was that?" Ted asked as he spun around in his seat, as much as the restraint harness would let him. But he saw for himself what *it* was. Through a relatively small hole just to the right of the rear door he could daylight. Through the smoke, the light coming in was like a laser. It illuminated the body of the soldier that had been in front of the door. His ACU uniform smoked as he lay motionless on the deck of the truck.

Dalton was holding the side of his head. The other soldier was hanging on with one hand and holding his head with the other. "You alright?" Ted shouted.

Dalton gave himself a quick check. The right side of his face was bleeding as well as his right arm. He rotated his shoulder, working his arm and judged the damage minor and gave Ted a thumbs up.

"What about him?" Ted asked, pointing at the man on the floor. The other soldier seemed dazed and out of it. To get his attention, Ted pulled a magazine from his vest and threw it at the guy. It bounced off him and brought him around. Pointing to the Guardsman on the floor, "He dead?" Ted asked the other Guardsman.

The soldier dropped to the floor and rolled him over. It was immediately obvious he was dead. He'd taken shrapnel to his face and head. Massive hemorrhaging from his head was covering the deck of the truck in blood. The soldier looked back at Ted and shook his head.

"Straighten this fucking thing out for a minute! Let me try and put a couple rounds on those pricks!" Dalton shouted.

"Alright, but you better do it quick!" Mike called back. "On three. One... two... three!"

Mike straightened the truck and Dalton lined the BTR up in his sights and pulled the trigger. The tungsten rounds impacted the road and he adjusted his fire. The second volley of shots saw two strike home. One in the front of the vehicle and one in the turret.

The M903 SLAP, or Saboted Light Armor Penetrator

can punch through up to thirty-four millimeters of armor, depending on the range. It's a tungsten penetrator held by a sacrificial sabot. The BTR's armor is thirteen millimeters on the front of the hull and only seven on the turret. When the two rounds hit, they left an impression.

The BTR jerked hard to the left before straightening out again. By that time, Mike was back to the swerve. The BTR didn't fire again though. It rolled along, slowing as it went. Dalton kept sending three round bursts at it, scoring a couple of additional hits. But they were glancing strikes at the side and probably had little effect.

Dalton had been lost in his video battle and hadn't even heard the radio chatter going on in his headset. Ted was giving the other trucks a SITREP of their condition when the BTR disappeared from his view as they started down a slope in the road.

Dalton heard Ted's voice. "We're good, just head for the barn."

"You sure you don't want to stop and check on your people?" An unfamiliar voice asked.

"Fuck no! Just drive!" Ted shouted back.

"We aren't stopping for anything or anyone!" Jamie called back from the now lead truck.

Dalton kept his eyes on the rise in the road. Waiting to see the turret crest it. He didn't have to wait long. But it wasn't the BTR. It was its tracked cousin, the BMP. It stopped at the crest of the hill.

"Contact rear! BMP setting up for a shot!" Dalton called out as he let a burst go from the Ma Deuce. The trucks immediately began the feeble evasive maneuvering. It was better than nothing.

As he fired, Dalton's view of the tank jumped as the big

Browning recoiled. Just as he let up on the trigger, he saw a flash from the one-hundred-millimeter barrel. Keying the radio, Dalton called out, "Shot out! Incoming!"

They were nearly three-thousand meters away by now. But the BMP wasn't firing conventional shells from its main gun. The gunner loosed an AT-10 Stabber anti-tank guided missile. Dalton could see it as it screamed towards them. It would cover the three-thousand meters in nine seconds.

"Hard left!" Dalton shouted into the mic.

The truck jerked left and Ted saw the missile as a flash as it passed just outside his window. Either they were very lucky, or they were not the intended target as the twenty-seven-inch-long rocket slammed into the middle MRAP. The explosion was fierce as both the rear and front doors were blown open. Mike swerved again to avoid running over the flaming body of the driver of the truck as it bounced out onto the road.

"Should I stop?" Mike asked. "We can't just leave them here!"

"What was that?" Jamie called over the radio.

"Go! Go, go go!" Ted shouted.

Mike looked over, "We cannot fucking leave them here, Ted!"

"They're dead, Mike! And we will be too if we fucking stay here! Now fucking drive! That gunner is probably loading another one right now!"

As they passed the MRAP that sat in the middle of the road, a burning pyre, Mike saw the front passenger roll out onto the ground. He was fully engulfed in flames and tried to get to his feet.

"Oh my fuck!" Mike screamed as he slammed on the brakes. "He's alive!"

"What are you doing?" Ted screamed as he looked past Mike out the window. "Go! We can't do anything for him!"

"He's fucking alive, Ted. We have to help him," Mike replied as he reached to unbuckle his harness.

The fifty-cal thundered above them. Mike had his eyes on the flailing man and saw the rounds as they slammed into him and he fell to the road.

"He's not alive anymore." It was Dalton's voice. Very calm and even over the intercom. "Now get moving before all we're roasted like he is."

"What's going on?" Jamie called over the radio. "Do we need to come back?"

"No! Keep going. We're coming," Ted replied.

Mike stared out the window. It took Ted hitting him in the shoulder with the butt of his rifle to get him back. Without saying a word, Mike pulled away from the horror. They rode in silence for a long time. They were back on the OBT before Dalton spoke.

"Why didn't they swerve?" He asked no one in particular.

"What?" Ted asked.

"Why didn't they swerve. I said to swerve. But they didn't."

There was a pause for a moment. Then Ted answered him. "You said it over the intercom. Not the radio. They didn't hear you."

Dalton looked at the PTT button. *I told them to swerve.*

CHAPTER 10

T
HE TRUCKS MADE IT BACK to town without any
further incidents. As they came down Bay Street
towards the armory, there was a lot of activity near
the police department. Many residents of Eustis were gathered
there, as well as a large presence from the armory. To include a
couple of gun trucks with men manning the turrets.

"What the hell is going on here?" Ted asked. But no one
answered him.

They made their way to the armory and parked the trucks.
Sarge, Sheffield and Livingston were coming out of the building
as they were getting out. Sarge looked at the two trucks and
asked the obvious, "Where's the other one?"

"Burning up on 429." Ted replied.

"What the hell happened?" Livingston asked.

Mike was standing beside the truck as Ted started to explain
what happened. Dalton climbed out of the rear and stepped
around. Jamie saw him and said, "You're bleeding." She turned
back to her truck and called out, "Doc!"

Ronnie came running up and took a look at Dalton. "We're
going to need to get you to the clinic."

Dalton waved them off and said, "I'm fine." He started to
walk away when Mike stepped in front of him.

"I can't believe you did that!" Mike shouted. This brought all other conversations to a halt.

"There was nothing we could do for him. Even if we had managed to get him in the truck, he was so badly burned he probably wouldn't have survived."

Mike was incensed. "That's not your fucking decision to make!"

"What the hell are you talking about?" Sarge asked.

Mike pointed at Dalton. "He fucking shot one our guys."

Sarge looked at Dalton and asked, "Why?"

"The guy was fully engulfed in flames." Ted replied, "There was nothing we could do for him. Not to mention that BMP was still there. If we had stopped, he would probably have gotten us too."

Doc looked at Dalton and said, "You just gunned him down?"

"You going to fucking shoot me too if I'm wounded?" Mike spat.

Dalton looked him in the eye, then each man in turn and said, "If you're really fucked up, yes I will. And I hope you will do the same for me. Our resources are limited. There's only so much care we can offer. If that was me back there on the road, I'd pray one of you shot me. Put me out of that kind of pain quickly and not let me die a slow, lingering, miserable death."

Everyone was silent for a moment. Doc was the one to speak up. "He's right. I didn't see him; but if he was burned that bad, there isn't much we could have done." He looked at Dalton and added, "I just don't know if I could do that," and shook his head.

"You think I liked it? You think I wanted to do it? But in this world there are no medivacs coming in. There is no *higher level of care*. It's ditch medicine, and there are many, many things you just can't treat with ditch medicine. It was the humane thing to do."

Sarge let out a long breath and said, "You're one hard son of a bitch, Dalton. I'll give you that."

"Who was it?" Livingston asked.

Dalton shook his head. "I don't know."

"Yeah," Livingston replied, "It's easy to kill a man when you don't know his name. But he was one of mine. I know his name. I know his wife and kids' names too."

"And you can go tell them that he is dead." Dalton replied, "Not that he was last seen burning alive on the fucking pavement as his comrades drove away. And if you want names, I can give you a fucking list."

Sarge reached out and put his arm around Dalton and turned him from the group. "You did the right thing, Dalton. Go with Doc to the clinic. You've got some iron that needs to be dug out."

Livingston looked at Sheffield and said, "We have to go talk to some people. Four of those men have families here."

Sheffield looked at Sarge's back as he led Dalton away. "That's why I don't want any part of these fools' missions." He shook his head and added, "We just need to stay here and try to keep our people alive."

"But it's you're fucking job," Mike said. Sheffield and Livingston both turned to see Mike sitting on an empty bucket. He rose to his feet and pointed at them. "Those uniforms you're wearing stand for something. It's your job to take care of people. You don't get to pick your fights." He pointed at Sheffield and added, "You took an oath. Honor it," and he walked away.

CHAPTER 11

WHEN I WOKE UP, I saw Mel sitting beside me. She was looking directly at me, as if she expected me to open my eyes. She didn't smile. In fact, her expression didn't change at all. I looked around, unsure where I was. After a moment, I realized I was in the clinic. Reaching down, I felt my side. I felt a small bandage, but there was little in the way of pain.

Mel took a deep breath and said, "They said it should heal. The doctor said it was a small hole."

"That's good." I replied. "I think." And sat up. Now there was some pain, though it was minor.

Mel shook her head. "Why don't you just stay home? Why are you always going out and getting into some kind of shit?"

I didn't know what to say. "Someone has to. I'd rather be part of the solution than part of the problem."

She rubbed her face and said, "I just wish you'd stay home. Because one day you're going to leave and never come back."

I reached out for her hand. Slowly, she reached out and took it. "People are dying every day. We're doing better than most."

"There's a lot of people that want to see you. It's a big day."

"Who's here? And why's it a big day?" I asked as I swung my legs off the bed.

"Everyone. Come outside, you'll see."

Getting on my feet, I held her hand as I walked to the tent flap. "How long was I out?"

"Three days."

"Three days!" I shouted.

"They kept you sedated. I told them to. I told them that as soon as you woke up you'd leave, and that you needed some time to get better first."

The sun was intense and I held my hand up to shield my face. "Damn. Wish I had my shades," I complained.

Mel was carrying a small bag and she unslung it from her shoulder. Reaching in, she handed them to me. "Thought you'd want them. Some of your other stuff is in here too."

"Where's all my gear?" I asked.

"Sarge has it," she replied and reached into the bag again. This time she took out a stainless bottle and handed it to me.

I opened it and took a sip. It was tea. I smiled and wrapped my arm around her and said, "You're an incredible woman."

She leaned into me and replied, "Then you better stick around a while." I looked at her and smiled and she added, "You ain't seen nothing yet."

The street was full of people and we fell into the crowd as it moved towards the park. "What's going on?" I asked.

A man passing me answered the question excitedly, "You ain't heard? There's going to be a hanging today!"

"A what?" I asked, looking at Mel.

She looked straight ahead as she spoke. "I guess after your excitement the other day there were some people you didn't kill." She gave me a snide look. "They rounded them up and tried them. They were found guilty and they're going to hang."

I took it in and thought about what she said. I remember the people there, but as I recall, they weren't doing anything. But then, there was all that shooting. "How many?" I asked.

Mel pointed and said, "There's your judge. You can ask him yourself."

She was pointing at Mitch. He was standing in the park with several of the folks from the ranch. As we drew closer, I saw the scaffold that was already erected. Three ropes hung from it, waiting patiently for their customers. Sarge was standing beside him, his arms folded over his chest. He was going on about something. He paused for a moment and looked over his shoulder. A smile spread over his face and he turned to face me.

He came up and slapped my shoulder. "I knew you'd get better." He grabbed my hand and shook it. "Glad to see you back on your feet."

Shaking his hand, I said, "Didn't realize I was out so long."

The old man pointed at Mel. "She insisted. Said it was the only way to keep you in the bed."

I smiled nervously, "She was probably right."

"I *was* right," Mel quipped.

I pointed at the scaffold and asked, "What's all this about?"

"I'll let the judge tell you about it."

"Good to see you back on your feet," Mitch said as we shook hands. "There were three people rounded up. Four others were shot and killed at the scene."

"Did you have a trial?" I asked.

Mitch nodded. "Indeed we did. So many people attended it, we had to move it to the amphitheater."

"There were spectators at the trial?"

"It was the biggest thing going on," Sarge said. "There's nothing else to do. So, hell yes, there were spectators aplenty."

"It was a circus," Mel retorted.

I looked at her, then back to Mitch and asked. "And how did that work out?"

Mitch looked embarrassed. "I admit; it did get out of hand."

Sarge laughed. "You think?"

Mitch smiled and nodded. "Yeah, I know. But we won't let it happen again. I mean, this was the first one."

I pointed at the nooses. "Then is this legit? Are we about to hang people as a result of a damn circus?"

Mitch shook his head. "No, no. It was proper."

Sarge nodded in support. "It was proper, Morgan. They all admitted to what was going on. In their own way."

"And what was going on?"

Mitch took a deep breath. "Well it seems Hyatt had his aim set on taking over the town. He really wanted to create his own little fiefdom. But you kept messing that up."

"I know he was a damn pain in the ass, but......"

"The people stated in the trial that he hated you. Since the first time the two of you met. They said he fixated on killing you. Said he wanted your star."

"Yeah," I replied. "He had it for a minute."

"We got it back," Sarge assured me.

"Where's my stuff?" I asked.

He pointed at the Hummer sitting in the parking lot of the park and said, "It's in there."

"You want me to go get it?" Shane asked.

I nodded and caught Mel's eye. She didn't look particularly happy about that. "Anyway," Mitch said. "He was plotting different ways to kill you. They said they were always elaborate plans."

Sean laughed and added, "Yeah, like something Wiley Coyote would dream up."

"I just don't get why though. Alright. So he hated me. But what did I do to him, really?" I asked.

"Hang on," Mitch said. "He was telling people that you and the guys at the armory were hoarding all the food in town.

That you guys lived in luxury, to use his words, while everyone else starved to death."

"We planted a fucking farm for these people!" I shouted, drawing looks from several people in the crowd.

"Calm down," Sarge said. "Everyone knows that. It was just his delusions. It don't matter now. It's over and settled."

"It's almost over," Shane said. "After this. It'll be over."

I looked up at the ropes hanging from the scaffold. The knots had thirteen turns on them. "Who tied those?" I asked.

"I did." Sarge barked.

Looking at him, I said, "Figures you would know how to tie a hangman's knot."

"Shit," Sarge snorted. "Every man should know how to tie a noose. Never know when you might have to hang someone."

"I guess it's time," Mitch said.

Sean nodded and he and Shane walked off. They went to the parking lot where an MRAP was parked. Two Guardsmen were standing at the rear doors and opened them as they walked up. Three pathetic looking people, two men and a woman, stepped down. Their hands bound in front of them. The crowd went silent and spread out to make a path for them. Shane, Sean and the two guards walked them to the platform.

The park, which moments ago was full of noise, remained silent. The kids that moments ago were running around playing like kids did long ago, were now hiding behind trees or looking out from behind their parents.

"Why are there kids here?" I asked.

"I asked the same thing," Mel said.

"Executions have always been a bit of a spectator sport, Morgan," Sarge said. "We're just going back to the way things used to be."

"Still doesn't make it right," Mel replied.

Sarge patted her back. "No, it doesn't, Mel. That's why Little Bit isn't here. You're a good mother."

We watched as those who were about to have their necks snapped walked up the makeshift stairs. Mitch was in the lead, a bullhorn in his hand. It was a bizarre scene.

"Who built that?" I asked.

"Oh, there were plenty of volunteers for the work," Sarge said. "Especially when they found out they'd be paid in meat."

"You paid them with the beef?" I asked.

"Don't worry, there's still plenty."

Shane and Sean placed each prisoner under a noose. One of the guards stood beside each as they were put in place. Once they were standing under their ropes, Mitch turned to face the crowd. He held the bullhorn to his lips and clicked it on. He read from a paper in his hand.

"These people have been found guilty of murder, attempted murder of a law enforcement officer and battery on a law enforcement officer. Tabitha Adams, Gordon Hollingsworth and Brad Adams have been tried and convicted of the aforementioned crimes. They have been sentenced to hang by the neck until they are dead. The sentence is to be carried out now." Looking at the condemned, he asked, "Do you have any final words?" None of them said a word.

Mitch turned and nodded to Sean. He pulled a blue pillowcase over Tabitha's head. She began to cry as the noose was draped around her neck and cinched tight. He repeated the process, placing a pillowcase over the men's heads before tightening the noose. Once all three had a rope around their necks, the men left the scaffold. I saw Mitch look at someone in front of the structure. I followed his gaze to see Dalton standing there. He held a two-by-four out in front of him horizontally. Three ropes ran through it and then up to the structure.

When Mitch nodded, Dalton stepped back on his right leg and jerked the board with all his might. Gordon and Brad fell through. Their necks cracked audibly. But Tabitha didn't. She let out a wail and the crowd gasped. Dalton straightened out the board and jerked again. This time, the floor fell out from beneath her. She dropped like the first two. At the end of the rope, her neck snapped as well.

The bodies hung there, swaying back and forth. Completely lifeless. A line began to form as people walked by to get an up-close look. As I stood there with Mel's hand in mine, watching the morbid scene, two large hands gripped my shoulders. I looked back to see Thad. He smiled broadly and said, "Good to see you again, Morgan."

I smiled, patted his hand, and said, "You too, old friend."

As the bodies swayed and the crowd slowly filed past the gruesome display, there was a sudden brightening of the sky to the southwest. Everyone noticed it and the all stopped in their tracks. The light grew in intensity until the horizon was nearly white. As the light faded, people began to whisper. A murmur spread across the park.

I felt Mel move in a little closer. I gripped her hand tight. She asked, "What was that?" Her voice nervous. Almost fearful.

"If I had to guess," I replied. "I'd say MacDill Air Force base in Tampa, is no longer there."

"I'd say you're right," Sarge added quietly.

"You think it was a nuke?" Mel asked.

I stared at the horizon. "No doubt about it."

"Who?" She whispered.

I shrugged. "Does it matter?"

65703723R00190

Made in the USA
San Bernardino, CA
05 January 2018